RUTHLESS

About the Author

Kerry Barnes, born in 1964, grew up on a council estate in the South East. Pushed by her parents to become a doctor at a time and in a place where women only dreamed of having a professional career, she started off as a microbiologist and then went into medicine.

She began writing when her daughter was born and she had free time. By the time her children were grown, she had written four novels.

Ruthless is the first to be published.

Kerry Barnes

RUTHLESS

Olympia Publishers
London

www.olympiapublishers.com
OLYMPIA PAPERBACK EDITION

A CIP catalogue record for this title is
available from the British Library.

ISBN: 978-1-84897-497-5

(Olympia Publishers is part of Ashwell Publishing Ltd)

First Published in 2016

Olympia Publishers
60 Cannon Street
London
EC4N 6NP
Printed in Great Britain

Dedication

To Carol Cussen, a beautiful woman inside and out.
To my Grandmother Elizabeth, who taught me so much and I miss every day.
You will always be in our hearts.

Acknowledgement

My family, who have always supported me. Without you there is no me.
My mum and dad, who taught me that family comes first, blood is thicker than water. My daughter, who has worked to achieve great heights in her career whom I am immensely proud of, and my son, who carries on no matter what life throws his way. My hubby, who pushed me to get this book published.
The characters in the book are based on my family members, although the story is fictional.

Chapter One

1998

Mary lay in her bed, listening to the birds outside. Bill, her husband, got up early, cooked himself a good fry-up, which he loved on a Sunday, and went to do the paperwork at the yard.

The phone was ringing and she heard Dan, her eldest, clamber down the stairs.

The arthritis in her spine had worsened over the years and some days the stiffening was too much to allow for rushing around – especially on a Sunday morning. Instead, she lay awake, relaxed and warm, wrapped in her bed sheets and daydreaming.

The boys, knowing how she suffered, tried to get up before her, just so she could rest rather than have to struggle to cook their breakfasts or iron their shirts. Even though they were grown up now, she still fussed and cared for them as if they were kids.

Mary looked tired; the years of anguish had taken their toll on her once bright and youthful skin. Raising four lively lads required mountains of energy, without the added worry of which one next would serve time at her majesty's pleasure. She was desperately scrambling to hold together what was left of her family. *God knows she had seen more prisons than she had beaches.* Nevertheless, they weren't that unruly in the grand scheme of things, and their stints in the clink were for minor issues. None of the boys had done any real bird – unlike their father, who had served a tidy lump.

But despite the fights and trials of raising four sons, her biggest worry was her daughter – not knowing from day to day how she fared, what she was doing or even what she looked like.

Mary, being the envy of most women in her neighbourhood, with her platinum blonde hair and hourglass figure, was never short of a date. Bill Vincent was a Face in the East End and the local men respected him. His business wasn't big, but then he was a youngster. A good head on his shoulders, and an eye for a money earner, he was going places – and to add to his financial status, he looked polished, with shiny, thick black locks and steel-blue eyes.

He had eyed her up for six months before he plucked up the courage to ask for a date. When he walked into the local club on a Friday night, followed by his mates, he drew attention from the girls. They would be gawking and whispering, checking themselves in the toilets, adding another layer of hair lacquer to their ever-increasing beehives, slapping on the lipstick and wiggling their way onto the dance floor, forever hoping they could catch his attention. Bill would gaze around to see who caught his eye, grab a pint, and stand at the bar with his gang.

He had the polished chromed motorbike, with the black leather jacket, as did his mates, yet he didn't class himself as a rocker. Mary was laid-back and easy going. She didn't bother flirting and she had no need to, as her good looks gave her respect. Her friends were undoubtedly very envious. "Where did you get that lovely frock?" they would ask, or, "I wish I could get away with wearing that," and, "Who does your hair?"

She was a kind person, who never liked to start trouble but, if it landed on her lap, she stood her own and chucked a right hook like a bloke. Living on a rough estate – and the hardship that went with it – gave her tenacity. Fortunately, however, the odd fight left no scars on her pretty face.

Bill watched her out of the corner of his eye. He loved to see her dance; she could twist like no other. Her figure, with ample bosom and small waist, was accentuated by the 1960s fashionable pencil dress. She looked glamorous. He waited for his moment before he made his move. The packed club, filled with blue smoke and excited women's chattering, rendered the atmosphere buzzing. He'd had two pints of beer, just enough to give him the courage to get on the dance floor. Full of confidence, Bill knew that whoever he asked to dance would never turn him down. Then there was Mary, the one he truly liked, but it took months before he had the guts to ask her for a date.

The club dated back to before the war and although the owner tried to brighten it up, painting the woodwork maroon and covering the seats in cheap red velvet, it was still a glorified wooden shed. The owner hadn't bothered with a complete overhaul; he just continued to rake in the money and wait for the building to collapse. He ignored the underage drinkers and patched up any aggro before anyone called the police. As their local haunt, everyone got themselves rigged out and ready for their Friday night dance.

Mary wore a red dress and her hair in a beehive with a silk poppy on the side. Her full lips, glossed with red lipstick, radiated her face. He watched her every move and noticed she was eyeing him too. He smiled her way and she coyly grinned back. The music played, and she danced with extra sensual moves. Just as the record came to an end, Bill got up from his bar stool and walked towards her.

Susan Leonard, another local girl from off the estate, had been eyeing up Bill for months, and told everyone to keep their hands off, as she wanted him for herself. The skinny redhead didn't stand an earthly getting a date with Bill. She had gained a reputation as a slag. The only time she got a date was if there were no other options and, deep in her heart, she knew that. The shag behind the big council bins made her feel special; she didn't realise that she was being used. She went away thinking that the boys fancied the arse off her.

Susan grew up in a small flat with four brothers, together in the same bedroom. Her mother kept her own bedroom to herself. She said to her daughter, 'You can't fucking share wiv me; my room is what makes us money.' By the time she reached twelve years old, she knew what her mother meant. The string of men in and out: fat or thin, pissed or sober, had one thing in common – a need for a Tom.

Susan hated sharing with the boys. They had no respect for her and she had none for them. Her middle brother, Denzel, named after his Jamaican father, born with mental problems, tried to help himself one night, lifting her nightie and having a nose around. She gave him a swift kick in the teeth and warned the others that if they even thought about it, she would stab them in their beds. Endless punch-ups with the boys gave her the reputation of being hard, and so when she told the girls to stay away from Bill, as he was hers, they did.

Susan spread the word far enough for it to land on Mary's ears, but she dismissed the whole idea, thinking it ridiculous that a girl could lay claim to a fella she wasn't even dating.

The crowd made room for Bill as he walked towards Mary. When she caught sight of him striding over, goosebumps covered her body. There was always a pause before the next record played.

"Hello, Mary, you look pretty tonight." Everyone's eyes were on her.

"So does that mean, Billy Vincent, that I don't usually?"

Poor Bill, taken aback, thought he had blown it.

She gently punched him on the arm. "I'm joking, thanks for the compliment."

Susan came out of the toilets to see Mary flirting with Bill on the dance floor. She was furious; *Who the fuck did she think she was?* Susan hated Mary more than she hated anyone. She watched her on the estate, thinking she was the fucking bee's knees, the boys offering to carry her bags, and the endless ogling. Just a common slag, teasing the blokes, leading them on like that. Susan wanted to give her a good kicking, and tonight it was going to happen. By putting the word out about her claim on Bill, and Mary ignoring her word of warning, by her standards she had the right to slap the bitch.

Bill's heart did a backflip. It was her hypnotic tone, the way she teased him and then kindly relieved his embarrassment, which he loved about Mary. He fell in love there and then.

"Would you like to dance with me, Mary?" He attempted to be sophisticated.

She teased again, "Well, Bill, that depends. Can you dance?"

He loved the half-smile and the way her eyes shone in the darkness.

"Can I dance?" he said loudly.

They both laughed – he had that reputation too.

The DJ deliberately played a slow number. Bill grabbed Mary round the waist and, with a nervous hand, he held hers and they swayed.

Susan shook with anger. It should have been her he asked to dance. She watched as Mary stared into Bill's eyes and Bill was giving her his charming smile. The sight was too much for Susan to handle. She marched through the crowd and grabbed Mary by the hair. It happened so fast that no one had time to stop it. Mary's flower fell to the floor. Mary, shocked by this turn of events, took a second before she realised what had happened. The first blow hit Mary hard in the eye. Bill grabbed the back of Susan's dress and pulled her off. As he let go of her to see to Mary's face, Susan lunged forward again to have another go, but Mary gave the girl her famous right hook and knocked Susan clean on her back.

"You fucking whore, Mary Mathews! You knew I had my eye on him but you couldn't keep your grubby fucking hands off!" shrieked Susan, at the top of her voice.

Bill picked up the flower and put his arm around Mary. "Come on, Mary, let's get out of here."

As they walked away, Bill was surprised by how calm Mary appeared. Susan, humiliated, sprang to her feet, and ripped a handful of Mary's hair from the back of her head, a right coward's move. Bill lost his cool. Although he never hit women, he made the odd exception, and this was one of them.

With a clenched fist, he punched Susan in the chest and sent her reeling across the floor.

"Now, you scumbag, stay away from her or I'll give you another dig." Susan sobbed, and the crowd just shook their heads. She had overstepped the mark and no one wanted to side with her.

"And one other thing, you stupid little bitch, if I'm taken for, it's by her." He pointed to Mary and continued, "I wouldn't touch you with a ten-foot barge pole, now fuck off home," he spat.

Susan gradually got to her feet. The punch winded her chest but, more importantly, her pride had suffered a momentous blow. To add insult to injury, the crowd applauded as she left.

*

They courted for a month before Mary took Bill to meet her father, Jim, who had brought up his two daughters single-handed. He was proud of them both, even though they were like chalk and cheese. The eldest sister, Anne, moved away from the East End to start a new life in Surrey and so Mary lived alone with her father. He knew of Bill and his past, who was well-known as a bit of a rogue, but he had money, which was something Jim never had.

He asked two things of Bill. "If you're walking out with my Mary, then you bring her home safe and sound by eleven at the latest and, when you're with her, you make sure no harm comes her way." Mary smiled at her father, who sat by the fire in his string vest and braces. Bill glanced around the tired-looking living room. Mary kept it clean with the odd touches, like the embroidered doilies and a small bunch of daffodils on the fireplace, something which a man would never consider. Her father looked tired too. He worked hard as a rag and bone man, and the years had not been kind, but he had been a good father, and so Mary was not embarrassed by her home or by her father's scruffy appearance.

Jim was as proud as punch when Bill asked him if he could marry his daughter. He knew in his heart she wouldn't have married a well-to-do fella, as she wasn't well to do or well-educated, but she had her looks and Bill happened to be as good a catch as any. The prospect of Mary living a life without the worry of poverty made Jim content and proud to lead her up the aisle.

"Now boy, all I ask of you is this. You take good care of my baby, never lay your hands on her and don't break her heart," he said.

Bill nodded furiously, as he happily agreed to all her father's demands. He wanted Mary on his arm and down the aisle.

It was well-known that Bill's business, the scrap metal yard, was not one hundred percent above board but what the mind did not know the heart would not grieve over, and that's how things remained for many years. Jimmy taught Mary never to look a gift horse in the mouth. By that he meant, don't question your husband's finances – just be wise with the money he gives you. Aware that his daughter was naive to the illegal underworld, he encouraged her to keep a good house, be a good mum, worry only over the issues in her home, and not get involved in the business. Jimmy wanted his daughter's marriage to work so he could live his last days knowing she would be looked after.

Mary bore her husband three stunning-looking boys. The first son, Dan, was the image of his father, propped up in the brand new Royale pram, with the large rear wheels and smaller front wheels and curved handle, in which Mary paraded him with pride. The neighbours commented on how smart she looked considering she had just given birth. They marvelled at the baby's angelic looks, with his jet-black curls and huge steel-blue eyes. Mary never stepped outside the door without her lipstick on and a fresh dress. She didn't entertain the idea of going out in her apron and slippers, as her Bill wouldn't like it.

Bill was proud to have a gorgeous wife and a son. A year later came Joseph; he too resembled his father, just a little chubbier with dimples. Mary secretly hoped for a girl, but was delighted when their third son, Sam, arrived; three boys, all happy, healthy and very handsome.

Bill kept her in a warm and comfortable house with money in the pot and food on the table. She was grateful not to have to use the electric meter money to pay the gas and have a rent man knocking at the door. Life was tough for most women, especially if their husband was a drinker. The poor wives had to scratch around saving pennies to pay the bills. Some went to Kent, having to go strawberry picking to earn enough for a bit of supper. Mary was so grateful that she didn't have to do this. Her husband was a very generous man who always put his family first.

The first man in the road to buy his council house, Bill turned this three bedroom semi into a small palace; they became the envy of the neighbourhood. Mary spent their money on expensive curtains, bed linen and even wall-to-wall carpets, which was a luxury that no one in the street could afford. The sixties were a tough period for people starting out and so, when the large vans pulled up outside Mary's house, delivering yet another new white good, tongues wagged.

Mary was oblivious to the gossip: as far as she knew, her husband owned a legitimate yard and earned an honest wage. She was so wrong. Bill became greedy – the more he had, the more he wanted. His yard covered up the importation and storage of firearms, which was the main bulk of his business. Having more responsibilities, he believed he needed more money. His contacts and his men trusted him and so the transactions were continuous.

When Mary became pregnant, Bill once again put in an offer to buy a larger four bedroom detached property in Kent, on the borders of South East of London.

"Oh, Bill, it's just beautiful." Her mouth was wide open, she had never dreamt that she could ever have lived in a place such as this. He smiled when he saw the wonder in her eyes. "Look, Bill, windows on both sides of the front door," she said, clapping in excitement.

"Yes, babe, it's called double-fronted," Bill stated.

"Like me then, Bill," she laughed, looking down at her rapidly growing bump.

Mary loved the new house and its surroundings. The boys played happily in the garden and Mary relaxed and enjoyed her pregnancy. But, as the months went by, she found coping with her three young boys – now two, three and four – too much so, towards the last month of her pregnancy, they were sent to her sister's in Surrey until the baby arrived. It was a matter of three weeks before she gave birth.

Bill came home later and later until, one night, he didn't come home at all. He looked tired and withdrawn. He had less time for nice things, lunchtimes in the local, and general small talk. She had believed that by sending her babies away she could relax, enjoy her husband's company, and not get so stressed, but she missed the kids and, what with Bill being away so much, she was left at home all alone. God knows she hated the loneliness and the isolation. Kent was picturesque but, with no neighbours to call on and no local gossip, she became bored and, no matter how attractive the house seemed, it was not home without her family.

Bill became impatient with her moaning and demanded she joined the boys at her sister's.

"Mare, you are not happy here. Go to your sister's and rest," he said.

"But I wanted to rest here with you. How am I gonna rest if I've got the little 'uns at me ankles?" she quibbled.

Bill looked annoyed. "Can't your sister take charge of 'em? I'm up to me eyeballs with work and I don't need to be worrying about you right now!" His voice was firm.

She felt so hurt: he wanted her to go, despite her pleas to the contrary. That afternoon, Bill helped her carry the bags to the car and off they went to Surrey. They spent the journey in silence. He appeared uneasy but Mary decided not to ask why.

Her sister, Anne, had done well for herself, having bought a reasonable sized home in a conservative street in Surrey. Bill pulled up outside the house.

"Now, my gal, I'm not coming in. The boys will get too excited, and I need to get back to the yard." She looked at her husband and for a second didn't recognise him.

"Come on then, Mare, let me get going and I'll see you soon."

He kissed her on the cheek and she got out of the car. He didn't even glance back. Her heart sank and she foolishly concluded that he didn't care for her or the kids anymore.

Her sister, Anne, five years older than Mary, left home at a young age, shortly after their mother had died. She had always been snobbish. She found the idea of living in a run-down council flat in the East End of London beneath her. Therefore, as soon as she could afford to move away, she did. She trained as a secretary and secured herself a job in a solicitor's office in Surrey, where she remained alone and unmarried.

Mary tried desperately to get along with Anne and understand her ways but their personalities were miles apart. With the gap between them too big to bridge, Mary resigned herself to the fact that they would never be close.

The short time Mary had been at her sister's, she got more stressed out than if she had coped with three lively boys on her own. After a blazing argument with Anne, she packed her bags and returned home.

Mary, relieved to be back home, had not enjoyed her sister's company. Nor had the boys. They could not move without having to ask permission first. Their hands had to be washed every five minutes in case they dirtied any of the furniture and, as for making a mess, well, they just didn't dare. Mary felt very sorry for her young boys. She had told them they were going on a short holiday, but it turned into a prison camp! Little did she realise that it was to be a salutary lesson to them for the future when they got themselves into bother and ended up in stir.

Anne's house was so clean and tidy, with everything in its place and not a finger mark in sight. She obsessively ran around with a cloth, wiping away any sticky finger marks or biscuit crumbs. Mary found it hard to relax; it wore her down watching Anne forever cleaning.

Dan tried to keep his little brothers occupied, even though he was only a baby himself. They had been sent to play in the garden by Aunt Anne. She had told them to be quiet, not to upset the neighbours and, she had added, to play nicely, *whatever that was supposed to mean*. As little boys would, they amused themselves. They mixed mud with the water from the garden tap, using the plant pots and sweet pea canes as stirrers. When the boys got bored with making mud pies, they poured the runny content over the newly laid patio, which previously had been beige, but was now transformed into a muddy grey colour, to the horror of their aunt.

Mary had been resting in the living room with her feet propped up on a stool when she heard the screeches coming from the kitchen.

"Look what your little shits have done to my new patio!" she screamed at the top of her voice, much to the surprise of the neighbours, who had never heard a peep before.

Mary jumped to her feet and rushed to the kitchen to see what all the commotion was.

"Anne, it's all right, calm down, it's only fucking mud," Mary snapped back.

Anne stormed past the three little boys, who were now standing in a line-up in the immaculate clean white kitchen, shamefully looking at the floor. They were not used to being shouted at. As she passed Joe, her hand accidentally caught his shoulder, and he lost his balance, falling back on to the oven door handle. He let out a scream which sent Mary over the edge. She grabbed Anne by her skinny shoulder, spun her around, and squeezed her throat.

"No wonder you ain't got kids and gawd help 'em if you ever did, you fucking spiteful cow."

It took five minutes for Mary to grab their belongings and march out of the house. She walked to the end of the road and used the phone box to call a taxi. The boys followed in silence, tightly holding each other's hands, as Mary stormed ahead, still seething. They had never seen their mum lose her temper and didn't quite know what to make of it. She felt the baby moving inside of her — *all arms and legs, this one*, she thought. It would not be long now before she could hold her fourth baby. The cab came and took them home.

*

Mary was not surprised to find the house empty. She allowed the boys to play for a while before she bathed them and tucked them up in their beds. Despite the day being long, tiring and extremely stressful, Mary still needed to talk to her husband, and so she waited up.

All the signs were there: the dry sheets, the affection they shared gone, and the excuses for working late.

The change in her husband convinced Mary he had been entertaining another woman. She loved her husband deeply and had no intention of giving him up without a damn good fight. Visions of her husband coming home with another woman went over and over in her head. What she would do to them made her heart race and her mouth dry. She thought of her new heavy pot set, made of cast iron, and how she would set about wrapping it around his mistress's head. Her mind ran away with her, such were her feelings of despondency at this moment

She sat waiting in darkness in the kitchen, sipping a hot cup of coffee. She silently prayed that he was being faithful, and that this was all a big misunderstanding. Her swollen ankles and heavy womb told her the baby would not be long coming, and she smiled to herself with the happy thought that, with her figure back, her husband would have eyes for her again.

Bill returned home, unaware she was there, sitting alone in the dark kitchen. With the boys in bed asleep, the house lay silent. He hated coming home to an empty house, but he decided it was the only way to protect his family.

Bill Vincent, a former small-time wheeler-dealer, now had a name for himself. His scrapyards occupied various parts of London, disguising other activities such as money laundering and gun imports. As his business developed, taking on shipping yards and hangars, interest from other villains grew. Bill stepped on a few too many toes and found his position in South East London now compromised. They had not taken too kindly to an East End boy raking it in on their manor. He hated violence and paid heavies to do any dirty work. Two of his hardest men had been removed, and two paid off, leaving the other men in his firm too afraid to work. They were now up against gangsters that would not just kill a man but torture him first.

His main man, Kenny, an ex-boxer from the famous East End boxing club, was a one punch knockout, and handy with a blade. He stuck by Bill through the ups and downs, but warned him of the dangers facing Bill and his men if they continued with these pressures on their business activities.

Kenny wanted out. "Bill, I'm jacking it in, mate. Minding your shipments is a dangerous game. I understand you've done good by me and, believe me,

I'm grateful, but it's me family like. I can't take the threats. They done in Nicky and Deano and they'll never work again, and I'm sure I'll be next." Those were the last words Kenny said to Bill.

Two days later, when Bill arrived at the yard, he found Kenny tied to his office chair. They had cut his tongue almost off and removed his thumbs. Used as a punch bag, he survived, but never spoke again.

Bill had made big mistakes and would soon pay the ultimate price. He regretted moving to the South East. It wasn't his manor, and it was time for him to return to the East End and live a more modest life. The South East firms were up in arms that the business had gone Bill's way. However, the Arabs liked the way Bill handled business and so, whether he lived in the East End, South East London or Timbuktu, they wanted to deal with him alone.

Mad Mick, the worst type of crook, had his businesses throughout the South East, yet he had come from the East End himself. He had no morals whatsoever. He didn't give a flying shit about anyone: if he wanted something, he'd take it. Watching Bill expanding his business, at the rate he did, left a nasty taste in Mick's mouth. He was older than Bill and, unbeknown to Bill, he had his eye on Mary for himself. When Bill and Mary dated, Mick married his current girlfriend, Betty. She loved a gangster but, after a while, the romantic notions of being a gangster's moll left her. It wasn't about being wined and dined and mixing with the rich and famous. Instead it was about lying to the Ole' Bill and everyone else, going on a hide-out, and putting up with the unpredictable nature of her husband. She loved Mick though – despite the fact that he was not everyone's cup of tea, with his white skin and ginger hair. Betty's sisters could never understand what she saw in him. "Bets, love, you can do better than him, fucking ugly bastard that he is, looks like a rat," her sisters used to say.

Her mother, however, would jump to her defence. "Come on, girls, leave our Bets alone. If she loves him, and he loves her, that's enough for me."

Little did they appreciate Mick's incapability to love anyone. 'Mad Mick', as he was otherwise known, was a fitting name for him, but his real name was Michael McManners, and he was descended from a real Irish family.

As soon as Betty had that ring on her finger and her first bun in the oven, Mad Mick became the bully. She was nothing but a sex toy, cleaner and a cook. She knew no different: the excitement of living with a gangster had addled her brain and for years she thought his behaviour normal. He chose the clothes she wore, which were expensive but not her choice. She had the latest gold watch and model of car, and of course she thought he was spoiling her. However, really he was doing it so he looked good, and to show his wealth and status by having a flash-looking dolly bird on his arm. Betty, not that way inclined, just wanted to be a good wife and mum. He made her bleach her hair and wear false eyelashes; he turned her into his fantasy. Then, he made her watch porno films, and demanded that she performed like them, regardless of what they entailed. She begged not to, but he reminded her daily that to be a good wife she must pander to his needs, or else he would find someone who was more willing to satisfy them. Terrified he would leave her, she did as he demanded. Eventually, she stopped when her sons were born, and she was old and wise enough to realise the distinction between love and control. Mick did not love her; she could see now that he controlled her. His problem was he had everything he wanted except for the treasure that Bill had, and his rival's good looks.

Mick, aware of his own spiteful face, knew women screwed their noses up at him, but the old prostitutes made him feel handsome; well, they had to – he paid them enough to say he was while they rode him. It was a fix to him because, as soon as he looked in the mirror and saw the milky rat face with white eyelashes staring back at him, he rushed to the nearest hooker. Betty stopped pampering him and just tolerated him for the sake of the children.

Even Mad Mick's own family hated him. When he reached the age of twenty they left London and headed back to Ireland. He brought them so much trouble and debt that their only way out was to leave for good. Mad Mick was so full of jealousy and hate that when he conducted business, he carried it out with extreme violence every time.

Mary remained in the kitchen in darkness. Bill was not alone, he had company. At first, convinced her husband was with another woman, she thought her suspicions had been proved right. But then she realised it was squeaky Sid. He was a hard man, a once top prize fighter, who had suffered a nasty blow to the throat, with a tracheotomy which left him with a squeaky voice. She listened intently to their conversation.

Bill poured two brandies and asked Sid for the second time, "You're sure it was Mad Mick himself who stabbed Joey?"

Mary almost gasped, but stayed quiet, listening to the rest of the conversation.

"It's like I said. Joey was fucking about, trying on your leather jacket and, while I was in the office, he pops outside for a quick roll-up. Then, next thing is I've heard a thud, you know what I mean, like when a head hits concrete. So, I've run outside and seen Joey on the floor, blood pumping out of his back, and some geezer taking off, all blacked up like a fucking cat burglar. So, I run after him, he slips, I grab him, spins him around, and it's Mad Mickey staring at me. Well, he tries to stab me, we struggle, he lets go of the knife and legs it. You know the rest." Sid was struggling for breath, and he found it hard enough to speak, let alone rant on, in his excitement.

Bill ran his fingers through his thick black mane and sighed, "I can't phone the Ole' Bill, the knife's got your finger prints on it."

"No it ain't, Bill. I had me gloves on ready to go home."

"So, did Mick have gloves on?" asked Bill.

Sid shook his head.

"Right then, Sid, put the knife back and leave the yard as you found it. I won't grass Mad Mick but I ain't fucking protecting him either. If the Ole' Bill check the knife for prints, and bet your bottom dollar they will, then he's nicked by his own mistake and I'm not the grass. Fucking Mad Mickey, the Irish Bastard, should never have killed little Joey – he was only a fucking kid."

Sid looked up from his glass of brandy and the blood drained from his face.

"Billy boy, think about what you are doing. Mickey ain't no small time." He paused for moment, as if in thought. "It's weird though."

"What is?" asked Bill, looking puzzled.

"Well, Mad Mick doing his own dirty work."

Bill laughed. "Not really, this is personal. He presumed it was me he had knifed, not poor Joey. He hates me. Think about it, Sid. He has practically knocked off all me men, I reckon it was him that burned down me hangar and I swear he wanted to have my Mary for himself. That ain't no secret. Look, if he can rob from his own mother, and beat his father near to death, I wouldn't put it past the man to have a good go at me himself! Well, there is one fucking thing for sure. He is not going to get away with this one, mark my words, Sid."

"Bill, me old son, you've really gotta think about fucking calling it a day. The other firms are getting too out of control, the game ain't fucking fair any more. When those Arabs see you on your fucking jack they won't trust their gear 'ere!"

Bill nodded. "Fuck it, I'm taking the business back to my manor. They won't fuck with me there." He resigned himself to the fact that he was off back to the East End.

Sid poured another brandy.

*

Mary, still listening, remembered Mad Mick from years ago. It was an incident she had desperately tried to bury deep in the back of her mind. No one was aware what he did to her, and she had kept it a secret since she was fifteen years old. She had a Saturday job in the shoe shop on the High Street. As pleased as punch, she collected her first wage packet and was going to treat her dad to fish and chips. It was a pleasant summer evening and still reasonably light outside. Mr Cooper locked the shop up and asked her leave through the back door, which she quite happily did. The back door opened into a long alley which Mary had to walk along and around the corner, before she reached the High Street to get to the chippy. Mr Cooper locked himself in the shop to carry out a stock check. He did not believe in staff leaving via the shop entrance. It was a rule he had kept up for twenty years, until the incident with Mary.

She skipped along the alley, oblivious to the man she later recognised as Mick McManners, standing there, obstructing her exit. She smiled and asked to pass him, but he stretched his arms and legs to touch each side of the wall, blocking her escape.

"What's up, little Mary Mathews? You look worried."

At fifteen, she was scared to death. Mad Mick's vile reputation had preceded him.

"Give me a kiss and I'll let you pass," grinned Mick. He could tell she found him repulsive by the way she looked at him.

Mary couldn't believe a man five years older than her was acting like a teenager.

"Please let me pass." She tried to push her way through but he grabbed her arms and pushed her to the wall. She searched either side of him, desperate to see someone to call for help.

"Let go of me!" she screamed in a panic.

He laughed at the young woman trying to struggle and writhing pathetically in his grip.

She kicked him hard in the shins, sending a piercing pain up his leg. His eyes narrowed and, in a rage, he shoved her to the ground and jumped on top of her. In terror, she tried to scream. He put his tobacco-stained hand over her mouth and, with the other hand, tore at her pants, tugging them away from her. She struggled to get away, punching and kicking, but not hitting him hard enough to escape. Clawing at his neck, she drew blood. He winced with the pain and, out of anger, shoved his hand up inside her. She let out an almighty blood-curdling scream, heard by Mr Cooper, who rushed to the back door to find Mary lying on the floor, sobbing uncontrollably, with blood on her skirt and a man fleeing in the distance. She had a red hand mark across her face and on her arms. Mr Cooper guessed from the state of Mary, that the attacker had either raped or attempted to rape her. He offered to call the police but she refused, insisting she was all right. Gingerly, she got to her feet, with help from Mr Cooper. Without too much conversation, he walked her to his car and drove her home. Once inside the safety of her flat, she rushed to the bathroom and sobbed for hours. Her father knew something had happened, but she insisted she was okay. She loved her dad and didn't want to add to his worries. He believed in his heart someone had tried to hurt her, and all he could do was make her a cup of tea, give her two aspirins and a hug. He wished his wife was present; she would have known what to do.

Mary kissed her dad on the cheek. "I'm all right, Dad, I can look after meself, but I'm not 'arf glad I got you here for a cuddle."

Jim gave his daughter another hug. "You're such a good gal, my Mare, you really are."

Mary remembered her father's hugs and felt a lump in her throat; she did miss him at times. She was glad he lived to see his first grandson born though and, although his first name was Dan, she named his middle name as Jim, after her father.

Mary stroked her bump, grateful that Mad Mick had not stopped her from having children. The internal injuries had healed up without going to the quacks and, after a while, her periods returned to normal. But she would be forever haunted by that awful experience in the alleyway and the putrid face of Mick jumping out at her, churning her stomach and bringing about a cold sweat.

*

"And what about all this?" said Sid, gesturing to the surrounding living room.

"To tell ya the truth, Sid, I'm conscious my Mare ain't happy 'ere. She doesn't know anyone. I've eyed up another house back in Bow. The old boy that lives there wants to get out of the East End and will do a straight swap. His house is worth the same as this and, well, it's mine if I want it."

"There ya go, what have you got to lose?" smiled Sid.

Bill knocked back his brandy and shuddered.

"Sid, I never wanted all this bloodshed, fucking turns me stomach. They're evil over 'ere- fucking cutting your tongue out. What sick bastard does that, eh?" And poor Joey didn't even reach his twenty-first. How the fuck can Mad Mick mistake him for me? What, is he blind an' all?"

"Listen, me ole mate, I'm gonna get off home. My Shirley worries, ya know. I'll put the knife back first though and leave the rest to the first person who finds poor Joey in the morning."

Bill nodded. He saw Sid to the door and headed to the kitchen for a coffee.

Chapter Two

Mary realised that she had been naive regarding the affair. She put what she heard to the back of her mind and, when Bill found her slumped in the kitchen, she pretended to be asleep. He gazed at her large bump and wondered how she coped carrying such a heavy weight around – and how she was such a patient, caring mother and wife. As he stroked her face, she opened her eyes and he helped her to her feet. "Come on, Mare, let's go to bed," he whispered.

She smiled at her faithful husband and, as she rose from her chair and into Bill's arms, she felt relieved.

The next day, Mary went into labour, but Bill stayed off work for the sake of his wife. Sid was left to sort out the mess at the yard. At first, Mary took it in her stride – this was her fourth pregnancy and she knew what lay ahead. The other births had been quick and Bill had always been there, pacing in the waiting room, eager for the doctor to call him after the messy bit was over. Most fathers didn't even go to the hospital in the sixties – that was something a woman would do without their spouse and was usually left to the mother and mother-in-law, neither of whom Mary had. Her mother died when she was thirteen and Bill was an orphan, so she was lucky to have Bill at the hospital and not at the pub, wetting the baby's head before it was even born.

Bill was a proud and loving father. He would often spend time taking the boys to the park or to the river, pushing the pram with pride, and even changing nappies, something that was a rarity in his neighbourhood – not that he cared what anyone else thought. He doted on his sons, and nothing gave him greater pleasure than to see them take their first steps or say their first words, but mostly he loved to tuck them up in bed and gaze at their sweet little faces as they drifted off to sleep.

After six hours of the worst labour pains, unlike the last three births, the screams could still be heard in every room of the maternity ward. Bill fretted and decided he should be by his wife's side. He wasn't sure how he could help, and hospitals were not his favourite place, but he stood up and marched straight into the delivery room to see his wife's legs high in stirrups. Her face was red and swollen from all the pushing, and sweat was running down her cheeks. She tried to smile at him but suddenly she felt the need to push the stubborn baby out. He gasped as he saw the mass of thick black hair, followed by the pink, screwed-up face, of his fourth son. The screaming instantly stopped as the nurses held the baby in the air, proudly announcing that Mary had produced a beautiful healthy son. Bill rushed to her side and kissed her on her hot, red cheek.

"Another boy," whispered Mary, who was not surprised, having had three already.

Bill nodded as he mopped Mary's brow.

Mary's face tightened and she let out another scream. "Oh, Bill! Help me! What's happening?"

The nurse placed the baby in the crib and turned to see Mary pushing again.

"Oh, my dear… it looks like you have twins. And here comes baby number two!"

Bill jumped back and let go of his wife's hand, which she had squeezed so tightly he felt the bones crushing together. He looked down to see another mass of black hair, complete with a pink, screwed-up face, identical to the other. Mary bore down hard again and finally her baby was out. She fell back with exhaustion and Bill stared in amazement. It was a shock for Bill, who hadn't witnessed his other children being born.

He tried to control his emotions but found it impossible. "Ah, Mare, we got two," he gasped, as a hot tear sprang from his eye.

The nurse wrapped both babies in blue blankets and handed them to Mary. Bill couldn't take his eyes from the precious bundles. "Ah, look at 'em. They are beautiful, and twin boys, eh? We've got ourselves a five-a-side football team!"

The nurse smiled at Bill. "Did you not notice something missing with your second born?"

Thinking the worst, Mary pushed herself up the bed in a panic. Bill and Mary both anxiously looked at the nurse, who, oddly, was grinning like a Cheshire cat. She took the second baby and opened the blanket. "Meet your daughter!"

Bill laughed and cried at the same time.

Mary was overwhelmed. She now had the chance to buy pink things she never dared consider before, just in case she jinxed her wish. Her family was now complete. Bill looked from one to the other. Although they were boy and girl, the resemblance was uncanny and, over the days that followed, Mary and Bill had to check their nappies to see who was who.

Bill bonded with his little girl, even more so than with his other children. He always said that she had waited for him to walk into the room before she made her first appearance. Both the babies had heart-shaped faces and the biggest dimples.

Mary was delighted that her children took on their father's features – they were stunning children, with tanned skin, steel-blue eyes and thick locks of jet-black hair. Daniel, the eldest boy, with a serious look, resembled Bill more than the others did. Joseph, the second born, was a joker and spent his waking hours giggling. Sammy, the third son, was the quiet child who loved to be by his mother's side. The twins were the brainy ones, and this was to become clear as they grew up. Francesca, the only girl among four brothers, was spoilt. 'Our Dolly', was her nickname.

*

Bill, devoted to his family, ditched the life of crime to return to the East End and manage his original scrap yard. He wanted to earn an honest wage and live a simple life. Mary was happy to go along with whatever Bill wanted. She was well aware why he wanted to move and sell up the yards. The return to the East End was not so tough. They moved to a modest house with a garden and, because the old man honoured his agreement and had done a straight swap, the move went smoothly. Mary once again redesigned the interior and had the builders extend and landscape the tiny garden, turning the house into a home in which she could comfortably bring up her five children.

It was never a quiet house, and that was how Mary liked it. The boys were boisterous and Mary thought it was normal. If the neighbours complained, she shrugged her shoulders and sighed. "Well, what do you do? I mean, boys will be boys."

The neighbours wouldn't push it as most of them still regarded Bill as a gangster, although he was far from being one now.

The twins were only eight months old when Mary noticed just how bright they were.

It was a hot summer's day and Bill had bought a plastic paddling pool, one which needed inflating. Mary filled the pool with water and watched as the three older boys played a game of running in and out of the pool, throwing water over each other, and screeching with excitement, while the twins sat on a blanket next to their mother and played contently with small toys. Mary had read somewhere that twins needed less attention because they had each other. It was certainly true of her two; not only did they have each other to play with, but they also had three older brothers to make a fuss of them and keep them amused. On one afternoon, the boys were having far too much fun to play with their twin siblings and so, after a period, the twins moaned. Francesca was the first to shout, "Me go!"

Instantly, the boys stopped playing and turned to look at the twins. They stood in disbelief, along with their mother.

Daniel rushed over. "Mummy, did you hear that? They want to play in the pool."

"Well, I'll be buggered!" spluttered Mary, flabbergasted. She scooped both babies up and gently placed them in the water. "Now, boys, no splashing, and careful they don't slip under the water."

Daniel, Sam and Joseph got in the pool with the twins and played gentle games, taking great care not to splash.

Mary watched with admiration at her children playing together. The fun had taken its toll on the pool and the sides deflated. It was then that Mary stared in awe as her daughter turned around, put her mouth on the cap, and blew.

When Bill returned from work, he hardly got his foot in the door when Mary was all over him, excitedly filling him in on the day's events. "Bill, she's only eight months – it's bloody amazing! Babies don't know things like that." Bill smiled. "It doesn't surprise me, Mary. I've always said she's gonna be the brains in our family."

"No you haven't, Bill!" Mary laughed, affectionately tapping him on the arm.

"Haven't I? Well, I've always thought it then." And with that, he kissed her on the cheek. "You're a good mum, Mare."

"My kids are my life, Bill, as you well know an' all!" she teased.

*

Moving back to the East End initially proved to be the right decision. The children were thriving and Mary enjoyed motherhood. Her figure returned to the curvaceous hourglass it was before, and again she walked the streets with grace and confidence.

However, Bill was uneasy. Mad Mick had been on remand at Brixton prison for a whole year, and now the time arrived for the trial at the old Bailey. Mad Mick was a raving nutter and made horrific threats. He hoped in vain that the Irish maniac would be locked away, long enough for his children to have grown up, especially Dolly. He put up a brave front and kept his business separate from his home life, praying that the gossip escaped his wife's ears.

Considering that Mick had spent a year on remand, he appeared in the dock as if he had been away on holiday. His complexion aired a glow; it was certainly not the usual grey prison pallor you would expect. He dressed impeccably in a neat, navy blue pin striped suit with a pale blue shirt that softened his spiteful features. To someone who had never met 'Mad Mickey', he seemed gentle and harmless. His bright ginger hair was cut short – an *'American GI crop'* they called it – unlike the usual mass of wild curls that matched his wild nature. In the dock he looked innocent, and not the evil, ruthless villain he was.

The trial ran for five days and on the sixth day the jury went out. Bill waited apprehensively in the gallery and sat as if he was a religious man praying.

The verdict was not guilty of murder but guilty of manslaughter. Mad Mick paid for the best lawyer money could buy to wangle a manslaughter charge on the grounds of self-defence and the judge sentenced him to eleven years. As the judge passed sentence, Mickey looked up from the stand across to the gallery and grinned. There was no fear or regret – just eyes full of revenge staring directly into Bill's face. Bill felt numb. The blood drained from his head and he thought he would be sick. The two men stared as if in a trance. Mickey's eyes were totally transfixed on Bill. He wanted to remember Bill's face every day he served in the nick because he needed to blame someone. Bill stared in fear. He wanted to know what was going through Mick's mind and what revenge he was undoubtedly planning. He was sure Mad Mickey would serve eleven years and return the same. Unless, of course, he became a born again Christian, which, in all fairness, the crankier ones did. Bill knew, in his heart, that when Mickey got out he would be a dead man, or worse. He put the whole business out of his mind. He was safe for now and decisions would be made nearer the time.

*

Five years later

Francesca and Fredrick spent their first year at school in the same class. Initially, neither one of the twins wanted to go to school and leave the security and comfort of their home, but having three older brothers turned out to be a real bonus and, after the first few days, it was similar to home. The children could play games, do puzzles and paint pictures. When it was break time, and they had to sit in the playground to drink their small bottles of silver top milk, their older brothers would join them to check they were okay, regardless of whether they needed permission or not. And so that's how their school life began.

Francesca and Fredrick became popular amongst their peers, although Francesca struggled to get used to her real name, having been called Dolly for so long.

It was the start of the new term, and Mary was removing the net curtains, when a very distraught Fred and Dolly came tearing along the path. Before they had a chance to knock, Mary was off the window ledge and at the door. "What on earth's happened?" she asked, holding her arms open to hug her two six-year-olds, who could barely speak from gasping for breath.

She sat both her children at the kitchen table and poured them a glass of milk. "Now then, my babies, calm down and, when you've got enough breath back, tell me what's happened."

As usual, Dolly spoke first. "I'm not going back to that school no more. I don't like it, it's nasty." She looked funny when she got cross, screwing her nose up and flaring her little nostrils.

Her mother smiled at the pair of them and admired the openness of her daughter.

"And, sweetness, why don't you like school anymore?" asked Mary, a caring tone in her voice.

Fred looked over his glass and said, less brazenly, "I'm not going back 'cos I don't like my teacher!"

"They won't let me and Fred be together," added Dolly.

Mary frowned. "Are you naughty in class then?" she asked, not believing it for a second.

The twins looked at each other and shook their heads.

Mary removed her apron, combed her hair, applied her pink shimmer lipstick, and headed out to the school, while the twins waited with a neighbour for her to return.

*

The whole school could hear the clip-clop of Mary's stilettos on the parquet flooring.

The corridor was not as long as Mary remembered it, but the wooden flooring was the same, the smell of wood polish still lingered, and the grey walls were still just as bleak as they were when she attended the school.

Mary was in a foul mood when she approached the headmistress's office, and didn't wait for an answer before barging in. The headmistress, Miss Peterson, was sitting upright in her chair with a look of disgust on her spiteful colourless face. She looked Mary up and down, surprised at how glamorous she looked for a mother. "Do you have any manners?" shrieked Miss Peterson, who was now on her feet.

She had been a headmistress at the primary school for three years and, before the East End, had taught at a private school in Kent. The change was a culture shock, and she soon learned to be on her feet when approached by an irate mother or she might well find herself on her arse.

Mary was fuming; she tried to hold her composure by tightly gripping her fists. "Manners? Fucking manners? Do you have any common sense or regard for the safety of the children at your school?" spat Mary, livid at the woman's tone.

"Of course I do, Madam, I can assure you of that… " Miss Peterson was now shaking, afraid of the woman standing in her office. Seeing the anger in her eyes, she feared that the Vincent twins had met with an accident. If that were the case, then she would surely lose her position as headteacher of the school. Her bowels moved and she could feel the blood pumping through the veins in her neck.

Glaring at the headmistress, Mary moved forward and placed both hands on the desk. The headmistress, who by now was weak at the knees and slumped back into her seat, tried to swallow. She looked like a chicken stretching its neck.

"Well, tell me then, how the fuck did my two kids manage to run out of your school and reach home? Now, Miss Peterson, I don't know about you, but I don't let my two six-year-olds play in the street outside my house, let alone fucking walk home from school on their own!"

Mary shocked the headmistress with her protectiveness over her children. Most of the other mothers would have slapped theirs and sent them back to school. Again, she looked Mary up and down, and realised that she was not like the other mothers. Apart from her East End accent, she was different. Her clothes and posture spoke of money – and lots of it. "Let me call the teacher who teaches your children," she said, in a more deferential tone.

Miss Lincoln was the teacher who separated the twins, and she was responsible for them running out of school. When she entered the room, Mary took a deep breath and waited for an explanation.

Miss Lincoln was a plump woman in her late twenties, who'd had her nose well and truly put out of joint when the school took on Miss Peterson as the headmistress and disregarded her application. Similar to Miss Peterson, Miss Lincoln had her hair pulled firmly back into a bun, hardening her facial features. Mary looked at both women and wondered why teachers lacked colour. It was the same when she was at school – all teachers ever wore was black or grey, and no lipstick. Her teacher called her a tart for wearing makeup and made her remove it before she was caned across the knuckles.

The way Miss Lincoln looked her up and down infuriated Mary.

"So you're Mrs Vincent. Well, I am glad you are here. I have got a few matters I need to clear with you..."

Before the teacher could continue, Mary jumped in. "And before you go on, lady, there is one thing I need to get clear with you. No one, and I mean no one, upsets my kids like that and, more to the point, no one fucking puts my kids in danger. Now, do we understand each other?"

"Now, now, Mrs Vincent. No one was in danger – your children simply went home." She looked up and with a tight grin, rolled her eyes.

With her head up and composing herself, Mary said, "Do you have children, Miss Lincoln?"

"No, actually," replied Miss Lincoln.

"Well, thank God for small mercies," shouted Mary, and before Miss Lincoln could reply, Mary lashed out with a sharp slap. "That's for upsetting my kids and if you upset any of my children ever again it won't be a fucking slap to wipe that evil grin off your face. Are we clear?"

The whole incident proved to be a lesson to both teachers. The Vincent children were treated with kid gloves and the twins could sit together in the same class – and not that of Miss Lincoln.

*

As their school years went on, Francesca and Fredrick became inseparable – God help any child that attempted to pick a fight with either twin because both joined in, and Francesca was as tough as her brothers were, if not tougher!

As young as she was, Francesca knew that she was lucky. Her family were better off than most, her parents were very much in love, and she was doing extremely well at school. Living in the East End, in a street a spit away from a real slum area, she spent a good few years playing with children who lived in houses with no inside toilet, and slept on old urine smelling mattresses with an old overcoat as a blanket. She thanked her lucky stars she had her clean, warm bed with her pretty candlewick bedspread and pink wall-to-wall carpet.

Although tough as old boots, Francesca had a soft and generous nature much like her mother. The children in the street were quite wary of her and didn't cross her, but they felt they could go to her for a chat or friendship; she did not care who was who and who had what.

Fredrick, however, was not as generous. He would give all the time in the world to his brothers and his sister but not the kids on the street – he was afraid of catching lice or, worse, 'the Slummies', as he called them.

There was one family in particular that repulsed him. Their names were the Reilly's – an Irish family brought to England by their father and left to fend for themselves after he drank himself to death. Mrs Reilly was a timid woman, and mother to seven children who ran the streets half-naked, full of sores from fleabites. Poor Nellie Reilly was run ragged, trying to feed and care for her brood; there wasn't a year between each child. Francesca befriended the two older girls, Ruth and Sarah, and encouraged Fredrick to play with their brother, David. Fredrick hung around because of his sister – he would play the odd game of football but would not play any game that meant contact.

It was some time before Francesca took her two new friends to her house for tea. It wasn't because she thought her mother would send them away; it was because she was embarrassed for having so much, knowing they had nothing. However, the Reilly girls were eager to go, as they longed for a sandwich with real filling like meat or cheese and a slice of cake – to them that would be a luxury.

Mary agreed that the girls could come for tea and listened to Dolly's demands.

"Mum, could you make special sandwiches please? And, oh yeah, can we have chocolate cup-cakes for afterwards? And Mum, can we have it in me bedroom away from the boys just this once?"

Mary looked up from her sewing machine, "Away from the boys, you say?" She frowned and awaited an explanation.

"Well, every time we have early tea, if Dad's working late, you let the boys bring their mates in, and they grab the sandwiches, gulp down the squash and leave. I just want it to be different for my friends."

Mary grinned. "It will be different! Your friends will come for tea as guests and your brothers can bring the whole street home with them!"

Francesca smiled. "So can we have tea in my room?"

Mary shook her head "No. I won't have food upstairs, but I will lay out the best tablecloth in the dining room just for you and your friends, how about that?"

Francesca nodded and kissed her mum on the cheek.

"What was that for, you daft thing?"

"You're the best, Mum."

Mary smiled as her sweet little girl, with such bright eyes, skipped away, full of life and love.

That afternoon, Ruth and Sarah got themselves ready. There weren't so many clothes to choose from – they barely owned two dresses that fitted them. They combed each other's hair and tied their hair back with elastic bands.

Meanwhile, Francesca helped her mother lay the table.

"Dolly, get your nice pink frock on, they will be here in a minute, love," said Mary.

Francesca shuffled from one foot to the other.

"Come on, girl, spit it out. What's wrong?" Mary had seen her daughter fidget when she was nervous.

"Mum, it's a lovely dress and everything but can I leave it for another day."

Mary guessed there was a good reason and agreed.

The two guests sat at the dinner table, admiring everything in the room, as they tried to imagine living in a house as pretty, warm, and posh as Francesca's. Mary knew why her daughter had stayed in her outdoor clothes and it warmed her heart to think that Dolly could be so considerate.

Mary brought the food into the wide-eyed guests. The sandwich fillings were as thick as the bread. The table was covered with delicious treats: scotch eggs, pork pies and crisps, and plenty of homemade lemonade. After they had eaten the savoury food and drunk the lemonade, Mary came into the room bearing a tray of cakes. Francesca looked at her mum and smiled. She overdid it with the cakes, but Mary had taken one look at her daughter's friends and felt obliged to fatten them up.

She couldn't believe the difference between Francesca and her friends. Her daughter had a healthy glow, hair that shone like a raven's wing and a plump face that still had a tiny dimple in each cheek. Dolly's two friends looked gaunt, with their thin, dirty blonde hair in desperate need of a cut and sores around their nose and mouth. Impetigo was a common problem among the poorer families and highly contagious. As were head lice, which Mary spotted crawling in the heads of the two young girls.

After they finished their food, Francesca took the girls up to her bedroom where they played every board game she had and dressed every doll at least four times. In the meantime, Mary took herself off to the chemist, and bought half a dozen bottles of flea shampoo and some pretty ribbons. There was no way she would allow her Dolly to have fleas – the thought made her shudder, as she remembered herself as a child and the consequences should the nit nurses find nits in her hair. The whole lot was cut off, and she cried for a week.

Bill arrived home around seven, his usual happy self and, as he entered the kitchen, he tapped his wife on the backside and ruffled Joseph's hair. "Where's all the others, Mare?"

"Danny's at football with his mates, Sammy's next door, Freddie's in his room, and Dolly's upstairs with two of her friends."

Bill sat at the kitchen table, sipping his freshly poured tea. "So, who are her two friends then?"

Joseph turned around to face his dad. "It's those Reilly girls, Dad. She's always knocking about wiv 'em!"

Bill sat upright. "Not bloody Nellie Reilly's girls?"

Mary bent down and pulled from the oven a large roasted chicken, as big as a turkey, and placed it on the stone tile before turning to face her husband. "Is there something I should know about those girls?" asked Mary, in a concerned tone of voice.

Bill, half-laughing, replied. "Only that Old Nellie's been selling her arse up the Dilly and it ain't such a good idea to encourage our Dolly to get involved with her daughters – get what I mean, Mare?"

Mary didn't quite understand what he was getting at and, in any case, her thoughts were now with poor Nellie, having to turn to prostitution to make ends meet.

After she dished up all the dinners, she got to work on the girls' hair.

The thought of nits disgusted Dolly, but Ruth and Sarah took it in their stride. They had suffered nits on and off for the last two or three years, and were lucky if they had shampoo, let alone flea shampoo. The three of them sat with towels around their heads, coughing and spluttering.

"Mum, how does it kill the fleas?" Francesca coughed again.

"Well, love, I think they choke to death, don't you?"

The girls giggled at Mary, both wishing they had a mother like her.

"Would your mum mind if I gave your hair just a little trim? It helps to keep it shiny."

By the end of the evening, both girls looked better than ever before, and were thrilled with Mary's attention to detail. Their hair was now shiny and neatly tied back with wide pink and white spotted ribbons. Before they left, Mary gave them a bag. Inside was the rest of the chicken and cakes they couldn't eat that afternoon. They skipped off down the road, giggling at each other's pretty ribbons.

*

As they burst through the door, their mother was waiting for them. "Where the fucking hell 'ave you two been? I've been waiting to go to work!" she yelled. They loved their mother but, over the few months since she worked the streets, her attitude had changed. She no longer had time or patience for her children, and the two older girls found they were now taking over the role as mother to their younger siblings.

Nellie took one last look in the mirror. She hated what she saw: her gaunt face, the scabs around her ears, the love bites on her neck, and the bruises — some of the men were heavy-handed bastards. The last punter tied a rope round her throat too tight and in fear of her life she wet herself, which made him despise her more. He tied her to his bed and, when he had finished with her, he sent his sons in, all three of them. The evil bastards watched and laughed as each one took his turn - they poked and prodded her as if she were a piece of meat. Nellie just closed her eyes and silently prayed they would hurry up and finish and let her go.

After a few hours, the old man came back. "Come on, boys, get out me room. You've had your fun!" he cruelly laughed.

Nellie opened her eyes, hoping that he would untie her and give her extra, for all the nasty games they played with her tiny body.

He climbed on the bed and grinned, showing his black teeth. His cheeks were fat and red with harsh stubble. "Now then, my turn." He slurred his words and his foul breath made her close her eyes and turn her head away. His finger dug deep into her thighs and she squealed. He yanked her legs apart so hard she felt the muscle tear. *Please let it be over soon*, she prayed.

"That'll teach ya to piss in my bed. Now, get outta me house and thank your lucky stars I didn't feed you to me dogs."

She grabbed her clothes and tried to run, but she could scarcely stand. The blood ran down her legs, and the rope was still round her neck. When she reached the safety of the street she hid behind a bush and put her clothes back on and untied the rope. All she earned that evening was a few bruises and a torn muscle. The only consolation was she escaped with her life. Behind the bush, where she put on her clothes, she found a bottle of brandy. She took a good gulp and allowed fire from the alcohol to warm her throat. It offered bitter relief, as a good drink always did, but it was still a luxury she couldn't afford.

That evening, she was more nervous than usual, and so she knocked back a large shot of the brandy she had found, before she went out.

Sarah rounded up the other children and sat them at the table. "What did Mum leave for dinner, Kathy?"

Kathy, at the tender age of six, was the clever, pretty one. She shrugged her shoulders and replied. "Nothing."

Ruth felt a real anger towards her mother. She vividly remembered her mother puffing away on a cigarette and taking a mouthful of brandy before she left. *If she could afford those things, then why did they not have food?* Her mind went to the bag Mrs Vincent had given them. They pulled from it a large foil-wrapped parcel. All the little ones gazed in wonder as their tiny stomachs ached with hunger. Mary had wrapped not just the chicken but the roast potatoes too. Bill wondered why Mary had given him two potatoes instead of four and why the slices of chicken were on the light side. He had a good idea, nevertheless, and so kept his mouth shut.

Sarah had a bag too, which contained flea shampoo and, to her amazement, more pretty ribbons. To most other people, being given flea shampoo would have been an insult, but to Sarah and her siblings it was a godsend. The children finished their chicken and potatoes and then savoured the chocolate cupcakes. The younger children went to bed and Kathy sat up with her two older sisters and listened to their day's events – she concluded that Francesca's mum was an angel.

*

During the summer holidays, the Reilly girls spent as much time with Francesca as possible, when they weren't looking after their younger brother and sisters.

Mary took a liking to the girls and, within a week, she had their impetigo cleared up. She also allowed them to take a bath once a week and, because her Dolly was a good size bigger than her friends were, she passed on all her old clothes – which in fact were not that old at all. Now that the girls looked clean and smelled as little girls should, Freddie decided that he too enjoyed their company. He and the girls spent many summer afternoons over at the small woods, building camps and having picnics.

Late one summer afternoon, Mary noticed that the twins were not home for their supper and so she took a walk over to the Reilly's to accompany them back. It was a still afternoon and Mary enjoyed the stroll. She nodded at the neighbours as she passed, and they greeted her with warm smiles. "Have you seen me twins?" she asked one woman, who was leaning on her garden gate gossiping to another neighbour.

"Oh yeah, let me think… Yes, love, they were with those Reilly girls walking down Herman Street."

Mary nodded and headed towards the Reilly's household. It wasn't until she turned the corner that she could see the smoke billowing out of their house.

Mary gasped. All she could picture was her twins trapped in a fire. A crowd had formed outside the house. Mary pushed her way through the crowd, hearing them swap evil comments. "Let the fucking house burn to the ground, it's a house of ill repute, the dirty fucking whore," one woman spat.

"Shut up! Just 'cause she was 'aving it away with your ol' man!" laughed another neighbour.

Mary reached the front door to see the firefighters dragging out two little children – both of them were limp in his arms. Mary barged past but two other firefighters pulled her back. "Get off me, my kids are in there!" she yelled in desperation.

"You can't go in there," the fireman warned her.

Mary collapsed to her knees, screaming, "Get my babies out!" Her throat was burning from the smoke billowing out of the door.

"Mum!" screamed the twins.

Mary looked up and, to her amazement, saw her children were safe. She jumped to her feet and grabbed them in her arms, crying, but otherwise so relieved that she was holding them. She was convinced she had lost them in the fire.

Francesca pushed her away. "Mum, Mum. Sarah, Ruth, Kathy – all of 'em are in there!"

Mary put her hands to her face. "Jesus…"

Mary heard a firefighter call out, "Back off now, the fire's out of control. Get the men out, now!"

She screamed in a panic, "How many have you pulled from the fire?"

"Six in all, love, but we didn't know how many were in there."

Mary's eyes widened. "But she has seven children."

The firefighter shrugged his shoulders and apologised. "There's nothing else I can do, love."

Mary looked up at the blazing house and, for a split second, she thought she saw a tiny head at the bedroom window. Instantaneously, she was through the door, her cardigan protecting her face from the smoke, as she tore up the stairs. Francesca and Freddie stood, clutching each other, praying that their mother would be okay.

There was an enormous blast, so huge that it threw Mary out of the bedroom window and onto the overgrown front lawn. She was clutching Kathy, the tiny six-year-old. Francesca screamed as she and the crowd ran to their aid, amazed to see both Mary and Kathy get to their feet.

Kathy's face was red, and it was clear she had suffered a burn.

The fireman helped Mary away from the blaze. "You could have died in there, whatever possessed you?"

Mary turned and faced the enormous man, who was concerned for her safety, but she couldn't stand the careless tone in his voice. "I don't give up on people's lives that bloody easily. She could 'ave been my girl and I would like to think someone would 'ave done the same for mine."

The firefighter walked away, knowing he called off the search too soon.

The children were taken to Hackney hospital to be assessed for lung damage but Mary refused, insisting she was all right.

*

Meanwhile, Nellie arrived home to discover her house burnt to the ground. No one knew if she was alive or dead and no one, except her children, would have cared. A neighbour saw Nellie standing there in a state of horror and total disbelief and quickly ran to her side.

"Nellie, dear, there's been a fire," said Mrs Landers, a sweet elderly woman.

Nellie's expression was pitiful. "My kids?" she whispered, afraid to hear the answer.

"They are all at the Hackney hospital, love. Checking them for smoke damage, they are."

Nellie fell to her knees; the shock had hit her hard, and it was a while before she could mumble a clear sentence. Another neighbour invited her in to her house and tried to give all the details, including the bravery of Mrs Vincent. "I'll tell you, Nellie Reilly, if it weren't for that Mary Vincent, one of your children would 'ave burned alive. I'll tell you this for nothing as well, Nellie, that woman, believe it or not, has been keeping an eye out for your kids while you were off selling yourself."

Nellie looked at Ivy Chambers as she sat opposite her in her kitchen, a cigarette in one hand, and the other tucked under her breast. There was no compassion in the woman's voice and all Nellie wanted to do was leave.

"I know you don't want to hear it, Nellie, but I'm gonna tell you anyway. If you had been at home with your children, where you should have been, your house would still be standing. Another thing – the social services were sniffing around here earlier. I wouldn't be surprised if you lose those kids. Mark my words, Nellie Reilly, if you don't get off the game you'll 'ave those nippers taken off you."

Ivy spoke with no compassion, yet her advice was sound. The social services had been asking questions but, as usual, no one knew a thing. The whole street knew that Nellie was out every night, but they also knew that she didn't physically hurt the kids or have any strange men in the home interfering with them. There were worse families on the estate, where the children were used as sex slaves by their own flesh and blood. However, they could never be proven and, besides, they looked okay. It was not like they weren't plump and healthy; they were just mentally disturbed, and so their parents got away with it.

Nellie visited her children in hospital – their tiny, frail bodies lost in the huge hospital beds, all seven lining the whole of the ward. The matron hadn't allowed the children to move. They lay there with the starched white sheets wrapped so securely around them that they were almost tied to the bed. She marched down the centre of the ward to meet the pathetic looking Nellie, who felt she didn't have the right to be there. After all, she had left her children alone to fend for themselves.

"I can see a family resemblance; you must be the mother." The matron, like all matrons, was a scary character, who ran the ward like an army unit. Everything and everyone had to be spotlessly clean so, even before the children could recover, she had the nurses give them all a bed bath. "Now then, you say hello but make it quick mind, I don't want you in the way when the doctor does his rounds." There was no compassion in her voice. She looked Nellie up and down and not discreetly either. If her intention was to make Nellie feel like shit, then she succeeded with flying colours.

Nellie wiped her nose with the back of her hand, as all the crying had set the snot running.

"Oh, for goodness sake! Here, girl, take a bloody tissue."

Nellie took the tissue from the matron and awkwardly smiled. She went to each child, kissing them, sobbing her apologies. Kathy was the last little one to be seen by her mother. Nellie gasped when she saw the huge bandage on her face.

Kathy tried to smile but her face was still sore. "I'm gonna be a nurse when I'm a big girl," whispered Kathy, through her dried and cracked lips.

Nellie kissed the top of her head, the only part free of dressings. "Course you are me little cherub, and a damn fine one you'll make an all," she whispered, her Irish accent soft and reassuring.

As she left, the matron looked at the little girl. *With a mother like that, she would be lucky if she ended up cleaning the hospital floors.*

Outside the hospital, Nellie sat on the bench, lit up a fag, and contemplated her next move. The house was burned to the ground, her kids had almost died, and she knew in her heart Mary had been their saviour, and not for the first time. She went nervously to pay Mary Vincent a visit.

Gingerly standing at the front door, Nellie waited for a reply. She wanted to apologise but was sure she would get a mouthful or a slap – not that she didn't deserve it. Mary was reputed for giving a right hook to anyone she felt took liberties with her or her family, yet Nellie had never laid eyes on the woman.

The ordeal had got the better of Mary and so, after a nice long bath and a hot cup of milk, she had drifted off to sleep. Bill, concerned for his wife, ordered all the children to play quietly and let their mother rest. As he answered the door, it startled Mary.

Nellie looked up at the tall handsome man standing before her. "Hello... Uh, I'm Nellie. Could I speak to your wife, Mr Vincent?"

Bill was angry that she had disturbed his wife but, more than that, he blamed her for his wife risking her own life to save Nellie Reilly's kids. "You'd better fuck off now before I kick you up the garden path meself!" he said.

The blood drained from Nellie's face and she turned to run.

Mary was in the hall now and pushed Bill aside. "Nellie, wait a minute."

Bill grunted and stepped back. Nellie stopped dead in her tracks.

"Come in, love, we'll have a little chat in the kitchen over a nice cuppa, aye?"

Nellie was on the verge of tears.

Bill walked on in front, rolling his eyes – typical of Mary to be so soft. He put the kettle on and left the women to it.

While Mary stood making the tea, Nellie admired her surroundings. Everything in the kitchen was beautiful. All the units had been replaced with solid wood, the blue and white wall tiles had patterns on, and the floor was covered with a blue marble-effect lino. On one wall there were wooden shelves, housing an expensive-looking array of plates. Even Mary was beautiful. She obviously had just had a bath but, standing in her lilac bathrobe with no make-up on, she would put most dolled-up women to shame. Looking into her cup, she said sheepishly, "I'm so very sorry Mrs Vincent, really I am," and a tear rolled down her cheek.

"Now then, Nellie, I did not ask you into my home to give you a lecture on morals. I thought it might be nice to get to know one another a bit more, especially since our kids are inseparable these days." Mary smiled.

Nellie was astonished at just how friendly and understanding Mrs Vincent was. She had met Francesca and Freddie and was impressed with how sweet and polite they were; now it was obvious they took after their mother. "Mrs Vincent..."

Before she could finish, Mary corrected Nellie. "No, please, call me Mary."

"Mary... I know you've done a lot for my kids these last few months and I know I should have thanked you before but, well, I guess I was too embarrassed. But I have really appreciated it."

Mary thought the tiny Irish woman was a truly pitiful sight.

"Listen to me, Nellie, I haven't done any more than you would have done for my kids if I'd needed it," she said.

"I love my kids, Mary, I do. I know people are talking about me and I know it hurts me little 'uns, but I haven't got much choice."

Mary topped up the tea and, in a quiet tone, asked gently, "Why don't you go to the state for money? It's gotta be better than... well you know."

Nellie looked up for a minute and sadly smiled. "Mary, I do claim the dole but it's not even enough to pay off the debts the ol' man left me." She shook her head. "I hate what I do, but it's the only way I can keep those loan men off me back – they broke two of me fingers already, and knocked out me back teeth."

"Oh my God, who are these men?" asked Mary.

Nellie looked at Mary in amazement. She was the only person in a whole year to take any interest in her. "Jack Mills and his boys. I knew nothing about it until they came knocking on me door, demanding four hundred pounds."

Mary gasped, "Four hundred?"

Bill walked into the kitchen to top up his tea "Did I hear you mention Jack Mills?"

"Do you know him, Bill?" Mary asked.

"I should cocoa – he works for me!" he replied, with a bitter grin.

"But Bill, he's a loan shark, how can he work for you?"

Bill frowned at Mary. "Now, girl, you don't get involved in my business."

Mary looked at her husband and gritted her teeth.

Bill realised then that he had upset her. "Anyway, what's that got to do with her?" Bill rudely pointed to Nellie.

Mary told Bill about the money and the broken fingers.

Bill looked at the women in disbelief. "No, no, no, Nellie, you've got it wrong. When I lend money to people like your ol' man, they have to pay a little extra as insurance and I always take life cover simply for that reason." Bill scratched his head and thought for a second, while Mary and Nellie waited in anticipation.

"Nellie, why did you think your ol' man owed me four hundred?"

Nellie looked at the floor as she muttered her answer, afraid she might say the wrong thing.

"Well?" said Bill. "Speak up." He was struggling to understand her Irish accent.

Nellie coughed and tried again. "Your men told me... They said he borrowed so much over the last four years that, with the interest, it amounted to a few hundred and, as I was his wife, it was my responsibility now that he was dead." She slowly lifted her head to see his reaction.

Bill shook his head. He looked down at Nellie and said in a soft voice, "Sorry, girl, you owe me nothing. His debt was only eighty quid, which was covered by the insurance. I'm sorry, love."

Bill left the room to use the phone. "Allo, Sid, I want you to get Jack Mills in the yard tonight. I'm gonna personally kick that fucking scummy ponce's arse myself. He's been running a right tidy racket at my fucking expense!"

Before Bill left for the yard, he popped back into the kitchen and grabbed Nellie's hand to inspect her deformed fingers. "Right, girl, how much have you given that scum bag since your ol' man died?"

Nellie rummaged around in her handbag and retrieved a small notebook. Each payment had been meticulously logged and signed by Jack.

Bill took the notebook. "Don't worry, girl, he won't be bothering you again. I'll get your money back," he promised.

Nellie put her head in her hands and sobbed as Mary placed a protective arm around her shoulders. "You can stay in our spare room tonight, and tomorrow we'll get you sorted out."

As Nellie lay on the sweet smelling bed, she closed her eyes and tried to sleep. She should have felt elated, but all she could think about was the neglect her children had endured. Filthy men relieving themselves for a quid or two. Her head was filled with horrific thoughts: the sick games some of the men played, the violent men that bit her, how they slapped her, tied her up, and then ran off with the night's earnings. Men despised her for what she was and woman despised her out of fear that their husbands might have been spending money on her.

*

Two days later, the kids were out of hospital, and each one had been given a clean bill of health. Mary had them at her house – of course. Bill agreed, feeling responsible. Meanwhile, next door but one, Mrs Thomas had passed away and left all the contents of the house to Mary. Over the past four years, Mary had cared for the old woman and would always cook an extra meal for her. Once a week she would do her housework and help her in and out of the bath. She liked the old woman and, not having a mother herself, treated the old girl like her own. The kids called her Granny Thomas, which delighted her, because all of her children had moved miles away, and she'd never heard from any of them again.

Although Mary was upset, she wasted no time in taking Nellie and her children down to the housing offices to ask for the house that once belonged to Mrs Thomas. This was common back in the sixties – most houses were owned by councils, and the tenancy was down to the discretion of the housing officers. Over the years, Nellie became a negative person, always expecting the worst. Nothing good had gone her way since she had left Ireland, and so she was overwhelmed when Mary offered to help in this huge way.

The young housing officer pertly sat behind a large oak table and listened to Mary with a nasty smirk spread across her face. She relished her position of power and enjoyed seeing potential tenants beg, plead and squirm.

"So, Mrs Ledbetter, when can Mrs Reilly move in?" Mary asked.

The woman, who was in her early twenties, and dressed in a cheap-looking suit, sat upright on her seat and looked down her nose at Mary. "No, I am afraid that the house is intended for another family – they have sixty points," she sneered.

Mary bit her lip for a few seconds and thought before she spoke. "No, Mrs Ledbetter, I do not think you have understood what I've just said."

Betty Ledbetter was taken aback by Mary's attitude, causing the corners of her mouth to twitch.

"You see, Mrs Ledbetter, Mrs Reilly here is offering you, or rather offering Hackney Council, the chance to make up for the major mistake it made."

The smirk disappeared as the young woman demanded to know what Mary was talking about.

"Oh dear, it's obvious that you haven't heard then? Well, let me be the bearer of bad news. You see the gas in the house, fitted by your own men, turned out to be faulty. That was what caused the fire and put all seven of Mrs Reilly's children in hospital."

Betty Ledbetter was now getting the picture, but she looked Nellie up and down and smirked again. She could never afford a court case as big as this one would undoubtedly be.

"Well, I'm sorry about that. I'm sure there will be a letter of apology in the post. Now, if that's all, ladies, I do have other matters to attend to."

Mary took a deep breath. "Excuse me, young lady, but I don't think you've grasped what I am saying to you. Firstly, if Mrs Reilly does not get that house, we will take you to court. Oh, and incidentally, my husband, Bill Vincent of Vincent's Yards, will cover the costs. His solicitors are on it as we speak. Secondly, I will also add that, during the proceedings you, Mrs Betty Ledbetter, were very unhelpful, and showed no compassion over such a delicate incident."

Betty nervously shuffled in her seat. She knew who the Vincents were, and she feared that she was in danger of losing the job she loved so much.

Mary then stood up to leave, along with Nellie, who kept her mouth shut the whole time. "Anyway, Mrs Ledbetter, you'd obviously prefer to pursue this matter in court, so we'll waste no more of your time, as you're apparently so busy."

Betty stood and pleaded with the two women to sit down.

"I can see your point. Now, it's the house in Green Street you say?"

Nellie nodded, as Betty took out a large ledger type book and filled out all Nellie's details. "Oh yeah, before I forget – the settlement offer was to include all the furniture destroyed in the fire."

Betty nodded. "Yes, I'll get the list from the fire damage report."

Mary smiled. "No need. We have a list and the cost of replacement with us." She was confident she was on a winning streak. The young woman gazed at the never-ending list of items, knowing that it would have been impossible for a woman like Nellie to have owned even half of them.

Mary and Nellie walked away from the housing department with the keys to a new home and a cheque for three hundred pounds.

"Nellie, you can move in now because the old girl left me all her gear. I don't need it but it's all right, I can tell you – I washed most of it meself." Mary grinned.

"I must have been in such a two and eight I don't remember the fireman's report saying the gas meter was the problem."

Mary laughed. "It probably didn't but, by the time the council get the report, it'll be too late – you've signed for that house, got your cheque, and anyway, ol' Mrs fancy pants Ledbetter is never going to own up to a mistake that big, is she?"

Nellie could not believe her luck and vowed to Mary that she would never forget all her family had done for her.

Meanwhile, Jack Mills lay in a hard hospital bed, thinking desperately of a way to get his own back on Bill Vincent. He was stunned that night when Bill gave him the kicking that nearly cost him his life. He had known Bill to do a bit of dirty work, but not on his own men. He thought his little scam was pretty much sewn-up, if it hadn't been for that slag, Nellie Reilly. He would have her too, and Mary Vincent. He looked down at his broken hands and cringed. That night would haunt him for the rest of his life; it was the first real beating he had ever had. The cracking sound of each finger breaking echoed around in his head. The thud of the hammer as it shattered his shins and vibrated along the length of his legs caused his stomach to churn. The final blow of the hammer to his forehead gave him instant relief. He was dumped at the side of the road and found by a passer-by two hours later. The doctors had told him he was lucky to be alive, and whoever did this to him had tried to kill him. He would make it his life's ambition to get back at Billy Vincent - one way or another.

*

Bill sat in his office, staring at yet another one of Mad Mickey's letters. This one was different, and he poured himself a large brandy and gulped it back. His thick black mane flopped forward and he quickly ran his hands through his hair as he tried fearfully to think how he could protect his family. There was no way they were going to live in fear for the rest of their lives.

Mad Mickey was due out next year and he was coming for his girl, the sick bastard. There was no point in even plotting to kill the mad Irishmen himself; it would do no good. Mad Mick brainwashed his four sons, who were all as nutty as he was, and they had been the ones dropping notes into Bill. He could see that they all resembled their dad, sharing his same mad expressions of anger and hate. They never actually spoke to Bill; instead they'd just handed him notes containing sick messages before they grinned and left.

As the days passed, Mary knew there was something bothering Bill. He was off his food, there were bags under his eyes, and he had kept her awake by tossing and turning. One evening, she sat upright in bed and demanded to know what exactly was on her husband's mind, what it was that worried him so much.

He shook his head. "Nothing much, love, only business."

"I'm going downstairs to make a nice cuppa. By the time I come back up, Bill Vincent, you are going to tell me all about it."

Before he could answer, she was gone – only to return five minutes later with a large tray of biscuits and a steaming pot of tea.

Bill wondered why he had never included his wife in some shape or form in the running of his business. She had a good head on her shoulders – more so than some of the men in his firm.

"Here you go, Bill." Mary handed him a strong cup of tea. "Now then, I've been married to you for seventeen years and you can't tell me it's business that's on your mind. Now, either it is an illness, another fucking woman, or it's something worse. So, Bill, what is it?"

Before Bill could think of a story to spin his wife, the words came tumbling out. "Mare, it's worse... Oh my God, what have I done?" Bill fell to the floor and sobbed like a baby.

Mary took her husband in her arms and whispered to him as if he was one of their children. "Whatever it is, we will deal with it together."

Bill told Mary everything. The happenings the night Joey died, the court case, the letters, and finally Mickey's threat. Mary sat in silence, trying to take it all in. A lump seemed to be wedged in her throat and, try as she might, she could not comprehend why Mad Mick wanted to harm her daughter. "But Bill, why our Dolly? Why?" she whimpered.

Bill looked directly into his wife's eyes. "Mary, he is fucking mental. He thinks I put him away for twelve years and he wants to hurt me badly. The worst thing he could do is harm the most precious thing in my life. Being as our Dolly is the only girl – well, he decided it's her."

Mary put her hands to her mouth as if it had just registered what her husband was saying to her. They sat in silence for a few minutes, letting the tea go cold.

"Well, Bill, we will just have to move."

Bill shook his head. "Babe, if it was that simple we'd be gone by now. He's sent me a message every week for twelve years – even if we moved he would find us." He cried again and so did Mary.

Mad Mick was not due out for another six months and so that gave them enough time to make arrangements. The atmosphere in the household was sombre, and it rubbed off on the children, who were oblivious to the looming problem. They bickered and fought, all except Dolly, who tried to keep the peace for her parents' sake. She could see there was anguish in her mother's eyes and could not fathom why.

The summer holidays were ending, and the children were getting ready to go back to school. The twins were due to start senior school but awaited the results of the eleven plus exam, to see which school they could attend. The postman finally came with the results, and the whole family gathered around the breakfast table, eagerly awaiting the opening of the two brown envelopes.

Francesca's results were first. Mary put her hand to her mouth as she read the attached letter. Quickly, she opened the second letter. All the children remained silent, and again she read the attached letter. "Oh, Bill," she squealed, beaming from ear to ear.

"Mum?" screeched the twins in unison, waiting for the verdict.

"Well, I be buggered," said Bill, "I never thought I had two geniuses on me hands!"

"Dad, did we pass?" asked Freddie, grinning at his sister.

"You did more than pass! You have been recommended by the school board and the examination board to go to a grammar school!"

The twins hugged each other and then their parents.

Although it was only nine in the morning, Mary decided to serve cake for breakfast – it was great finally to have something to celebrate! The past few months had been an unbearable worry. Mary, who always looked impeccable, was looking tired and tatty around the edges, and Bill looked completely washed out. This morning, however, their spirits were lifted, and they laughed and joked with each other. That was, until they heard an unexpected knock at the door.

Two smartly dressed men demanded to come in.

"What is it exactly you want?" asked Mary, in her polite but firm manner.

"Your husband, Mrs Vincent." The police officers paused, grinned and went on. "We've come to make an arrest. He can come peacefully or not, the choice is his."

Mary thought they had made a mistake and called Bill to the door.

Bill looked them up and down, as he tried desperately to remember his last criminal activity.

"Mr Vincent?"

Bill nodded.

"Mr Vincent, I am arresting you for the attempted murder of Mr Jack Mills."

Bill felt his knees go weak as he looked at his wife. He knew she couldn't take much more.

*

She watched her husband go peacefully with the two detectives along her garden path. When she returned to the kitchen, the kids sat silently. They had heard the policemen and awaited some reassurance from their mother. She sat at the table, poured herself another cup of tea, and spoke very calmly and with a smile on her face, "We are a family that sticks together and that is what we will do now. Before we know it, Daddy will be home," she said, biting her lip. She had known about the Jack Mills incident, but neither of them believed that Bill would be arrested for it. Men like Jack Mills didn't grass – they would take any kicking on the chin and, if scores needed to be settled, then it would be done with fists, not by getting the police involved. Mary knew a stunt like this would mean the end for a man like Jack. He could never hold his head up. He would be forever looking over his shoulder. But Jack couldn't care less. He had just been offered a few grand by Mad Mick to grass up Bill. The money would see him all right in Spain, and his revenge would be sweet.

Mad Mick made sure he knew everything concerning Bill, even from inside the prison and so, when told about Jack Mills, Mick smiled. He had a lump sum of money stashed away, and it was worth paying a low-life like Jack just to see Bill inside the slammer.

Dan, the eldest boy, who looked more like his father every day, announced that he would make sure that, if the worst came to the worst, he would look after his family. Mary studied her first born. He had grown so much and for the first time she realised he was becoming a man. His voice had broken and he had even begun to shave. The odd spot and other teenage traits did not deter him from looking handsome. He was now almost seventeen.

Then she looked at Joe who, at nearly sixteen, was almost a man. He towered above his elder brother and his stocky frame rippled with muscle. These were precious and vulnerable years for her sons. If Bill was found guilty of attempted murder, it would mean that they had lost the years of nurturing her boys would need. Mary sent the younger children out to play, after she had made them promise not to tell a soul, and then got to work tracking down Sid and Bill's solicitor.

Sid arrived and sat for a while in Mary's kitchen while she told him the whole sorry story. "Sid, I don't know what I'm gonna do. If he gets banged up for this, he could be looking at an eight stretch, and Mad Mick is out soon."

Sid nearly choked on his tea. "Mary, what do you know about Mad Mick?"

"Everything, Sid. Bill told me everything." She bowed her head and looked defeated.

"Oh, Mare, what can I say? If I can do anything just give me a bell, yeah?" He patted Mary on the shoulder and slowly stood to go.

"Sid, what would I do without you and your Shirley? You're good to me, ya know."

Sid smiled and his fat face lit up. "Bill has done good by me enough times. Me and Shirl, we never could 'ave kids, and the money I've earned at the yard has given me and her a fair few holidays that have taken our minds off it, know what I mean? And look at you. You've always let me treat the kids as if they were me own. What I'm trying to say, gal, is that I see you as family." He bent down and kissed her on the cheek. "And family stick together."

Mary patted his hand and saw him to the door.

Bill was remanded in custody pending the trial. Mary realised she had to make arrangements for Dolly before that nutter Mick was released. She looked out of the window, and tears rolled down her cheeks as she watched her twins sitting on the front wall. They had gone over every avenue looking for a way they could protect their family, but there was still no obvious answer.

Chapter Three

Mary sat at the kitchen table, alone. The morning cuppa, which she usually enjoyed in the company of her husband, would be a lonely experience for the next few years. She had done all the crying she could do, and now she had to be head of the family and make decisions. She needed to be mum and dad. She sighed aloud. How was she going to cope with the house, the business and four young men – not to mention the ever-looming threat that her only daughter could be taken from her - if she didn't come up with a plan soon?

Bill constantly told her, "Get Dolly away. How can I do my bird worrying about my girl every minute of the day?"

He was right; the only way to protect their daughter was to send her away and never make contact. The idea churned her stomach – she would die for her children but, if Francesca stayed, God knows what fate would bestow on her. It was funny; when she thought of her daughter brought up by another family she looked upon her as Francesca and not Dolly. That was their special name for her because, as a tiny child, she looked as fragile and precious as a china doll.

As her sons gathered around the kitchen table, she stared at each one individually: she was so proud of her brood. All these years her husband had been the man of the house and she had seen the boys as children – as her babies. Sure, they were loud, and they might have a fight now and then, but when Bill said jump they asked how high. He'd worked them in the yard from a young age, teaching them to graft and showing them how to earn a few quid.

Dan especially loved having money in his back pocket and he used it to buy smart clothes to pull the birds. Joe was a hard worker with muscle, bigger than most of the men at the yard. They were all tough and could fight as if grown men – even Fred could brawl. Joe was more sensitive than the others, although they all agreed he was the hardest, always winning at arm wrestling and coming out on top when it came to play fighting with his brothers. In the years that followed, the pain of losing their sister made them close and dangerous.

Dan, the image of his father, pleaded with his mother to let him take over the yard. His father had taught him well: organising orders, paying wages and learning the ropes to the business in a mature fashion. He wanted to be an adult, play like the big boys – have the cash, the name and, most importantly, the respect.

Mary shook her head. "I can't let you take on so much. You're too young, love. Besides, I've got good ole Sid to give us a hand."

Dan jumped up from the table and, in a raised voice, said, "I'm not a baby anymore! I've worked with Dad. I know the business and Sid will help me." After a deep breath, he lowered his voice and whispered, "You don't need to worry over yards and the finances – just concentrate on our Doll."

Sam and Joseph looked up to their older brother. His sophistication bordered on arrogance, yet he still managed to be charming. Mary loved her boys equally and felt comfortable boasting their individual qualities. Often she remarked on how smartly her eldest boy dressed. 'Could charm the birds out of the trees, but rub him up the wrong way and his words will cut you like a knife.'

Knowing she no longer needed to worry, Mary felt proud as she watched her son become the head of the house. Dan was right – he knew more about the business than she did. It needed a man with muscle and he was certainly strong, both mentally and physically.

Mary nodded. "All above board though, boys, no funny business. Besides, I can't have both my men inside now, can I?"

Dan leant over and kissed his mother gently on the cheek. "Don't worry about us, Mum," he reassured her as he gestured to his younger brothers. "Just sort out Dolly and Freddie."

Sam took his mother's hand and said in a quiet voice, "When Dolly goes, Freddie's gonna need you, Mum – really need you."

His words stuck deep in her mind as it dawned on her that not only would Dolly suffer, but Freddie too; they had never been apart, ever.

"This will be the hardest thing we will ever have to do, but we have no choice. We must be there for each other no, matter what." Mary took another deep breath to stop the tears from flowing. Her heart ached from the absence of her husband. Like Fred with Dolly, she wasn't used to being without Bill, and, as she slipped into her bed at night, she curled into a ball, hugging herself to sleep. She missed his big strong arms wrapped round her waist and every night she shed a tear.

Dolly and Freddie lay sleeping in their rooms, oblivious to the fear faced by the rest of the family. The older brothers looked at each other; there was a special bond amongst them – instilled by their parents – to care for one another. The fact that Bill was an orphan, who dragged himself up, made him a real family man, and he ensured that his boys learnt to put each other first. The kids watched each other's backs and never sided with anyone outside the family.

*

Mary's sister never kept in contact with her; they were just too different. The boys did not recall the visit with their aunt when they were younger and Dolly had never met her. In fact, Anne wasn't aware she existed. This situation would be ideal. No one knew about Anne, as it had been so long ago that the locals forgot about her. It was the perfect place for Dolly to go to be safe from Mick — she just prayed that Anne wouldn't make her life a misery. Now the only problem she faced was talking her sister into looking after her daughter.

All the worrying for Dolly's safety had left Mary exhausted, but the idea of her one and only girl being sent to live with her estranged sister changed the worry into grief. She placed her head in her hands and sobbed for what seemed an eternity. *Poor Dolly, away from her brothers, to a life so different.* The images of her being controlled and stifled distressed Mary, but what kept her going was that one day they would be a family again.

Monday morning, Dolly went with her mother to visit her father for the last time, although Dolly didn't know this. She was surprised that her mother had let her take the day off school because she usually booked any visits for a Saturday so the kids wouldn't miss their education — but still, she didn't question it.

Dolly loved her father so much that each day he was away it got harder and harder. She missed his comforting smile and reassuring hugs. The rigmarole at the prison was the same old story. The queue went on forever outside the gate and then, when the doors eventually opened, the visitors poured in. They were squashed into a small room that stank of urine until the doors at the front were locked, before finally being allowed to move once the door at the opposite end swung open. Dolly hated the noise of the chains that rattled when each door opened or shut. She gripped her mum's hand throughout the long drawn-out process. She remembered the search room, but luckily they never bothered with Mary or her. Perhaps they guessed that Bill wasn't smuggling anything. Nor was he the type to shove a wrap of Lebanese up his arse to trade off on the wing. Bill watched with amusement; he understood why the screws turned a blind eye — after all, it kept some of the men calm, especially the Rastas. There was a good reason they grew those enormous dreadlocks — it was the perfect place to stash ganja. Drinking the odd glass of throat burning, prison-made hooch was the only illicit activity Bill tried. It tasted like shit but helped to pass the time away – either sleeping it off, or with your head down the pan chucking up the contents of your stomach!

Finally, they unlocked the visiting room, and Dolly eagerly scanned the tables to see where her father was sitting. When she spotted him she was shocked: he looked older, and had the grey pallor typical of the other inmates, who lacked sunshine and decent food. When he saw her, his eyes lit up, and a quivering smile appeared across his pale face. Dolly ran into her father's arms and hugged him tightly. Bill looked over his daughter's shoulder at his wife as tears flowed down his cheeks. In a comforting gesture, Mary rubbed Bill's back. She winced as she felt his protruding bones.

"What's up, Dad?" asked Dolly, as she looked from her mother to her father and back again.

"Sit down here, love," Mary said, patting the chair next to her.

Instantly, Dolly sat and waited for an explanation as to why her parents looked so sad.

"I love you with all my heart – I probably loved you too much!" Bill laughed a sentimental laugh.

Dolly frowned, not understanding the awful tension between them.

"There is a man who, in a few weeks, will be coming for you," Bill said in a trembling voice, and another tear rolled down her father's face. "He wants to take the most precious thing away from me – to hurt me in the worst way possible... And my most precious thing in the world is you, Dolly."

There was silence for a few minutes while Dolly tried to take it all in. "Why does he want to hurt you so bad, Dad?"

"Well, my darling, he went to prison because he killed my best friend and the police found out it was him – but he believes it was me that told them." Bill gazed into his daughter's big, innocent eyes, wondering if his little girl, as bright as she was, could really comprehend what he was saying.

"It's all right, Dad, we can move." She faced her mother and smiled, waiting for agreement.

The sweet naivety of his child burned deep in Bill's chest. He was forced to explain something that was so far removed from a child's world that not even adults should have to comprehend it. However, the threat was so real he could not afford to call Mick's bluff. He would never take that gamble with his Dolly's life. "No, my darling. Wherever we move he will track us down, so you need to be very brave and grown up." His voice began to crack and he couldn't speak, as the words were too painful. "We can't come with you..."

Dolly had never seen her father so devastated – she didn't recognise him, for he had always been strong and in control.

Mary held her daughter's hand, took a deep breath, and continued. "We need to protect you and get you away to a safe place where he won't find you."

"Where?" Dolly almost screamed, her eyes widening in total disbelief.

"My sister's," Mary said, through gritted teeth. Bill nodded.

"I didn't know you had a sister," she replied in a flat tone. Her heart sank.

The vision of her parents that day remained with her as she grew into a woman. She had never seen such hurt and sadness in a person's eyes as she did then and never forgot it. It returned on many a lonely night to haunt her. Despite the fact that they were sending her away, demanding she had no future contact with them or her brothers, she understood why and loved them even more.

*

The morning came for Dolly to leave, and each brother had red rings around their eyes as if they had just walked into a gas chamber. Poor Freddie was sick and inconsolable, Sam could not speak, and Joe and Danny kept repeating, "It will be okay, it will be okay."

Mary wondered who they were trying to convince.

Dolly tried to look as if she was coping and hovered about the house collecting pictures and small sentimental items. Mary noticed how grown up and sophisticated her daughter had become. Her heart wrenched. She would never see her grow into a beautiful woman. Mary, racked with guilt and an inconsolable heartache, didn't have a choice – she knew she had to let Dolly go and just pray that the monster that had threatened her daughter's life would have a change of heart. If there was no Mad Mick or his devoted sons, there was no threat.

The long drive to Surrey was silent. Mary could not speak for the choking lump in her throat. Freddie held Dolly's hand as he stared out of the window. He was old enough to understand the situation and, as he looked out across the fields at the never-ending countryside, he thought of how he would kill Mad Mick. As he closed his eyes he pictured a different scene every time – watching as Mick was hung, stabbed or shot, and begging for his life. Then he would drift into a sleep and dream about his family, all together, building sandcastles on the beach, as they did when they were younger.

Sid had borrowed a car and offered to drive them there, praying all the while that no one would guess where they were headed.

Chapter Four

Mary was amazed at the beautiful surroundings. She rarely ventured out of town except for the coastal trips during the school holidays, and was struck to find that Surrey was certainly more colourful than London. All the gardens she passed seemed to be heaving with an array of exotic flowers, the lawns were carefully cut, and the trees pruned, with not a twig out of place.

"Cor, there's money 'ere all right," noted Sam.

Mary nodded in the front seat. She was desperately trying to see all the benefits that would help her sleep at night, hoping her Dolly was in a good place.

Dolly sensed her family's guilt, and she tried to make them comfortable by commenting on how much cleaner the surroundings were and how much she liked the countryside.

Sid was almost silent throughout the trip, too choked to talk. Dolly was the nearest he had to a daughter and he would miss her. He couldn't imagine what they would all go through, largely because he'd heard that this Anne was a tyrant, and he was well aware that little Dolly could be cheeky, although that just added to her charm. Sid sniffed as he fought back the tears that were quickly appearing. Holding the steering wheel with one hand, he reached across and held Mary's hand.

The pebbles crunched underneath the wheels as he drove along the drive, around the ornamental font, and parked outside the grand oak door. Sid announced their arrival to the stunned occupants in the car. Anne had moved on from her home in Dorking after her promotion. She was in a good position to buy a decent sized house that most professional couples would be happy to own. It stood as proud as it did back in the 1700s, with its oak beams and leaded windows.

Mary stood back, admiring the impressive building, and smiled to herself. *Well, the old spinster has made a right nice home for herself.* All that hard work had paid off.

Anne opened the door, expecting to see a bunch of scruffy beggars but instead, and to her great surprise, she saw a spotless-looking family. She gestured for them to come in and Mary straight away noticed her sister appeared to have softened; her expression lacked spite and her smile reached her eyes. As they each passed their aunt, the boys nodded in a polite manner. Dolly almost curtsied and, to Mary's surprise, Anne leaned forward and kissed her on the cheek. Mary instantly felt a strong sense of family love and sobbed irrepressibly in her sister's arms.

"There, there, love, come into the kitchen. We'll get this sorted."

Mary's shoulders lightened, as if the overwhelming guilt she carried since making that final decision had lifted. Anne had markedly transformed over the years. Life had not been cruel to her. In fact, the hard work that she enjoyed so much enabled her to have this beautiful home in lovely surroundings. Mary was shocked. Her perception of her sister – a sad, lonely old witch, who hated all kids and mess – had certainly changed, and for the better! Anne smiled and greeted each child, ruffling their hair, pinching their cheeks, and commenting on how handsome they were.

Overwhelmed with jealousy by her sister's looks and popularity, Anne had viewed Mary as a second-class citizen. This was purely a defence mechanism to enable her to feel good about herself. Mary likewise, had assumed Anne was a snob, so the years spent apart had left ghosts in both of their minds. Although Anne was happy in her own private world, keeping herself to herself, she did from time to time dream of what it would have been like to have had a child. Gone were the days that Anne looked down on her sister – in fact she secretly admired her, and her loving children, and she wished that she had been a part of their lives too. She realised, too late, that she should never have been jealous of her sister, that everyone is born with something special. Whilst Mary possessed beauty, Anne had the brains, and she hadn't realised that being clever had its own attractions.

*

Dolly stared at her aunt for a while. She expected her to look like her mother, but instead she saw a skinny woman with sharper features and brown straight hair, unlike her own mother, who Dolly considered the most beautiful woman in the world. Dolly gazed, as Anne's smile changed her face from a sour appearance to a gentle, kind expression. Mary also noticed that her serious-looking sister had sweetened in her old age.

She led Mary and the children into the kitchen, whilst Sid wandered around the garden. The large kitchen had everything in its place and was spotless. Mary, who was still crying, stopped and giggled, pointing at a set of mugs lined up on a chunky oak shelf. In bold letters along each mug read, 'Do not remove: property of HM Prison Wormwood Scrubs'. All the boys looked and erupted with laughter. Anne decided to join in and asked if anyone fancied a cuppa, waving a teapot that said 'Property of HM Prison Brixton'.

Dolly, being too young to understand, innocently asked, "Aunty Anne, did you go to prison?"

"No, no, Dolly. I bought these on an outing to the coast. I thought they would give my friends a laugh when they came for tea – well, they sure gave you lot a laugh."

Mary's brood fascinated Anne. They naturally referred to her as Aunty and behaved in such a friendly manner. Anne wondered whether Mary had told them about the time they came to stay when she had been horrible to them all. However, she was different now; all the jealous demons had gone. She faced Mary and winked. Mary was dumbfounded by the shift in her sister's personality – even her East End accent had returned.

Anne showed Dolly to her room and left her with her brothers to explore the house and the surroundings. Fred marvelled at the spacious pink room with views from the window, which reached for miles, showing the Surrey countryside at its best. Under the window was a long seat covered in crochet blankets and, in the corner of the room, there was a white rocking chair with pink cushions. Dolly opened the enormous wardrobes to see clothes rails and, below the rails, sets of draws. The bed was larger than a single but smaller than a double. Dolly felt grown up in her new room but, without her things, she felt like a visitor. Even though still young, she understood that unpacking her belongings straight away would give her the chance to settle with her family around her. Sam and Joseph helped to unpack her clothes, put the photos out on the bedside cabinets, and placed the dolls and teddy bears around the room.

Mary sat in the living room with her sister Anne. "Anne..." Mary paused.

Anne guessed what her sister wanted to say. "Mary, I know what you are thinking, and I understand I'm not you, but I will try. God help me, I will try to be like you and when I'm not I will encourage Dolly to show me how because, Mary, you are the best mother a child could have. To be so selfless to hand her over for her own safety... you are a wonderful woman."

Mary's head bowed in pain. "God, it's killing me – well, it's killing all of us, me boys, my Bill... But I know now you will take care of me gal."

Anne nodded. "Mare, I never had kids of my own. I was too much of a control freak for things to work, for one thing... but every day I regretted not having you and the little ones in my life. But now, with God as my witness, I will do right by Dolly. I will give her all the things she needs, I'll make sure she has a good education, that she's well dressed, and has lots of friends and..."

Mary put her hand up to stop her sister going on. "Anne, all I want you to do is to keep her safe and love her like a mother would love her daughter. Anne, you have to be her mum."

Anne looked at her sister and realised that she had at last been given the opportunity to have a child of her own. She would be her mother. "Mary, I will love her as if I gave birth to her meself, I promise you that."

Mary nodded. She knew that her sister meant it.

When the time came to leave, each brother hugged their sister, each with their own loving message, not knowing when they would meet again. Mary, although weak with grief, still felt reassured that Dolly would be safe and that kept her going. Dan stayed strong although, still so young to suffer this heartache, he became an angry young man. Joe, the joker, was solemn for months and found everything irritating. Inconsolable Fred couldn't speak; in fact, he wouldn't speak for the next four weeks until he visited his father in prison and one guard rubbed him up the wrong way. In a fleeting rage, he jumped in the air and broke the guard's nose. Luckily, being only twelve, he got a telling off and a six-week ban from prison visits. Dan was proud of the fact that his youngest brother was a rucker, but Fred was sad and lonely and so Sammy, the mummy's boy, played more with him and that pleased everyone.

*

It didn't take long for Dolly to bond with her aunt, and by the end of the week they had become fond of each other. She had not expected to feel for her niece so quickly, but Dolly's open nature, eagerness to please, and laid-back attitude made it very easy and also a joy to have in her home. She liked her aunt and enjoyed their morning chats. She was particularly interested to hear about the antics her aunt and mother got up to in their younger days. Dolly, however, still grieved for her family. She felt that she had lost more than any of them, and so the quiet, empty house, with the sound of the birds or the odd passing farm animal, was sometimes too much, and she would have to go to her room and put the radio on full blast to cheer herself up. Anne, of course, knew at these times that Dolly suffered from withdrawal symptoms for her family in London, and so decided on these occasions that she would take her into town.

The main high street was busy on a Saturday afternoon, although not as busy as London. But sitting in the Wimpy, and watching the people go by, helped Dolly with her loneliness.

Anne sat opposite, sipping her coffee, and wishing she could change the sad expression on Dolly's face. She admired the child's strength, intelligence and beauty. "Dolly, we must start thinking about a school for you. You can have the pick since you have passed the exams to go to a grammar."

Dolly turned to face her aunt. "I guess that means making new friends."

Turning it into something positive, she replied, "Dolly, that's exactly what you need – friends to go out with, to have fun and smile again."

Dolly thought for a minute and agreed. Aunty Anne was not so bad to live with but she needed friends of her own age. She desperately missed the camaraderie and banter of her brothers and their friends, and so she saw that going to a new school might not only be exciting but could offer her something different in her life.

*

Ballington House, the best grammar school in Surrey, was renowned for its outstanding academic success, turning out top lawyers, doctors and businesswomen. The pupils were lucky to be selected to go to the school and many of the parents spent time and money prepping their children to pass the exam to get in. So Anne was proud as punch to be enrolling her niece into such a well-respected establishment. At heart, Anne was a bit of a snob, so the thought of her niece going to a top school reflected well on her! The school uniform shop was a focus for excited parents and pupils. It was difficult to work out which group of people were enjoying the occasion the most! The list for the uniform was endless: school bags, PE kits, jumpers, tunics, blazers – all of which required the official emblem embroidered on them. Dolly looked around, eyeing up all the girls that looked her age. She listened to the way they spoke. They were so different from her; it reminded her more of her aunt's friends that came over for afternoon tea. *It's all right*, she told herself. Her mother's voice was in the back of her mind, saying, '*Just be yourself and you'll be fine.*' She looked around at the proud mothers and missed her own dearly. None had the same charisma, the good looks, or warm manner, that her mum had, but her aunt was there, doing her upmost to make her happy and help her fit in with the crowd.

Anne, who was talking with one mother, beckoned Dolly over. "Now, Dol... uh, um, Launa."

Dolly froze for a moment; she forgot about her new identity and so had her aunt for a second – this was a mistake they would never repeat.

Having worked up through the ranks in the solicitor's office to become a legal executive, Anne could change Dolly's identity to Launa Mathews and, until she became a woman, she would never refer to herself as Francesca or Dolly again – well, so she thought.

The family made all the arrangements. Before Dolly even met her aunt, they let Dolly choose the name she would be known as in the future. Her favourite doll, with the nylon hair that grew when you pushed a button, was called Launa. No one in her neighbourhood was called that, and so she thought it was probably French or something romantic and so Launa it was.

The girl standing next to Anne said in a clear voice, "What were you going to call her?" rudely pointing to Dolly. The girl's voice was high-pitched with an arrogant tone.

Before Anne got her words out, Dolly answered. "Me aunty often muddles me name with our cat's name… Hi, me name's Launa, pleased to meet you."

The girl stared for a second and turned to her mother and asked, "Am I allowed to talk to her? Only she seems awfully common, Mother."

The girl's mother apologised immediately, making the excuse that her daughter had not met a girl with a London accent before.

To Dolly's surprise, her aunt launched an attack. "Well, I'm not sure I want my niece to mix with your daughter, since good manners are of paramount importance in my home and we pride ourselves on that."

The girl's mother blushed red with embarrassment as Anne stood her ground and maintained her dignity without losing her East End temper.

Dolly felt elated, for when it came down to it, her aunt was much like her mother; *it stood to reason – blood is blood.*

Outside the school shop, she slid her arm through her aunt's, and together they walked home. The bond between them was sealed.

Anne grinned at Launa. "What you grinning at, Aunt Anne?" she asked.

"You are so like your mother when she was growing up, let no one get the better of her." Anne winked at Dolly

Despite Launa's background differing greatly from the girls that would attend the school, she was bright and intelligent, as well as having a quickness about her and a smart mind which would make her very popular. Anne thought back to her own school years, her own sister's popularity, and how she envied her. Now she stood and admired with pride her niece whom, in a short space of time, she had grown to love.

*

Meanwhile, Mary was grief-stricken, knowing it would be a long time before she would see her daughter. She tried to keep herself busy but, without Bill and her dear Dolly, it was hard. The boys often found her with her head in her hands, sobbing into a tea towel. They soon learned to make a good cup of tea. "'Ere you go, Mum, get that down ya – and remember, our Dolly is safe. There's nothing else you can do!" exclaimed Sam, trying to comfort his mum. Mary thought deep and hard. Fed up with feeling so helpless, she decided to face the demon himself. He hadn't been out of prison long when Mary turned up at his yard.

The cab dropped her outside. She stepped out, straightened her dress, and threw her shoulders back. Her heart thumped, knowing he was dangerous, and could swiftly do away with her if the need arose. But, in her mind, nothing could make her more frightened than the thought of not seeing her daughter again. As she walked up to the office, she planned how she would talk him around but, before she even got there, he appeared like a bat out of hell, fiercely grabbing her by her arm as he marched her to the warehouse.

"Hey, Mr McManners, I just wanted to 'ave a little chat." Her nerves, and the fact he was dragging her along, caught her breath. "Please, let go of me," she pleaded as his grip tightened. She looked around, desperate to grab someone's attention, but there was no one in sight. Her shoes came off and the glass and shingle cut her feet, but she couldn't break free, as he was too intent on getting her into the warehouse. She tripped and almost dragged him on top of her. Without a word, he scuffed her up by her hair and continued to pull her inside.

The large metal door slid open and slammed hard shut behind them. He pushed Mary onto the floor, where she remained, trying to get herself together. The building was stacked with boxes and wooden crates and, in the corner, she saw a large grappling hook dangling from the ceiling underneath which lay a pool of blood. Gripped with fear, her eyes widened and she gasped. Mad Mick was staring at her as if he was watching an alien and then he laughed.

Mary got to her feet. "Look, Mr McManners, I just wanted to talk with you about my gal," she begged him.

"I know, I know," he said in a whisper. "It must be hard for you," said Mick in an understanding voice as Mary furiously nodded.

"I can't tell ya how hard it's been for us all. We all miss her so much…
it's killing me."

Mick put a gentle arm around her shoulder and walked her over to a
chair. Pulling up another chair, he sat opposite her. "Tell me, Mary, how
much do you want your daughter home safe and sound with not a hair on her
head harmed?"

Mary took a deep breath, thinking maybe he wanted sex as a payoff, and
she deliberated whether perhaps this might be the best course of action just to
save her family. "Anything, Mick, anything."

Her voice sounded so desperate that Mick smirked. He would have fun
and games this afternoon. He looked her up and down. She wasn't the feisty
young teenager he nearly raped years before, she was rounder and older. He
liked his girls young - really young. Even thirteen was too old for Mick.

He ran his hand down her face and Mary shuddered. He was disgusting.
He smelt of fags and his teeth were growing a fur coat with breath that could
cook a joint of beef.

Suddenly, Mick pushed her head away. "I wouldn't fuck you, you're too
fucking old." He paused and then went on to say, "But when I get hold of your
daughter, and I will find her, this is what I'm gonna do." He grabbed her by
the arm and once again dragged her, this time towards the hook.

In a split second, he lifted Mary up and onto the terrifying-looking curved
spike. She felt the sharp metal tear at her skin and let out a blood-curdling
scream before the pain subsided. She was lucky, he had only managed to hook
her up by her dress and the spike had just given her a superficial cut.

As skinny as Mad Mick was, he still had the strength of ten men, and he
was so fast she had never seen it coming. Now she dangled there as he laughed
and watched Mary plead for her daughter's life. "Oh, Mary, you look so ugly
when you cry. Now then, listen carefully. When I find your daughter, I will
show her how a real man can give her a good time, know what I mean? She's
gonna love me and then, when I'm done, she will be hooked up just like you
are and I will cut off her feet so she can't run away. Then… well, I don't
know. We shall just have to wait and see!" He laughed loudly.

Mary stopped struggling and listened with total resignation. There was no
way she would risk her daughter's life. He was the sickest person she had ever
come across.

"So, Mary, are you going to tell me where she is or shall I rip off each of
your finger nails?"

Mary retched and emptied the contents of her stomach before she went
limp and passed out.

Mick heard the workmen returning from lunch so he pressed the release button. The hook and chain, along with Mary, hit the floor, leaving her battered and bruised. As she regained consciousness, she realised where she was and, without nursing her wounds, scrambled to her feet, hurrying out of the warehouse and out of the gates of the yard. Mick looked out of his office and laughed. As she ran, Mary glanced back and caught a glimpse of his grin and that frightened her more than ever. She was terrified – not for herself but for her family.

That dreadful event assured her that there would be no bargaining with Mick. He was hell bent on revenge and, now she knew he was mentally sick, there would be no calling his bluff. She walked a good part of the way home before jumping on a bus. She was so numb with pain and heartache she didn't realise that she looked as if she had been run over by a truck. Her hair was sticking up, she had no shoes on, and the soles of her feet were bleeding. There was a bloodstain on the back of her dress from the hook, and her face was black and blue from the heavy chain. And yet her pain wasn't physical.

The passengers on the bus were staring, but Mary didn't see them as she sat shaking. One old lady got up from her seat and sat next to Mary. Without a word she put a frail arm around the buxom woman. Mary snapped out of her trance and looked at the old lady. She nodded a silent thank you and tried to tidy herself before she reached her bus stop. Another woman opposite handed her a brush and a mirror. Mary looked around her and then saw her surroundings with conscious eyes. She thanked the woman with the brush and painfully got herself off the bus just at the end of her road. As she stepped on the pavement, she felt the sores on the soles of her feet, smelt the vomit on her dress, and clutched her throbbing head.

"Mum!" screamed Joe, who had been on his way to the bus stop. "Mum, what happened?" He looked his mother up and down in disbelief as she held onto his arm whilst they walked along the street. Seeing her brutally beaten – her pretty face swollen, the gaping wound on her back when she took off her dress, the look of resignation and despair, stayed with him for many years. What haunted him the most was the eerie silence that spoke volumes, as well as the shame and the deepest sorrow in her eyes. Joe knew then she had been to see Mad Mick.

In the years that followed, Mary drummed into her sons' heads they were to keep well away from Mick and his brood. So disturbed was she by the incident that day, she begged her boys not to go for revenge, no matter how bad it got and instead just to stay well away. For, while she was hanging from that hook, and Mick laughed at her from her below, he didn't know that it was the dress that was saving her – he thought the hook was buried in her ribs, and yet he still laughed. It was all part of his makeup and, when he laughed, she believed she was staring into the eyes of a demon.

Chapter Five

As Launa walked to school with her aunt, the September breeze blew strands free from her tightly pulled ponytail, framing her face with black curls, and the cool air brought her rosy cheeks to life. There was a comfortable silence between them as Anne, not wanting to interrupt Launa's thoughts, strolled proudly by her niece's side. Launa looked perfect, and Anne felt honoured to be walking her to secondary school on her first day.

The schoolhouse was a mansion full of period character, with an impressive entrance and grand stone steps leading to two large oak doors, already open to welcome the new intake, due to start later than the older pupils.

Launa felt relieved that most of the girls, walking through the doors, were close to her age and many smiled at each other. They were like her, nervous yet excited. She still felt the pain of not having her family there — especially Freddie, her dearest twin. A big part of her was missing and, looking at all the girls, she missed the company of her brothers, and the rough and tumble which bound them together.

It was strange to be at this new school, yet she marvelled at being part of something so big, the newness of everything, and being independent. She was going to get used to it. From now on, she would be her own person. There would be no more looking behind her to see a brother, or to the side of her to see her twin. Her brothers had taught her one thing — and that was how to be strong. If she wanted to be heard, she must speak up. That wasn't hard; she often had to shout over the noise of the boys. She remembered fighting her way to get first pick of the ice-lollies and running to be first up the stairs to have a bath. Joe or Sam had tried to drag her back down in fits of laughter.

Anne hugged her and whispered, "One word of advice — never sit alone, always join other people, in case of any nasty bullies!"

Launa giggled. "You wanna hope it's not me that's the nasty bully!"

Anne tutted. She ought to have known that Launa would have made a comment like that. It was her way of saying 'don't worry, I can look after myself.'

Eventually, the parents departed, and the pupils sat in the main hall. The headmistress, a short, stout woman, with thick-rimmed glasses and dressed in a Chanel tweed suit, welcomed the new pupils. Her voice was sharp and, as far as Launa was concerned, haughty – a right plum in her mouth. The other girls found the accent perfectly natural.

The headmistress began by listing off the school rules: the list seemed to go on forever. So much so, that Launa decided instead to focus on the enormous room, with its high ceiling, and breathe in the smell of strong furniture polish. The pupils were immaculate and well kept – as her mother would have said, *'Well turned out'*. Launa felt alone in the room full of people and hoped she could make friends soon – good friends like the Reilly sisters.

The girls were taken to their classrooms, with each assigned to her own desk. "Launa Mathews, you sit there, next to Cynthia Hamilton," said Miss Masters, her new form tutor.

Launa smiled at Cynthia, who confidently smiled back. She liked the appearance of her new classmate, who had blonde hair and bright blue eyes, a gene she got from her father, who was a very famous rugby player. Launa had no idea who he was, but Cynthia boasted frequently he was well known, and that anyone who was anyone would know him. Launa decided that, although she liked the way Cynthia looked, she didn't like her personality very much.

When it was lunchtime, the girls in the class were encouraged to socialise and make friends. To encourage them to do this, their break was set at a different time from the older girls, so younger siblings couldn't go running to their sisters.

Launa sat next to Miranda Hemingway-Brown, a girl who looked shy and not so much of a show-off. However, once she spoke, Launa found herself bored to tears by the constant talk of ponies. At this point she felt different. It seemed most of the girls on her table had their own horse and had won awards for show jumping. They all got excited about their hobbies and so she sat back, observing and listening to their accents. They all spoke with a plum in their mouths and used different words to her, like 'gosh' and 'jolly this' and 'jolly that'. She found most of them highly articulate and assured but different from her; they liked to show-off and boast about their parents and their occupations.

"My father's a surgeon, he saves lots of lives," said Amelia Ledbetter.

"My father's a judge, and he sends bad people to prison," said Sophia Smyth excitedly, and it went on and on. The relief came with the end of the lunch bell.

Launa sat back on her chair, wondering how the hell she would fit in. She never knew what her father did for a living. As far as she was concerned, he was a dad and to her that was his job. She bit down on her lip as she thought back to the last time she saw him. '*I must not cry, I must not cry,*' she said to herself over again. If the girls asked about her father's profession she would tell them he died along with her mother when she was tiny and that her aunt brought her up. *How hard that would be.*

After the timetables were handed out and the rules re-read, the classroom door suddenly opened and in walked the headmistress, followed by a bedraggled, unhappy pupil.

Miss Masters knew instantly who she was as she informed them, "Class, this is Thomasine Horsham."

A whisper circled the class. Launa had no idea why everyone made such a fuss about Thomasine, who was, to the other members of the class, clearly regarded as someone of importance. As far as Launa was concerned, there didn't seem to be anything particularly special about her at all. Launa looked around the room, realising the only empty seat was next to her own. Cynthia had sat next to another girl instead.

"Class, I want you to make Thomasine welcome. She has travelled a long way to be here today and I'm sure you will all help in updating her regarding how the school runs," said Miss Masters, gesturing to Launa.

Afternoon break came and the form tutor called Launa and Thomasine to the desk. "I want you to show Thomasine the canteen and locker rooms," she directed, smiling sweetly in Thomasine's direction.

*

As soon as the girls left the classroom, Launa turned to her new classmate. "So are you a princess then or what?"

Thomasine laughed. "No, they have to be good to me because my daddy paid for the renovation at the school to make sure I got in!"

"Loaded then, is he?" said Launa sarcastically.

"Yep, stinking rich." She laughed before asking, "So where do you come from – only your accent is different?"

"You can talk – yours is really weird!"

Both girls laughed. Thomasine had travelled and lived in France, America and Germany, so she had a cosmopolitan accent.

"Please, call me Tom. I hate Thomasine – it's so pompous."

She decided she liked Tom and, from then on, they became good friends.

Launa had been conscious of her appearance and wanted to fit in with the other girls. Tom, however, had a rebellious streak in her and so her long curly hair flowed wild and her blouse hung out of her skirt. Launa liked that, she wasn't a show off and she hated ponies — motorbikes were more up her street! She didn't own one of course, but she had a bowling alley in her basement and the girls would go there after school and bowl. Tom and Launa were inseparable, which Anne approved of immensely, since her Launa was best friends with the daughter of one of the wealthiest men in England. However, Launa didn't care how much money Tom had — what meant more to her was that they had the same sense of humour and enjoyed each other's company.

Thomasine's father, Alfie Horsham, a widower, raised Tom on his own. He found it difficult at times because, like most young teenagers, she had her fair share of problems, and they were not always sorted out by throwing cash her way.

"Hi, Mr 'Orsham. Pleased to meet ya." Launa put her hand out to shake his. He was important and so she guessed she should shake his hand, which was the next best thing to a curtsey.

He gracefully took her elegant hand and replied, "The pleasure is all mine."

Launa went pink. He was like a prince: tall, dark and handsome.

"So Launa, I guess you come from the East End then."

She giggled nervously. "That's right."

Alfie was especially intrigued by his daughter's new friend. Her round blue eyes were full of life and eagerness but her accent surprised him since she appeared so demure. "Well, it makes me jubilant that Tommy here has finally found a nice friend. You are welcome in my home anytime you like." He spoke slowly and deliberately, giving Launa goosebumps. She thought about his tone and made a promise to herself that, by hook or by crook, she would speak just like him one day.

As they walked away, Launa whispered, "Is your dad a prince then? From Arabia or somewhere like that?"

Alfie grinned to himself at the innocence of the child that she had thought him a prince.

"No, Launa, he isn't a prince... he is a lord. His full name is Lord Alfred William Horsham, but he hates all that stuff."

They both laughed.

"Come on, Launa, let's go to my room." Tom tugged her by the arm.

She didn't know it then, but Alfie and Tom would be responsible for shaping her into the sophisticated woman she was to become.

Launa worked hard at school and she excelled in all her subjects, particularly English and Maths. She learned to speak with a perfect English accent, yet never with a plum in her mouth. As she blossomed into a woman, with no pretence, people warmed to her.

Alfie and Tom invited Launa on holiday to the most exotic places around the world, which delighted Anne, who would sit for hours listening to the stories when Launa returned, bringing with her a colourful neck scarf as a present.

The experiences she had with Alfie and Tom taught her more than the school ever could. In a way, it provided her with a social education. She watched Alfie's every move, taking it all in. Alfie noticed what Launa was doing, and admired her for trying to better herself. He taught her how to choose wine and, although she was still young, he allowed the girls to experience the taste.

Before long, Launa could order food in French, Spanish and German. She knew which spoon she should use for soup, desserts, and even figured out how to handle the escargot tongs. Ordering wine to go with the meal was a pleasure for her and it became a ritual. She no longer said 'yeah' but 'yes', having the ability to speak slowly and eloquently.

Over the years, Alfie watched as the two girls grew into beautiful and well educated women, who displayed self-confidence, etiquette and charm. He adored Launa as his own daughter and saw her friendship as a huge blessing. It had been hard to control Tom when her mother died – her sadness manifested into a rebellious streak but, as soon as Launa was on the scene, Tom mellowed and enjoyed life again.

When Launa looked back on those school years, and the privileges she had experienced, she understood that it was Thomasine and her father who had brought so much pleasure and worldly experiences into her life. The day she got the news they had died in a boating accident, she was totally bereft. She was beside herself with grief, and lonelier than ever. She couldn't bear the pain and so for a while she stayed in her room.

Anne tried to help, but it was time she needed to get over it. "Sweetheart, come on, you need to live again. You have been through worse," whispered Anne, as Launa lay face down on the bed.

Launa spun around, annoyed with her aunt. "Worse? How did you work that out? I don't even know anyone who has died – tell me what's worse than that?" she spat.

"When you came here to live, you grieved for your whole family." Anne tried to be compassionate.

Launa took a deep breath and sighed. "One day I will have the chance to see my family again. They are not dead. One day it will be safe for me to return... one day that Mick will be dead." Her voice was a monotone, as though she read the words from a newspaper.

It left Anne cold. Nevertheless, she could understand that her niece needed to grieve in her own fashion.

*

It was a month after the funeral that the Horshams' solicitor contacted Launa and invited her along to the reading of the will. This was usual practice in America but, considering Alfie had property worldwide, the meeting went ahead in England. The office was grand; she had never been inside a solicitor's office before. She liked the luxurious surroundings, and the people were friendly in a busy way. Launa went along with her aunt, unsure of the whole matter. Launa wasn't a relative or anything, but the solicitor had requested her presence by sending a member of staff to her home.

The secretary showed both Anne and Launa into the room where the will was to be read. Already seated were five people. Launa smiled and gracefully sat herself down, followed by Anne.

The will took an hour to read, most of which Launa didn't understand, until the solicitor addressed her by name. "Launa Mathews, Mr Horsham has, in his last will and testament, left a sum of two hundred thousand pounds, to be paid when you reach twenty-one. This was put into a trust when you were fifteen, to be paid regardless whether Mr Horsham had passed away. So this part of the will cannot, I'm afraid, be contested."

Launa gasped, along with her aunt. She had no idea that Alfie had left anything to her. Anne squeezed her niece's hand in excitement. Launa wasn't excited: she had lost her best friend and a father-like figure — even a month on, she was still grieving.

The people in the front row turned to see who Launa was and the large man sitting dead opposite the solicitor, practically reading the papers himself, coughed. "And what relationship to Mr Horsham is this Launa Mathews?" His voice was full of scorn.

"I am afraid, Mr Mumford, since this part of the will cannot be contested, that information is confidential."

"I suppose he left his yacht to the dolphin protection league?" Mr Mumford was a cousin of Alfie Horsham's, a cousin that Alfie had no time for.

The solicitor had been a good friend of Alfie's for many years and knew the situation between Alfie and Mr Mumford.

"Look, Mr Mumford, if you keep interrupting me, it will take a long time to get to your part." The solicitor wasn't at all posh; he probably came from the East End himself, thought Launa.

The uptight Mr Mumford nestled himself back into the chair.

"And now we come to Mr Reginald Mumford. Oh look, there is a letter attached." The solicitor already knew what it said. "This letter I must point out is signed and counter signed." Reginald looked up and frowned. Why would Alfie want to write a letter? He knew Alf hated him but he hoped that he had left at least a portion of his estate to his cousin.

"I'm afraid Mr Horsham had left everything he owned to his daughter and, in the event she died at the same time, which is what tragically happened, then his assets will be divided up and shared equally amongst his loyal staff and I have a list here… Your name's not on it."

"But that's preposterous!" he shouted. "I will contest the will."

The solicitor nodded. "Well, he must have guessed you would and so this letter outlines that you are not his blood cousin and therefore not entitled to a sausage."

The fat man jumped from his seat and left the room fuming.

Launa decided there and then that she would be a lawyer.

She pledged to work hard and use the money to get herself through university and make Alfie and Thomasine Horsham proud.

Chapter Six

Anne sat in the kitchen as the September sun pierced through the blinds and the coffee steam faded into the sunbeams. Placing the letter opposite her on the table, she shuffled her feet and wished that Launa would hurry.

"Launa," she called in her sweetest voice, controlling her excitement.

"I'm coming, let me finish peeing."

"Well, there's no need for that," mumbled Annie under her breath. She was anxious. This letter contained good news and would give Launa the start she needed to begin her career.

Launa appeared, still in her pyjamas, her hair tied up in a rough ponytail, the light giving her raven curls more movement. With her cheeks pink and her eyes shining, Anne just wished for a second that she looked perfect first thing in the morning.

Launa slowly slid onto the kitchen chair and, with half a smile, picked up the letter and teased her aunt. "I'll have a coffee first."

Anne shuffled her feet again. Her excitement and frustration building, she thought she would explode.

"Here, Aunt, you open it," giggled Launa.

Anne looked up from her coffee, feeling honoured, and she took the envelope and tore it open. Standing with her back to her aunt, Launa made herself a coffee. The screech made her jump so much she spilled the powder all over the side.

"You're in, you're in!" Anne screamed at the top of her voice and jumped up and down. Launa spun around with a huge uncontrolled grin and, like two school kids, they danced around the kitchen. Launa had grown into a graceful woman, but right now she was like a child with ADHD. Annie was proud beyond belief. Her niece had made it – she was to be working as a junior barrister at one of the oldest chambers in London. She had worked so hard and deserved to get a first in her law degree.

"I knew you would get in though," stated Anne.

"No you never," laughed Launa.

"Yes I did, you excel in everything you do."

Launa looked over the letter and smiled. "I wish my mum and dad could be here now," she sighed.

Anne bowed her head. She had tried to be the best parent to Launa, but nothing would ever change the love Launa had for her own mother – not that Anne would want anything different because she cared so deeply for her. When Launa felt sad, she did too.

"I wouldn't want anyone else to know before you though, Aunt. Besides, you helped me get there, and I do appreciate all you do for me. I love you like I love my mum." Leaning forward, she rubbed Anne's hand.

For a moment Anne could not speak, since a large lump had risen in her throat. Eventually she managed, "Oh, I almost forgot, I have arranged for a friend of mine to come over tonight to take measurements."

Launa, was flicking through a girly magazine, not paying much attention to her aunt. "Oh yeah?" she mumbled.

"Launa, I'm talking to you!" She put down her magazine and sat to attention. "Sorry, Aunt. So what are you going for – new curtains, carpet?"

Anne paused, "No, Launa, you will be measured."

Launa inclined her head to the side.

"My friend is a dressmaker and he will come all the way from Saville Row to measure you up for a suit for your new job." Anne clapped her hands together in excitement as if it was for herself.

"You are so kind, you spoil me."

"Well, I can't have my niece going off to work in any ol' fing," she laughed, exaggerating her East End accent. "And your money's still tied up in that trust."

Working as a legal executive for years, Anne was fully acquainted with how lawyers dressed, what worked and what didn't. The legal system was male dominated, and she knew that her niece needed to present herself in a confident manner, and power dressing gave her the best start. Her designer friend, a master at tailoring, had measured up the rich and famous. He knew how to make the perfect suit for every shape and size.

Anne had suggested a pinstripe and the designer, a Jewish man, agreed. "Nothing is more striking than a woman in a navy blue pinstripe. You'll be guaranteed to turn a head or two," he said as he winked.

Anne met David Moss at the office years ago and they had an understanding that remained a secret between them. David, a gay man and Anne a spinster, both had needs. She liked to be wined and dined with no strings attached, and he needed to be seen as straight, particularly in the earlier days, when his clients could not be associated with gays.

David acted camp in front of Anne, which amused her. Launa, thrilled by the attention, spent ages looking through the samples, trying to imagine the suit in each shade. "You know what? I will leave the choice of fabric up to you two. I have no idea."

When she left the room, Annie leaned over to David and whispered, "Make up two – one in the blue pin and one in charcoal grey."

"I tell you what, I'll charge you for the blue, but I've got loads of charcoal back at the shop, and I'll knock her up something special, on me."

Anne was thrilled. "You're too generous, David."

He laughed. "Don't tell me brothers, they'll disown me!" he laughed, winking as he left.

The suits arrived one week later and Anne couldn't wait to see them on her niece. "Anne," she called downstairs, "David has sent the wrong box."

Anne rushed upstairs to see Launa holding two suits, and laid across the bed was also a refined wool dress.

"He's sent the wrong stuff – look."

She walked over to her niece and said, "No, my love, these are for you."

The navy pinstriped outfit fitted her like a glove and, with her hair pulled back and wearing her high-heeled shoes, she looked a sophisticated, business-like young woman.

The grey suit was, as David said, 'very special'; the long jacket had silver buttons from the collar to hem and, under the jacket, a shift dress, tailored trousers, and a skirt.

"This is too much, it must have cost a fortune," blushed Launa.

"A present from David," said Anne, smiling from ear-to-ear.

"If I didn't believe David was gay, I would think that you and he had a thing going on."

Anne sighed. "He is just a friend… Now then, have a look in the mirror, young lady, and tell me what you think."

Launa was amazed at how professional she appeared once dressed in her suit. The clothes, along with her new shoes and handbag, made Launa feel grown up. "I absolutely love them! Now I can't wait to start my new job."

*

Her first day at work began with a formal introduction to all the office staff. As she entered the building and introduced herself, she met first Susan, the receptionist, who showed no interest in Launa at all. Susan pointed to a sofa with her long painted red nails and said William would be with her when he arrived. Launa smiled sweetly and thanked Susan, but there was no response, so she took a paper from the casual table next to her, and looked over the day's news. Susan peered over her desk and took a good gawk at Launa. She gazed with green eyes and sighed with dismay. Her days as the best-looking girl in the office were over, as the attention would be on Launa. She had been told the new junior was the best candidate on paper, but she didn't expect her to be so young and pretty. Launa was going to put a spanner in the works because Susan had been slowly working her way into the heart of a certain young barrister. It would only be a short time before Charles asked her out on a proper date – not the odd pint at the pub at lunchtime and the quick snog in the storeroom. She had fallen in love with him, and spent much of her hard-earned cash on new clothes and makeup to wind him in and, so far, it had worked. She loved the way he flirted with her; he would bite his bottom lip, flash his long eyelashes and wink at her as he made his way to their secret place. Susan swallowed hard. Looking at Launa now gave her a bitter taste in her mouth, and she must make more of an effort to be certain that Charles' eyes didn't wander in Launa's direction. She had been the main receptionist for three years and, as the time went by, her skirts had got shorter and her tops lower. She fantasised about men fancying her and flirted with every man who entered the building, even the couriers. She was, nevertheless, hooked on Charles, and when he returned from his yearlong sabbatical in the States, she would be there, waiting for him.

Eventually, William Enright arrived, looking fit for a man of his age and, like most judges, he walked with an air of authority. The silver streaks in his hair accentuated his green eyes. He spotted Launa straight away, perched gracefully on the entrance sofa, looking fresh and vibrant. "Ah, you must be Launa." He carefully looked her up and down. She was presentable, but he just couldn't imagine her in a courtroom; her face was too soft and, with her eyes so round and bright, her expression seemed permanently fixed, one of innocent naivety.

As he held out his hand, she confidently shook it. "I am so looking forward to working with you, Mr Enright!" she said cheerfully, remembering the saying 'first impressions count'. Deliberately, she spoke with confidence, and yet she did not seem arrogant. It was a lesson her linguistic teacher had taught her, a lesson that would carry her well through her advocacy career.

William, pleasantly surprised by Launa's countenance, accepted her right away. He had an exceptional reputation as a judge which he had inherited from his father. His brother was also a judge and his son a successful barrister.

Launa felt honoured to be working with the best, unaware that they had carefully scrutinized her application. They discovered she had two hundred thousand in the bank, and she had the highest achievement award from university. William tested her intelligence by throwing odd questions or speaking in French – she answered back in the same language and never queried it. She was perfect; firstly, she held him in high esteem and secondly she was intelligent – just the skills that William required for a particular job he had in mind.

Launa excelled herself yet again and managed to reach the bar in the shortest time possible. Her cases were small to start with, burglary mainly, which then accelerated to more serious litigations, such as GBH and armed robbery. Highly dedicated, she worked late; sometimes she crawled into bed at four in the morning. Even when she wasn't working, her days were spent in the courtroom, following higher profile cases. Soon, her ratio of positive verdicts outweighed the negative ones, her reputation began to spread fast amongst the solicitors, and the work came in to the office with her name on it – a huge accomplishment for such a young barrister.

*

One summer afternoon, when Launa was busy ploughing through a pile of old cases looking for a slant angle on her latest one, she was startled by a knock on the door.

She expected Susan, who usually brought the post, but instead, she was pleasantly surprised. The door opened abruptly and in stepped a striking man, dressed in an extremely smart suit, white collars and a fetching tan. His face beamed, "Oh, sorry, have you seen my father, William Enright?"

Launa tried to remove the hair that had fallen from her ponytail and gathered messily around her unmade face. "Oh yes, well he was here a moment ago." She got to her feet and held a hand out to introduce herself. He was gorgeous, with a striking family resemblance. The office girls had often spoken of his good looks and they weren't wrong. Launa suddenly became conscious of her scruffy appearance.

"I'm Charles, the prodigal son. And you must be our new barrister, Launa, I believe?" He eyed her up and down, amused by her formal handshake, so unfitting for such a charming young woman. She looked pretty in a plain way, until she smiled, and then he saw her beauty. Her eyes were unusually deep, round and baby-like, with dimples that deepened as her smile grew.

"I'm very pleased to meet you, I have heard a lot about you and I must say it's rather impressive," Launa gushed.

Charles raised his eyebrows and, utterly charmed, chuckled. "Impressive, you say?"

Launa blushed. She had forgotten herself for a second. "Yes, I mean your record for guilty verdicts."

"Oh those?" He laughed again, his face glowing. He knew exactly what she meant, and he was going to have fun teasing the junior. "Look, seeing that my father has more pressing business than lunching with his one and only son, how about you come and join me? We can get to know more about each other. Err... in a professional sense of course." Perched on her desk, he grinned from ear to ear.

Launa stuttered, taken in by his flirtation, but she needed to get the case ready for the next morning. "I would like that very much, but I'm afraid I have to get this case ready." She pointed at the pile of folders on the office chair.

Not used to being turned down, Charles assumed that she was genuinely busy.

"Oh, I see. Okay, maybe another time then," he said. Before he left her office, he turned to give her a sexy wink that gave her an odd feeling in her stomach.

"*Damn!*" she said aloud. So handsome, and he had just asked her out; the bloody case could have waited. She found the rest of the afternoon such a chore and, every time she tried to read another case, his face popped into her head. *Never mind, he probably didn't fancy me anyway* and, after all, he did say strictly professional. He worked for the Crown Prosecution Service and as she was a defence lawyer, she thought, they might end up head-to-head in the courtroom.

*

The next morning, she got up ten minutes early to make more of an effort. All the hours she had put into working left her little to no time for herself. She blow-dried her hair, so her natural waves had more energy, and applied mascara to give more definition to her eyes. With a shimmer of pink lipstick and a very pretty pink blouse she set off for work. Anne spotted her presentation over the top of her newspaper. "Who is he then?"

Launa was startled. "Aunty Anne, you made me jump!"

"Well, spill the beans. It must be a man — you're done up like a dog's dinner!" she chuckled.

"Can't a girl make the effort without a man being involved?" Launa raised her eyebrows.

"All right, all right, if you don't want to tell me…" She waved her hands.

"I'll tell you tonight," said Launa, guessing it would wind her aunt up because she hated not knowing the latest gossip. Even after all these years, she still loved to taunt her.

"You little bitch!" laughed Anne.

"Yeah, I know," teased Launa.

*

Susan glared at Launa as she walked past reception. *What was she up to?* She did not normally come into work with makeup on and high heel shoes — she often looked quite dowdy, shuffling along, head down with a pile of folders under her arm. *If she thinks she can get her claws into my Charles, thought Susan, well she has another thing coming.*

"Morning, Susan," beamed Launa, determined to be acknowledged this time.

"Yeah, morning," replied Susan, who, despite her feelings, still had to be polite.

Launa spun around on her heels and walked over to the desk. Susan, who was busy filing her nails, instantly put the nail file away.

"You look nice today, going anywhere special?" she said with a fake smile. She didn't give a shit, as long as it wasn't with Charles.

"Oh, thank you, Susan. No, I am not, just thought it time I made more of an effort; well you know what it is like. You get snowed under with work and next thing you know your roots need doing." Her sarcastic comment dug deep. Aware that her own needed bleaching, Susan growled under her breath.

She bit her lip and flared her nostrils. Bitch, she thought. As if she ever needed her roots touching up.

"Susan, when you have a minute, ask Charles to see me in my office?"

Susan jumped. *Did she say Charles?* Without thinking, she said, "What for?"

Launa raised her eyebrows, taken aback with the question.

"Oh sorry, Launa, I mean shall I tell him what it's about or…" She paused, waiting for a reply.

"No, Susan, I will discuss what needs to be discussed in my office." With that, she turned on her heels and walked along the corridor.

Usually Launa was polite and soft, and too sweet as far as she was concerned. Today she seemed different.

Susan was fuming. *Who the fuck did she think she was, dishing out orders?* As the new member of staff, she should be the underdog. As if being treated like a secretary wasn't bad enough, the new kid on the block was outdoing her. The only time Susan gained control was in the store cupboard. Legs astride of her victim, she loved to see their lips quiver, and the funny face they pulled just as they reached their climax. She did consider being a Dominatrix but thought about the clientele she might have to whip and then thought about Charles. Whenever he walked into the building, her heart pounded like a love-struck teenager, and when he flicked his head in the direction of the store cupboard, she went running.

Launa walked confidently along the corridor, her shining black curls bouncing on her shoulders as her hips swayed, accentuated by her black fitted skirt.

"Hi, Susan, who is that?" said Charles, pointing to Launa. He had walked into the foyer without Susan noticing; she had been too intent in throwing daggers into Launa's back. Charles admired the graceful figure breezing her way into the offices.

"That's Launa, the new barrister." Susan replied in a flat tone. By the look on Charles' face, there was an obvious attraction. He stared until Launa was out of sight. "Oh yeah, she said she wanted to see you in her office."

Charles smiled. "Oh, she did, did she? Well, you can tell her I'm too busy." he laughed.

Susan was annoyed there had obviously been an earlier discussion, and she sensed something going on. *There had to be more to the change in Launa's appearance – her flicked-up hair, the makeup and the cocky attitude.*

"Fancy lunch today?" asked Susan, trying to get his attention.

"No, I am genuinely busy. Old Johnson was rushed to hospital, appendix or something, and I have to stand in. I need to read through the case rather sharpish before the court resumes at two o'clock." As he walked away, Susan jumped off her seat and headed for Launa's office; she was itching to give her the bad news. *That'll teach her getting cocky with my fella.*

Launa sat as usual, head in a pile of notes; "Oh sorry, Susan, I didn't hear you knock," she said arrogantly.

"Sorry, I forgot. Anyway, Charles can't meet you today as he is busy." Susan stood in the doorway with her arms folded and a large chip on her shoulder.

Launa laughed. "Oh, I see." She chuckled again at the frustration on Susan's face. With her lips pursed together, Susan took a deep breath and tried to be calm.

"What's so funny?"

Launa looked up and smiled. "Oh, it's nothing, Susan, just a private joke, I guess."

Susan spun on her heels and slammed the door behind her.

Launa's heart sank. She felt a fool; there was no private joke, just a chance to piss off Susan. Hearing her march down the corridor in her stilettos, she felt a tinge of guilt. Just because she was disappointed it was not a good enough reason to upset the woman. It was evident that she had an interest in Charles and, besides, Launa had heard the other admin girls talking behind Susan's back, regarding her overly friendly way with Charles. Launa sighed heavily and thought about cutting her some slack.

*

She enjoyed the challenge of the work. Her eagerness to win was the reason she got up in the mornings. Her present case involved a ninety-three-year-old woman who had shot and killed a burglar. The Crown proposed a murder charge since the woman had used a firearm. However, Launa pleaded for an acquittal; a risky approach as it meant all or nothing with no manslaughter to fall back on. She sensed the worry had affected the old girl and hoped she could cope with the court proceedings. She had good cases up her sleeve, dating back as far as 1935, and she wanted to set a precedent today, believing whole-heartedly that she would.

As two o'clock approached, Launa entered the courtroom. Amongst the packed gallery sat reputable solicitors writing notes. Suddenly, to her horror, she realised that the senior barrister, Mr Johnson, had been replaced with Charles Enright. Caught off guard, her nerves got the better of her, leaving her mouth dry and her hand sticky. Charles turned to his left and spotted Launa. He straightened his head and smiled.

"All rise, the Honourable Judge Freeman presiding," addressed the clerk.

The judge called the briefs to the front. It was a formality to begin the case, covering any changes, including the absence of Barrister Johnson.

"Do you have any objections, Miss Mathews?" He firstly addressed Launa, who politely replied, "No, Your Honour."

"And you, Mr Enright, have you had enough time to commence or shall we adjourn for a later date?"

"No, I have had enough time, thank you, Your Honour."

Launa's body shook as she returned to her seat.

The case continued, with Launa to examine her client.

Agnes Bishop, a frail, thin old lady, stood in the dock, hunched with osteoporosis and with hair so fine it showed her scalp. It had taken five minutes for her to get to the witness stand and be sworn in.

Launa spoke slowly and carefully, trying to use simple words so as not to confuse the bewildered woman.

"Now then, Agnes, if I can begin by asking you to tell the court in your own words as much as you can remember about the night in question. Please speak loudly and clearly, but take your time."

Charles admired her every move. The tone in her voice was professional and yet sexy, and he could see why the male jurors stared at her rather than at the witness.

Agnes attempted to describe the evening in as much detail as she could but her memory was not on her side.

"So, Agnes, you were awoken suddenly by the sound of your dog yelping?"

The old lady nodded.

"You have to answer the question with a yes or a no," snapped the judge.

"Yes," she croaked.

"And, as you stepped out of your bed a man, in your words a very big man, came into your bedroom, clenching his fists, demanding to know where your money was?" Launa's words were simple yet precise.

Agnes shook her head. "No."

Launa was pleased the old girl was paying attention.

"No, Miss Bishop? Then whose bed did you get out of?"

"Well, my son's bed. You see, I was staying on his farm, while he was in Spain, looking after the place for him."

Launa smiled and nodded.

"And the gun? Please tell the court how you managed to have possession of a gun?"

Agnes began to shake, as she had been standing for too long.

"Please get a chair for Mrs Bishop." The judge softened his tone.

"Now then, take your time, Agnes. Please tell the court about the gun."

She looked around the courtroom, which looked so formal and daunting. Clearing her throat, she carried on. "My son has problems with the foxes you see, and so when he thinks they are upsetting his chickens he shoots them from out of the window." She paused to get her breath; emphysema and nerves made it hard. "When that robber came in, I just picked it up. It was on the bedside table and I lifted it up to stop him coming near me but it just went off – I didn't even pull the trigger."

There was a murmur in the courtroom.

"Agnes, did you drop the gun before it fired or were you still holding it?"

The old lady now looked pale, and it was clear to the jury that she was unsure.

"Thank you, Agnes. That will be all from me." Launa looked at Charles. He smiled at her and she looked the other way. He was even more attractive in his magpie's suit and wig.

Charles approached the witness stand with bags of confidence. He had this case sewn up; clearly, she shot him – she must have cocked the gun for it to fire, so whether she pulled the trigger or dropped it, it had to have been cocked. "So, Agnes, may I call you Agnes?" He spoke softly, presenting himself as a caring person. It was a common method to get the old lady to follow his train of questioning without becoming defensive.

She nodded.

"Now, when the robber," he relayed her exact words, "came in with his fists clenched, demanding money, you picked up the gun, engaged the barrel, and pulled the trigger, or did you..."

Before he was able to continue, Launa jumped up. "Your Honour, the council is leading the witness."

The young barrister did not impress the judge. He knew Charles and his family well and this was an open and shut case. He didn't believe it necessary to make such a meal of it. The old lady shot dead a burglar, period.

"Sorry, Your Honour. I'll choose my words more carefully."

The judge smiled gratefully at the counsel and the case continued.

"Agnes, did you fire the gun or did you drop the gun?"

Still unsure. "I didn't do anything – it shot the man on its own."

"Do you honestly believe the gun went off by itself, or a ghost fired the bullet?" he chuckled.

Angry, Launa spun to glare at Charles, who was amused by her facial expression. She looked cute. As soon as he had won this case, he would take her to lunch and order the best champagne to drown her sorrows.

"Do you have any more questions, Mr Enright?" asked the judge, who hoped to wrap the case up by four o'clock.

Charles smiled at Agnes. "No further questions, Your Honour."

"Please call your next witness, Miss Mathews."

Colonel Hemmingway entered the courtroom, a smartly dressed man and grand in his attire, with an old-fashioned handlebar moustache, a tweed jacket, and a distinctive smell of cigars. He nodded at the judge as they had met on various occasions at the gun club. As he was sworn in and stood confidently in the witness box, the jury assumed him to be extremely important as his accent was comparable with royalty, yet it was deep and husky, from all the Cuban cigars he smoked.

Charles, unprepared for this witness, frantically read his brief, but there was no note regarding a witness by the name of Colonel Hemmingway. He looked through the latest paper work on the case and there, at the back, he found the details. He felt foolish – his father had always taught him to leave no stone unturned, to check and double check the evidence to be presented by the defence, and never, ever, to rely on your own affirmation to get a guilty verdict. He had been too cocky and assumed that this new barrister was an amateur. He didn't expect her to be so thorough.

Launa knew Cedric Hemmingway through Alfie Horsham. He belonged to the same gun club as Launa, and her then best friend Thomasine, where they all enjoyed a round of clay pigeon shooting – in fact it was Cedric who had taught Launa to shoot.

"Colonel Hemmingway, please tell the court your background and your expertise in firearms."

Cedric beamed, and his cheeks, rosy from years of red wine, glowed. He admired Launa and watched her in action, a far cry from the first day he met her – a thirteen-year-old with a cockney accent but full of fun and determination. Cedric was proud of his achievements and he proceeded to tell the jury about his roles in the army, and as chairman of the gun club association, and also his knowledge of guns.

"So, Colonel, is it at all possible that the gun could have been fired without it ever being cocked?"

Charles predicted exactly where this would lead. Launa only asked the questions to which she already surmised the answer. However, in his case the facts stood, the old lady still pointed the gun, and it was highly likely that the jury would find her guilty through intention.

"The gun was a hundred-year-old relic," replied Cedric. "I'm afraid those guns should be destroyed, as they are unpredictable and, if it had hit the floor hard enough, it would have discharged a bullet without the gun being cocked and the trigger being pulled."

Charles saw no point in cross-examining the witness and instead he waited for the summing up. He would make it obvious to the jury that she held a loaded gun to the man's head — whether it had fired on its own, or she had pulled the trigger and killed him.

A doctor, the next witness called, had examined Agnes and run a strength test, which proved unequivocally that she could not have lifted the gun; it was beyond her capability according to the weight.

The final summing up was the grand finale. Launa, in her element, paraded around in front of the jury, outlining the relevant points. "It has been shown quite clearly today by our expert witnesses that Agnes Bishop did not physically have the strength to lift the gun and, as it slipped from her fragile clutches, the impact with the floor was enough to fire the bullet, sadly hitting the robber in the head. This amounts to an accident and will result in Agnes Bishop being cleared of the charge of murder."

Charles resigned himself to the fact that he had failed. The judge summed up in favour of the prosecution, which infuriated Launa. *What the hell did they want to lock a ninety-three-year-old woman up for?* Then she realised it was a power issue. She grinned to herself; *surely, a young, female junior barrister didn't bother them?* Launa lifted her head and pushed her shoulders back. *Welcome to the world of the big boys.*

The jury came in after one hour — such a short time that she predicted the verdict would be unanimous. "Not guilty."

Launa turned to the old lady. Clutching her hand, she whispered, "You are free to go home now, Agnes."

The old lady looked into Launa's eyes and for a second Launa saw a young woman staring back. "You are so clever; don't ever let a man drag you down. Remember those words, my dear, and thank you so very much. I can now spend my last days with my son."

Launa had been taught not to get involved with her clients, but creating a relationship with them gave her the passion to fight for their liberty. Charles eyed his opponent with mixed feelings. She was everything he admired in a woman: grace, beauty and intelligence, yet he had only ever dated soppy tarts with big tits and short skirts. Dating such a gem was going to be difficult.

*

Afterwards, the judge called Charles into his office. "Now then, Charles, just a bloody word of warning. You have been back five minutes, and you have taken your eye off the ball. Read your cases thoroughly and stop watching the barrister's arse."

He stepped back in disgust. "I don't know what you mean…" His voice was over the top.

"Charles, over the years I have witnessed you become a bloody good barrister and your father and uncle are very proud – we have protected you. Now don't bloody well lose your excellent reputation over a silly slip of a girl."

Charles tutted. "There's nothing going on between Launa and me, I can assure you."

The judge took off his robe, hung up his wig and sat down. "Look, Charles, watch yourself. That Launa Mathews is damn good; her defending is the best I have seen in a long time. The solicitors are giving her plenty of work, and big cases too. Just be careful that, when you're up against her in court, you look at the case and not her. Or, if you are infatuated with her, bed her and get her out of your system."

Charles listened intently. Launa was a go-getter and could one day professionally humiliate him. He decided to bed her and take her out of the picture.

*

As Launa walked gracefully down the steps of the grand old court, she heard footsteps running behind her.

"Launa," called Charles, without raising his voice too much.

She spun round, not expecting to see Charles.

"Well done," he said, trying desperately hard to contain himself. He wanted to tell her it was luck and he would beat her next time, but instead he asked her out for dinner.

"So, do you like French or Italian?"

Launa, still on a high from the court result, chose to play it cool. "Actually, I love Italian, and the Pomederra Mozzarella restaurant is very good."

"Yes it is, and I am partial to Italian myself." Charles had forgotten about the case already and was more than happy with the idea of spending the evening with Launa.

*

By the time they reached the restaurant, it was seven o'clock. Luckily, they didn't have to book in advance and the waitress showed them to a cosy table for two. Launa sat elegantly opposite Charles. They looked through the menu, stealing the odd glance at each other. He was even more handsome close up and she became immersed in his green eyes. A tingle ran through her body.

Her wine choice did not go unnoticed and instantly Charles was intrigued. "So, do you know a lot about wine?"

Not wanting to appear a show-off, she smiled coyly and replied, "I wouldn't say a connoisseur, but I like wine and enjoy trying to match the grape with the food."

Charles hung on to her every word, sucked in by the way she spoke slowly and deliberately. He enjoyed the way her mouth moved and how her full lips sipped the wine. Equally, Launa burned inside with desire for him. His gorgeous smile made her want to pull him across the table and lick his lips, but she managed to contain herself.

They chatted away for the whole evening, with the odd flirty comment or slow wink from him and blush from her.

"So how did you find the gun expert? Bloody good one, I thought. I might use him myself in the future." He was actually being genuine.

"Oh, well, he is a friend of mine," she smiled.

"I must say, Launa, you do not cease to amaze me. I find you fascinating. To call an old colonel your friend – well, it's hard to imagine you two being pals!" he laughed.

"I have friends of all ages and backgrounds. I used to go to the gun club when I was younger with my best friend Thomasine Horsham. Actually, it was her father who was friends with the colonel, but I guess after all the years we sat in the Horsham's garden drinking wine and telling silly jokes," she paused, "and still having telephone conversations even after the death of Alfie, I suppose then, yes, I can call him my friend."

Charles was touched by the way she viewed herself. She spoke as if it was an honour to have good friends, amazed by the fact that she had been so close to one of the most influential businessmen in the country, and yet she didn't boast. To her, Alfie and his daughter were kind people who cared for her.

"Let me take you home. It's rather late and you can never be too careful." He wrapped her cardigan around her shoulders and she felt his hands linger around her neck.

"Oh no, it's fine, honestly. I often jump on the tube at this time of night," she said.

"No, I insist. Besides, you would have gone home long before now if I hadn't asked you for dinner. If anything bad should happen, can you imagine how I would feel?" He clutched his heart as she giggled.

"Charles, you can't take me home. I live in Surrey."

He looked up at the stars. It was a clear night, and he felt like a schoolboy again. "You know what, it's Friday. I have nothing to prepare for Monday; in fact, my weekend is free. How about you? Please tell me you are not working this weekend."

Launa beamed with excitement. He was obviously going to ask to see her again. She smiled, "Actually, I planned to do nothing and have a bit of a break."

"It's settled then," he stated, as he marched her out of the restaurant and towards the taxi rank.

"What's settled?" giggled Launa.

"You can stay with me at my home in Chelsea and tomorrow we can go and have fun, such as a picnic, a boat ride, or whatever your heart desires."

Launa stopped dead in her tracks. "Hey, Mr Enright, I might have enjoyed the meal, but I'm afraid I'm not in the habit of jumping into bed with the first man that buys me pasta." She pulled the cardigan tighter around her shoulders. *How dare he treat her like a common garden slut!* Her heart sank.

"Good God, you didn't think I meant sleep with me? No, no, I have a large apartment up the road and it has three large bedrooms, all en-suite, and I thought, if it was agreeable to you, you might like to take one of the rooms. Then we can spend tomorrow together, chilling." He held his hands up. "No funny business."

She smiled and blushed. Perhaps she had have been too presumptuous. "I'm sorry, I didn't mean to jump down your throat. It sounds a great idea. The only problem is, I don't have an overnight bag."

Charles was elated; he didn't want her to go home. "I have spare PJs, bath robes, and you can always use the washer and dryer."

*

The apartment was lavish, and it did have three huge bedrooms and bathrooms. The spacious lounge was extravagant and the floor to ceiling windows allowed the best views over London.

"This is beautiful, Charles, did you plan this or…"

"No, not me. I employed an exceptional designer. I just write the cheques!" He walked over to the bar. "Can I interest you in a glass of wine or a wonderfully cold glass of bubbly with chocolate-dipped strawberries?"

Launa nodded, totally absorbed in the moment, gazing around the room and admiring the wonderful ornaments and pictures. A couple of the sculptures stood as tall as she did, and the oil paintings that adorned the walls, although huge, fitted in well amongst the luxurious soft furnishings. She sat on the enormous suede sofa and felt comfortable right away. Charles had dashed into the bedroom, taken off his jacket and tie, and returned with his white shirt undone at the top two buttons, enough to show off his tan. He grabbed the champagne and strawberries from the fridge, along with two flutes, and casually walked into the lounge. To his delight, Launa had removed her shoes and cardigan and sat cheekily draped on his sofa.

"Here we go." He laid the goods out on the glass table and knelt opposite.

Launa's eyes lit up when she saw him dressed casually. He looked even sexier. Gazing at his neck and the way his dark brown hair flicked up behind his very neat ears gave her goosebumps, and that funny feeling in her stomach. After Charles handed her a full glass of champagne, they made a toast, keeping their eyes firmly on each other. She wanted to rip his shirt off and look at what else he had to offer. Never had she felt so attracted to anyone; *if this is what they mean by lust, then I'm lusting,* she thought, and took another sip of the freezing cold bubbly.

"To a good friendship," said Charles, hoping desperately that she changed the toast to more than friends

"To fun in the courtroom." She started to giggle, and her cheeks glowed pink.

Launa enjoyed the champagne. It eased the conversation and intensified the seduction.

Charles too was partially sloshed and was just three feet away. He imagined grabbing her by the arms, pinning her to the settee, and kissing her neck and those plump lips.

"Let me play some music." Charles jumped up and put on a slow number. Launa realised he was making a move. She tried to think rationally, but the champagne was leaving a marked effect on her brain, and she was unable to think straight. *So, I guess this is what happens when you drink too much — your brain stops working and your heart kicks in.*

He sat next to her on the sofa and she suddenly felt awkward. "Are you enjoying this music?" he whispered in her ear.

She could smell his aftershave and feel his breath on her skin. The warm effects from the alcohol had enhanced the tingling sensation, and she closed her eyes to enjoy the moment. "Hmm, it's pretty cool," she mumbled, as she slid further back into the sofa.

He moved her hair away from her face with one finger and flicked it around her ear. She didn't move: excited yet stunned, she remained still.

He leaned forward and, with his other hand, he stroked her cheek, looking her up and down. She shyly looked into his eyes, not knowing what to do next. It was too soon. She hardly knew him yet he was so sexy, so gentle. Her urges were becoming more powerful, and she turned to face him. He ran his finger from her forehead to the nape of her neck, staring intently at her lips. Her heart started to pound and she closed her eyes, waiting for the second he put his lips on hers.

Gently, he spoke. "You are the most beautiful creature I have ever met. I want to take you to bed, but I want us to be friends." All the while, he stroked her face and neck. "Just let me kiss you; your lips are so luscious, so perfect."

His words spun around in her head; she felt beautiful and sexy, and she wanted him. She opened her eyes and was dazzled by his stare. His face so close to hers, she could almost taste his breath. He touched her lips so gently; she wanted more. Closing her eyes and arching her back, she grabbed his hair, pulling him closer. Their first kiss was so intense that, before she knew it, she had ripped at his shirt and bitten his neck. He pulled her to her feet to slow her down, whilst simultaneously kissing her lips, as he unbuttoned her blouse and slipped it off her shoulders. He kissed her with passion.

She stood naked and, with the lights dim, she looked like the twenty-thousand-pound sculpture that stood in the room; her body was of perfect proportion. He held her away so he could see her. Never had he touched such a tidy-looking figure – her skin smooth and shiny, her waist tiny and her breasts full and neat. She was a goddess.

He carried her to his bedroom and laid her on the bed. Launa was in ecstasy, quivering as he traced ever contour of her body. Inexperienced as she was, she enjoyed the pleasure beyond belief. She wanted him as much as he wanted her.

She didn't tell him that she was a virgin but, as he entered her, she squealed and he guessed. "This is your first time, my angel, isn't it?" he whispered.

She bit her bottom lip and nodded, feeling a fool – a virgin at her age.

"I will not hurt you, I promise."

She trusted him when he said those words.

The next day they enjoyed a long breakfast together, gazing into each other's eyes and giggling as though they had done something naughty. She fascinated Charles; she was charming and graceful with an abundance of knowledge and interesting conversation.

He wanted to finish with the quick shags and one-night stands and settle down with this little beauty.

Sunday, she got up from her own bed and, with a spring in her step, she skipped down the stairs for breakfast with her aunt. Anne was unimpressed with Launa. "You could have phoned, at least," she said crossly.

"Sorry, only I had too much to drink, and by the time I realised I should have called, it was too late. Any tea in the pot?"

Anne, still annoyed, gestured to the cup on the side.

"Oh, thanks. You already poured one for me." Launa didn't let Anne's mood perturb her. "So do you want all the details or just the best bits?" Launa could hardly contain herself. Anne was not just her aunt these days but her friend too and she enjoyed their Sunday morning chats.

She smiled, giving in. "Okay, tell me everything!" She leaned forward on her seat with eager anticipation.

"Well, he is gorgeous, Aunt. I mean, extremely handsome with the most amazing green eyes I have ever seen and his face, when he smiles, just lights up. And…"

Her voice was high-pitched from the excitement.

"Slowly, Launa. Now tell me from the beginning. Who is he and how did you meet?"

Launa took a deep breath. "His name is Charles Enright Junior." Her face beamed with pride; he wasn't any old soul.

Anne threw her hands to her mouth in shock. "Launa Mathews, don't tell me you're dating the judge's son?"

She nodded enthusiastically.

"Well, my word, you have struck gold there, my girl. You want to make sure he doesn't slip through the net."

"I really like him. He is very sweet and kind and, well, maybe I have fallen in love." She stared out of the window, smiling.

Anne shuffled on her seat. "Launa, be careful, my love. Make sure he is the right one before you…" She stopped herself saying the words 'have sex'.

Launa knew what she was trying to say and laughed. "Too late for that, I'm afraid. Don't look at me like that – I'm not a teenager and it was bound to happen one day."

"Yeah, but not on the first bloody date, young lady."

"Well, it did, and I would do it again. Anne, he is everything I dreamed of."

Anne rolled her eyes. "And what about him? Are you everything he wants? Obviously sex, yes, but are you enough for him?" Anne looked at her niece and thought she would be every man's cup of tea, but she was disappointed that he had taken her to bed so soon, and was concerned that, although Launa was very clever and bright, she was still very naive when it came to men. "I am happy for you."

Launa was still in a world of her own, dreaming about him.

*

A year on, Launa picked out her wedding dress. Charles had asked her to marry him, since they had spent every spare moment together. Her work increased along with her reputation, and it was only on very few occasions that she faced her fiancé in the courtroom. It was not a good place to be, since the majority of the time the cases were won by her and so the mood turned sombre, but a good session in the bedroom put everything right again.

William Enright and Charles Senior were pleased that the youngest member of the family was to be married to a very good barrister, and not one of the tarts he generally dated. William still had a particular case that he had planned for Launa in the next couple of years.

Anne, beside herself with excitement, invited all the relevant people along to the occasion. Launa walked down the aisle, wearing the gown designed by Anne's close friend Davis Moss. The dress was made of ivory raw silk, a simple design from the front, nipped in at the waist, and covered in tiny pearls, all hand sewn. The back was stunning. It was cut away to show her figure with a large bow as a bustle and a thin layer of lace to cover the skin. With her hair piled up on her head, she looked like a Grecian goddess with tiny pearls sewn into each wave.

Anne cried as she walked Launa down the aisle, while Launa fought desperately hard to stop the tears from flooding her face. She wished her father was here by her side and her heart ached for her mother. She should have been there with her, helping to choose the dress, design the flowers, and do all the things a mother of the bride should do.

The reception was held at Hever Castle in Kent, a picturesque venue with a lake and fantastic gardens, and anyone who was anyone in the legal system attended. Charles paraded Launa like a trophy. The champagne flowed as everyone enjoyed themselves. It was the first time Launa met Mackenzie, Charles' stepmother. Halfway through their first dance, a tall woman with blonde hair, wearing a very expensive summer suit, approached them. As

Charles made the formal introduction, Launa noticed he was nervous and embarrassed by the woman's odd behaviour.

"Well, hello, darlings. Sorry I'm late, blasted chauffeur got pissed and we got pulled over by the police." She threw her head back and laughed a very false laugh. "Fancy that, eh? There I was, trying to explain that I was off to the wedding of the century, where every judge in the land would be, and do you know what the daft police officer said?"

Launa and Charles had stopped dancing – they were dumbfounded at the woman's manner. Launa could not imagine why this so-called stepmother of Charles was drunk already and on the verge of making a scene.

"Go on, try to guess what the bloody man in blue said?" She laughed unnecessarily whilst waving a champagne glass around. Some of the contents splashed over Launa, much to her disgust, but she held her tongue and politely smiled it off.

"Come on, have a bloody guess."

"Listen, Mackenzie, it doesn't matter. Anyway you are here now so go and have another glass of champagne and enjoy yourself." Charles tried to steer Launa away but Mackenzie followed.

"I must say, Charles, your bride is just perfect." Her voice was loud from the drink and attracting stares from the other guests. Launa turned to face Mackenzie to thank her for the compliment, but was surprised by the sneer she got from this woman.

William hurried over to take his wife away but, as he grabbed her arm, she shrugged him off and headed for the exit.

"Charles, what was all that about?" asked Launa.

"Oh, she likes a drink, my stepmother. Just ignore her."

He led Launa over to the buffet. "Don't worry about her." He picked up another glass of champagne.

"She is very young to be your stepmother. She looks as young as me."

Her indirect question irritated him. "Well, she isn't as young as you. Now let's go and enjoy our wedding – after all, it is our special day!" With that, he gulped back the champagne and walked off.

Launa turned to see where Mackenzie had gone and spotted her by the bar, perched on a stool, staring right back at her. William asked if Launa wanted to dance with him, and she gracefully accepted, but her heart ached. She had dreamed of a dance on her wedding day with her father and each brother, but sadly she realised she couldn't, and so she put the thought to the back of her mind.

One-day, Mad Mick will pay, she thought.

Chapter Seven

Three years on

Married life was not a bed of roses, but Launa had nothing to compare hers to. Her aunt lived alone, never married, and what she remembered from her parent's relationship was perfection, but that was a long time ago now.

After Launa's wedding, Anne decided to up sticks and move to Australia with David Moss to start a tailoring company. She had promised Mary to love Launa as her own, and she had kept that promise. When Launa married and moved out, Anne believed that she had done her job and so pursued her new life venture.

Launa decided, for her own security, to buy a home by the sea, and found the perfect cottage. A large sum of money remained after her university fees from the trust money left to her by Alfie Horsham.

She bought the cottage just before she tied the knot and so, when they moved into his Chelsea pad, they had a wonderful retreat to go to on weekends. The house remained in her original name, Francesca Vincent. She told her husband the truth about everything, except the past, as it was an unbreakable solemn promise she made to her parents. Her marriage was a fake, well, in name only. Launa loved her husband deeply and acted the good dutiful wife. Charles, however, had a strange side to him. He blew hot and cold, which Launa could not comprehend, and she questioned his true feelings.

They both worked hard and before long Launa became one of the best defence lawyers. They agreed to disagree when it came to their clients, and tried not to go against each other in the courtroom or to discuss each other's cases.

Weekends, they ditched everything and went off either to the coast or abroad for a couple of days. Their flourishing income allowed for a lavish lifestyle, with good food, fine wine and exotic holidays. Yet there was something missing. The sex was still good, and he was sometimes attentive, but often he appeared miles away, in a world of his own. She felt particularly insecure when he came home late, and worried when he returned home in different clothes, but she kept her concerns to herself.

It was the mood swings which bothered her the most. She was uneasy when he sulked but, no matter what she tried to do to cheer him up, it wasn't enough and, as time went by, he took his misery out on her. However, when he was happy their marriage was wonderful; it was just that she just wished he was always that way.

Launa arrived late for work Monday morning, having started her period with unbearable cramps. Charles had left his breakfast plates on the side with the spilt milk dripping onto the floor. *Inconsiderate pig,* she thought. *He wasn't the only one who had a job to get to.* She cleaned the mess and left the apartment in a foul mood.

Susan nodded at Launa, who swept by, looking white and bedraggled.

"Susan, bring me a café latté, please?"

She grunted, pissed off with Launa for stealing her man. It might have been four years ago, but she still hadn't forgiven her.

Her office door was open and there, behind her desk, sat her father-in-law, William. "Good morning, Launa, and how are you this fine morning?"

Launa was dumbfounded; never before had she seen him so happy or, for that matter, in her office.

"Good morning, William. I'm fine," she sighed, feeling the worse for wear.

"Good, good. Now then, my dear, the chambers have been given a case here." He pointed to a red folder on her desk. He got up from the seat and walked around the office, with his hands behind his back like a schoolteacher. Launa's eyes followed.

"This case is the highest profile we have ever covered in these chambers." After emphasising the word ever, he smiled, almost sarcastically.

Launa's heart raced in anticipation.

Eagerly, she nodded.

"I want you to represent the client but..." He paused, taking a deep breath. "But, this must be done under my supervision." He glanced her way to see her reaction.

Her heart sank; she felt undermined. She could handle the best cases on her own, as a senior barrister with an excellent record of accomplishment. Bravely, she asked, "Is there any particular reason for overseeing this?" She didn't want to come across as being too frank but the words just fell out of her mouth.

William was struck by her brashness. "Yes, there is a reason. This is the highest profile case you have been given, and I don't think you have enough experience, so it will be under my supervision. Is that all right with you, Launa, or should I hand it to someone else?" His jolly tone turned threatening.

Launa chewed the inside of her mouth. Her cramps worsened. She despised William. With his arrogant and sharp-tongued nature, he took on the role of the interfering father-in-law.

"That's fine," she replied, desperate to sit down.

"Good. Now we have that straight, I want you to read the case. There will be no need to search any other evidence for this client, as it is an open and shut case. We will not win this one."

Launa frowned, what did he mean? *We will not win this one.*

"Who is our client?"

"He is a serial killer. The killings — prostitutes, I might add — have been sensationalised in the newspaper. Well, he was caught two nights ago, and we have been asked to represent him."

Launa folded her arms. "So they have definitely got the right man?"

William snorted. "Launa, I'd never suggest we would lose if there was any chance they had arrested the wrong man, now would I, you silly girl?"

Furious, she bit down on her lip to stop any more words popping out, like, '*Fuck you, you pompous, patronising fucking faggot*'.

"I'll read the case this morning and meet with our client tomorrow."

William gave her a stern nod before he left the room.

Launa secretly hated William. He thought he had a right to interfere in all aspects of her life, even to the point of walking into her home and requesting that she made more of an effort to clean up. He enquired where she went for lunch and who she mixed with, making suggestions — or should that be issuing edicts — that she shouldn't frequent particular establishments and socialise with certain colleagues. She had to accept his criticism at work since he was still her boss.

Susan stood in the doorway with a smug smile across her face.

Launa snapped, "Susan, how dare you stand listening to our conversations? It is not for receptionists to be privy to. Now, put the coffee down and leave!"

Susan, gobsmacked, had never seen Launa lose her temper, and she left feeling rather belittled.

Mauricio Luciani was the name on the folder, arrested for the murders of seven prostitutes, and the evidence was overwhelming. He was found with a dead prostitute in the boot of his car. The victim's face had been slashed twice on each side, a trademark of the serial prostitute killer. Each of the other victims had been brutally murdered — stabbed and sliced.

Launa pulled out the photos and gasped; the contents of her stomach rose, and she dashed for the toilet. Before she could endure reading on, she took two painkillers and finished her coffee.

The prostitutes were young, in their early twenties, dark-haired and probably very attractive at one point.

Strands of Mr Luciani's hair were found on the victim and a small bloodstain on his shirt.

The statement from the police – 'No comment'. *Not a good start*, she thought.

Her few years of experience taught her that 'no comment' was advised by solicitors when they had no idea as to which direction the case would go, or by criminals who familiarised themselves with the law.

William was right as far as she could see. The evidence against him was overwhelming and it would be difficult to get an acquittal. Her success in the past was largely down to loopholes and overlooked small segments, but in this particular case she thought her chances of winning the case were highly improbable.

Reading the statements from the police, and seeing the horrific pictures, she prepared herself to meet a monster. Her mind conjured up all kinds of images: a big, fat, greasy, Italian devil with horns and breathing fire.

*

When she returned home that evening, again to an empty house, she filled the bath and soaked herself with lavender bubbles. Lying back, sensing each tense muscle turn to jelly, she dreamt of her family. Her thoughts were rudely interrupted, however, by the sound of the door being flung open, snapping her out of her introspection.

"Hello, honey, I've bought you some flowers." Charles' face beamed; he knelt by the bath and kissed his wife on the cheek, shoving the posy under her nose.

"Hey, my sweet, you look pale. Are you okay?"

She smiled, enjoying the attention. "I'm just a little tired."

Charles raised his eyebrows. "Any reason why?"

"My period," said Launa flatly.

"Oh, not because you have a tough case ahead of you now, is it?" Charles, fully aware of the Luciani case, wanted Launa to share the details with him.

"Oh, that. I guess your father told you then?" responded Launa flippantly.

Charles didn't understand his wife's reaction and put it down to hormones.

"I'll go and start dinner then," he said, as he walked away.

Launa was still unhappy with the whole affair and mumbled under her breath, "Yeah, you fucking do that."

They sat silently over dinner until Charles crashed his knife and fork down. "What's the fucking matter? I'm not coming home to a miserable wife."

Launa – for the first time – shouted back. "Well, what difference does it make? Most weeknights you come home so late I'm asleep in bed anyway."

She felt her head getting hot; she wished for the second time that day that she had kept her mouth shut.

"For goodness sake, I do work, you know." His eyes glared at her and then he got up from the table, knocked over his chair and left.

Launa felt empty and alone. Maybe she should try harder to make her husband happier. The great saying *'you have to work at a marriage'* only applied if both tried, but that wasn't going to happen. She sipped a glass of wine and laid on the bed, contemplating her new approach to the whole marriage business.

She missed her family more than ever. Anne was in Australia, and her mum and dad – *well, would they even recognise her in the street?* And Fred, her twin brother, *was he thinking of her too? Did he miss her or had they moved on and forgotten her?* A big tear plopped on the beige satin sheets and left a dark circle, followed steadily by many more.

*

The next morning, she awoke to discover her husband had slept in one of the spare rooms. She made herself a strong coffee and left the bathroom door open when she took her shower, hoping that he would join her, but to no avail.

He remained in his bed until she left for work.

Determined not to let the last night's argument turn her into a miserable wife, Launa decided to wear a cheerful-looking blouse and apply a small amount of makeup.

Susan grunted at her as she passed the reception but Launa, too busy contemplating the Luciani case, didn't notice. As soon as she entered the office, she called the remand centre at Brixton to arrange a visit.

Firstly, she must meet with his solicitor and then visit her client at the prison.

Mr Hackly, a bit of a drip, always wore the same green raincoat, and spoke through his large pointed nose. He reminded her of a cartoon character.

He went over the evidence in an unusually flippant manner, which somewhat surprised Launa, because she had worked with him on several occasions, and he always appeared to be thorough. However, there was something very odd about him today; he could not look Launa in the eyes.

Before they closed the meeting, Launa asked him if there was anything wrong, to which he replied, "No, not at all. Anyway, must dash. People to see, places to go, and all that..."

Launa left his office uneasy, and with suspicion on her mind.

*

The next visit was the prison at Brixton. She had visited there before when her father was on remand and it always gave her the shivers.

She knew the drill and, without too much fuss, she was in and ready to meet her client. The large, heavy, grey metal door slowly slid to the side and there, sitting on a chair with a table in front of him, was Mauricio.

Launa expected to see a horned, middle-aged monster, but instead she saw a handsome, young Italian man, who looked pale and bewildered.

He eyed her every step as she walked over to the spare chair opposite. He stood, as a gentleman would, but the chunky officer shouted, "Sit down, Lucy anee."

Mauricio was insulted. "If you want to call me by my surname, it's Luciani."

He watched her sit gracefully and put her hand out. "I am Launa, your barrister."

Mauricio looked on in amazement. She was attractive, charming and sexy, but far too young to be representing him.

"Good afternoon, Launa. It's good of you to come, but there must be a mistake. I can see you are a nice lady, but my father, he has paid a lot of money for one of the best lawyers, and look at you."

Launa, still shocked at the fact that he was so good-looking – and not breathing fire – smiled at his lovely accent and his naïve presumption. Under normal circumstances, she would have taken offence at this type of comment but Mauricio wasn't being derogatory, just honest.

"Mr Luciani, looks can be deceiving. I have a good track record. I win more than I lose so don't judge a book by its cover."

Mauricio loved her accent and the way the words left her mouth with complete confidence.

"But you are so young."

"I know, and that's because I'm not old and past it. In fact, I love being young, with a fresh mind and the intelligence to use it." She gave him a reassuring smile.

"Well I don't know, you English are so different. In America we have older lawyers and a big team, you know."

She nodded.

"Now then, are you happy to continue with me as your representative in court or would you prefer an old fuddy-duddy."

He laughed and nodded. "I guess you will have to do."

For a second she realised that she was laughing along with a man accused of being a serial killer…

"So, first I have to ask, did you murder Miss Elizabeth Jane Chapman?"

Carefully, she observed his body language as he answered. "No, I never."

He didn't touch his face, run his fingers through his hair, bite his lip; in fact, he didn't show any signs of lying.

"Did you put the body of Elizabeth into the back of your car?"

Again, she watched his face as he replied. "No."

"How did it get to be there then, and with your hair in her hands, and her blood on your shirt?" she casually asked.

"I do not know any of these things. One minute I was in the nightclub talking to a girl, the next thing my car is surrounded by police."

Launa had studied body language at university and used this skill when it came to judging her client's character. In thirty seconds she concluded he was innocent.

Mauricio clutched his head.

"Do you know what, Mauricio, I think I believe you." Again, for the umpteenth time, Launa let the words trip off her tongue; *she should never have said that, it was so unprofessional, but something inside told her he was.*

Mauricio looked up and straight into her eyes. "You do?" The surprise knocked him back on his seat. They smiled at each other, sealing an understanding.

"You say one minute you were talking with a woman in the nightclub, but the next you were surrounded by police, so tell me this – how did you get to your car?"

He shrugged his shoulders. "I swear to God, I sat in this club. My car was parked in the car park. I talked to a girl, I don't know her name, and then I felt drunk, but I only drank one beer, then I woke up in my car with the police saying I murdered this girl."

"Okay, let's go back to the beginning and – do you mind if I tape this as I'm not a fast writer?" Launa was intrigued; her notes did not say he was drunk or even asleep in the car.

"I came to England four weeks ago, on business."

"What business?"

"My father, he owns a shipping company, and I came over here to buy more ships."

Launa inclined her head to the side. "Did you say ships?"

He laughed. "Yes, ships. Launa, I tell you now I come from a wealthy Italian family. We have lots of businesses, including ships, and so I often have to come to England, as well as other countries, to do business."

Launa already knew that her client's passport showed various trips oversees. However, a major concern was that Mauricio was in England every time there was a signature killing.

She took a deep breath. This did not add up at all – a good-looking young guy with lots of money over here on business wouldn't be a typical serial killer. *Then again, what determined a typical serial killer?* All her training in criminology had taught her that most serial killers are deeply disturbed in one way or another and the man opposite her now showed no signs of any deviances.

"Go on, Mauricio."

"Oh yeah, I was staying at one of our houses in Surrey when Mr Courtney of Courtney Shipping asked to have a meeting in London. There was nothing odd about that so obviously I went along. I like London, it's so different to New York and Chicago, eh, so I decided to stay over and go to a club. The Violet Club was recommended by Mr Courtney and, well, the rest is history."

Launa was confused. "So you came to England a month ago, alone, and had one meeting with one man, and then, bingo, banged to rights on a murder charge."

Mauricio shook his head. "No, I came with my associates and we met with lots of ship owners. Only Mr Courtney was staying the weekend in London and asked me to join him."

"And you met him alone?" Her questioning was soft, unlike the police.

"No, my associates come everywhere with me, except the Violet Club."

"Look, this story is not making sense. Firstly, please make it clear who your associates are and secondly, I need to know why, if they go with you everywhere, do they not accompany you to the Violet Club?"

"My associates are…" He paused. "I am very rich, yeah, and I have associates that help me with business decisions and as you say in England, watch my back."

Launa knew what he meant and nodded. "And the reason they didn't come to the club was?"

"Oh yes, sometimes I like female company, you know, so I sent them home and hoped to have some fun, but I ended up in here."

"So you searched for a prostitute to have female company?"

Mauricio, insulted frowned, "Hey, I do not look so bad, I don't need prostitutes. I can find myself a lovely English lady to have fun with."

Launa could tell he was being truthful.

"I have enough here to be getting on with so, if you don't mind, I will go back to my office and try to unravel this mess."

She got up from her seat and went to shake his hand, but the officer stepped forward. Launa put her hand up in Mauricio's defence. "It's okay." Leaning forward, she shook his firm hand and smiled.

"Oh, before you go, Launa, I just want you to know, you may be young but I believe in you too," the cheeky Italian said, winking.

The officer followed her out to the gate, *a proper jobs-worth, smug-faced git*, she thought.

"He thinks we are stupid. Caught in the act and he thinks he is innocent – still amazes me. How do they do it?" Clearly, he was expecting Launa to agree with him.

She felt her chest inflate.

"Listen, Officer Jones, it's for courts to decide whether he is innocent or not, and for you to look after the inmates, so I suggest you keep your fucking comments to yourself. And if I find he has been hung drawn and quartered while on remand, I'll have your fucking guts for garters. Got it?" Her well-spoken accent disappeared and the old East End twang returned, to the total shock of Jones, who knew of Launa's impeccable reputation and her influential-in-laws.

Instantly, he apologised, and made a mental note not to upset her again.

*

She drove on autopilot back to the office, her mind filled with niggling concerns. *Mauricio, a mass murderer? It did not add up. With that amount of wealth, if he really was a killer he would not leave a sloppy mess in the nightclub car park. This wasn't an open and shut case. She was going to find the evidence that would free him, regardless of what the system believed.*

Mauricio had been escorted back to his cell. He hated the nick and, what was worse, he just couldn't fathom out who had set him up and why. He sat back heavily on the itchy grey blanket and hoped that his barrister was good enough to get him released. The one positive thing was that she believed him. She was the one person who spoke to him as a human being and not an animal. He closed his eyes and tried hard to remember every tiny detail that could help his case.

Launa went over the statements again and found nothing to suggest he was innocent. There was the possibility he was framed, *but why and how?* It was early days to make a case without all the statements. The Crown Prosecution had plenty of time to take more statements and collect further evidence.

William came into the office as soon as Launa returned, still wearing his gown, eager to hear what Mauricio had to say.

Launa was again surprised at how determined he was to oversee this one.

"So how are we doing then, Launa?"

"Well, I have read the brief so far and it looks like an open and shut case."

William grinned sadistically. She could not work out if he was smug or pleased.

"Well, that's if he wasn't set up of course," she remarked.

William spun around. "Don't be ridiculous, girl, you are living in a fantasy world. Sounds to me as if you've been watching too much TV."

The words hit Launa like a thousand needles. She frowned and bowed her head.

His voice softened. "Now then, I know it's easy to get carried away with such a high-profile case. However, there are times when we as representatives, and judges like myself, have to resign ourselves to the fact that, as smart as we are, we must allow the system to take care of real evil characters like the Lucianis of this world." Before he left the room, he made a very odd comment. "Don't be fooled by his charming, innocent appearance."

Launa realised that to make that comment, William must have previously met Mauricio.

She decided not to pursue it. He oversaw the case, so he may have seen a photo or something, and besides he had given her the most significant case to date.

She ascertained that, while agreeing with William, she would do her best to prove he was innocent and win this case.

Charles arrived early from work and they sat together, enjoying a meal and a bottle of wine. He was unusually attentive and she lapped it up.

"Your hair smells nice," he said, as he twirled it around his fingers.

She giggled like a schoolgirl. Back to being happy, their argument was over and they cemented their bond with a night of passion.

*

The next morning over breakfast, Charles asked, in a matter of fact way, "So, how's the Mauricio case going? Found out any juicy gossip?"

Launa wagged her finger whilst pulling funny faces over the sharpness of the grapefruit she had just shoved in her mouth. "I thought we agreed not to discuss our cases," she replied light-heartedly, so as not to spoil the mood.

He bit his lip in annoyance. "What difference does it make? I'm not on the case."

"Ah yes, but you could pass on any titbits I share with you," she laughed.

Charles was angry and his eyes twitched. "I wouldn't do that now, would I?"

"How do I know?" she replied, still trying to keep the atmosphere jolly.

"Well, because I am supposed to be your fucking husband, that's why." He stormed away.

Launa looked at her grapefruit segments and sighed. *Why did he have to push it?*

She had made every effort to look good when he came home from work each evening and to be cheerful, but it made no difference. He was spiteful and obnoxious, like a spoilt child.

Launa arranged to visit Mauricio again, and this time she wanted to know more about his character and get the addresses of his associates.

The visit was granted and again she found herself in the same room with the same officer present.

"Good morning, Mauricio." She put her hand out to shake his and again he stood up. This time Jones stood still, not saying a word.

"How have you been, are they treating you okay?"

Mauricio was nodding. "Yeah, they are okay. Why, what did you do?"

Launa looked at Jones, who had a resigned expression on his face.

"So today I want to get to know the real you," she stated.

Mauricio grinned, "Oh yeah?" His Italian-American accent was apparent.

"Yes, I need to get a good understanding of your character so that I am able to represent you in the best light."

Mauricio liked his brief even more.

They went over his childhood and she found no reason to suspect he had been abused in any shape or form, an indication of deep-seated mental problems.

"Jones, please fetch us two teas," said Launa, without even looking over.

Jones nodded at the other officer by the door, who instantly left to fetch the refreshments.

"So you have a cousin, and you grew up together like brothers?"

He nodded.

"No jealousy, favouritism?" She searched for one clue that could put a tiny doubt in her mind.

"Jealous? No way, we had whatever we wanted. He is my best friend as well as family, and I trust him with my life."

"So what about girls?"

"I love the girls. I'm not gay, you know."

She laughed at the expression on his face. "So tell me, what has been your worst experience with a woman?" Launa looked at her list of questions but still had the tape recorder running.

"Getting caught by the husband."

Launa looked up and laughed. "No, I mean mentally."

He looked over at the officer and leaned forward to whisper in Launa's ear.

"Well, once I couldn't get it up and I felt pretty bad."

"In what way bad?"

"Hey, I'm Italian! It's my duty to give a good time, ya know."

"So what did you do?"

"I made a mental note not to drink too much before making love," he chuckled.

"I am going to get a psychiatrist to prove that you're not nuts." She stood up to leave. He accepted everything without question. He trusted her, and hoped that his instincts would be proven right.

Meanwhile, his associates were busy trying to find out who had set him up.

Another Italian family, the Bertolli's, had moved to England from New York to escape persecution from the Aldini family. The Aldini family were known for their violent methods of resolution and had made many enemies, including the Luciani family, but that was a feud that had lasted twenty-five years and was supposed to be resolved.

Joe Aldini had believed that Luka Bertolli had double-crossed him in a cocaine deal and so threatened to cut off Luka's head.

Mauricio thought that maybe Joe had struck a deal with Luka to have him locked away. He was warned by his father never to think a war is over, always to be ready for it to begin again. He was referring to the Aldinis.

Mauricio's men visited Bertolli and, after interrogation, they let him go, convinced that he was not involved.

Mauricio prayed that the men would find whoever was responsible soon, so that he wouldn't rot in jail.

*

As the weeks rolled by, Launa did her utmost to find the clues to save her client, whilst all the time pretending to everyone that it was an open and shut case.

She had the hair examined and enlarged the photo of the hair in the girl's hand. She had the blood tested on his shirt and examined the pictures of the corpse.

Her regular visits with Mauricio had left her with a clear conclusion that he was innocent, and she ached to win. She liked Mauricio and their relationship grew into a friendship.

William had not noticed the amount of time she had spent with Mauricio or the evidence she was uncovering. When he asked, she smiled sweetly and told him what he wanted to hear. Her smile masked a deep yearning to prove that she was a good barrister and, one way or another, she was determined to win the case and give the biggest credit to her chambers. William and her husband would be so proud – she tingled with excitement.

Two weeks before the trial, a statement turned up from an eyewitness, which William dropped on her desk with an annoyed glare.

"I've heard from the forensic department that you had some evidence looked at." He had both knuckles on the desk and was tight-mouthed.

Launa leaned back, away from her menacing-looking father-in-law.

"Well yes, I thought it best we had it done again just to be on the safe side."

"Safe side, what do you mean safe side?" He spat the words so aggressively.

"Well, if our client asks, then we have done our bit."

William threw his hands in the air. "In future, Launa, take orders from me, or I will hand the brief over to another barrister."

Launa gulped, "Oh, I'm sorry; I assumed you wouldn't want to be bothered with the trivialities," she replied, trying to ease the tension.

"Just do as I say!" he shouted as he left the room.

Susan was in the doorway when Launa looked up.

"Hey, before you shout at me, I just brought you a coffee. I didn't listen, and, to be honest, Launa, I don't give a shit what your briefs talk about, as long as it ain't me."

Launa looked white and Susan noticed she was shaking.

She felt sorry for Launa. Charles had gone back to his old ways, shagging any old tart, including her for that matter. He flashed his long black eyelashes and, before she could say Ann Summers, she was there giving Charles the ride of his life in the broom cupboard.

After he left, she realised that he had never truly liked her. She was just a quick shag and, when she looked back over the last few years and how she had given Launa such a hard time, she disliked herself.

"Come in, Susan. I'm going out for a break. Why don't you join me for a coffee and a nice cream cake? My treat."

Susan could not believe it. She nodded.

"I'll grab me coat."

Launa missed female company. Anne had gone overseas, her best friend had died, and all she had was Charles, William, and a pile of papers. *Oh, yes, she did have Mauricio. But, what was she thinking? Mauricio was nothing more than a client.*

*

The coffee shop was quiet, with the lunchtime trade finished, so the two women had the place more or less to themselves.

"Launa, are you all right? You look pale."

Launa bit her lip, not used to anyone talking to her sympathetically — especially Susan.

She fought to stop the tears from falling but to no avail. She put her hands over her face and sobbed quietly.

"Hey, hey. Come on, now, whatever it is it can't be so bad." Susan's voice was low and gentle as she slipped an arm around her shoulder.

Launa blew her nose and apologised.

"Oh look at me, a fucking wet weekend. I'm sorry. I didn't bring you here for coffee to cry over me cream cake," she half-cried and half-laughed.

Susan hated herself. Launa was sweet, and she had just fucked her husband.

"It's all right, Launa. Look, I know I'm sometimes a bitch an' all, but I don't like to see ya like this. Besides, you've smudged your mascara."

Launa laughed and touched Susan's hand. "Thanks," she whispered.

"What are you doing tonight? Fancy a jar after work?"

Launa didn't even think about what she needed to be doing. Instantly, she nodded. "Yes, fuck it. Why not? I would love to go!"

After work, they went to the local pub. Unlike the usual posh restaurants and wine bars, it was a real, old-fashioned pub, with characteristic thick blue smoke in the air, dog-eared carpet, and barmaids with big tits and rotten teeth.

"Cor, 'ello, darling. Get ya coat, you've pulled," said one fat drunk builder.

Susan's eyes widened when she heard him, but she was relieved to hear Launa laugh and, with a traditional cockney accent, reply, "The only thing I've pulled, darling, is a muscle."

The night was full of laughter. Susan had enjoyed Launa's company. She wasn't the typical snooty barrister, looking down her nose at the office staff. She accepted everyone for who they were, without judging them. Launa's thoughts drifted a little to her career. It was going to be difficult for her when she did get to be a judge and, at the rate she was going, it would only be a few years before she reached position as a silk – a common expression for Queen's Counsel – and then possibly a circuit judge.

*

Launa arrived home, well after twelve o'clock, to find Charles watching a late-night film, having drunk half a bottle of brandy.

"Where have you been? I called the office, no fucking answer. So have you have been slutting around then, queen fucking bee?"

"Charles, I'm not going to talk to you when you've had a drink."

He had never spoken to her in that ugly tone before; her feelings were truly kicked in the teeth.

"Before you go to bed, just a little word of wisdom, don't try to undermine my father again!"

Launa was dumbfounded. "What do you mean, Charles?"

He slurred his words. "You know what I mean."

Launa went to bed with her tail between her legs. She never discussed cases with her husband and expected William to have more discretion. They controlled her and supported each other. She was the outsider.

*

The next morning, she got up early and left before Charles awoke.

As soon as she arrived in the office, Susan rushed along the corridor with a coffee. "Hello, Launa. Here you go, freshly brewed. Just wanted to say I had a fab time last night."

Launa looked up from her notes and smiled at Susan, who looked very different. Her hair was tied back, the orange face replaced with soft makeup, and she wore a pale blue shift dress just below the knee.

Launa's eyes widened. "Look at you!"

Susan nodded. "I have decided to turn over a new leaf — no more glamorous Susan." Launa tried hard not to laugh; *surely, she didn't see herself as glamorous.*

"This is the new me: intelligent, sophisticated and no more quick shags."

Launa then burst out laughing. "Susan, you definitely look the part."

Pleased with herself, she held her head high and walked back to the reception.

*

Launa looked over the new statement.

Ms Daisy Burrows, a thirty-five-year-old woman. Occupation: unemployed. She had given the statement on the night of the murder to the Sergeant.

She described a man fitting Mauricio's description standing by the car. He was talking on the phone and, at the same time, trying to squash something into the boot.

The statement did not add up either.

Daisy Burrows was in the car next to Mauricio's, having had a nap. She was not sure what was going on because she only peeped once but she was very clear on what was said. And the man by the car was asking about a man called Gianluca — obviously Italian. He then asked about a bonnie and where to put it. She distinctively remembered him talking about the gates of Rome and messing up a boat deal.

Launa studied the statement. *There were many loopholes here and she could rip this witness to pieces. Yet, the Crown could use this to sew up the case. There were so many links to the fact he is Italian.*

She left the statement until her next appointment with Mauricio.

With the court case nearly upon them, she still couldn't assure him that she would get him off, but she did promise to do her best.

Mauricio looked defeated. "Launa, I don't understand this statement. I don't even speak this way, I don't know a Gianluca and I didn't have a conversation by the car. How could I?"

Launa nodded. She spun the statement back to face herself and went over the words, gates of Rome. Suddenly it dawned on her what it meant; *they were out of the woods*. She was so excited, but decided to keep the reason to herself just in case she was wrong. She left Mauricio sooner than planned and headed to Surrey to meet an old friend of Alfie's by the name of Gordon Smyth.

As she approached the drive, she had flashbacks of her childhood. She had spent many happy days here along with her friend Thomasine. Tom had called him Uncle Gordie, but he was not strictly an uncle, just a very good friend of Alfie. He didn't have children of his own and loved the company of the girls. His huge kitchen hosted a small wine making set-up and often they were allowed to sample the latest batch. He also bred a rare breed of cat and sold them to the rich and famous for huge amounts of money. Launa had enjoyed playing with the kittens. When she looked back over her teenage years she realised she was more privileged than most. She'd had so many wonderful experiences and met some genuinely good people, Gordon being one of them.

He opened the door, excited to be visited by Launa, who had grown into a sophisticated young woman.

"Thank you for seeing me at such short notice." Launa felt like a child again. He had been the man who taught her how to change her accent.

Gordon hadn't altered much. He was still rotund, wore his trademark bow tie, and his hair was still cut very short – he was definitely a quirky character and no mistake.

"Always such a pleasure to see you, my dear. Wonderful to hear you're doing so well."

"Thank you," she replied.

They sat, enjoying small talk over a cup of Earl Grey.

"Now then, I am representing a client in a difficult case."

Gordon rubbed his hands together. Bored these days since his retirement, and wanting fresh challenges and excitement in a life which had suddenly become rather humdrum, he had contemplated climbing the Himalayas but his doctor said unequivocally that it would kill him.

"He has been accused of murder."

Gordon stared intently.

"I have a statement from a witness and the Crown Prosecution is going to be calling this woman. I have only just received it, which is very naughty of the Crown, since I should have had this on my desk over ten months ago."

Gordon looked perplexed and shrugged his shoulders. "Is that important?"

"Yes," she said eagerly. "This means that I can present my evidence at the last minute. It gives the Crown less time to make a case against my findings."

"Oh, I see," he said, itching to see where he fitted into the whole scenario.

"This is where you might be able to help." She handed him the statement as if she were handing over a new-born baby.

Gracefully, he took it and – plonking his glasses on to his chunky nose – he read on. "Yes, I can see this woman was either drunk or semi-comatose, the way she remembers certain words."

Launa wanted him to tell her the meaning of the words to prove herself right. Her heart raced in anticipation.

"From this statement, I guess the man standing by the car was a cockney."

Launa jumped from her seat, threw her hands around his neck, and kissed him on the cheek. "You bloody genius, Gordon."

Gordon went pink and smiled. "Well, I am a linguistic expert."

"Would you mind if I called you as a witness?"

Gordon clapped his hands together. "I would be honoured. Oh, what fun!" His laugh was loud and haughty. "Let's have a drink. I have been desperate to share a glass of my latest raspberry red."

Launa really missed her old friends, and her heart still ached when she thought of Alfie and Tom.

They sat and drank the new wine, chatted over old times and caught up on the new ones and, before she left, she promised to see more of Gordon in the future.

Launa drove home, beaming. *She had the secret weapon now to get Mauricio acquitted, and she was not going to share it until the last moment. She was going to play dirty,* as *the Crown had.* The evidence she uncovered pointed to a set up; the only thing she didn't have in her possession was a reason why, but that wasn't her job anyway.

The case was held at the Old Bailey. The story had been in the papers for quite some time as the grisly details had entered the public domain. The great British public loved this type of case and the papers, especially *The Daily Mirror*, were more than willing to feed their version of the facts with sensational headlines. This was a huge case for Launa. She knew in her heart that if she lost, her client would never see the light of day. Judges were influenced by the media, and they needed to be seen to be taking a very firm line on the most public cases.

William had arrived at their home early that morning to accompany her to the courtroom.

She heard her husband and William whispering in the entrance hall, but couldn't quite work out what they were saying, except the words, "He will serve a twenty-five-year recommended. Stevens will see to that." Launa was sure they were talking about Mauricio and felt a twinge of guilt for him. If she lost the case, he would do a twenty-five-stretch, and she hadn't even discussed the possibility of pleading guilty and doing a fifteen. She had to go with her gut instinct — an all-out acquittal.

William hugged his son tightly, as if they had just won the lottery, and both were looking decidedly pleased with themselves, displaying a rather smug expression. Launa was made uneasy by the way William acted towards her, as if she was his best friend.

The oddness of it made her uncomfortable — in fact, she felt queasy, and couldn't, for the life of her, think why. But it was definitely one of those moments, when you experience a sense of dread about to prevail, but with no way of determining the course of events — like a car crash waiting to happen. Launa, now in court, was facing the biggest case of her career, with unspeakable and dire consequences for Mauricio if she messed the final part of her case up. If she encountered any last minute curveballs she would just have to rely on her wits.

William, still unaware of her defence strategy, naturally assumed that Launa was following his orders.

Charles had been pleasant and as she left for the court that day, he took her into his arms, kissed her neck and whispered, "I love you, my queen bee."

She melted for a moment. "I love you too, my lovely lashes." He kissed her again and patted her on the bum before she left. She enjoyed the attention but the nasty taste in her mouth remained.

William was present in the courtroom but not on the stand. Her junior barrister, Nettelwood, was the gofer for the continuation of the court, a privilege which he honoured.

Barrister Henry Weirs, leading for the Crown Prosecution, was known not to mince his words – he was one of the best advocates in the legal system. He was a tall man with grey hair, roughly sixty years old, with a high class accent. He often came across as very arrogant and snooty.

"All rise. The Judge Philip Manson presiding," shouted the clerk.

Launa surveyed the courtroom to see the jury. They were also looking around and many of their eyes were on her, especially the men. She smiled sweetly and looked ahead at the judge. He had a reputation for being firm yet fair. During her break, William showed up and demonstrated his disdain. "Damn, I thought we would have Stevens; he's a good fellow."

Launa ignored his comment. She knew Stevens to be a good friend of William's, as they often played golf and lunched together.

The morning session was devoted largely to the formal ceremonies and swearing in. This was the boring part and most of the jurors were finding the experience tedious to say the least.

The case began in the afternoon. First, the Crown Prosecutor explained to the jury how they intended to proceed with the case, followed by Launa acting for the defence.

After the first day, when the Crown had presented a damning case, William smiled endlessly and Launa just bit her lip and bided her time. She was unable to work out exactly what angle William was coming from. It was very perplexing and, considering the stakes, quite unnerving. *It was as if they wanted to lose the case, but why?* Mauricio was a stranger and this was the case of the century. *Surely, her firm's reputation would be enhanced if they could win the case and Mauricio would be elated and indebted to them.* The evidence against Mauricio was presented rather flippantly, and in a manner that would look to the jury as incontrovertible – a straightforward open and shut case. The fact that the defendant was there at the scene, with blood on his shirt and the dead girl's hand clutching his hair, spoke volumes. Launa hoped that they would pay attention to her evidence before they made up their mind, but she was getting increasingly despondent about the way events were heading.

Mauricio was in the courtroom the next day to give his account of the events.

He was very nervous on the stand and Launa had to keep urging him to focus on his side of the story and answer her questions concisely and confidently. The jury, though, was beginning to warm to Launa's approach and the Italian, who didn't look at all like a vicious killer, was conjuring up all sorts of thoughts in the jury's minds and certainly giving them reason to question whether this was in fact such an open and shut case.

By the third day, William had seen enough to believe one hundred percent that Launa had done as he asked and was just allowing the Crown to take control. In fact, she didn't seem to fight his corner at all. What William didn't know, however, was that Launa was playing a crafty game herself and had decided to leave the best until last. She wanted and needed the last piece of evidence to stand out the most in the jury's minds.

*

That evening, Charles was fussing around Launa as if she was pregnant or something. Whatever he was doing, she couldn't put her finger on it.

"There you go, my angel." He pointed to a bath full of bubbles, with candles lit everywhere.

Launa kissed her husband and enjoyed the pampering.

As they sat at the candlelit table, savouring the chicken chasseur, there was a knocking at the door. Launa pulled the bathrobe tighter around her shoulders as Charles let the visitor in.

It was William.

"Oh, I am sorry to interrupt your evening."

William eyed Launa up and down. He had noticed just how sexy she looked in her robe – her skin was glowing and her fresh face looked so inviting. He could see why Charles wanted to bed the beauty even though he had initially been told not to. She was supposed to be primed just for this case, not to end up as his wife. However, she was very different from his previous tarts and she was now the perfect candidate to manipulate. This was the case, the one that the Enrights had dreamed about, planned to the finest detail, and were about to execute for their own purposes. She was perfect for this position. Her respect and loyalty to William and Charles would ensure she did as she was told; *well, so they believed.*

"That's all right," grinned Charles as he pulled up another chair, suggesting that he joined them.

"Look, I won't stay – just wanted to say you are doing a fantastic job, Launa, and, seeing that you have everything under control, I wondered if I might steal my son away for a few days on a yachting trip, since Charles Senior has booked the trip as a surprise for my birthday tomorrow."

Launa smiled politely. She was secretly glad he was going to be out of her hair. Of course, she would miss her husband, but William was a pain in the arse right now.

"Hey, that's wonderful, I don't mind. You go and enjoy a boys' holiday."

Charles was surprised she seemed so keen, but he decided it was better than being nagged.

William ogled a little longer than necessary and Launa pulled her robe tighter around herself, to the annoyance of William — *as if she would think I would go after his son's wife*. But he would have — he had done it before with Charles' many girlfriends.

*

The next morning, the men went off and Launa could relax.

Having William around made her nervous.

She entered the court and handed the evidence she had to the crown and made the same apologies they had when they handed her copy late.

"Sorry, must have got stuck to the bottom of my file."

Barrister Weirs snatched it from her without even a thank you.

Launa looked at Mauricio, who appeared sickly in the stand. His thick, curly hair looked flat and the sparkle in his eyes had gone. He looked gaunt and resigned.

She managed to get his attention. She gave him a huge smile and a wink. His face lit up; *there was light at the end of the tunnel*. He could see from her countenance that she looked excited and confident, but he had no idea why.

"Please call your next witness, Barrister Weirs."

"The Crown calls Daisy Burrows," exclaimed Weirs.

Launa had not met the witness until now, and could see instantly she was a prostitute. She grinned again.

As she was sworn in, Launa recognised her accent as being northern.

Daisy looked more fifty-five than thirty-five. Her skin was wrinkled from too much drink and fags, she was slightly tipsy, and the skinny woman, with dyed ginger hair, was shaking from withdrawals of some kind. Her appearance looked distinctly shambolic but perfectly in sync with her position in life. Her lipstick was bright red and bleeding up the creases in her lips, and she was wearing an animal print fake fur coat that looked like it had been used as a rug at one time. However, she thought she looked good.

"So, Ms Burrows, you were asleep in the car next to the defendant's and were awoken by the noise?" Launa questioned in a polite way, with respect.

"Yes, that's right." Daisy's words were slightly slurred but what gave it away were the eyes – they seemed to drift off of their own accord.

"Now then, Daisy – may I call you Daisy?"

She nodded. "Daisy, please tell the court what you do for a living?" Launa directed, giving the witness an encouraging smile.

"I'm currently unemployed." She tried to put on a well-to-do voice but putting an h in the wrong place was sending slightly strange signals to the court.

"Daisy, whatever you tell us here today will remain here, okay? Now, because you are a witness in a very serious case, please don't feel you will be in any trouble if you tell the court your occupation."

Daisy looked at the judge for reassurance. He nodded.

"I am a call girl. A high class one, mind." She wagged a finger at Launa.

There was a snigger from the gallery.

"Yes, Daisy. Thank you for being so honest."

"Now then, Daisy, as a call girl, you know how important it is to find the right man who has been killing the local prostitutes, as I am sure you must have been terrified for your own safety."

Daisy looked around the courtroom and back to Launa. "Yeah, of course."

"Okay. As you know, our suspect is Italian."

Daisy nodded.

"Did the police tell you he was Italian?"

"Objection, Your Honour. The defence is suggesting collaboration."

The judge frowned at Weirs. "Overruled. Continue."

"Please, Daisy, try to remember how you knew he was Italian."

Daisy felt uncomfortable. The police had dragged her in that night, threatened to nick her if she didn't make a statement, and then they had told her he was Italian.

"I can't remember."

"Daisy, please tell the court how you knew he was Italian. You need to tell the truth; it's so important that we have the right man."

Daisy remembered seeing the poor girl sliced to pieces in the boot of the car; it could have been her.

"The police told me he was Italian," she said in a low voice.

"Did you hear him speak?" questioned Launa.

"Yeah, of course I did."

"And you are sure he was Italian?"

"Yeah."

"What makes you so sure?"

Daisy recalled the conversation she heard. "He was talking about the gates of Rome and some Italian name. I've heard the name before it was... Uh, Gianluca, and he said where shall I put the bonnie – well, Bonnie's Italian for something, ain't it?"

"So from that conversation you heard, you assumed he was Italian?"

"Well, yeah, and 'cause he was sitting in the car asleep you could see he was Italian."

"So, Daisy, the man you heard on the phone was the man asleep in the car."

Daisy nodded, very proud of herself. She had drunk a small bottle of cheap vodka before she had entered the court, and could not remember who was the good guy and who was the bad guy. *The young, sweet barrister must have been on her side.*

"During the night in question, how much did you have to drink? It's okay, Daisy, please feel free to be honest and tell the court."

"Well, I did, in all honesty, have a small bottle of vodka. Ya know, to give me a bit of confidence."

Weirs could not interrupt; he would have looked a fool.

"One last question, Daisy. Would you recognise an Italian accent if you heard one?"

"Oh yes, I've seen The Godfather three times."

"That's all, Your Honour. May I call my next witness?"

Weirs was fuming; *his witness was pissed and had completely fucked it up.* He still had the Italian lingo to use though.

The defence calls Gordon Smyth.

Weirs rolled his eyes, a fucking linguistic *expert? Whatever next.* He smiled at Launa in a patronising way.

"Mr Smyth, would you please tell the ladies and gentlemen of the jury your occupation."

He stood proud in the witness stand. "I am a linguistic specialist and have been for over forty years. I specialise in accents and dialects."

"Thank you, Mr Smyth. Now please tell the court your findings from the statement you have been asked to study." Launa had the statement passed around as exhibit one. Weirs was tapping his fingers on the desk, thinking how he was going to get around this one.

"Yes, the statement suggests that the conversation that took place was not by an Italian but a true East End cockney."

Weirs took a sharp intake of breath. What the hell did she have up her sleeve?

"When the man said gates of Rome, he was referring to 'home'. This is true cockney rhyming slang but not modern, so I guess this man to have been around fifty years old."

"Objection, Your Honour. This witness is not here to establish the man's age."

The judge faced Smyth. "Is this true, or does your expertise cover such matters?"

"Yes, of course, Your Honour. I can tell a person's age, background, sex and colour by the words they use – that is my job."

The judge asked him to continue.

"The rhyming slang for hair is 'bonnie fayre' and a more modern term in slang is 'Gianluca Vialli' which means 'Charlie' – another term for cocaine. In my professional opinion, it would be very highly unlikely that the man was Italian and would, as I said, be around fifty to sixty years old. And just one more point, the boat is not literal – it means 'face'. So when the man said, and I quote, 'the boat's a mess', he meant the victim's face was a mess."

Weirs was up in a flash to cross-examine. "Now, you say the man was fifty years old or more, but you cannot be certain. Explain to the court why."

"He may, of course, be older. That particular slang dates back so far that, yes, he could be older."

This wasn't the answer Weirs was expecting. Launa sat back and smiled; she looked up at Mauricio, who looked baffled. It was obvious it was beyond him.

"And, of course, you cannot be certain that he wasn't younger, around twenty-six, say."

Gordon didn't like Weirs – not because he was a prosecution lawyer and his dear friend was the defence lawyer. No, it was because he could not stand condescending individuals.

"It is with the knowledge and skill gained with forty years' experience, that I can assure you that those words would not have been spoken by a man in his twenties."

Launa was excited; *it was going the right way*.

The final day was the showdown. She went to see Mauricio just before the hearing was to commence, and he looked as if he hadn't slept a wink.

"I can't promise anything but my best," she whispered.

Mauricio had one hand cuffed to the officer and put the other around her neck and kissed her on the cheek.

"Whatever happens, Bella, I know you have tried your hardest for me."

She nodded and left.

Weirs was there ready. It was the day the forensic evidence was to be revealed.

"The Crown calls Doctor Lipman."

Launa smiled. *She was going to eat him alive.*

Weirs began the questions and Launa left him to it. The photos were shown to the jury and the most important one was the clump of hair found in the victim's hand. The photo was clear – it showed the long, thick bunch of hair protruding from the clenched fist of the victim.

"So, Doctor, on identification, the hair of the victim was a match?"

"Yes, the DNA is exactly the same, there is no doubt."

"The blood on the shirt of the suspect, does that match that of the victim?"

Weirs obviously knew the answer. "Yes, one hundred percent match."

Weirs turned to the jury and smiled. He strongly believed he had sewn it up.

Launa was so excited; *she was going to wipe that smug smile off his face.* Slowly, she approached the bench.

"Mr Lipman, when you looked at the hair, did you notice anything strange?"

He shook his head, not sure where she was going with the question.

"Well, are you sure that the victim pulled that clump of hair from the suspect's head?" she emphasised the word pulled.

"Yes," he answered nervously.

"Then please explain to the court why you are so certain because – on close examination of the photo – I can clearly see the hair does not have roots and the ends are a clean cut!"

Mr Lipman blushed and Weirs nearly choked.

"If in a frenzied attack the victim pulled from her assailant a clump of hair, would you or would you not expect to see roots?"

"Well it depends."

"Depends on what, Doctor?" She knew he had no answer.

"Well, no, I suppose there would be some signs of roots."

Weirs glanced around the courtroom, wide-eyed and worried. He couldn't see William or Charles Enright anywhere, and he knew they would be angry. This was supposed to be an open and shut case – a slam dunk. He believed that William had prepared Launa; *there should be no doubt as to his guilt.* Weirs didn't mind the other witnesses. Besides, the case had to look like there was some defence, but now she was questioning the prosecution witness, and she was bloody good. The case was starting to wobble, along with Weirs' legs.

"The blood on the shirt. In your opinion, Doctor – if the defendant had indeed murdered the victim in such a brutal fashion, slicing her face, stabbing her groin area – would you not see splatters of blood, because clearly she had bled to death? A major artery was hit. Surely the blood would have left a spray mark rather than smudges?"

"If the defendant stepped aside he could easily miss the spray." Lipman looked and felt stupid. He had been asked not to delve too much into the evidence, and now he could see why. The police had wanted a quick arrest – their name was mud, and they had been accused of not doing enough to catch the killer.

He looked down in shame.

"So, if the suspect, in his frenzied attack, watched carefully enough to see as to where the blood was going to squirt, he could have cleverly anticipated in which direction to move?"

Mr Lipman realised it sounded preposterous.

"No further questions, Your Honour."

The court adjourned and, over a fresh salad, she prepared herself for the summing up.

Her heart was pounding, and she sensed the adrenaline surging through her body. It was like being on stage and every time she summed any case up, that's exactly who she became – *a bloody good actress.*

Back in the court, there was a buzz coming from the jury. Weirs looked pissed off and Launa was anxious. The summing up was the most important part. It would be the last thing the jury heard from her, and so every point needed to be precise and short.

She glanced up at the gallery, knowing that there would be reporters and other solicitors watching, but she was surprised to see it packed with men in suits. They all looked Italian and worried to death. She smiled sweetly, and they nodded in unison. She looked back at Mauricio, who felt a strange sense of being looked after. *She knew that he would walk free.*

"So, members of the jury," – she paused and smiled sweetly – "I would like you to think about this very carefully – if Mauricio Luciani is guilty of the brutal killing of those seven woman, then he should go to prison for a long time. But if he is not guilty, as I will clearly demonstrate, then the real killer will still be out there preying on his next victim. It is up to you to be clear in your mind that there is no doubt, not one tiny piece of doubt, because if there is, then you must find the defendant not guilty. It is my job to show clear evidence that the defendant was not the man who killed the victim, and put the body in the boot of the car, or the man who made the phone call.

"Firstly, let us look at the witness. She was drunk, yet she made a clear statement regarding the conversation that took place that evening. She only identified the defendant when the police pointed him out and, looking at the defendant, yes, it is obvious he is Italian.

"We have heard from the experts that the man by the car was presumed to be a fifty-year-old East End man.

"We heard all the evidence from the police, including the blood results, which showed a small amount of alcohol in his blood stream and yet, when they found him, he was barely conscious. We know that a date rape drug has the same effect but is not traceable in the blood after so many hours.

"We know that the hair found on the victim was cut from the defendant, and placed into the victim's hands, rather neatly I might add, and so we come to the last piece of evidence – the blood. I ask you, members of the jury, to think back to the pictures of the butchered victim and the defendant's blood-stained shirt. I put it to you that Mauricio Luciani was drugged and put in his car. This is the same car in which the body of the victim had already been placed in the boot. The hair was cut with a sharp object and placed in the victim's hand. This is clearly a set up! By whom, we don't know, but that's not for us to consider. We are only concerned with the facts, and the main and crucial fact is this – there is too much doubt in this case to convict Mauricio Luciani of murder."

Weirs knew straight away that the case was lost and so he gave a flat summing up.

The judge, surprisingly, gave a fair representation, and the jury were led away.

Mauricio was shaking when Launa approached him. She grabbed his arm. "I'm not going to say you will get a not guilty but keep your fingers crossed." She was shaking too.

The jury returned three hours later, and it was extremely difficult to tell from their expressions what they had decided.

Launa stared at the dock, holding up her crossed fingers. Mauricio smiled.

"Foreman of the jury, have you reached a verdict?"

"Yes, Your Honour."

"Go ahead."

"We, the jury, find Mauricio Luciani... not guilty."

Mauricio bowed his head and Launa almost cried.

Weirs snorted, giving Launa a filthy look.

*

After the paper signing and formal red tape, she led her client to her car. They raced away from the flashing cameras of the paparazzi.

She felt like she was in a film escaping a mob or something.

"Hey, Bella, you can slow down now. I think we have managed to lose them."

Launa laughed. "Well, how do you feel?"

He laughed. "Free. I feel free."

They stopped at a country pub and enjoyed a celebratory drink.

Getting carried away in the moment, he forgot about his associates, who had been sitting throughout the case in the gallery.

"I must go now, back to the States. I know we haven't known each other very long — only ten months — but you have been my rock and I love you for that. I will be forever in your debt." He grabbed her cheeks and kissed her on the lips — not a passionate kiss, but a kiss that said 'I love you like a sister'.

Before he left for good, he handed her a piece of paper.

"If ever you need me, call me on that number."

And he was gone.

Launa looked at the numbers and instantly memorised them. They were easy to remember. She had worked hard over the years to remember case dates and names, so phone numbers were simple.

Launa was high as a kite on her success. She imagined the triumphant look on her husband's face — he would be so proud of her and, of course, her father-in-law, who clearly doubted her ability. Tomorrow would see their return, and she couldn't wait.

Chapter Eight

His face was contorted with rage, and the anger in his eyes was so deep that she felt it burn her very soul. She hardly recognised her husband. Charles had once been the ideal man for her, the same profession, the same tastes, and the same desires. They both enjoyed material things, being fortunate to be able to afford a nice house, a yacht and all the lavish things that money could buy. Now he stood towering over her, screaming obscenities, while spit sprayed from his mouth. Launa trembled: holding her breath, she silently prayed to herself that he would continue to shout and scream for, all the while his anger came out in words, she knew he wouldn't hit her again. Only when he was calm and calculating would he throw a punch or a brutal kick — it was always premeditated, a controlled rage.

What the hell did he have in mind for her now? Her heart thumped furiously and her stomach's contents rose up to burn the back of her throat.

He had brought her to their seaside home, supposedly for a weekend break, yet his silence throughout the journey from their home in Chelsea to West Sussex spoke volumes. He was angry. Now, inside her eighteenth century cottage, gulping back two large brandies, he taunted her, called her names and belittled her. The more he shouted, the greater he intensified his own anger; again and again he accused her of wanting to leave him. Ashamed of herself for being so weak, she shook her head, denying all his accusations and thinking, *Please, God, let him stop.* Then he became silent. He walked towards the kitchen whilst she slumped in the chair for a few minutes, and then he returned to the sitting room, holding two glasses. "Here, Launa, have a drink." His calm manner unnerved her as she took the glass.

He eyed her up and down, revolted by his perception of a wife who had become boring, miserable and untidy. She had once been the envy of all woman lawyers, both admired and fancied by her colleagues for her brains and charm.

Now, however, all that had changed, since she won the Mauricio Luciani murder case. She remembered her husband being disgusted with her and, most troubling to her, she never did find the underlying cause of his anger and obvious hatred. Her husband's family reacted to the victory as if she had taken down the entire legal system.

She vividly recollected the evening as if it was yesterday. She prepared supper, hoping that William would pop in so that she could revel in the news. The radio blared out 'Wake Me Up Before You Go-Go' and Launa danced around the lounge.

The door opened and in bounded Charles, followed by his father and his uncle. They looked windswept and tanned. With beaming smiles, they held up three large, smelly fish.

"How's my wonderful wife?" Charles scooped her up and kissed her hard on the lips.

"You can wait until we have gone before you start all that," said William light-heartedly

"Hi, Charles, good to see you." Launa pecked her husband's uncle on the cheek. She did it for show. There was no real affection for him or her father-in-law. *Secretly, she despised them.* Charles Senior was pompous and cocky; he paraded around the chambers like a peacock. She couldn't deny he was attractive for a man of his age. In fact, they all were, but they also knew it and that took away the appeal.

"Now then, forget cooking. I thought I would treat us all to a meal at the Ivy. It's my birthday and I'm sure Launa would enjoy a bit of company." Launa was excited, and wanted to blurt it out there and then, but decided she should probably wait until she reached the restaurant. *They could toast her victory.*

"And I suppose you probably need a good drink to drown your sorrows. Not that you should worry – there are some cases we need to let the Crown Prosecution Service take control." He grabbed her hand, a sign of affection.

"And I promise you, young lady, this will not affect your excellent reputation."

Launa's heart pounded: she was unable to contain her excitement any longer.

"Well, haven't you heard? I'm sure it has done my reputation the world of good." She tried to slow her breathing, to speak clearly and calmly, but the words tumbled out.

"What do you mean?" spat Charles, his face like thunder.

William let go of her hand as if it was on fire.

She stood, facing the three Enrights, whose furious expressions looked almost identical.

She thought they misheard her.

"Yes, I won the case. Mauricio Luciani is free."

Charles Senior threw his hands to his mouth and William turned a deathly grey colour.

"You stupid fucking tramp!" shouted her husband.

William hurriedly dragged Charles into the kitchen, away from Launa, before he flew in a rage and said something they would all regret.

Charles Senior looked at the floor, shaking his head.

"Charles, what have I done?" Launa pleaded for an answer.

He stared at her for what seemed an eternity. "What you have done, you foolish woman, is that you have let a guilty man go free." His voice was low and flat.

William left Charles in the kitchen, having told him to keep calm, and joined his brother, Charles Senior. Incensed, he pointed his finger at Launa.

"I hope you are satisfied with yourself when you read the headlines, 'Another woman found butchered to death'."

Launa's lips quivered, and her ears burned, as she tried so hard to absorb their reaction.

"But he was innocent, I know he was," she pleaded like a schoolchild.

William was almost nose-to-nose when he shouted. "How dare you undermine me? How dare you think for one second that you are better equipped than I to judge? I will not let you loose on another case that might jeopardise the public. Do you understand me?" His angry words came with arrows that hit her deep. She sensed her world blow apart around her. But she couldn't explain why.

*

As the months rolled by, Charles, her once loving husband, looked cruelly upon her: there were no more affectionate glances or sweet words, no more good times.

He constantly argued with her – putting her down, belittling her appearance, undermining her confidence and, worse, letting her believe that she was a laughing stock in the courtroom. Even his father and uncle, now high court judges, laughed at her, and the constant nagging to quit her job became too much and she gave in. He controlled her every move – what she wore, who she socialised with, and how she spent her day. Now she had nothing in her life. Her so called friends – really they were Charles' friends more than hers – saw her as damaged goods, and with no family on whom she could rely, her life appeared to be over, or so she thought, so depressed was her state of mind. Trapped in a loveless marriage, Launa longed for her husband to have a change of heart and to go back to how things used to be.

He sat on the edge of the chair and placed an arm around her shoulders, his strong aftershave almost choking her. Glancing up at her husband, she felt a tinge of pain. He was handsome, strong boned, muscular and tanned. His eyes, although still reddened from rage, had that brilliant green glare. She had always admired the way he looked, and in the early days would tease him about his girly eyes, as she called them. The thick, black, long lashes would blink slowly, like a teenage girl flirting. Even though his attractive features remained the same, his personality had changed beyond belief.

After taking a final mouthful of his brandy, he placed the glass on the coffee table, threw his head back, and laughed. His wavy locks bounced on his shoulders and, with his mouth wide open, he showed his perfect white teeth. "So, my dear queen bee, you decided to take it upon yourself to have an abortion, to kill my baby. Or was it even my baby? Who knows?"

Shaking his head, he went on. "You, a mother? Don't make me laugh, you evil slut, you fucking scummy whore. And you thought you could hide your sordid little secret."

Her heart pounded and once again the back of her throat burned. *How could he have possibly known that she had attended the clinic?* She racked her brains. It was not for an abortion, not at all – her body began to tremble, her limbs became weak. Her ears burned and tingled until finally her head was numb.

"Well, well, Launa, who's not such a clever girl then?"

Launa, paralysed by fear, remained silent. She wanted to explain that she had been to the clinic, *but for a different reason.* She had waited for the right moment to tell him she was pregnant, hoping that her new baby would change everything – *or give her back some respect at least.*

In a calculated voice, he went on. "Well, Launa, there is only one thing left to do. So you don't want a baby, eh?" He grabbed her by the shoulders and threw her to the ground. So terrified she could barely move, she saw with horror a sickly, evil poise had swept over his face.

His fist came crushing down on her dainty cheekbone like a nutcracker. The pain slowly hit her, the fear so great that her adrenaline pumped fiercely around her body, and her stomach contents rose and ejected from her nose and mouth. She started to choke as he held her down, but she was spared further distress, as he had to release his weighty arm from her shoulder when the vomit splattered his much coveted Rolex watch. "You fucking dirty bitch," he spat as he slapped the side of her face, which was already throbbing in pain.

Catching her breath, she screamed, "Please, please, Charles! I'm so sorry, you've got it wrong!"

Her words meant absolutely nothing. He thought of how she betrayed him and how the punishment would fit the crime, and again he smiled. Gripping both her arms tightly above her head, he grabbed at her pants, ripping them away from her.

She closed her eyes, bit her lip and waited for Charles to carry out his vile sex acts, a ritual she had bitterly learned to accept.

She heard him laugh as a cold, sharp instrument scraped the inside of her leg. She opened her eyes to the sick grin of her husband and the object thrusting up inside her. The pain was not delayed – the unbearable torturous pain gripped and burned as she let out a blood curdling scream. The warm liquid poured away from her crotch. Charles sat up, brandishing a knife dripping with blood. "There, now you can't have children."

She stared at her husband and then her eyes focused on the knife, and the blood which was pouring from her, and she let out a terrified scream. "No, no, my baby!" Overwhelmed with grief and agonising pain, she passed out.

He regarded his wife's face. She looked at peace – no torment in her expression – *and she should be tormented because she had aborted their child*, well, so he thought. Anger engulfed his mind, but his mental state, at that precise moment, went into lawyer mode – she was the mother who had terminated her unborn child. That fact alone justified finishing his actions. A life for a life.

He smiled at the blood leaving her crotch, thick and almost black. She remained unconscious. Slowly and deliberately he lifted the sharpened knife, and, like a heated blade through butter, he carved the first slice in her left cheek. He watched the tiny dimple fall apart as it left a gaping, gruesome hole. He matched the slice on the other cheek and decided to add two more, but he paused, conscious of a buzzing sound in amongst the eerie silence. His phone was ringing. He got to his feet and answered the caller. "Oh, hi, honey. No, I'm not with Launa but I am busy, so I will call you later." He hung up the phone and returned to his wife, who was still in the same position, but now her face had swollen appreciably. He then realised she wasn't dead, just unconscious. He pushed open the back door. Scooping her up in his arms, he carried her to the cliff edge. The blood ran down his arm as he stood there, towering above the sheer drop. As his mind flashed back to discovering her betrayal, the thought repulsed him, and he released her body into the freezing sea. Coldly, as if he had just thrown a stick to a dog, he walked back to the cottage and ran himself a bath. The water was hot and, while he let it cool, he attempted to clean the carpet rug. He scrubbed for ages, but it made matters worse so he rolled it up to dispose of it later. The bath was perfect. He soaked for an hour, listening to Pink Floyd's 'The Wall'.

*

For a moment, she regained consciousness, aware of a strange, unearthly floating sensation, ice cold and eerie. *Was this what it feels like when you're dead,* she thought. The strong salty taste at the back of her throat made her gag. As her eyes opened, she saw nothing but blackness. Realisation hit her; she was in the sea, freezing, weak and in pain. It wouldn't be long before she died.

Longing to say goodbye to the people she loved, believing it was the end, she whispered, "*Goodbye, Mum and Dad, I know I did not get the chance to see you again but thank you for loving me so much. Goodbye, my dearest brothers.* She saw her brother Fred's face when they were twelve. *Will you feel my life leave me, Fred, my twin?*" She drifted back into a state of unconsciousness.

She was dreaming she was on the beach with Fred, building sandcastles, with the waves washing over them both – her mum and dad laughing, whilst Dan, Joe and Sam were eating ice creams. Feeling her mother's arms around her shoulders and the sweet smell of her white linen perfume, she drifted away from the realms of reality and into the depths of another world, where she was safe. In the distance shone a bright light. It was time: the light was going to take her to meet her maker.

*

She finally regained consciousness, in a room which gleamed brilliant white. Her eyes blinked fiercely as she tried to make out where she was.

"She's coming around, dim the lights."

Doctor Harrison had been on duty for almost thirty-six hours and was about to go to his room for a nap when nurse Reilly called him. She had received a call stating that a young woman was on her way to the hospital via ambulance. A fisherman had found the poor woman in the sea, but her injuries needed to be seen to by a doctor who was neat with sutures.

Dr Harrison spun around and said, "Oh no, not a shark attack," and instantly felt a fool. The long day had left him tired and, for a split second, he forgot where he was – *Australia was a long time ago.*

The nurse frowned.

"I'm sorry, Nurse Reilly, forget I just said that."

She grinned and nodded. "She will be here in two minutes, Doctor. Shall I prepare to scrub up?"

Dr Harrison nodded.

Dead on time, the ambulance arrived and the doors flew open as the rain began to pour. The paramedics wheeled into the accident and emergency department a young woman barely gripping on to life.

They listed the girl's vital statistics to the doctor, whilst running the trolley up to the crash room.

"I can see the girl's face is a mess, but this wouldn't cause her blood pressure to hit the floor. She has lost too much blood — she needs a transfusion now. We are going to lose her." Dr Harrison frantically pulled back the blankets.

"Christ, she's haemorrhaging. I need to stop this bleeding."

Doctor Richards, another surgeon on duty, attended the crash unit, and together they worked hard for three hours, desperately trying to save the life and the womb of this butchered young woman.

Five o'clock and Launa's eyes flickered again. All was dark except a small, dim light in the distance. For a minute, she thought she was still in the sea with the fisherman's boat approaching. However, she could feel the bed and the warmth and she let out a juddering sigh. She was placed in a separate room, not a ward, just as a precaution. The pain gripped her when she tried to move. Putting her hand to her head, she felt the bandages wrapped around her face and her neck.

"Hello, my name's Doctor Harrison. It's okay, you are at Hastings and Rother Hospital, and you were found last night at sea. I am afraid we don't know your name."

Launa tried desperately to recall what had happened, and then it hit her. *Her husband's face, the knife, the dripping blood* — she gasped for air. Seized by fear, Launa fell into unconsciousness.

Dr Harrison left the room and approached the policemen waiting outside. "I am afraid she is still asleep, and it's my guess that she will continue to be for at least another twenty-four hours." He glared at the two officers who, after waiting three hours, were told that it would not be possible to speak to her for at least another day.

"Twenty-four hours, my arse," said Sergeant Simms to the young PC.

"Well, Sarge, he wouldn't lie, and she did look like a train wreck."

"Listen to me, Phipps, there's a bloody lot you need to learn and one thing is, doctors do not like us taking up their time, their patients' time, or their bloody corridor space. Now then, I want you to stay here and phone me when she has come to, okay!" bellowed Simms, as he flew off along the corridor.

PC Phipps nervously hovered outside Launa's room. He felt uncomfortable being there, knowing the doctor had, in effect, asked him to leave.

Nurse Reilly hurried to the room, laden with bandages and dressings. She eyed PC Phipps up and down and, with one eyebrow raised, she said, "If I were you, I would make myself scarce. Dr Harrison will not be pleased if he finds you here."

Phipps, now irritated, had a job to do, and no doctor was going to stop him. "What's the big deal here? I only want to ask that girl in there a few questions." He pointed to the darkened room.

Nurse Reilly turned and realised the blinds to the large window were open and that the PC could see straight in. Quickly, she went in, closed the blinds, and left the bandages and dressings at the end of the bed.

PC Phipps tutted. "It's all right, I wasn't going to pounce on her the minute she woke up," he said sarcastically.

"It's not you I'm concerned about, Officer, it's the nutter who did this to her," she sighed.

"Of course, yes. I'm sorry. Look, I will wait in the canteen – if she wakes up, would you please call me?"

"Yes, but only if she comes to and wants to talk to you."

The young PC tutted again and walked away.

Nurse Reilly had been requested by Dr Harrison to watch the girl and be very gentle because not only was her face destroyed, but her womanhood too, and she would need extra help and understanding in the days and weeks ahead. In the fifteen years of nursing, Kathy Reilly had never seen such butchering and dreaded the poor girl looking in the mirror.

She had gone into nursing as soon as she was old enough. She had always wanted to be a nurse and not a doctor. It was the full responsibility that put her off, along with lower than expected grades at school. She had never married, despite a few offers when she was in her early-twenties. Unfortunately, a fire accident when she was six years old had left her with scars on her face, and had also mentally scarred her confidence. So she moved from London down to the South coast and tried to start a new life, where nobody had known the once very pretty Kathy, who was now a shy, plain and plump twenty-seven-year-old. In fact, she was now the antithesis of who she had been in another life.

Kathy did not realise at first that the reason Dr Harrison had assigned her responsibility for the girl with the slashed face was because she would be the most understanding.

She carefully removed the bandages, trying not to wake her, but it was tough as some of the dressing had slipped and stuck to her stitches. Kathy cringed, almost feeling the pain herself.

Launa stirred again. This time she began to speak, calling a name. Her eyes remained shut as she started to shake and scream.

"It's all right," said Kathy in a panic. She wanted Launa to wake up from her nightmares. "You're safe now," she whispered, as Launa's screams subsided.

Kathy continued to stroke the girl's hand whilst whispering words of comfort. Eventually, Launa's eyes began to open. The bandages hid the marks on her face but not the swelling. Peering through slits, Launa tried to focus on the nurse.

"Hello there," whispered Kathy.

Instantly, Launa put her hands to her head, just as Kathy grabbed them.

"No, don't touch your face," Kathy said, making herself jump. She did not want Launa to tear at the bandages, as she had done after her accident. Kathy placed a straw to Launa's mouth and slowly Launa sipped – she could still taste the sea, combined with anaesthetic.

"Who did this to you, love?" asked Kathy.

Launa's eyes widened; the memories came flooding back. *Her husband, the knife and the sea.* Fighting through the haze of the anaesthetic, she had to think straight. Her thoughts were becoming clearer. *Charles had left her for dead: he must never know she survived, ever.*

Sergeant Simms entered the room and Kathy instantly spun around. "How dare you just barge in here? Please leave," she spat.

"I heard you speaking to the girl and I thought she was ready to talk."

Launa closed her eyes, pretending to drift back off to sleep.

Kathy marched the sergeant out of the room. "Now, you listen to me. I am responsible for this patient and I will not have you or your drippy PC interrogate her until Dr Harrison or myself decide, without any doubt, that she is up to it. Now, I suggest that you and him," she said, pointing to PC Phipps, who was now running up the corridor, "go back to your station and wait for a call from me. Trust me, Sergeant, this young woman won't be going anywhere for at least a week; her injuries are too severe."

"You bloody nurses think it's a game. I have some nutter on the bloody loose who's sliced her up and thrown her into the bloody sea, and for all we know he could be slicing up his next victim as we bloody speak. It might even be that London slicer who killed seven prostitutes. Now do you understand why we have to question her?"

"Yes, sergeant, this 'bloody' nurse can see why you need to speak with her. Unless you want to run around like a headless chicken, looking for the wrong person, I suggest you wait until she has fully regained consciousness. Hopefully, she can gather her thoughts without being hounded by you, and then maybe you will have all the facts to catch the bloody butcher!" With that, she turned on her heels and went back to her patient, ensuring the door was securely closed behind her.

Launa sat up and sipped some more water. Her head thumped and her face throbbed. "Is my face…" She could not bring herself to finish.

The nurse nodded. There was no point in denying it. "Yes, you have been cut several times across your face." She paused, waiting for a reaction from Launa, who just stared back.

"How bad is it?" whispered Launa in a childlike voice, afraid to hear the truth.

"Let's wait until Dr Harrison gets here and he can answer all your questions."

She guessed then that it was bad.

"The police want to ask a few questions when you're up to it," smiled Kathy.

Launa shook her head. "No, I'm not up to it, not yet." She had to stall them until she had made a plan. *No way could they ever know the truth.* Even if they arrested her husband, he would never go to prison. Even if his family didn't control the legal system, they were definitely able to exploit it for their own ends. She witnessed first-hand how they'd manipulated, coerced, and got away with everything. They had the police, lawyers, and even the forensic team eating out of their hands. *She would never win. They had broken her, and it would take a power greater than theirs to beat them.*

For a moment, Kathy thought she recognised those eyes staring back at her.

"Can I get you anything…?" Kathy raised her eyebrows, waiting for the girl to reveal her name.

"My name is Francesca." For a while Launa felt as though she had lied but she hadn't. Her real name was Francesca, yet no one except her family knew that.

"Please would you pass me the phone? I have to make a call."

Kathy couldn't believe what she was saying to her. She was amazed how quickly this young woman got herself together. A few moments ago, she was just coming around from a horrific ordeal where, in the crash room, they had nearly lost her twice. Now this young woman, who looked worse than a car crash victim, was getting herself together, as cool as anything.

"Are you up to this, Francesca? Really, you should rest, you know."

"Please, Nurse, I need to make this call now while I still can." Launa's voice sounded desperately tired and Kathy predicted she would be out again for the next few hours.

Quickly, she grabbed the phone and sat with it on her lap. "What's the number?"

Launa, like a robot, reeled off a London number and reached for the receiver. Kathy quickly dialled it and left the room. She didn't hurry to call the police – *there was something stopping her, maybe what she saw in the girl's eyes.*

Dan was recovering from the worst hangover for some months, but didn't shout for his mother to answer the phone. He knew her arthritis was bad.

A slow voice at the other end irritated Dan. "What did you say? Speak up, I can't hear you."

Francesca heard her brother's voice for the first time in over fifteen years. Her heart pounded. "Dan, it's me, Dolly." Her voice faded but not before he heard her. Goosebumps covered his body, a lump rose in his throat.

"Dolly, is that really you?" Dan, now a large man, tall and handsome like his father, hard as nails, shrank in his chair. Like speaking to a baby, his tone was low and soft.

"Yes, Dan, I need your help. I'm in the hospital in Hastings, and I need you to get me out and home." Her energy level plummeted and, unable to continue, she hung up the phone and flopped back on the pillow.

*

Mary walked into the room, shocked to find her eldest son grey. "What's up, love?"

"It's our Dolly. She... she's in the hospital."

Mary flung her hands to her face. "My God, what's happened?"

Dan shook his head. "I don't know, but I am going to get her."

"Where is she? What's happened?" she shrieked.

"I don't know, Mum. I need to go and get her now. She sounded so sick, Mum." He bit his lip, forcing himself to hold back the tears. He needed to pull himself together. Snatching the keys from the table, his kissed his mother and jumped into the Jag, heading for Hastings. As he drove along the motorway, many thoughts ran through his mind. Since Dolly had gone to live with his aunt, the house always seemed quiet. Even after all these years, they still missed her. The only news they ever received was that she was safe – too much information would have given her away. He didn't ask God for anything ever but, just this one time, he begged for her to be okay. Her words echoed inside his head, the soft, weak voice of a woman. He only imagined her as a child, the cheeky little sister, with as much gumption as her brothers, the pretty little Dolly with the biggest heart. He blinked away the tears and forced down the lump in his throat.

The car park was empty, unlike the London hospitals. As he walked through the main reception, he realised that he wouldn't know what she looked like, or what name she went under. In fact, he didn't know where to start. Standing outside A&E, puffing on a cigarette and contemplating his next move, a familiar voice greeted him.

"'Allo, stranger," said Kathy.

Dan turned around and smiled. "'Allo, Kathy." He kissed her on the cheek. Her being there was not good for him right now. He didn't want to make small talk or go over old times; he needed to concentrate on a plan to get his sister out of the hospital.

Kathy pulled out a packet of Rothmans and asked for a light. "So, Dan, what brings you down to this neck of the woods?"

Dan shuffled from one foot to the other thinking of what to say. His words did not come in time.

"It's been a long time since I was in the East End. I enjoyed growing up there. Your mum's a real gem, and Dolly..." She paused as she saw his eyes widen. Kathy stared into his face and, as if she had seen a ghost, she blurted, "Oh my God, Dan, it's Dolly, ain't it? Fuck, it's your Dolly in there! Jesus, Dan, I thought I knew those Vincents' eyes."

Dan, desperate to get in to see his sister, paused to collect his thoughts. "Kath, I need your help," he exclaimed, with his head tilted and his eyes watering.

Kathy nodded. "Whatever, mate. Remember, I owe your family. Your mother saved me life once, so whatever." Her words almost tripped over themselves, she was so eager to assist.

"I have got to get her out of the hospital. She called me and asked me to take her home." He shrugged his shoulders. It was clear that he was oblivious to the nature of her gruesome injuries. "I haven't seen her since she was twelve. I don't think I would recognise her."

Without meaning to be callous, Kathy said, "Well, love, you definitely won't now with all her facial injuries."

Dan cried aloud and held on to the wall. He pulled himself together as soon as Kathy hugged him. She had never seen him or any of the brothers so vulnerable. The street knew not to mess with them; they stuck together like glue. The brothers had changed so much though, since Francesca, their Dolly, had gone. Tougher and fearless, they took no nonsense and trusted no one.

Neighbours, friends and colleagues were told that Dolly lived in Spain with her uncle. Of course, no one asked any more than that.

"Dan, she is sick. She's lost loads of blood; her injuries are horrendous." She took another drag on the cigarette.

He swallowed hard, forcing back the vomit that lodged in the back of his throat. "Accident?"

Kathy looked at the floor. "By her injuries, no, some bastard has done this to her, but she don't want the Ol' Bill to know who it is, that's for sure."

"Kathy, I have to get her home."

"Dan, there's no way she can leave the hospital. She is really sick, mate."

"I have let my sister down for the last fifteen years. I have to get her out of here and home, Kath. This is the first time I have spoken with Dolly since she was fucking twelve years old. Out the blue, she calls me to take her home. There's no way I'm leaving her; she has never asked anything of me." The tears rolled down his face.

Holding his arm, she nodded.

*

The plan was arranged very carefully. Night fell and the police were once again told there would be no interviews that evening, as she was still sedated. As the hours passed, Francesca regained full consciousness.

Kathy hugged her, whispering, "Remember me?"

As Francesca pulled away, she looked at the unforgettable face of the Reilly sister and a hot tear sprang from her swollen eyes. "Yes, Kathy, I do."

She explained the plan to get her out of the hospital. Not a problem for Kathy, no one would question her — besides, she had booked two weeks off work starting tomorrow. She was going to go with Dan and take care of Francesca in London. She also knew how to keep her mouth shut.

Kathy gently helped her into a wheelchair, packing her bag with antibiotics, anti-inflammatories, lots of dressings and painkillers. Getting her out of the hospital was easy. She opened the fire exit and went around the side. No one saw a thing. All she had to do now was to hand over the patients' notes to the next nurses on duty. How was she going to do that when the patient had gone? She needed an excuse to leave before the changeover. Good at making herself sick, she approached the nurses' station, retched and then vomited all over the floor.

The sister ran to her at once, shocked at the total vile act of vomiting, and sent Kathy home immediately. Without even considering the hand over, the sister realised the mistake but thought a sick nurse on the ward was a liability.

Dan looked at the frail figure sitting in the wheelchair – her face heavily bandaged and her eyes sunken and lifeless. Tears streamed down his cheeks as he held her gently, whispering her childhood name, Dolly.

He opened the back door of the Jag, glad that he had just had it valeted and it was clean for his dear sister to lie in. Francesca tried not to appear in too much pain but it was hard – the painkillers had worn off, and the deep throbbing pain inside her womb became immense. She couldn't speak just yet.

Luckily, the transfer from the wheelchair into the car took a little longer, and so Kathy had time to catch them up before they took off. Quickly, she searched through the bag for another shot of morphine, to help Francesca relax through the journey home. In fact, it knocked her out. She had administered too much.

Kathy hopped into the front seat and they headed for the East End of London – home.

"I appreciate this, Kath, but promise me you will not breathe a word to a living soul." He stared out of the window.

"My mother said to us kids, when we were growing up, that your mother was an angel sent from heaven. We will always be indebted to her. She saved my life, we know that, but God help her, she probably saved all of us. My sisters are doing well for themselves, and we may not have been 'ere if it weren't for your mum, so I promise you faithfully I will do all I can to help and never breathe a word – your family is my family."

Kathy stared straight ahead too, just like Dan.

Trust was paramount and a blanket of relief covered him. He liked Kathy – she was just like her sisters. They all made something of their lives. His mother had become good friends with Nellie over the years, and in fact Nellie became a bit of a rock, and her daughters too. They often popped in with flowers and an update of the latest saga in their lives. He knew it helped to keep his mother going. Mary loved her sons and enjoyed bringing them up. However, her world was a man's world – with no fresh girly company due to the absence of her precious daughter. It was hard, so she appreciated the visits from the Reilly sisters.

Kathy had always been a bit special to her, being the youngest and the one she saved from the burning house. She hadn't married or entertained the idea of having children. Dan thought about himself and the fact that he didn't have children – well, even a wife for that matter – but he did, however, enjoy his lifestyle, holidays abroad, flash cars, fast woman and the comfort of living at home with his mum, which meant good food. Fred was the same. He seemed to follow his brother, buying the same cars, frequenting the clubs, and enjoying the same lifestyle. Fred was clever like his sister, so he took time to invest money and, although he lived at home, his bank balance was fat and he could have lived in a luxury house in town if he'd wanted.

The four brothers, now men, looked similar, all handsome, yet their appearance changed once their personalities emerged. Dan was suave and sophisticated. He walked with ease – not an ounce of clumsiness, his hair immaculately swept back, yet he was sharp enough to dodge a bullet. His calm manner was sometimes seen as chilling, whereas Fred was more lively and, although he wasn't suave like Dan, his personality was more aggressive when he got angry, which surprised people because he was the cutest-looking of the brothers, with dimples and round eyes. The girls called him 'sweet', which provoked long-term teasing by his brothers. The biggest teaser was Joseph. He was dark like his father but built like a brick shit house and as daft as they come. With a permanent smile, he giggled at everything; he would light up a room with his laid-back, jolly presence. Sam was the worrier, so different from the other three who, when in trouble, wouldn't have laughed it off. Fred was the worst for trouble but, being so clever, he could manipulate his way out of most situations. He could fight and with good reason – he had three big brothers to practise on.

Bill had sent them to the boxing club. It was the done thing in the East End. 'Boys, you'd better get some meat on those arms, never know when you might need it,' he would say.

His sons did as they were told. They never back-chatted or disrespected their parents. Mary and Bill knew full well their boys got up to mischief – a bit of puff now and then, a few fights – but the details were always left outside the house. Each brother watched the others' backs. If the police ever came to the door, Dan or Sam got there first, saving their mother the distress.

It was usually Fred who was up to no good. He loved a good tear-up.

Dan's dealings were more serious. He was into more heavy shit, taking on the role his father had years before but with more muscle on board. The Vincents managed to reclaim their share in the Arab trading. This time they kept it in the East End. The legitimate business was the nightclub, their pride and joy, but more of a pastime than a job. All the brothers worked there – until Sam was sucked in by some stinking junkie, and ended up serving time to take the rap for her fuck-up.

As the car approached the East End, Dan felt nervous, but not for himself, though. He worried for his sister. He had no idea what had happened to her. *Why did she fear the police? Why was she found in the sea and why did she call home?* Nothing seemed to make sense. He did, however, sense that she wasn't afraid of her hunter, Mad Mick, the man who had haunted their lives for years – the reason Dolly was sent away.

He lit up a cigarette, inhaled deeply but quickly, and put it out when he heard his sister moan. Kathy turned to find Dolly trying to sit up. "No, no, lie down until we reach home and I can see to you," said Kathy, in the tone you would use to speak to a child.

Mary paced the floor. She had tried hard to contact her husband, who had gone up north to secure a waste disposal site. She needed him here with her to take care of their daughter. Bill never got over the fact that his daughter wasn't there anymore. He blamed himself. Mary wanted her daughter to come home to her mum and dad together.

She watched at the window to see her son pull into the driveway. She rushed to the car and, as tears streamed down her face, a mixture of emotions overwhelmed her to see her grown daughter in such a terrible state.

Although she was delighted Francesca was back home with her family, and she was able to hold the daughter she loved so much but didn't know any more, she was distraught that this was happening in such terrible circumstances.

All three of them helped to get Dolly into the house as quickly as they could. Kathy was amazed by how much strength Dolly had considering she was so ill. She lay on the couch and her mother stared, whilst Dan sat in the armchair shaking his head, and Kathy searched her medical supplies for fresh dressings. The two-hour drive had caused the bleeding to start again.

"Mare, get us a bowl of boiled water." She leant over Dolly, addressing the situation; there was no movement. Kathy turned around to see Mary still staring.

"Mary, are you okay?"

Mary snapped out of her gaze and ran to the kitchen. All the aches and pains from her arthritis seemed to have gone. She was racked with guilt: her daughter had been sent away, had suffered horribly in circumstances of which she was unaware and, so much worse, she had not been there to help her.

*

Kathy got to work. Slowly, she unwrapped the bandages. Dolly kept her eyes closed; the sedation allowed her to go in and out of consciousness. As her injuries were revealed to everyone, Mary threw her hands to her mouth to stop the gasp that so wanted to escape. Dan looked away in utter disbelief. The blood seeped from her deep wounds. Some evil bastard had slashed her face in what looked like a frenzied attack. *But who, questioned Dan.* Anger started to build up inside. He clenched his fists. God help whoever did this to her. He was now angry. Whoever had done this to his wonderful and precious sister would suffer the direst consequences for this despicable act of cowardice and brutality. He would tear them limb from limb and laugh in their faces whilst he did so. He reached for the brandy bottle and downed a large glass. Mary kissed her daughter's hands, begging for forgiveness. "Dolly, I am so sorry, my angel. I'm so sorry."

Dolly opened her eyes and looked for the first time in so many years at her mother, and the feeling of safety overwhelmed her. She touched her mother's face as tears welled up. "Mum, shush. It's okay," she whispered.

Her voice was so sophisticated and mature that Mary saw her daughter as a woman and not a little girl. Seeing past the lacerations, she imagined how beautiful she was. Her sons were handsome but her daughter was beautiful; her eyes were big, round, and so full of love for her mother.

Kathy redressed her wound and changed the painkillers to non-sedative ones, so that Dolly would come around completely.

Mary and Dan sat in the kitchen whilst Kathy slept upstairs. She needed to sleep. The last shift was a double, and to be able to care for Dolly, she had to be sharp.

"Dan, call your brothers and tell them to get home. Don't tell them why. I'll keep trying to get hold of your father."

The house was in silence, with just the crackle of the fire and soft ticking of the clock pervading the room.

Joseph walked through the door, oblivious to the situation. "Dan, what's all the fucking fuss. I was just ready to tuck into a right nice fry up." He stopped as he entered the living room to see a woman completely hidden by bandages lying on the couch. "Who the fuck are you?" He was half-laughing at the sight before him, not having the slightest clue that it was his sister. He thought it was probably one of the girls from the club resting from plastic surgery.

Mary rushed to the doorway. "Joseph, keep you voice down."

Dolly opened her eyes. "You must be Joe," she whispered.

His half laugh turned to an expression of shock and compassion, and then his bottom lip began to quiver. Joseph recognised her the second she spoke, and he rushed to her side. "Oh my God, what the fuck!" He paused and tried to hug her, afraid that he might crush her, his delicate sister. "Did that fucking bastard get to you?"

She shook her head.

Dan came over to kneel on the floor beside Joseph. "Sweetheart, what happened?"

Dolly bowed her head. "Give me time and I will explain it all if I can. Please help me; I need to get well first." The tears streamed and her body shook uncontrollably. Instantly, her mother was there by her side, rocking her as she had done years before.

Bill arrived at six in the evening. He had no idea what was awaiting him, and, just like Joseph, Bill had the same reaction. Mary, Dan and Joe were in the kitchen, Mary cooking a chicken stew — it was all she could do to stop the tears flowing, and she needed to be strong to help her daughter.

"Mary, who's on the couch?" asked Bill as he entered the kitchen. He had not noticed the eyes of the frail woman lying on the settee. The room fell silent. And then Bill guessed, as his eyes focused on each face of his family.

He slowly walked back to the sitting room to see his daughter struggle to her feet. She wanted to greet her dad properly; *the vision of his face the day she left him behind in the prison had haunted her.* Now she wanted the strength to hug him, to see him smile. The expression on his face was the same; he looked into her sunken eyes and, just like the day he said goodbye, his heart ached and he broke down. His precious daughter looked so damaged — a smashed china doll. Like Joseph, he too thought that she had been attacked by Mad Mick or his sons.

He raised his head and looked at Dan. "So after all these fucking years they still got to her."

Dolly shook her head. "No, Dad."

Bill looked at the others for answers. They shrugged their shoulders.

Not wanting to push his daughter for an explanation, he left her to rest. There would be plenty of time to talk once she was better.

Fred was the last brother to come home and, by the time he got the message, it was nearly ten o'clock. The house was unusually quiet as he walked through the door. The telly was off, a low flame flickered in the fireplace, and the lights dimmed. *Had he walked into the wrong house?* Lying motionless in front of him was a woman wrapped in bandages. His heart thumped so hard he thought it would jump out of his rib cage; the immense familiarity engulfed him. His chest tightened as he walked towards her. The smell of anaesthetic and antiseptic did not mask her own smell; he knew it was her. She lay there lifeless but, like Fred, she sensed his presence. She was his other half, his twin. She may not look the same but it was her. She put her arms out to hug him. Together, they cried.

"My Dolly." His voice cracked in between the sobs. His body shook with the intensity of his emotions. The last fifteen years, Fred had ached for his sister. His brothers tried to compensate for his loss but his bond with her had left a chasm in his heart. The last years of pain came streaming down his face. All the tears he wanted to cry came at once and it was some time before he calmed down. Dolly, too, could not hold back; with her brother in her arms, she was whole again. He hadn't forgotten her, he still loved her as she did him.

They sat gathered around the kitchen table whilst Dolly slept peacefully for the first time. As if there had been a death in the family, each member silently cried, sipping brandy and hugging each other. The hours passed and Kathy, after a much needed sleep, joined them.

"Oh, Kathy, I am so glad your 'ere, love. You gonna stay and help our Dolly?" cried Mary.

"Damn right I am, she needs a lot of medications," she quipped, and smiled at Mary. "And a lot of loving from her family!"

Mary put her arms around Kathy. "Thank you, my darling," she whispered.

The non-drowsy painkillers had taken effect, allowing Dolly to be more awake and now able to sit up.

Chicken stew was the first meal they had together. With one member of the family missing, Dolly asked about Sam, hoping that he was just on holiday.

"Now, don't you go worrying about Sammy. He has just got himself into a bit of bother and, well, he will be home soon, fingers crossed."

Joseph rolled his eyes and laughed, trying to put Dolly's mind at rest.

Her family treated her with kid gloves and she was so not used to it!

She had been abused by her husband and yet before that, she had been one of the country's top defence lawyers, and her angelic face and childlike dimples had deceived many a prosecution barrister. However, they soon learned not to underestimate her, and she became respected. No one in her profession afterwards spoke to her like a child but, right now, she felt protected by her family, surrounded with love and security.

They hadn't changed. The close bond between them still existed. Her memories of them had been so perfect, she thought that maybe she had created them or even glorified them, but she hadn't and that was obvious.

*

Kathy had done a wonderful job looking after Dolly's medical needs and, after four days, she was able to walk around and bathe, but it was now time to unravel the bandages. Kathy had warned them that this would be when Dolly might have a relapse because the scarring was so bad and, since she had not seen herself in a mirror yet, the shock could set her into a trauma.

Precariously, the dressings were removed. A family affair – they all gathered around, not knowing how to react, what to say, or what to do. Dolly took a deep breath and looked in the mirror. She stared for ages and gently nodded.

"Thank you all so much for helping me get this far and now I need to do the rest myself."

Fred looked on in disbelief. His sister's face destroyed, her beautiful dimples gone – in their place were the most horrific scars – he was at a loss to find words to support his treasured sister. He wished it had been him. Dan and Bill felt the same, a deep anger – like father like son. Bill had given up a life of violence and crime for the past fifteen years, but now it would change. *Whoever did this would pay with their lives.* Dan's anger nearly choked him; *no one would be forgiven for this.*

Joseph wanted to lighten the situation. He wanted to say something that would make her feel better, but no comments would ease the most horrific ordeal that his sister had to endure.

The men realised at this point that Dolly was not an average woman; her reaction was so calm, perhaps too calm. She was brave but there was more; it was something so intangible that they could not quite put their finger on what it was. They did not realise that the pain she felt was not from her disfigurement but from inside her. The loss of her womanhood was far worse than her scarred face. She would have a life with no children and, coming from a family so loving, the reality that she would never be able to have one of her own was a shattering revelation. But there was no hiding from the fact that the one dream she'd had was now gone forever.

Dolly decided not to tell her family about her internal injuries. *Why pass on the pain when there was no need?*

Her family went about their business and her mother returned to the kitchen - still shocked that her daughter had remained so calm.

Dolly sat, trying to remember a number she had stored in her memory for so long. She dialled long distance. "Hello," she said rather sheepishly.

"Hello, Launa," replied the voice at the other end in a thick New York-cum-Italian accent.

"How did you know my name?" asked Dolly.

"There are only two people that have this number and the other person is a man. Now you have called, I am at your service. How can I help?"

"I am sorry, but who am I talking to?" replied Dolly, in an unassuming manner.

"I am Mauricio's father and my name is Roberto."

"Oh, okay then, Roberto. Please may I ask if you could arrange for me to come to New York and stay awhile? I need to leave England, I need..." She paused, afraid to ask.

"Launa, anything, my child. Just ask." His voice was deep and husky, yet soft. He could tell, from the frailty of her voice, that that there was something so desperately wrong with this young woman.

She paused. The man was very familiar with her, yet she felt comforted by that.

"I need a new identity." Her voice rose as if she was asking a question. Had she asked the impossible?

"Launa, this I can do and, my child, I do it very well. I will make all the necessary arrangements. Call this number tomorrow morning and I will have everything ready. Can you wait that long or...?"

"That will be fine. Thank you."

"No, Launa. I must thank you. You gave me back the most precious thing in life and I am indebted to you for that." His voice wavered.

"Roberto, your son is a lovely man, and I was just doing my job."

"No, you did so much more. I am forever in your debt." With that, he hung up.

Mary walked in the room.

"Oh, Mum, did you hear that?"

Before she could continue, her mother nodded.

*

The next day she sat her family down and, without too much detail, explained that her life was in danger from two people now, and that the person that tried to kill her must never know that she was still alive, so no one must mention that they saw her – even her aunt must be kept totally in the dark. Mary was surprised by this and said, "But I thought you were happy with your aunt. Why shouldn't she know what's happened?"

"Aunty Anne is very dear to me and yes, Mum, I was as happy as I could be under the circumstances. She did her best to give me a good life but, Mum, she is not like you, and if I said to her, 'Please don't mention any of this', she wouldn't be able to cope. Trust me, Mum, my life depends on it."

"Oh, fucking 'ell, Doll, tell us who did this and I swear that they will be gone, fucked, finito," spat Fred.

"No, Fred. I can deal with him. I just need to go away for a year – maybe two – but I promise I will be back and everything will be fine. I will see to it." She paused. "I promise."

Although Dolly was the little sister and the darling daughter, she had a way of addressing people that enabled her to be heard without interruption. That was, until a year ago.

Right now, her brothers were so proud; she seemed tougher than they did, a chip off each block. And they sat back listening, knowing that whatever she had been through, she would get her revenge, and they would be there to run to her aid whenever she called.

Bill took it the hardest to say goodbye again, but she promised she would contact him every so often to let him know she was safe, and soon they would be a whole family again.

Kathy agreed to go with her. All the fees were paid and besides, she needed to get out of the UK and see the world. Little did she know right then that she would not return – life in the States was too good to be true, and she had no hubby or any kids to rush back to.

She proved to be worth her weight in gold, especially when the captain questioned whether Dolly was fit to fly. Kathy ascertained her authority as a nurse – well, actually as Dolly's nurse, explaining Dolly's medical condition in such a way as to leave the captain confused and somewhat baffled, but he decided to take Kathy at her word, and so they both managed to overcome the red tape and have a comfortable flight.

It was on the plane that Dolly and Kathy really had a chance to catch up, and the more Kathy got to know Dolly, the more she became intrigued by her. Dolly was an East End girl but her posh, educated voice made her captivating.

Kathy couldn't quite work her out. It was as if she were two people. On the one hand she was the adorable young friend back in the East End with possible traits of her brothers' wild ways, and on the other she was this very sleek, very well spoken, and intelligent young woman. It didn't matter to Kathy though; as far as she was concerned it was her opportunity to pay back some of the debt in her life which she owed to Mary, as well as the fact that she also cared deeply for Dolly.

Dolly was at her most vulnerable, so her companion and soon-to-be trusted friend was a real asset, and this gave her the confidence to flee England and plan her future – *including the promises she made to her family.*

New York was so different from London, with the speed, the colours, and the different accents. For Dolly, it was also too tiring, and she was relieved when a gorgeous Italian guy stood in front of her holding a sign with her name – just 'Launa'. Kathy was used to Dolly or Francesca, so she walked by him. By this point, she had taken on the motherly role, so she stated, "Right, Dolly, you sit down over there, and I will sort out everything."

Dolly pointed to the tall, dark Italian and, to her dismay, was told by Kathy that there wasn't time to play 'Spot the Hunk'. Spinning around, Kathy searched for the name of Francesca but Dolly laughed and explained that Launa was her new name – well, not so much new. In fact, the name was very familiar to her now, since she had been called it for the last fifteen years or so.

The Italian's name was Tony, and he made it very clear that his job was to take them wherever they needed to go and whenever they felt up to it. Kathy felt special: a fabulous car, a man to carry the luggage, and a new city. Dolly was just relieved to get to the hotel and rest. The long flight and the amount of blood she had lost over the past few days had left her weak and exhausted.

Kathy did tell her that if she had stayed in the hospital, they would have given her another blood transfusion, so it would take time to build her strength, but she would be there by her side.

The best hotel in Manhattan – the New York Palace – oozed luxury from every brick in the wall. The front of the building was alight with magnificent colours and two concierges, dressed in traditional, deep navy blue suits edged with gold, staffed the enormous glass doors. As they pulled up to the entrance, Tony rushed to open the door for Dolly and the concierge was there in an instant to take the luggage. However, he was surprised they only had a small holdall and that most of the contents were medical supplies but, as a concierge, his job was to assist with his customers' needs. Kathy helped Dolly out of the car whilst Tony spoke with the doorman. It was apparent that they knew each other and instantly the concierge fussed over the two new guests. Kathy, astounded by the interior of the hotel, had never been in such a beautiful place. Her eyes remained wide and her smile permanent. Dolly was used to five star hotels, but she was not used to so much attention from the staff. For the first time since she had left the East End, the stares stopped. Dolly had noticed that her disfigurement caused people to glare, especially since it was still swollen and raw, yet not here, not in this hotel. The hotel seemed different; the surroundings felt very comfortable – even the ride up in the lift was a comfort. At the back was a velvet settee on which she plonked herself down; she was still so weak she couldn't stand for too long. Roberto had organised the penthouse suite for her and Kathy to stay in indefinitely. The suite was only used by him, unless, of course, the Queen arrived. Since he only ever stayed there maybe three months out of the year, he decided she should make use of it, and it had the advantage of being the one place no one could get to her. Although he lived not too far from the hotel, he never liked to conduct any business from home. He trusted no one enough to come into his house – only family or his own men. Therefore, the penthouse was available for Francesca and Kathy for as long as necessary.

Kathy was so excited, like a child, running into every room.

"Doll, have you seen the kitchen? Fuck me, it's even got a jazzy whatsit in the bathroom."

Dolly sat in the huge lounger that would seat about ten people – white, soft leather, which went around in a semi-circle, surrounded by thick fur rugs, all in a soft cream.

"Dolly, look at that view. You can see all over America." Kathy was walking from one room to another, giving Dolly a run-down on all the suite had to offer. She was still chatting on when Dolly drifted off to sleep.

*

She awoke eight hours later to find herself draped in a soft blanket, still curled up on the settee. The strong smell of fresh coffee and eggs filled the air. "Kathy," she called in a croaky voice.

Instantly, Kathy was there, coffee in one hand, eggs on toast in the other.

"How do you feel, love?"

"Well, actually, I feel much better. Did you sleep well yourself, Kathy?"

Kathy grinned, nodding profusely. "What a place, Doll, eh! I've never stayed in a hotel before. I can't get over this; it's like being a fucking film star."

Dolly gracefully nodded. She liked to see Kathy happy and so went along with her excitement.

They spent the morning having breakfast, reading the papers, and getting acquainted with their new home.

Roberto called and enquired about their well-being. Kathy requested a doctor to check Dolly over, just in case there were any further problems, and it was agreed.

Midday, the doctor arrived, along with Mauricio.

Kathy opened the door and welcomed them in.

"I'm Mauricio." He put out his hand to Kathy.

Her face blushed as she took his hand – she felt stupid.

"I'm, I'm, um, uh... Kathy, a friend of Doll, I mean Launa, no, I mean I'm her nurse."

Mauricio realised Kathy was nervous, so he cheekily put his arm around her shoulders and whispered, "So, Nurse Kathy, would you like to take me to see your patient?"

Kathy could feel her skin burning. He was so gorgeous, *too handsome for her. No man as good-looking as him would have ever looked at her, especially with the scars she had on her face.*

Yet oddly, Mauricio didn't look at her like most men did.

As Kathy led Mauricio to Dolly's room, he gasped at the sight of her. Goosebumps covered his body. He hugged her, kissing her cheek. "Launa. My lovely Launa, who has done this to you?"

He stopped to see tears stream from her eyes. He hugged her again. "Hush, hush, it will be okay, I will make it okay. You are safe now; you are here with me and my family." They held each other for what seemed an eternity.

Kathy came back into the room with the doctor and saw the two of them embrace, and she felt guilty for having thoughts about Mauricio when he was obviously Launa's boyfriend.

Leaving the doctor to look Launa over, she joined Mauricio in the kitchen for a coffee.

"Kathy, did Launa tell you who had done this to her?"

She shook her head. "No, she will not speak about it."

Mauricio looked up from his coffee and spoke softly. "She is like a sister. I never had one, you know, and I will kill the person who did this."

Kathy's ears pricked up.

"Sister, you say. I thought you were, well..." She paused. "I'm sorry, I shouldn't presume."

Mauricio smiled. "Oh, you thought that maybe Launa and I were having an affair?"

Kathy blushed again.

Taking a sip of her coffee, she suddenly realised what he had just said – *an affair – well, that would suggest she was married.*

"Mauricio?"

Mauricio looked up.

"Mauricio, is Launa married?"

"Yes, of course." Mauricio frowned, bewildered by the fact that her so-called friend did not know she was married.

"Kathy, if you are friends, how did you not know she is married?"

Kathy, afraid to say any more, asked to be excused. She left the kitchen and sat in her room. There was so much she didn't know about Dolly and neither did her family, as there was no mention of a husband. Her mind raced. Maybe it was to do with him, only Launa hadn't asked to contact her husband. She decided to speak with Launa once the doctor had gone.

Mauricio was polite and decided not to press her for any more information, but instead gave her two credit cards – one with her name and the other with Launa's.

"You will need some cash. Please, spend as much as you need to. Don't worry about a thing." He winked at Kathy, which made her stomach feel like it was in her mouth.

Launa was watching from the doorway. "Well, Kathy, if I'm not mistaken, I would guess you were flirting with Maury."

Kathy blushed again.

As they sat down for lunch, Kathy admitted to Launa that she did like Mauricio, but a man as handsome and charming – as well as stinking rich – would never look twice at a Plain Jane like her.

"Kathy, I'm not going to pretend you're a Miss World potential, but I think that you would look more attractive if you believed you were."

Kathy was confused and curled her lip.

"Don't look at me like that. What I mean is, you dress down; under those baggy clothes is a neat figure and you don't do yourself any justice. Your hair is boring and you lack the confidence to wear any makeup. But, Kathy, your beauty is skin-deep. You are such a good person and your kindness shines through. If you want to look physically attractive, then start believing you are."

Kathy began to cry. "Look at me. I'm so lucky, Dolly. I haven't been through what you've been through and look at your face; you're the bravest woman I know."

Launa took a deep breath. "Kathy, I must tell you now, I could – if I wanted to – live with the way I look. These are scars that I will, with the help of good makeup, be able to cover up, but what I can't cope with - and will change me - is how I got them." Launa broke off and stared into space.

Kathy wanted to ask, but she felt as though she was prying. "Dolly, I will be here when you want to talk about it."

"I know, Kathy."

*

The next day the doctor arrived again, this time with a plastic surgeon, Dr Weller.

The four of them sat around a table and it was put to Dolly that a change of identity was possible, but the surgery would be very intense and the results drastic. The question was, could Dolly endure the stress and pain in her current condition?

"Mental pain affects me more than physical, so it's fine." She turned to Kathy. "I have a wonderful nurse who will look after me, and so I am happy to begin the process as soon as possible."

Kathy questioned Launa about the operation being so soon after her recent ordeal but Launa insisted, the sooner the better. She had promises she needed to keep, including the one she made to herself.

The next day Kathy ventured out, escorted by the chauffeur, to a very posh shopping mall. Dolly stayed behind; she had not brought any clothes with her, only the ones which her mother had given her, and they were all too big for her now frail figure. The last week had left Launa a stone lighter.

Kathy, not wanting to leave Launa for too long, whizzed around the shops looking for suitable clothes for Launa to be comfortable in. Tony, the very patient chauffeur, followed her attentively and carried the bags. The shopping spree was full of pleasure for Kathy. Firstly, she was spending money that wasn't hers, and secondly she was buying clothes with a handsome Italian holding the shopping.

The bags were placed in the boot of the car and off they went. Instead of going to the hotel, Tony took Kathy to a road lined with top designer shops.

She gasped then laughed. "Tony, we can't shop here. Mauricio said I was to spend money on things we needed."

"Kathy, it's my job to see to it that you girls have the best of everything. These orders are from Roberto, and when they say 'get what you need', they mean only the best. Now, Uncle Tony here will show you how to shop. I am Italian and we know about fashion." He looked her up and down and waved his hand.

The outfits he chose for Kathy and Launa were perfect; yes, he knew how a woman should be dressed.

*

When Kathy returned to the hotel, she was pleased to see Launa up and about, preparing dinner. She had sent the concierge out for a list of groceries. Both women laughed liked schoolgirls when they tried on the clothes. Launa was very intrigued by the outfits picked by Tony. Kathy had no idea what Launa liked to wear, since she had only seen her in the hospital gown or Mary's clothes. But she looked comfortable in the Chanel suit he had chosen. Kathy was surprised at herself – she could see how much better she looked in tighter fitting clothes, and she decided that she would show off more of her figure.

The operation was scheduled for the next day, providing Launa's blood pressure was stable.

Roberto himself paid Launa a visit; he was intrigued yet very grateful to her. Therefore, he wanted to meet her personally and wish her the best. Mauricio had sung her praises and held her totally responsible for his freedom.

She was sitting on the sofa, looking very relaxed, when he entered. His eyes were not as good as they had been in his younger days so, without his glasses, he saw a very graceful woman dressed in silk pyjamas. Her hair, the colour of black tulips, shone from the light of the chandeliers. As he got closer, he could see the weave of scars across her once-beautiful face and he felt a deep sorrow for this young woman to whom he owed so much.

Launa saw a heavyset man, impeccably dressed in a navy blue suit, and a soft smile. She got to her feet to greet Roberto but, instead of a handshake, he put out his arms. She hugged him and felt instantly warm and safe.

She could smell the strong, expensive aftershave mixed with cigars and brandy. His voice was deep and husky. "I am so glad we can finally meet, but I am so sad it is under these circumstances."

Launa nodded. "I am grateful…"

Before she could finish, he interrupted her. "My home is yours, my family is yours, you are very welcome to all I can offer, and I will make sure you are looked after."

He paused. "I will always owe you."

Kathy stood back, still astonished by the presence of this large, assured man.

As soon as he had gone, Kathy laughed. "Cor blimey, he was like one of those men out of the mafia films... Italian an' all." She paused for a moment. "He's not, is he? Uh, mafia, I mean?"

"Who cares, Kathy? Roberto is Mauricio's father, and I just happened to help him out a long time ago and, well, he has agreed to return the favour. That's all there is to it."

Kathy nodded as if to say 'okay', but she still mused over the idea that they could be mafia.

*

Dr Weller met Launa at the entrance of the hospital and wheeled her to a private room. He explained that they would use the room for recovery and then, as soon as she came round from the operation and her pain was controlled, they would transfer her back to the hotel where he would monitor her progress.

They sat and discussed again, in more depth, the transformation. She had made it very clear that she must look different, so that no one would recognise her. He had suggested changing her bone structure by placing implants into her cheeks and reshaping her nose. Her appearance would be very different. The only thing to give her away would be her eyes but, even then, if she wanted to, she could wear coloured lenses.

The operation itself was a success. With skin grafting, as well as laser treatment, Dr Weller managed to hide the scars and, for the skilful and humane way he conducted the operation and the subsequent aftercare, Roberto rewarded him well. His own private clinic needed a boost, and he certainly received one, as the work on Launa proved to be a great success.

When Launa awoke, a little dazed, she realised that she was still alive and on the road to a new life as a new person. She had to gain her strength, tone her body and train her mind. It was time to put a plan together. She hated the smell of the hospital anaesthetic, and antiseptic was a too familiar reminder. Waking up in a hospital with the same sound and smell drove her back to the pain she had gone through. *She saw her husband's face again, the evil grin and bright green eyes as the knife plunged towards her.* A tear sprang from her eyes but not through sadness this time – she was angry. Fighting back the tears, she needed to be strong: *No more crying, no more senseless emotions.*

As she lay in recovery, her thoughts drifted back to her past, the kindness she had shown people – she liked to be helpful – and her time as a top city lawyer, where she had progressed so quickly, and had earned such a high reputation.

She had also been a caring and loving person, taking after her mother in that respect. Launa knew now that she had been denied a life rich in purpose and promise for the future.

As she looked around this splendidly finished bedroom, in one of the most luxurious hotels in the world, she reflected on what she had to show for life up to this point. Nothing... but strong feelings of revenge.

Chapter Nine

The total holistic pampering aided her recovery. Doctor Weller redressed every bandage himself and carefully monitored her transformation. This was an enormous undertaking for him, but there was a suggestion that if he could bring about the physical changes in Launa that she both wanted and needed, he would be well rewarded. Roberto, in so many words, had promised to fund the practice until it was fully up and running and he was a man who was always true to his word. Roberto only dealt with men he believed he could trust.

Back in the seventies, when the young doctor graduated, Roberto befriended him, and their relationship led eventually to Doctor Weller's success. It all happened unexpectedly.

Roberto, for one reason or another, got into a situation where he thought he was being double-crossed and mistakenly shot the wrong person. The young victim wasn't going to press charges for fear of the consequences. Luckily, in those days, Roberto was a bad shot and so the damage wasn't too severe; he didn't kill him. However, the young lad was left disfigured. Of course, any gunshot wound needed to be reported to the police. Roberto called Calton Weller. The deal was straightforward – you scratch my back and I'll scratch yours.

Coming from a poor background, Calton's university fees amounted to far more than he could repay and he would struggle for a long time. All those years of training, and then qualifying, one would assume there would be a respite but, no, so the offer made by Roberto was too good to turn down, and helped him on the road to financial recovery.

He remembered the gangster only too well. He had been brought to him later that evening after the conversation with Roberto. He didn't waste time. As he arrived at the hospital, the blood was still pouring from his face and neck. Luckily, the shots had missed his vital arteries, but it had still left a nasty mess. He stitched the wounds, patched the guy up, and got him out of the hospital before anyone noticed. Roberto contacted him again a few days after and asked him to perform a maxillae facial reconstruction. The young man, who went by the name of Stallion to those who knew him personally before the shooting, needed more than a quick patchwork if he was ever to resemble anything like his former appearance.

"So, Doctor, can you mould me into Elvis Presley?"

Calton laughed and replied, "All I can do is make you look fucking human. How about that, eh?"

The young Italian pulled out a picture and handed it to the doctor. "Hey, Doc, please do your best."

Calton remembered looking closely at the photo and staring at a face that looked so different from the one staring at him now. He took out his rosary beads and kissed the cross.

It was the most nerve-racking operation Calton Weller ever performed, but the results were far greater than he expected, which led to the cementing of a long-term relationship with Roberto.

*

"Good morning," greeted the doctor. He tried to raise the tone of his voice every time he greeted her; it made him and his patients feel positive. Launa nodded, acknowledging his presence.

She sat upright in the armchair, feeling strong this morning. "Calton, I wish to see my face today," she said, matter-of-factly.

Calton felt sick; *now his whole future would be mapped out.* If she wasn't satisfied with his work, Roberto would not fund his new practice. He gazed at the slight body, so sophisticatedly dressed in a long lambswool dress. He was aware of her soft nature and the graceful way in which she moved. It was her eyes he loved; *he dare not go there for she was very special to Roberto and Mauricio,* so he looked away.

His nerves got the better of him, so apprehensively he replied, "No, not yet, you will not see any benefit until the swelling goes down."

Launa's stomach turned over. *Why was he delaying, and why did he sound so cold?* Four weeks was long enough to wait. Her face itched where the stitches dissolved, the swelling had subsided and she felt no pain, not even a twinge. She suspected he was stalling because he had fucked up. And, in a flash of temper, she turned her head towards Calton, grabbed his chin and spat, "Get me my mirror, and I will be the judge, not you." She let go to see the blood drain from his face.

Calton was shocked by Launa's reaction. He found it unbelievable that sweet Launa almost bit his head off; her eyes portrayed a chilling screen that left him cold to his bones.

"I'm sorry, Launa. I just thought…" Before he could finish, more words flew from her mouth.

"That's the fucking problem with men; they seem to know what's best for me. Well guess what, you don't, so get me a mirror now."

Calton stepped back, angry for feeling intimidated by a woman – who had acted so differently that even her accent had changed. He decided to put it down to a bit of depression; most women in her shoes would be depressed by now, having gone through what she had been put through, trapped inside an apartment for weeks on end.

Calton rushed to the bathroom and grabbed the large oval mirror on the stand. As he ran back to her, he almost tripped over. Launa tutted, she was anxious – she so desperately wanted to emerge from the bandages completely different. The notion of going through all this pain and misery for nothing was too much for her to bear right now.

"You bumbling fucking idiot, leave the damn mirror. I'll see to it myself." She jumped to her feet. "You wait there!" She pointed and disappeared into the bathroom. Calton shook from head to toe; he desperately needed the money offered by Roberto. He would be ruined – *no money, no job, no face.* The past four weeks had been difficult for him. He had been very aware that, when he took on the work, he'd been asked the impossible. The facial alterations were so extreme that, in reality, no woman would like it. He had worked with so many clients that had undergone excessive facial changes and then needed psychotherapy to get over the experience. Launa only had to express her distaste and, well, he dreaded to think. He got to his feet, strolled over to the small bar in the corner of the room, and poured himself a large vodka.

Before he got back to his seat, the glass was empty. He walked back to the bar and poured another. This time, he sat back into the softness of the couch and allowed the warm feeling to go through his body and the light waves of insignificance circle his mind. *To hell with it all, if she doesn't like it, well, tough.* His stomach churned, the comfort of the sofa was wearing off, and the glass once again was empty. He poured a bit more for the third time and slowly sipped as he waited.

Launa had gotten herself so angry that, once inside the privacy of the bathroom, she ripped the bandages away. Her hair was sticking to the last one, but she managed to use the showerhead to release the hair and wash off all the creams that had been continually plastered on her face day and night.

As she looked in the mirror she gasped, more shocked than anything, by seeing the scars for the first time. There was so much to absorb, and so she stood for some time, staring at herself, looking at every detail. As she smiled, a tear left her eye and rolled down her new high cheek. The change was so dramatic that she would not possibly have recognised herself. Now she could get on with her life.

Before she left the bathroom, she applied a touch of makeup, combed her hair, put on her black high heels, and walked tall towards her slightly pissed doctor. He stared, looking for a sign. *Did she like it?* Launa had a twinge of guilt so, slowly, she raised her eyebrow and, with her hands on her hips, said in a New York accent, "Well, Doc, do I look good or do I look damn good?" she smiled.

Calton felt his whole world come back to him. "You look fucking good." He laughed with a tone of hysteria.

She walked over to the brandy glasses and for a split second her husband's face entered her thoughts, but she didn't leave the glass. No, nothing would stop her from doing what she wanted to do now, so she poured a decent measure, walked back to Calton, and made a toast. "Cheers, here's to a new me. And a very sexy me at that." She chuckled for the first time in what seemed like an eternity.

"I'll definitely drink to that," grinned Calton.

Of course, Launa was joking about the sexy part, but Calton wasn't. She looked every bit a sexy woman; her face had been sculpted to perfection and her skin had healed incredibly well.

*

With Kathy out for the day sightseeing, it was an ideal opportunity for Launa to go and complete her other alterations.

The chilly air outside cooled her skin, so she put on her new cashmere jacket. Her face felt fresh, not weighted down with bandages and thick cream that made her sweat. Hailing down a taxi, she asked to be taken to a top hairdresser. The young taxi driver looked Launa up and down and asked, "How good a hairdresser?"

"The best."

The taxi pulled up outside a glamorous, sleek beauty salon and, with a spring in her step, she entered, hoping that they could squeeze her in.

The assistant behind the glass desk looked up and smiled from ear to ear. "Hi, ma'am, how can I help you?"

"I would like my hair cut and dyed."

The young assistant smiled again and said, "Well, if you would take a seat for one little moment, I will speak with Andre and see if he can fit you in today, as I believe he had a cancellation. I think he is otherwise fully booked for the next two months."

Launa was bemused by the girl's accent which appeared to be a deep southern drawl. She hoped that this would be a lucky day for her. Andre was free for the next three hours. Two clients, booked in together, cancelled at the last minute.

Dressing the heads of the rich and famous, he was pleasantly surprised by Launa; she obviously had money, but she lacked the celebrity diva attitude. Her well-spoken, demure English accent brought to his mind the royal family. Andre, a typical gay hairdresser, knew exactly what looked good and what didn't, and he refused to cut a style that wouldn't suit a person. He would protest, 'It's more than my reputation is worth to send a client out of my shop looking worse than when they came in'.

As Launa sat in the chair, Andre started to play with her hair. As he scooped it all back, he saw the pink scars around her ears. "Oh, sweetie, what a neat job! You must give me his name," whispered Andre, in his very camp voice.

Launa smiled. She liked him.

"So now then, darling, this tumble of curls could do with a trim, but other than that…"

Before he finished, Launa jumped in. "No, I want it all off, as short as you can but with a certain style to it, and I want to go blonde."

Andre did an exaggerated gasp. "You must be joking."

"No, I'm perfectly serious. I want my hair to look completely the opposite to the way it looks now," she said, as she grabbed a bunch of her black waves.

Andre mused for a moment, and then took out a magazine. He cupped her chin in his hand and moved her head from one side to the other. "Um, um…"

"Andre, just do whatever you like as long as it's completely different."

"Okay, princess."

Her cheekbones were high and her face resembled perfect proportions. Only those features could get away with a pixie crop style and it would emphasise her beautiful eyes. He got to work while Launa flicked through the magazines. The assistants manicured her hands and made her lemon teas, unlike the treatment back in England. The washing and bleaching, conditioning and cutting, had left Launa looking a bit bedraggled. Andre called over to the beautician to give Launa a fresh make over to go with her new style.

The shop closed, so the usual salon chatter died down, leaving Andre and the beautician alone to complete the final changes.

As he spun the chair around, Launa put her hands to her mouth. Totally assured no one would recognise her, she gasped with delight to see all traces of her former self had gone — all except her eyes.

"Well," squealed Andre, "Do you like?"

"I love it, I really love it." Her voice was slow and husky.

Andre flicked the sides of her short pixie bob, running his finger down her cheekbones. "This makes you look like a supermodel and, princess, if I didn't have my eye on Ernie the butcher, I'd probably have my eye on you."

Launa laughed for the second time in one day.

He presented her with a bill for eight hundred dollars and waited for a gasp. He was expensive but it was their standard price. Francesca gave him the credit card which had her name and Roberto's on it. Andre's eyes widened, and he smiled nervously. If he had known this beautiful young woman was connected with the Lucianis, he would have pretended he was fully booked. Their reputation preceded them, and Andre was relieved that his client had left the salon with a smile on her face.

*

All the way back to the apartment, Launa tingled with elation and anticipation. She could not wait for Kathy and Mauricio to see the new Launa look! She was and felt a different person although, beneath the cosmetic changes, she was still the same Francesca who was loved by her family so dearly.

With the first part of her plan in place, she sighed with relief. The aches and pains gone, the operation a success, she looked better than okay.

Her first test would be Kathy. She should be back from her sightseeing escapade and as Kathy hadn't seen Launa without her bandages, not even once, this would be a real life measurement.

As she arrived at the hotel, her decision to surprise Kathy right away was curtailed briefly while the new Launa tested her appearance, and her own self-belief by having a drink in the bar first. She hadn't been to the bar in the hotel. Full of men and woman in business dress, having the wind-down drink from the day's work, she missed being a part of it. The waiter took her order and, just like the movies, the man next to her offered to pay. She smiled but turned the offer down. He was tall, roughly thirty, and quite handsome. Launa was flattered; *it must be the new look*, she thought, as she sipped a glass of champagne.

About to head upstairs, she spotted in the corner, behind a group of portly businessmen, her dear friend Kathy. She was sitting on a leather sofa, a short distance from the bar. Launa leant further back on her seat to get a better view and, yes, she was right, it was Kathy. She was dressed to the nines, her hair styled, and she even had makeup on. Launa giggled to herself, *what a dark horse you really are*. Kathy was obviously chatting or possibly flirting with someone, but too many men blocked her sight. So she wandered casually over to see for herself, completely forgetting about her own big surprise. Wow! Mauricio, dressed in a drop dead gorgeous suit, was charming the pants off Kathy.

Launa paused for a moment, pondering whether maybe she shouldn't interrupt. Too late, Kathy looked up to see a huge grin across Launa's face. Mauricio glared at Launa, who was by now stunned that even her own friend didn't recognise her at all.

"Can I help you?" he asked.

Launa shook her head. She walked back to the apartment with mixed emotions, pleased that she really was unrecognisable, but also afraid of the odd lonely emotion that clouded her happiness.

Kathy came in about an hour later, alone, and called out for Launa. "I'm home, lovey, and guess what? I have had a brill day, got lots to tell... Launa, where are you?" Kathy was busy taking off her shoes and putting all her new parcels away. She really had made the most of her credit card.

Launa walked into the living room, grinning from ear to ear. Kathy leapt out of her skin. "Oh, you made me jump. Who are you, and what are you doing here?" She could tell the woman wasn't a burglar or there to hurt anyone.

Launa smiled again and it dawned on Kathy who she was.

"Jesus!" shrieked Kathy. "Fuck me, you're so... well, not you."

"How did you guess it was me then?" asked Launa.

"When I left this morning you wore that very same dress... fucking 'ell, Dolly, I can't believe it's you. Your hair, your face – it's beautiful."

Rooted to the spot, she looked Launa up and down in shock.

"You really didn't recognise me down in the bar?"

Then she recalled Launa standing in the bar and Mauricio asking if she wanted something. Suddenly, she was embarrassed, as it was now obvious that Launa saw her and Mauricio.

"Dolly, I'm sorry. I should have told you about Mauricio and me, but I wanted to wait until you were back on your feet."

Launa laughed. "Kathy, I think it's wonderful. I love to see my closest friend having fun."

Relieved, but still bemused by Launa's new look, she remarked, "Dolly, excuse me for staring, love, but I can't get over how different you look."

Hugging Launa, she said, "Now you are as beautiful on the outside as you are on the inside."

Launa felt guilty. Regrettably, Kathy's comment wasn't true anymore. She had decided to drop the loving and forgiving nature and become a lot harder, a sure way to protect herself. It was a break from the past but a necessary one all the same.

*

As the evening came in, the sun disappeared from the sky. The huge floor to ceiling glass windows became another picture frame to the amazing view of the lights that speckled Manhattan. Launa gazed out and wondered if all those tiny lights were rooms maybe, with people – families – sitting down to a meal, discussing the day's events. *She imagined herself one day enjoying a romantic dinner with a husband but, of course, there would be no children.* Her heart always ruled her head, so the way she loved her husband was based on feelings she had for him in the early stages of their relationship and not what he really stood for. *If only she had seen the change in him, if only she had known how much the Mauricio case meant to Charles' family.* Then, she realised, if she had gone along with them, where would she be right now? The plain fact was that she would be with her evil husband, connected to his evil family, and probably cocooned in utter misery, and controlled to the point where she could not have escaped from the relationship. She pictured her family life as it would have been – two, possibly three, children sitting around the dinner table, ill at ease, as her husband walked through the door, anticipating the fallout if the meal fell below his ridiculously high expectations. And her children – how would they have coped, and what would they have turned out like?

She recollected a court case where her husband had represented his friend – a simple custody battle and, by the time they had finished, the man's wife had practically been committed to a mental home and the kids awarded to the father with no contact granted to the mother. She remembered feeling disgusted how her husband had bragged about his methods. He had exaggerated the truth so much, and the poor girl had been so worn down, that she had in fact become a bumbling wreck and needed tranquilizers from the doctor to help her cope. Launa visualised Charles doing the same to her.

For all the pain and suffering she had been through, her mind remained sane. *From now on, her head, and not her heart, would govern her.* Her thoughts returned to her husband, *his callous debauchery turning her love for him to pure hate.* An uncontrolled sensation started in the pit of her stomach and rose to her throat. Her cheeks burned, and her heart raced – a warm feeling tingled in the back of her neck. *He wasn't handsome at all, he was the ugliest man alive...* blackness started to close in around her eyes and the lights dimmed.

Luckily, the thick, shag, pile rug softened her fall. She came to with Kathy waving a copy of *Vogue* over her face. "Wiv us now, then?"

Launa blinked, her head hurt, and she could just make out Kathy's face.

"I fainted, eh?" croaked Launa.

"You've overdone things today. I mean, look at yourself. A fucking transformation like yours is a lot to take in. Fuck me, Doll, I nearly fainted when I saw ya meself."

"It's not shock though, surely?" asked Launa as she struggled to her feet.

Kathy grabbed her arm and helped her to the sofa.

"No, no, now then, the problem is you are not aware of how much your body has been through. When you arrived in the hospital, you were so near the brink, well, actually you did snuff it."

"What?" cried Launa.

Kathy nodded. "It's true, love, the bruising over your chest was from the paddles. You had to be resuscitated. Not just the once, either."

Launa slumped in the chair. "Shit, Kathy, I didn't know."

With a gentle arm around Launa, she whispered, "Listen, girly, you are nothing like that sick now, so just take it easy, but bear in mind you can't overdo it."

Launa realised that her husband had meant to kill her and she must let him believe she was dead.

Kathy ran a hot bath full of bubbles and relaxing oils, lit a few candles, and helped Launa into the tub. She left the door ajar and every so often would call out to Launa as if she was a five-year-old.

With the fridge full of delicious meals ready to be cooked, Kathy chose a steak with fresh salad and set about making a succulent dish to whet Launa's appetite. Launa relaxed in the bath, her muscles unwound in the water, and the lavender aroma soothed her mind. She thought about how Kathy had helped her so much during the last four or five weeks and a tinge of guilt swept through her. Kathy had lost her job due to not returning after her two-week vacation, and Launa had no means of supporting them.

Sitting down enjoying their evening meal, Launa asked, "How long do you think it will take before I am a hundred percent better?"

Kathy sipped her glass of wine and replied, "How long is a piece of string?"

"Only, I'm thinking of going to work here for a while, just to pay back what I owe to Roberto and to support us."

Kathy was confused. As far as she was concerned, Roberto did not want paying back – it must have shown on her face.

"I know Roberto doesn't want any money but I need to be independent."

Kathy shrugged her shoulders. She could see the determination in Launa's eyes.

"Well, you could work part-time for a while if it helps and if you don't need me, then I could get a job here too. After all, I'm a qualified nurse."

*

The next morning, Kathy was on the phone to Mauricio. Excitedly, she told him about Launa, her new face, and that their relationship was no longer a secret. Before she hung up, she said, "And Launa wants to see you."

Mauricio was pleased he had been invited over. He had not seen her for over three weeks and had started to miss her. Being so inquisitive, he wanted to see her new look and hoped she really was as beautiful as Kathy had made out. He remembered her sweet expression, her round face with dimples, and a glow to her cheeks.

Before Mauricio arrived, Launa had got herself up, dressed – putting on her Chanel suit – and applied some light makeup. Kathy looked over from the kitchen area and whistled.

"What do you think?" asked Launa as she spun around.

"Very professional. Where are you going, dressed like that?"

"A job calls me," replied Launa.

Kathy assumed she had looked through the local paper, unaware that Launa had spent half the night on the phone with Roberto. The job would pay a substantial amount of money but required a lot of work.

Before she had breakfast, she worked out the time difference and decided to call home.

Her father answered.

"Hello, Dad," she said endearingly, longing to hear his voice.

There was a pause.

"Is that you, babe?" he whispered. Mary heard him and came rushing in from the kitchen.

"Who's that?" she said, thinking he was talking to another woman although, to be fair to Bill, she had never had any reason to doubt him.

"Dad, are you there? It's me, Dolly."

"It's our Doll, Mare, she's on the phone."

Mary laughed. "Well she's not on the bloody sofa." Walking over to him, she said, "Let me say hello."

Bill held on to the phone. "Hello, babes, how are ya?"

Launa's eyes filled up. Her dad sounded so homely – she wanted to be there to hug him. She wanted them to see her new face and see that she was okay now.

"Dad, I'm well. I'm really well. Give me some time and I will be back, I promise."

Mary snatched the phone. "Dolly, it's me, Mum. How are you, love?"

"Hello, Mum. I'm fine, honestly. I'm very well. In fact, I look so well you wouldn't recognise me."

Mary began to cry. Bill put his big, meaty arm around her shoulder and they held the phone together.

"Mum, I want you to know that things will be different when I come back. I'm not staying away again."

Mary sobbed. She missed her daughter even more since she had seen her so recently.

"Before I go, there's one thing I need you to remember – for now I don't exist, you haven't seen me." Her voice was firmer.

Bill jumped in, afraid he wouldn't get another chance.

"Dolly, whatever you say, babe, we are here always, whenever you need us, that includes your brothers, and – before you go – we love you, princess. Take good care and please stay in touch, even if it's just once a week." His voice began to crack. He had the biggest lump in his throat.

"Dad, I love you, all of you, and I will call once a week, I promise. I have to go now."

"Goodnight, babe," whispered Bill, followed by Mary.

"Yeah, goodnight, Dad. Goodnight, Mum," Launa whispered back. They hadn't realised that in America it was daylight, a five-hour time difference, but that was okay; she felt a sense of comfort hearing her mum and dad say goodnight.

Mauricio came bounding through the door like a puppy. "Well, Kathy, where is the blonde bombshell?"

Launa emerged from her bedroom to see Mauricio standing there. His first reaction was one of concern, and then he choked, shaking his head.

"Maury!" screamed Launa. "What's the matter?" Her heart sank.

Slowly, he looked up, and then he stared. "It's not you."

"Of course it's me," she grimaced. As much as she liked Mauricio, he did have a knack of winding her up occasionally.

"No, Launa, I mean it doesn't fit your personality. What I mean to say is, I always see you with kidlike dimples and round, full eyes, and now, well... you just look like a woman."

"Maury, these tits have never belonged to a man. I've always been a woman."

He tutted. "Yeah, I know that, but instead of being pretty, cuddly, you're, well, more... different, that's all."

Mauricio walked over and hugged her. He kissed her face and whispered, "You are still beautiful, though."

Launa kissed him back. "Thank you."

*

Mauricio helped Launa into his black Mercedes. The cream leather interior had that distinctive new leather smell. Launa felt excited; she had a purpose, a job, and, at long last, she had her independence back.

She had called Roberto to thank him for all his kindness and to ask if he could recommend any legal firms she could apply to for work. After ten minutes of insisting that she didn't need to work and he would look after her like a daughter, the weaker of the two caved in and Launa got her way. He offered her a position with his own legal team. The vast companies he owned had a legal firm dedicated solely to his businesses, so he was sure to find her a position. He then considered her for an alternative role. He trusted her completely and the idea that she could be his eyes for underhand dealings put a smile on his face. As they headed towards Roberto's home, the car phone rang. Mauricio spoke in Italian. Launa began to enjoy the excitable rambling; it sounded as though they were arguing. Mauricio pulled the car over to the side of the highway, to the disgust of other drivers that flew past beeping their horns. His voice got louder and his facial expression changed. Launa couldn't help herself.

"What's up, Maury?"

He put his hand over the phone. "It's my father — he wants us to meet him somewhere else. There's been an incident."

Launa nodded. She was nervous yet excited — *what was the incident?* In the back of her mind, she, like Kathy, thought that maybe Roberto was part of the mafia. However, this was the early nineties and, well, it was probably too far-fetched. She should not assume, just because he was Sicilian, extremely wealthy, and walked around with bodyguards, that he was The Godfather. The plain truth was that Launa was bored and quite liked the fantasy idea of being part of a mafia underworld. She wondered whether criminality was in her genes.

Before Mauricio could pull away, a cop car drew in behind them, and a large, heavyset police officer came over. He was different from the English Bobbies. He peered in, looked at Launa and smiled. "Morning, ma'am." He tilted his hat, and then looked at Mauricio, who looked angry. "Morning, sir."

Mauricio nodded in acknowledgment.

"Sir, unless you have broken down, you are violating the road traffic law by stopping on a highway." The smug officer knew Mauricio hadn't broken down because the car was still running.

Launa immediately jumped in and used her feminine charms. "It's my fault, Officer. I'm off to an interview and, as you can see, I'm dressed in my best suit." The officer looked her up and down. She looked sophisticated, and he was drawn in by her elegant English accent. "I sometimes get travel sick and, well, you can imagine, what with the nerves and the long travel, I had to pull over. He did insist we shouldn't, but I'm afraid I'm not familiar with the road laws. Officer, I'm very sorry and it won't happen again."

The officer's face changed. His smug expression faded and he smiled sweetly. "Well, ma'am, I can see your predicament. Are you okay now?"

She nodded.

"Well, you can't be late for an interview. Now then, off you go."

As they drove away, Mauricio laughed. "That's never happened to me before. Those traffic cops are right sons of bitches."

Launa laughed. "Nor me. Must be my new face."

"To be frank, Launa, the way you look now, not many men would say no to you."

"What's that's supposed to mean?"

"Well, I was trying to explain to you back at the hotel, your face is different, but your personality is the same. You have always been graceful and elegant but now, with your face chiselled, your eyes slightly narrowed, and those lips all puffy and juicy …" he giggled.

"Juicy," laughed Launa.

"Yeah, fucking juicy, really fucking horny." Mauricio tried not to keep looking at her because, although he had feelings for Kathy and regarded Launa as a friend, it was hard not to fancy her.

"Maury, that's disgusting."

He laughed. "It's not disgusting, it's a damn right fact."

*

The drive to the hotel for the secret meet with Roberto was spent teasing each other. Launa teased Mauricio about Kathy, and Mauricio joked with her about all the boyfriends she could kiss with her 'juicy lips', as he called them.

Mauricio stopped at a sidewalk as they approached the hotel and there in front of them, just like in the movies, was an external metal stairway, protruding down the side of a tall building.

Mauricio turned to Launa. "I want you to get out here. Wait about fifteen minutes and walk into the hotel. Then, order five or six drinks, ask for the drinks to be put on a tray, and then take them to Room 702… do you mind?"

Launa frowned. "No, I don't mind doing anything to help, but why don't we go together?"

"I don't want anyone to know who you are, or, for that matter, that you have any connection to us. If you look like a hotel manager or something, then no one will notice you."

After weeks of resting, watching American soaps, and reading every magazine she could find, Launa was ready for some excitement.

She nodded. "That's fine."

Mauricio kissed her on the cheek just before she left the comfort of the warm car.

As he drove away, she felt vulnerable; these alleyways in the films were always portrayed in a dark light and were the ideal location for a mugging or a rape. Launa pulled the warm, wool jacket more tightly, as she slowly began to walk towards the hotel. She could see Mauricio in the distance, walking through the hotel entrance.

Although not as grand as the hotel she stayed in, it was four or five star and looked very grand and busy.

The reception staff didn't notice her as she slipped quietly into the bar. There were a few people dotted here and there — *no one looking conspicuous.* Launa then realised she was acting rather foolish — looking for potential villains; she wasn't a detective, and this wasn't a film. The barman, an ordinary guy, wasn't perturbed when she ordered six drinks including two cocktails. She paid in cash, thinking it best not to leave credit card details, just in case.

"Oh, and please will you put them on a tray?" She thought it a good idea to put on an American accent too, just so she didn't appear out of place.

The barman just nodded, gave her the tray with the drinks on it, and away she went, heading for Room 702.

As soon as she knocked, a deep, husky voice asked, "Who is it?"

Launa, recognising the voice, almost said 'Launa' but bit her lip, paused, and then replied, "Your drinks, sir."

The door opened and sitting at a desk facing her was Roberto, with Mauricio by his side. Sitting across the room was another man who was very similar in appearance to Mauricio.

As Launa entered, Roberto stood up and Mauricio took from her the tray of drinks. Quickly, he closed the door.

"My beautiful daughter, look at you. You are so gorgeous."

Launa embraced Roberto as he kissed her gently on both cheeks.

"This is my nephew, Sergio." Roberto nodded in Sergio's direction.

The young Italian gave a friendly smile.

"Get to your feet, Sergio!" Roberto shouted. "You must greet our Launa as your own sister."

Sergio did not hesitate. He was on his feet in a second and kissing both of her cheeks.

"I am honoured."

Launa expected him to be annoyed by his uncle's outburst and a touch resentful, but he wasn't. He seemed genuinely pleased to meet her. She liked his friendly face — he looked so open. Mauricio and Sergio could be mistaken for brothers, except Sergio had a more refined, slimmer face; a little more reserved than Mauricio who, like her own brother Fred, had more immature features.

Roberto sat back down and shook his head; he was looking at the papers in front of him. Everyone seemed to be on the edge of their seats.

Launa sat, awaiting some conversation, completely unaware of the seriousness of the situation.

Slowly, Roberto looked up and stared Launa in the face. "Nobody knows you and, certainly since your operation, knows that you have any connection with me."

Launa was uneasy. *What did he mean?* Her thoughts ran away with her and again she felt vulnerable. *Was he going to kill her, get rid of her body?* She shook the thought from her head.

"What's going on?" she demanded, shocked at the assertive tone of her own voice.

Roberto liked the confidence in his new adopted daughter. "My Launa, I find myself in a position of, how you may say, being sailed down the river."

She frowned. "I'm sorry, I don't understand."

Roberto placed the piece of paper towards her so she could read it.

Launa read the fax sent to Roberto which, from the contents, was obviously meant for someone else. After reading it again, Launa asked in her serious, professional tone, "Who are Enright & Bradshaw?"

Roberto looked at his son and nephew, then back to Launa, and replied in a voice of resignation, "They are supposed to be my lawyers."

Stunned by the fax in front of her, it was apparent that there had been a double-cross going on involving Roberto's lawyers. The fax suggested that Roberto and his son were involved in a criminal activity. Details concerning shipments and cargo had been recorded, and it appeared that the Lucianis were being set up. Was this supposed to read like this?

She looked up to find Roberto's face deflated.

As he shrugged his shoulders, Mauricio jumped up. "I'm going to fucking kill the sly bastards." He banged the table.

Instantly, Roberto jumped to his feet. "Wait, my son, we will not go in heavy. We will wait first and seek good advice."

He paused and turned to Launa. "What do you suggest?"

"Well, you are right, Roberto, nobody can associate you with me, and I guess from your thoughts, not that I'm a mind reader, that this situation needs investigating, right?"

Roberto smiled and nodded enthusiastically.

Mauricio had wanted to go in all guns blazing and wipe out the whole company, but the new plan was a better option and besides, he wasn't going to argue with his father.

Enright & Bradshaw had advertised for a secretary. It had become a regular thing, since one of the partners was such a pervert, that most girls would not last more than six months before they would leave. None of them would attempt to file for sexual harassment charges, for who would believe a young secretary over a lawyer from one of the best legal firms in New York? So the ad was there again.

Launa nodded. With a mischievous look on her face, she went on to say, "A secretary in a legal firm? Roberto, I would be the best goddamn fucking spy in the world."

Roberto raised his eyebrows and Mauricio giggled. They had never heard her speak with such attitude, or even such profanity.

Roberto grabbed the cocktail to drink a toast to their plan and laughed when the umbrella nearly shot up his nose. "Where's the brandy? No, no, where's the champagne?" he squealed. "I have the best weapon to nail these bastards." He put his two hands out and turned them over as if he had just revealed a new prize.

Launa had become fond of Roberto and had always been close to Mauricio, the latter reminding her of her twin brother – their personalities so similar, always ready for a punch-up.

The fax had mistakenly been sent to the wrong place. Roberto read it, he photocopied it, left the original in the tray in his office, and walked away, leaving no evidence that he had even been to work that morning. The information on the fax message was so incriminating that for sure the firm would send someone over to find it and explore the possibility that Roberto had seen it. However, if the office was still locked, and the fax in the tray, they would remove it, expecting Roberto to be none the wiser.

The one thing that did concern Roberto was the doubt as to whether anyone in his company was in cahoots, so now he would become more vigilant and trust only the three people in the room with him.

The timing was perfect, because no one had seen Launa with her new guise, including his own minders, so he didn't anticipate anyone recognising her and associating Launa with him.

Roberto pulled out a huge bunch of keys and slowly unclipped one, handing it to Launa. "This is yours. It is a key to one of my homes, now your home. It would be a good idea to move into it and then, if you're really happy to still go ahead and investigate this problem for me, you must keep away from us and we will have contact on the quiet."

"I am going to enjoy this assignment. Trust me; I will get to the bottom of this. Fancy that, eh? Me, a barrister, playing a secretary."

Before she left, she said very seriously, "I want to start using my real name."

Mauricio frowned and Roberto looked on in surprise. "But your real name is Launa Mathews, or is there more to you than what we know?"

Roberto was concerned. *Who was Launa if she wasn't the barrister, Launa Mathews, who represented his son in England?* He did not like surprises. He liked to feel he knew a person and became unnerved when skeletons fell out of the closet.

"Don't worry, I am Launa Mathews. Well, actually Launa Enright – well, I was since the age of thirteen when I was sent to my aunt's for my own safety, but I was born Francesca Vincent. No one in the States would know me by that name."

Launa looked at the three men, who appeared to be shocked. She smiled but her smile was not returned. She felt that she should explain her names. Besides, she was safe with Roberto – *he was not about to turn her over to Mad Mick or his mad sons back in London.*

"It's okay; I will not keep any secrets from you." She paused, gathering her thoughts. It was strange telling someone about her childhood secret. "When I was born, my father got tangled up with some gangster and ended up having this man, Mad Mick, put behind bars. This madman threatened that he would kill the most precious thing to my dad, which was me. So my parents decided to change my identity and sent me to live with my aunt, and so my name was changed from Francesca Vincent to Launa Mathews." Launa was bemused by the look on Roberto's face – he was slightly pale.

He was frustrated with himself for not being able to unravel this baffling coincidence. *Was this woman he saw as a daughter the ultimate in deception, or was the name just a genuine coincidence?*

"Roberto, what's the matter?"

"Enright... You said your name was Enright, and you – as we know – are a barrister."

Launa nodded, still not understanding what was concerning Roberto. She didn't like the way he spoke. She felt interrogated.

"Are you in any way related to Tyler Enright?"

Launa recalled the name.

She sat back, crossing her arms and legs. The blood began to drain from Roberto's face and his lips went thin.

Launa was more confused than ever, but still she went on. "Roberto, I was – well, I still am married to Charles Enright, and I believe he has an uncle called Tyler."

Mauricio and Roberto glanced at each other. Launa sat on the edge of her seat. The soft expression on Roberto's face when he looked at her changed, and he was angry as he sat staring at her. "Are you fucking serious? My God, I have had you in my home, with my family, and you are married to an Enright.

Tell me, Launa, Francesca, whatever your fucking name is, what is it you and your damn family want?"

The room fell silent.

Roberto stood up and walked to the window. Mauricio knocked back a large brandy and Sergio looked more confused than anyone.

"Please would someone tell me what the fuck's going on?" Launa was nervous; her dear friends were acting very strange. "I don't understand what you mean by me and my family. Why are you so concerned with the Enrights, for Christ's sake? They are practically the English legal system but what's that got to do with you?"

She turned to Mauricio. "Maury, why are you so surprised? You knew I was married to Charles Enright, so what's the big deal here?"

Roberto turned slowly to face her. "This does not make sense. You have represented my son in England and you are married to my lawyer's nephew…"

Launa shrugged her shoulders.

"My lawyer is fucking Tyler Enright, for fuck's sake. Look at the fax, it's from my lawyer." Roberto was screaming now, his veins were protruding from his neck, and his fist pounded the desk.

Launa, collecting her thoughts, calmly replied, "Roberto, I have never met Tyler Enright. I was led to believe he was a second-hand car salesman in the north of England who the family disowned."

Roberto shook his head. "This is too much of a coincidence. Tell me this, exactly what do your husband and his father do for a living?"

Launa stared at Mauricio. "You knew, Mauricio, didn't you?"

In a flat tone, Mauricio said, "No! How would I know what your husband did for a living? You never spoke of him."

Launa went back in her mind to the court case and recollected being told by Charles she was not to let him know that she was married to him. He let her believe that barristers, especially defence lawyers, never gave any information out to their clients regarding families because some previous convictions had not been handled too well by the clients who, when released from prison, had taken revenge on a lawyer's family. She remembered thinking at the time that it was very rare for instances like that to happen. However, she decided to continue with her maiden name and not let any future clients know that she was married. It then dawned on her that he had said it at the start of Mauricio's case.

"My husband is a barrister and his father, William Enright, is a judge, and the other uncle, Charles, whom my husband is named after, is also a judge."

Roberto looked angrier. He lit a cigar and blew the smoke directly into Launa's face. She coughed and waved her hands.

As much as she liked Roberto and Mauricio, she was angry at how she was made to feel right now, and the fact that Roberto had blown smoke in her face enraged her.

She jumped to her feet and banged a fist on the table. "I don't know what the fuck's going on here but one thing is for sure, I'm not putting up with any more shit from Charles bloody Enright or the fucking Mario Brothers. If you wanna intimidate someone, pick someone who gives a shit. I'm off." Launa marched towards the door but was swiftly intercepted by Sergio. "Get out of my fucking way."

"Hey, Launa – I mean Francesca – please calm yourself. It's okay."

Launa was surprised to hear Sergio speak with such a gentle command. He had just gone up in her estimation. He held her arms, without any aggression.

Roberto shouted, "Launa, please wait! There is a great deal of confusion and my mind is full of deception right now. I'm sorry, please sit down. We are family; we must get to the bottom of this."

Launa turned around to see Roberto's eyes loaded with tears. He was so sad his voice sounded deflated.

They sat back down. "My Launa, I am sorry. It is obvious you have no idea who Tyler is. I also believe, when you represented my son, you did your very best to defend him, so I trust you. It is, however, a huge coincidence and so strange that you are related to the Enrights."

Launa nodded. She flashed back to the past and remembered her father-in-law commenting on the upcoming court case with Mauricio. The first comment was a subtle hint that the likes of the mafia should be behind bars, so Launa would be doing the world a service by relaxing a bit and letting the Crown Prosecution have a field day.

She took the glass of brandy offered to her. After taking a large swig, she said, "Looking back on Maury's court case, I was under immense pressure to fuck up and let him face prison." She paused and took another swig. "It was gentle hints at first, but then I was being bullied, especially by my husband. It was then that he started to be abusive and when Mauricio was found not guilty, well, the abuse increased and eventually I gave up work."

Roberto took her hand and kissed it. "My daughter, it was your husband that cut your beautiful face, wasn't it?"

Mauricio was now on the edge of his seat. The pause seemed like eternity. She nodded and hung her head in shame. "He wanted to kill me. He must think I'm dead, and I want it kept that way."

The room fell silent for a while as Mauricio hugged Launa.

"I'm gonna kill him with my bare hands, so help me God."

Launa pushed Mauricio back into his seat and said very firmly, "No, you will not. Someone else is going to do that." Her voice was cold.

Roberto was astonished by all he had heard that day, and so it was imperative that Launa got inside the firm to find out exactly what was going on and why the Enrights would want Mauricio in prison.

The pure fact that this whole situation had already affected her life gave her more reason to get in there and find out the truth. When Launa left that day, Roberto commented to the boys that they must take great care of her. Mauricio laughed and said, "Father, she can look after herself. Did you see the hardness in her eyes? I don't think I would like to cross her."

Roberto agreed. "I love to see a strong woman, especially when she is on my side, because — trust me, my son — a woman like her can be very dangerous. If there is one thing I have learned in this life, it is this — do not ever try to understand a woman. Us men, we think we are tough, but women go through the worse pain, childbirth, and why is that? Well, it's simple, they are so much stronger than us. They have feelings that we do not have and will never understand, so remember this — never underestimate the power of an angry woman."

A sorry smile adorned Mauricio's face. "She is tough but, before her husband slashed her face, she was so soft and gentle. I would love to know who she has in mind to kill that cruel bastard."

Roberto laughed. "Maury, my son, you have a lot to learn. Did you not see the look in her eyes?"

He gasped. "She can't!"

"She will," replied Roberto.

Sergio jumped in. "She is so cool, but I agree with Uncle, there is more to her and I don't want to cross her. I think she will be good for business."

Roberto put out his cigar and gazed at the two boys before him. "I have searched deep into Launa's eyes and I know that she has changed. She has changed because of what life has served her. Women eventually have a bottom line, and when they reach it, there is no turning back. From the little she has said, life has been cruel." He paused, then finally he muttered, "She reminds me of me when I was younger."

Mauricio and Sergio left the hotel with a lot to think about.

There was a lot unsaid between Roberto and Launa, but they both understood – she had been a pawn in both her husband's and his family's game and Roberto had been double-crossed by the Enrights, but neither of them knew why. Roberto was very confident that Launa would find the underlying cause of it. She was as passionate about the downfall of the Enrights as he was.

*

The house was not a contemporary, luxurious pad like the penthouse suite, but it was more than she could have afforded herself. The style was more traditional, in keeping with the design of the house. The bedrooms were large and airy with thick, heavy curtains, well-dressed beds, and plenty of cushions in all shades of pastel colours. Looking around, she found it hard to imagine a man lived here; *it definitely had a woman's touch*. Little did she know, Roberto had never even stayed there – it had been taken from a wealthy businesswoman who had owed him money. He was a fair man but a very good negotiator, and what was owed to him, he would take.

She spent a day rearranging things to suit her style and generally getting used to her new home.

Kathy was completely smitten with Mauricio, so she moved into his home, which was ideal, because if she had moved in with Launa, then it would have been apparent who Launa was. For now, Launa lived alone, and she was happy with that. All the relevant papers were put together to make a fake career history, and the application for the job as a secretary was sent off.

She was surprised at how quickly she received a reply. The interview was set for Friday but it was already Wednesday. *Never mind,* she thought. She decided to keep her English accent. Besides, she wasn't sure if she could keep up the imitation America drawl. Funny, all Brits imitating the Yanks would always exaggerate a deep southern accent, and yet in New York they spoke very differently.

Friday arrived not soon enough. She was anxious to get this right. If she messed up now, she would not only be letting herself down but everyone else.

A less expensive suit would be more appropriate. *Realistically, a secretary would not turn up to work in a thousand dollar Chanel two-piece*. She opted for a plain shift dress with a matching jacket in a deep green – no jewellery, just a nice pair of plain black shoes. She looked taller than the average sized woman did, and so she stood out without the designer labels. *That was fine though.* Roberto had stressed that most of the secretaries were employed mainly for their aesthetic appeal, rather than the number of words they could type in a minute.

With the taxi hooting outside, Launa grabbed her folder and left the house quickly. A chill in the air hit her, and so she skipped back into the house, snatched a scarf, took one last glance in the hallway mirror, and darted down the garden path.

The traffic was not too bad for the time of day. Launa checked her watch and realised she was wearing a gold and diamond Rolex, a get-well gift from Roberto – well, actually, it was one of many. She pulled her sleeve further down her arm to hide the extravagant piece.

Nine o'clock on the dot, she arrived in the foyer of Bradshaw and Enright.

The receptionist greeted her with a huge smile, showing off her pristine white teeth, "Hi, you must be Francesca Vincent."

She nodded.

The entrance was large, with glass everywhere, and she felt as though she was in a goldfish bowl.

Before she had the chance to take a seat, a man arrived to meet her. "Hi, I'm Tyler Enright."

Francesca's knees wobbled. Her mouth went dry and she could barely reply. "Pleased to meet you." She gulped very nervously.

Tyler looked her up and down and, as he opened the large chrome framed glass door for her to walk on ahead, he managed to have a better gawk at her figure.

He had made his mind up already – she had the job. Just to be able to gaze at her every day was worth paying a wage.

Francesca tried desperately to get herself together. Tyler Enright was Charles' uncle, of that she was sure. His eyes, his eyelashes and that smile; it was her husband all over again. The only difference was that he was older, but that didn't change the same expression and neither did his vocals. She tried to hold down the vomit that was rising in her throat. The back of her head was getting hot, and she prayed she would not faint.

Tyler guided Francesca to a room halfway down the corridor and offered her a drink. Quickly, she answered, "Oh, yes please, I would love a glass of water." *Great*, she thought, *I can cool down, relax and get on with this interview.*

He walked over to a bar with filtered water on tap. He poured her a large glass and added a slice of lemon, and took this opportunity to have a sneaky peek at her. "There you go."

He sat on the edge of his desk, a position of relaxation. Francesca quickly but gracefully drank the water and her hot feeling began to subside. Tyler watched her, intrigued. He was mesmerised by the way she looked. Secretaries had come and gone but this young lady was not like them; she had a certain sophisticated glamour about her.

"Now then, Francesca, I'm not the type to do formal interviews, so tell me a bit about yourself, and feel free to ask me anything you want."

Francesca was amused by him, particularly by the manner in which he spoke down to her, the way he perched on the desk, and his silly grin, as if he was talking to a schoolgirl. *He had no idea.*

The uncomfortable sensation had gone. Now she felt in control. On a winning streak – she reeled off various small companies that she had worked for, added a bit of bullshit and flirtatiously giggled, whilst remembering to keep her skills to a minimum. If she had let on that she was more skilled than him in law, and could probably handle a computer better than anyone in his company, then he would wonder what the hell she was doing sitting in an interview with him. She wanted this job more than anything and, the way Tyler responded to her, she knew she had it in the bag. *Amazing,* she thought, *even an intelligent man like Tyler was sold.* It all paid off, and he offered her the position there and then.

She stood up to shake hands and thought for a second; *did secretaries shake hands?* Before she could change her mind, Tyler was there. He grabbed her hand and shook it. He acted as though he had just won a court case, but little did she know that he was just as keen to get her on board as she was.

Tyler had plans for Francesca, and he really couldn't give a hoot if she was good at her job or not. He just had one thing on his mind, but Francesca wasn't dumb and she knew of his intentions.

They negotiated salary, and she tested the water by asking far more than she thought most secretaries would earn, but he agreed. It was all in the fluttering of the eyelashes and the newfound lip pout. Tyler was putty in her hands.

He couldn't wait until she was to start work on Monday and decided to have a haircut, buy some new aftershave, and collect his best suits from the dry cleaners. He wanted this woman and planned how he would get her into bed.

Francesca felt lonely over the weekend. She missed the companionship of Kathy and the odd visit from Roberto or Mauricio. Even Tony, the driver-come-cook-come-cleaner, wasn't to see her again; he hadn't seen her new look either. She had become fond of him, with his silly jokes, but, although he pleaded he was as straight as they come, it was clear that he was too naïve when it came to female matters not to be gay.

Saturday, she shopped for a computer and by the afternoon she had it set up and already linked up to the internet.

Francesca decided to have a break and go for a jog. The house was situated in a perfect position. It was far enough away from any neighbours but close enough to town for work. The area was lovely to take a run, with plenty of greenery and huge trees. Just as she began to pace herself, she heard a commotion coming from the main road. As she turned the corner, she saw two white vans parked and four men trying desperately to capture what appeared at first glance to be a large dog. They were shouting and trying to surround the animal. Each man had a noose and the poor thing was obviously distressed. It had a wound on its back leg and was struggling to stand. As she came into view of the animal, it bolted and headed for her. Not knowing right away what it was, she froze.

"Don't move!" shouted the men.

Francesca looked into the dog's eyes and realised it was seriously injured. The very scruffy, large dog sat by her feet and bowed its head. On closer inspection, she saw deep lacerations on the dog's face and, before she had time to think, she bent down and stroked the trembling animal. He licked her hand and collapsed. The men rushed over and began tying the noose around its neck.

Francesca was horrified. "Get your hands off my dog!" Her voice was loud and demanding, to the surprise of the wardens.

The man bending over the dog stood up immediately. "Your dog, ma'am?"

The second man laughed. "You must be mistaken."

Francesca felt a little foolish. *Of course it wasn't hers.*

"This dog has been reported by this neighbourhood for over a week for causing mayhem, and we have to take it to the pound to be destroyed."

The second, bigger, guy was not so polite. "Listen to me; this isn't some friendly pooch that you can rescue off the streets. It's a goddamn dangerous animal."

Francesca was fuming; her temper was under control but she was not going to be spoken to like this by a couple of dog hunters.

"Listen to me, you fuckwit, this is my dog and I'm taking him home. I lost him ten days ago at my sister's across town, and now the poor thing has somehow found his way home, but I wasn't here so, if you don't mind, I will take what's mine and handle this from here."

The men looked the woman up and down and decided she wasn't a woman to fuck with. She was very firm and, with a well-to-do English accent, she could have been anyone. It was best to leave the situation alone. As they walked away, Francesca looked down at the trembling wreck that lay on the ground, obviously ready to die. When the vans were out of sight, she sat by his side and asked him in a very soft voice to try to muster the strength to walk home with her.

He didn't move.

She looked at the size of him and knew that she could not carry him, so she held his head and whispered again, "Please, my little friend, get up."

The dog struggled to his feet. Launa slowly but surely walked on, showing the dog she was by his side.

As they reached the house, the dog stopped at the doorstep and waited for Francesca to let him in. He wandered through to the lounge, flopped down, and fell asleep.

Francesca quickly fetched some water and slowly dribbled it into the side of the dog's mouth.

'*What the hell am I doing? I have no idea about dogs,*' she said to herself.

The dog came to and gained enough strength to lap up the water from a bowl.

Francesca called the vet and was surprised by his attitude. The dog wasn't registered and so he was reluctant to come out.

She panicked and called Kathy, but there was no answer. She was obviously on another sightseeing trip.

Francesca made the decision to nurse him herself. She felt over his body to see if he had any broken bones, but she didn't exactly know how to assess her new friend. The wounds were awful; *someone had cut this dog.* She went back to the kitchen and searched for some antiseptic. Luckily, the medicine cabinet was full. She grabbed some bandages and set about cleaning all the lacerations. Too weak to complain, he lay still. Francesca realised he had stopped trembling and his eyes were open.

She tried her hardest to bandage the dog's head, but it was difficult, with a big mouth and two large ears in the way.

Back in the kitchen, she scoured the cupboards for something suitable for this very sick dog to eat. *Nothing.* The cupboards were bare, but the fridge had a lovely fat steak. She was intending to have that for her own dinner, but his need was greater than hers was.

She pushed the steak through the mincer. It would be easier for him to eat that way if he had any energy at all.

She cooked the meat and took it into the lounge. He was still there, not moving, poor thing. His coat wasn't matted, just tangled in places. Francesca tried to work out what breed he was, but she hadn't seen a dog of this kind before. However, he did resemble a large snow-type dog – well, he was the size of one, but his nose was longer and his fur thinner.

She placed the meat on the floor by the fireplace and sat staring at her newfound friend.

She hoped he wouldn't turn and bite her.

As time ticked by, Francesca fell asleep in her armchair and, for two hours, the pair of them slept on. She was woken by something nudging her hand. Slowly she opened her eyes and saw the dog standing there. He looked so peaceful.

"Hello, my friend," she whispered, as she ran a finger gently over his nose. She then noticed he hadn't touched the meat.

She walked over to the dish.

"Here, boy," she called, patting her knees. He walked over to her and lunged into the bowl, devouring every morsel. This meant he probably was starving, and yet he still had manners and respect enough for his new owner to wait for her command.

She tried to be the best nurse for her new pet and so, as the vet wouldn't come to her, she went to the vet. She called a cab and headed to the clinic. The one thing she learned, living in America, was that money could buy you anything. The nearest veterinary surgery was closed, and so she had to go out of town, to a grotty hovel that was open until late.

What a place: a smelly clinic with a grubby receptionist and a vet with dirty fingernails.

"What can I do for you?" asked the disinterested vet.

"I need some painkillers for a large dog."

The vet was a fat man with yellow teeth and bad breath. "Well, I can't give you any medication without seeing your dog."

"Right, how much does it cost for a consultation?"

"One hundred dollars," he spat back. It had been a long day for him and he was looking forward to a stiff drink or ten.

Francesca knew he was lying. *No way did they charge a hundred dollars*, but she was desperate to help her dog.

"There you are." She pulled out a wedge of notes and slapped it on the desk. "Now, I need some painkillers for my dog."

The vet looked at the money and decided not to argue. "Okay. Is there anything else you need?"

Francesca realised she had no idea what she needed. With a bewildered expression on her face, she suddenly lost her confidence.

The vet asked, "What is wrong with your dog?"

"He has some deep cuts on his face and legs," she replied and then paused, not sure of herself. "He is a rescue dog, so I'm not sure what's wrong with him."

The vet looked Francesca up and down and decided she was a kind woman to rescue a dog.

"You will need some antibiotics, some anti-inflammatories and possibly some flea drops."

Francesca nodded. "How much?"

The vet waved his hands. "It's okay."

Francesca thanked him, grabbed the paper bag and returned home.

The dog was still there, lying by the fireplace in the lounge, just where she left him.

She was amazed how easy he was to handle. He took the pills without a fuss and lay down again.

"Well, my friend, we are two damaged souls on the road to recovery. I'm going to call you Bear, because you are so strong and yet so soft."

Chapter Ten

Over the weekend, Francesca found herself surprisingly busy, looking after her newfound friend. His recovery would be slow but the look in his eyes told a story of determination.

When Monday morning arrived, she was confident that Bear would be safe left alone for the day. The small room adjoining the kitchen had access to the garden – perfect for him to rest but enough space not to be too cramped. She could leave the back door open and lock the kitchen door so the house would be safe from intruders, but it also allowed Bear to be comfortable and take a walk outside if he needed to relieve himself.

The New York streets in rush hour were far busier than those in London. The bumper-to-bumper taxis hooted for no reason other than to make a noise. For a person unused to city life in down town New York, the streets were a hive of activity, with high energy and purpose. Hotdog stands were on every corner of every sidewalk, people rushing from cabs to tall buildings carrying briefcases and papers, casual workers with hard hats, and steaming cups of coffee – *Welcome to New York, and your first day at work as a secretary*, she thought.

She sat back, enjoying the ride as New York daily business sped past her. It was the first time she had seen New York with her eyes fully open. *Always in her previous working life she had rushed around on a mission, but not today.* Savouring the experience and absorbing her surroundings, she relaxed in the confines of the taxi as she watched the world go by.

The offices of Bradshaw and Enright were markedly busier this Monday morning, which took her by surprise. When she had been for her interview the week before, it was pleasantly quiet, but today the foyer resembled Piccadilly Circus.

The receptionist recognised her at once and, with the same huge smile, offered to show Francesca to her new office. A different room from where she had been interviewed, it was much bigger with two desks and two large, black leather sofas.

Francesca looked at the receptionist with a puzzled expression.

"I thought you would be surprised," she said, still grinning from ear-to-ear. "Tyler, I mean Mr Enright, said to get yourself comfortable in his office as he needed a PA rather than a secretary and, well, since it means working more closely together, he has had the rooms changed, and so here you are." She threw her hands in the air and smiled.

Francesca was thrilled. *This would make her job a doddle.* All the files were neatly aligned along one wall and a computer sat on his desk. She could access everything, every scrap of information, and without her motives ever being in question.

"Thank you, uh..." Francesca tried to read the receptionist's nametag.

"Oh, it's Melanie, but you can call me Mel – and if you're stuck for lunch, just give me a call and we can go together."

As a lawyer, the receptionists and secretaries never dreamt of asking her to join them for lunch – except Susan. As a secretary, it was different.

Francesca nodded. She thought it a good idea if she fitted in with the admin staff and talked girly talk, just to keep the Enrights off the scent.

She wandered around the office, looking at pictures, photos and general decoration. She was determined to be properly prepared, in order to take on her project seriously and find out everything about her new boss, Tyler Enright. She needed to know all there was to learn from the contents of his office.

There was what looked like a coat of arms in blue and red on a small plaque, on top of the filing cabinet. Francesca picked it up recognising it as the plaque found in all the homes of the Enrights, including her husband's.

The door opened, which startled her. Instantly, she turned around to see Tyler standing there, looking pleased with himself. "Good morning, Francesca. Good to see you are nice and early." He winked.

Francesca looked at her watch. She wasn't early, he was late.

"So then, let's start by having a cup of coffee."

She eyed him up and down and grinned to herself. *So obvious that he had made a special effort*; his hair was cut into a style much suited to a younger man. He wore an expensive suit with diamond cufflinks and not even a crease in his new shoes. The winking irritated her, *Who did he think he was?* She imagined him wearing a huge gold medallion under his shirt.

"Where do I go for coffee?" asked Francesca sweetly, as she looked around the room searching for the refreshments table.

"Allow me," answered Tyler, again with a wink.

He walked over to a large wall cabinet, where he pulled the door open, to reveal a bar with a water cooler and a coffee machine. Underneath was displayed an extensive array of alcoholic drinks.

He poured two cups of coffee, placed them on his desk, and gestured for her to sit beside him.

"I am assuming Melanie explained the change in arrangements. I decided it's more appropriate, as we will be working in the same room and, having regarded your experience, it seemed pointless to have you sit in the corridor answering calls and managing my diary." He smiled again, pleased with himself.

"That is wonderful, Mr Enright. I will certainly try my best to be an efficient personal assistant," said Francesca in her sweetest voice. All the while, she was thinking that this performance could win an Oscar.

He winked again.

Watching Tyler was a constant reminder of her husband. The way he walked and all his mannerisms were identical. However, she tried not to hate Tyler — *after all, he wasn't Charles, and for all she knew, the whole issue of the fax may well be a misunderstanding*. She tried to treat him as a client and not judge him just yet. The key to success was to stay calm and gather as much information as possible on exactly what Tyler was up to, get it out of the office and then study it at home.

Tyler complimented Francesca without words. He smiled approvingly every time she looked his way and she could feel his eyes on her when she worked.

He admired the way she answered the phone and addressed the caller. He got aroused when she twiddled the telephone coil round her fingers.

She had his diary in front of her, and it was her job to manage the meetings and appointments. He had explained that his client was the Luciani family — he worked only for them.

Francesca acted surprised. "Mr Enright, I am somewhat confused. Only, I have worked for many lawyers and they have many clients, hundreds in fact. Some are more important than others, but never just one."

Tyler laughed; he wanted to act the big man in front of her by showing how important he was, in the scheme of things.

"Francesca, the Lucianis are a very large concern and, with their type of business, it takes a certain type of lawyer to protect their assets, and that man is me." He put his shoulders back and puffed out his chest.

Flash twat, she thought.

Francesca played with her pen and tried to act dumb. "So what is their business?"

His total confidence in his ability, his smug disparaging view of his employer, together with Launa's obvious charm and beauty, lowered his guard on a professional level. Launa wasn't serious, the flirting was an act, but he fell for it hook, line and sinker.

He walked over to her desk and bent down to whisper in her ear. "If I tell you, I'd have to kill you."

She enjoyed playing the game. "Well, you'll have to kill me then because I'm sure, working in this office with me by your side, I will have a pretty good idea."

Tyler laughed, probably more than he should have.

As he strolled back to his desk, he agreed that, as his right hand woman, she should become familiar with his client's business.

"The main businesses are concrete, haulage, waste disposal, construction and shipping. Oh, and also casinos." Tyler looked at Francesca's expression; he expected her to be impressed.

She sat, amazed, but for her own reasons, and not because she thought he was trying to massage his own ego. She had guessed that Roberto was very wealthy, but had no idea to what extent.

"Shit, that's a lot," she gasped. "And so diverse. I mean, it's unusual to have businesses that have no relation to each other."

Tyler nodded enthusiastically. "They are companies that make the city go around, and I ensure they are all legal and above board. I also decide whether or not they are a good investment."

Francesca frowned. "What do you mean, above board? Are these businesses illegal?" She tried to sound innocent but realised maybe she was asking too many unnecessary questions.

"Of course they are legal. What I mean is, contracts concerning any large business, contract of employment, ownership revenue, that sort of thing."

Francesca felt stupid; it was the idea of Roberto being part of the mafia again, and for a moment, she forgot where she was. *How daft; of course company lawyers make all transactions legal.* She had studied company law but favoured criminal law and so, whilst at university, she had decided to pursue that career.

Tyler tried to impress Launa by admission of his own self-importance. "I am their advisor, and nothing goes ahead without my say so."

Francesca wide eyed, to add to the role-play, replied, "They must trust you, then!"

"Trust? Without me they wouldn't have half of their businesses. I have built them up from nothing," he revealed. His tone was firm and the look on his face said it all. *Tyler was a bitter man.*

The office became busy, men came and went. They all had New York accents, dressed in smart suits, and looked Italian. One very short fat man, with a pin-stripe suit and a fat cigar protruding from his mouth, was accompanied by a tall meathead who kept his hand inside his jacket the whole time the short guy was talking business. Francesca kept looking over expecting a gun to be pulled any moment. At first he argued with Tyler and then, after Tyler grabbed the papers that the fat guy was holding and threw them in the bin, the fat guy nodded, kissed Tyler on each cheek and left.

Francesca was surprised to hear Tyler speak Italian and to receive so much respect – *it was as if he was a godfather or something*. Every time clients left, he looked over at Francesca and winked. Of course, she pretended not to notice.

By the end of her day's work, she had come to some serious conclusions. Tyler was not as dumb and stupid as she thought, and the men that visited the office that day respected him. Whatever he said, they agreed and not one of them left the office in dispute. Such a different world: Sicilians, pin stripe suites, gold watches, and not a hand shake but a kiss. Her mind running away with her, she reeled it back in. She concluded that they were businessmen within a Sicilian community and were culturally different. In fact, it was a breath of fresh air, so very far removed from the English legal system, full of pomp and ceremony.

Before she went home, she offered to put away the files that piled up beside Tyler's desk.

"No, it's fine, I'll put those away."

"Actually, Mr Enright, I can't find the key to the filing cabinets – it's not in my drawer."

Tyler glared at Francesca; it was the first disdaining look he had given her.

"Listen to me. You do not need to go into the filing cabinets. That is my territory; your job is to look after my diary." As soon as he had spat the words out, he realised he had been harsh and jeopardised his chances with her.

Like water off a duck's back, Francesca shrugged her shoulders. "No problem, Mr Enright, I'll see you tomorrow. Have a great evening."

Before he had a chance to gather his thoughts, she was gone.

*

Tyler sat back with his feet on his desk and savoured his well-earned brandy. *Business today was good.* He had managed to convince the Fredo brothers to take a shipment from his other client, Carlos Enrico, otherwise known as Charles Enright, his own brother.

The Fredo brothers had worked for Roberto for twenty years and the loyalty they had given him had been rewarded with their promotion to running the shipping business. Their father had also worked for Roberto in the early days and had been the go-between with the Onassis family.

Roberto's shipping company began with two cargo vessels back in 1951. The alcohol business had dried up since they lifted the Prohibition. Luckily for him, a Sicilian family, the Bioccis, had tied all their revenue up in alcohol, well-known for their serious amount of cash flow. Having no cash flow would leave a Sicilian family powerless and desperate.

One of the Biocci sons wanted to break into shipping so, behind his father's back, he went to Roberto and borrowed the money to buy two ships. Young Frankie, in his naivety, had blackmailed the ship owner with information that he had heard regarding the shipping owners' double-cross over a deal with another Italian family. Afraid for his life, the ship owner sold his two ships for a fraction of the price.

When the deal was done and Frankie Biocci went to his father to break the news, his father broke his nose. The shipping owner was a friend of Frankie's father and the company imported wares from overseas. Now the ships belonged to his son. With no money to invest in goods to import, the vessels were useless.

Frankie's father, Orlando Biocci, had seen the mess his own business was in and was outraged by his son's stupidity, but even angrier that he had disrespected his own father by going to another Sicilian man for money. Orlando had known the businessman for years and they had a mutual respect. However, Frankie was very naïve about these relationships. When the demand for drink had gone, the Bioccis could not repay the loan. The market had crashed, and the ships were handed over to Roberto. His family disowned Frankie, who had made the biggest mistake of all, by undermining his father and his father's consigliore.

Roberto's business, however, was also in danger of failing. His profits had begun to fall, and he needed to get on the ladder again. Although he had built a reputation, without a cash flow, he would be nothing.

Luckily, the shipping was very lucrative. He already had the local politicians in his back pocket, so they turned a blind eye to the cargo from Cuba.

He made enough money through the concrete business and through contracts to supply the building work after the Depression. Once the Depression was long over, the money he made he poured into the businesses, partly to hide the not-so-legal rackets. He took advice from a very good source and one who he never revealed to a living soul – *his dear and beloved wife*. She showed him the future, and they would sit for hours in bed at night looking at the papers. She knew the country could not be serviced without waste disposal, construction and, of course, entertainment – in other words, casinos.

When his wife died, part of Roberto died too, so he lived each day for his family. In many ways, he had become softer – very different from the young man that left Sicily and started his new life in New York. Not that he was any less respected. He was more inclined to think before he jumped.

Fewer men died these days.

Years after she passed away, Roberto watched as his investments made more and more money and looked to the sky. '*You were right, my Angelina.*'

She had advised in safe investments – businesses that the country couldn't do without.

He could still hear her voice. '*Roberto, people in America will always make garbage and they want their cities to be clean. There will always be a need, just like the old days, eh; there was always a need for the drink.*' All the years she had lived in America, she still could not speak English, and so her gentle Italian voice sang in his ears. He heard her late at night, whispering his name, before he drifted into sleep.

*

Francesca asked the cabbie to go to a bookshop on the way home. Once inside, she easily found the section on languages. 'Speak Italian in a week' was the title of the first book she picked up. By the time she put it back on the shelf, a shop assistant appeared.

"Good afternoon, ma'am, how can I help you?" A young lad in his early twenties, eager to please, stood in front of her, grinning.

"Oh, well, I'm looking for a book on speaking Italian, but not for a holiday trip. I want to learn to speak Italian fluently."

The young man was taken aback by her accent. "Are you from England, ma'am?"

Francesca nodded.

"Come with me, I have something better than a book. We have just taken on a series of tapes and, I must say, they are excellent. In fact, I'm almost fluent in French."

Francesca decided to tease the young man and asked in French, "I can already speak good French, but I want to know how to ask a handsome Italian if he fancies a fuck."

The assistant had obviously learned a great deal from the tapes and answered in a cheeky English accent. "Just say it in English because you're sure to get him where you want him."

Francesca laughed. "Cheeky."

She bought the complete set and set off home.

*

Bear was just where she had left him, but he was definitely stronger. He got to his feet and greeted her, and she gave him a treat and walked around the garden with him. The garden comprised two acres and was fenced off for safety with trees dotted here and there. It definitely was not typical of an American garden at all, but very much like the English gardens with flowerbeds and evergreen shrubs, a fishpond and a pergola. Bear walked slowly but with more control. She threw a ball to see if he would fetch it but he gazed up at her as if she was mad. She tried a stick and again he showed no interest. However, as she ran herself to fetch the ball, he ran too. He was by her side, and that's just where he wanted to be.

After making herself a cup of tea, she returned to the garden, got herself comfortable, and put on the first of the Italian tapes. The teacher on the tape would say a word and then Francesca repeated it. At first, Francesca was more amused by the dog. He looked at the tape player and then at Francesca, as if he knew it was her turn to speak.

She found the lesson easy and enjoyed exaggerating the accent. After her evening meal, she decided to report to Roberto on how her first day had gone.

She dialled the secret number – a phone that was only for her, Mauricio and Sergio.

"Hello."

"Roberto, good evening. It's me, Francesca."

"How are you, my daughter?" His voice was soft.

"I am very well. There are just some things I need to clarify with you."

"Go ahead," he replied.

"First of all, if Tyler is your lawyer does he know you own this house that I am living in? Only, he has my address."

Roberto laughed. "You are quick. Don't worry, there are many things Tyler does not know about, including the house. Listen to me, I will not put you in unnecessary danger, and please remember this, you do not have to go through with anything – remember, you owe me nothing."

Francesca was not going to quit; she enjoyed the thrill.

"Also, I do not know how much information is relevant at this stage. I think most of the material I need is in his filing cabinets, which – I might add – he keeps closely guarded. And one more thing, I cannot access his computer files because he has a password, so I'm afraid I'm going to need some help."

"What do you need?" His voice was so calming.

"A serious distraction."

They put a plan into place for the following week but, in the meantime, Roberto wanted her to keep an eye on who went into the office.

Before she said goodbye, she remembered one of the meetings.

"Roberto, I remember the two men that had a long meeting with Tyler today. The Fredo Brothers."

"What were they doing there? They have not discussed any business with me."

"I couldn't understand the conversation, it was in Italian, but they mentioned a Carlos Enrico."

There was a silence.

"I do not know of any Enricos. Please, Francesca, keep your ears and eyes open and call me every night, because what you may not understand, I may. Goodnight, and be safe."

Before she could reply, he was gone. She wanted to tell him she was learning Italian but maybe it would be best to surprise him.

Before the week was over, Francesca got to grips with the language, but she was not fluent enough, not by a long way. So, when she discovered there was a meeting booked in the diary with the Fredo brothers, she decided to invest in a tape recorder, a slim model that was easily concealable and didn't make a whirring sound when taping. The recording time was four hours, and the meeting was arranged for nine o'clock. *Perfect,* she thought.

The tape would be on record before Tyler arrived, so she wouldn't have to fumble around in her bag and draw attention. Friday, the day of the Fredo meeting, she decided to dress differently. She wore trousers and a plain polo neck jumper, just to stop the glances from Tyler. He was forever ogling her, and she needed to be invisible. Her bag had to remain open to pick up the voices.

Tyler arrived just before the Fredos and seemed flustered. He poured himself a coffee and gulped it back, even before he said good morning to Francesca.

The Fredos arrived a while later. They sat opposite, looking relaxed. One of them pointed to Francesca and spoke in Italian. Tyler waved his hand and replied in Italian.

Francesca wasn't frustrated this time by her lack of understanding of the Italian language; she had her new toy.

After ten minutes or so, she walked over to Tyler's desk and offered refreshments. Gino Fredo, the older brother, a fat man with a bald head, spoke up first. "Yeah, I'll have hot chocolate and a doughnut if you've got any."

The other brother, Bobby Fredo, smiled nicely and asked for a black coffee, no sugar, no doughnuts. He was the healthy one; he still had a full head of hair and possibly a six-pack under his trim black suit.

Francesca tried to see the paperwork on the desk, but too many eyes were on her.

The meeting went on for two hours and it seemed that Tyler was uncomfortable. He ran his fingers through his hair and kept pulling out a handkerchief from his pocket to wipe his brow. His nervousness was clear when he offered the Fredos a brandy – it was only eleven o'clock.

Francesca left the office at twelve to use the bathroom and carefully locked away the tape.

*

At last she was in her own home, with the tapes safely in her hand and Tyler none the wiser.

Roberto was pleased with her job today and sent over a car to pick up the tape and deliver a huge bunch of flowers.

Saturday, Roberto had Sergio pick her up to take her to a meeting place. It was another one of his secret properties, kept away from even his closest friends; only his family knew of it.

Sergio was dressed very casually in a pair of Levis and a plaid shirt, and he wore glasses; he looked very different from the first meeting.

He greeted her with a warm smile and a gentle kiss on the cheek. She wondered if the kiss had lingered or whether she'd imagined it.

Quickly, she jumped in the car and, with very few words spoken, they headed up the highway towards Roberto's place.

"Francesca, it's good to have you on board. I know we haven't really spent much time together but my family have told me so much about you that I feel I know you. So, if I seem familiar with you at times, please do not think of me as being rude, just family." His voice was soft and smooth, unlike Mauricio, who was excitable most of the time.

Francesca smiled. "It's good to be part of your family, Sergio."

They drove to a secret location. She was intrigued and astounded by the amount of grand properties Roberto owned.

Turning off the highway, there was a large apartment complex, beautifully set in ornamental gardens. Sergio drove to an underground car park and looked back to see if anyone was following.

He hurried Francesca into the lift. They got out on the third floor and entered a corridor which was absolutely beautiful, with gold plaster cherubs protruding from the ceilings, and deep burgundy flock wallpaper decorating the walls.

Yet again, the apartment was lavish. Roberto got to his feet and greeted Francesca with a kiss to both cheeks followed by Mauricio.

Gathered around a white and gold marble table, Roberto offered everyone a drink, and each took a glass and drank.

"My family, look at you, you're so young and healthy." The three sat in silence, waiting.

"I am older than you, I am wiser, but quicker, I am not." He paused and took another mouthful of brandy. "It appears that we do have a serious problem with our lawyer."

Both Mauricio and Sergio looked at Francesca, who shrugged her shoulders. She was just as much in the dark as they were.

"Francesca gave me a tape with a conversation between the Fredos and Tyler."

Mauricio's eyes widened.

"I have always considered myself a fair man and when my own lawyer, the man I trusted with my life with, is undermining me, well, I want to know why." He shook his head and tutted.

"Father, you do not need to know why. Just let me deal with him."

Roberto leaned back on his chair and paused for a while.

"Tell me, what is the most powerful possession?" Roberto made a hand gesture for all three of them to respond.

Sergio smiled. "Money. Money is power."

Roberto nodded.

Mauricio laughed. "No, it's not. A gun is power; no one wants to argue when they have a gun shoved up their ass." He looked to his father for an approving nod, but he didn't receive one.

"Francesca, what do you think?" Roberto smiled. He knew she would have the answer.

"Knowledge is power," she replied.

"You see, knowledge is power. Without it, you have nothing." As Mauricio went to speak, he put his hands up in objection. "Listen, I have not finished. Tyler is up to no good behind my back. We knew that anyway, and now we have knowledge about how he proposes to do that, but…" He banged his fists on the table. "I need to fucking know why."

Mauricio resigned himself to the fact that he couldn't resolve this problem with a shotgun. He would have to bide his time and wait for the answers to come.

As if Roberto had read Mauricio's mind, he went on. "I understand your frustration, my son, but without the full facts we do not know if there is more to come. This name, Carlos Enrico, I have never heard of him. I have made enquiries, but the name is unknown."

Mauricio asked to listen to the tape and Sergio nodded. "It may give us some clues."

They played the tape and the anger was displayed very clearly on Mauricio and Sergio's faces. "The fucking bastard – and the Fredos. What in God's name did they think they were doing, going behind your back?" shouted Mauricio. "Have they no fucking honour?"

Roberto stood up. "Sit, my son. You did not listen properly to the tape. The Fredos believe Tyler called them in on my behalf. Look, I do not bother the Fredos for months. They work well, they keep the business running, I make lots of money and any issues they deal with Tyler. So now, the Fredos think this is my idea and why would they argue?"

"Father, are you going to tell them now? Or do we wait?"

"We wait, but when the time is right we go in and stop this shipment."

Francesca felt left out. She still didn't understand the conversation on the tape as her Italian was still not fluent.

Roberto looked at her and realised that she wasn't in the picture. He very quickly translated the conversation, and she felt in a better position to comment. "Tyler has asked the Fredos to pick up a shipment from a man called Enrico and bring it back here. I often instruct Tyler to organise shipments from various places but I didn't organise this, you understand."

Francesca nodded.

Her skills as a barrister coming into play, she stood up and walked to the window, giving this latest information some thought. "I think the best thing I can do right now is to find out who Carlos Enrico is and when the transaction is to take place. If you can manage it, I would have Tyler followed too, because Carlos Enrico hasn't been to the office, and he has not spoken with him on the phone." When she turned around, all three were staring at her. Sergio shot a look in Roberto's direction. *Never before had anyone ever dared to tell Roberto what to do.* Roberto himself gave direction and, if challenged, then a pat on their left shoulder meant death, and a gentle slap on the left cheek signalled a beating.

Mauricio felt for Francesca; *she didn't know the rules and why should she, her world was so different from his.* His way of life was based on honour and respect. The only men who could gently challenge his father and get away with it was himself and Sergio but, once he raised his hand, they shut their mouths.

Roberto nodded. "Francesca, you are on the same road as me. I wanted to ask you if you remember any visits by Enrico, but I see you have already thought of that." He gulped back another brandy and cleared his throat. "It is very clear to me that you are going to be my eyes and ears around Tyler, and so I want you to understand that Tyler is not a kind man, and can be dangerous. If you think he has uncovered your position, get out of the office and head here."

Roberto surprised Mauricio and Sergio. He was talking to Francesca as if she were his advisor.

Mauricio didn't mind and Sergio was relieved. Sergio loved being so high up in his uncle's business, but he never had the stomach for the aggression that needed to go with it. He enjoyed running the casinos, making lots of money, and leaving the heavy mob to deal with the unpaid debts and any unpleasant characters.

Mauricio, however, was completely different. He had the code of honour embedded in his head, so he was very quick to take down any force that got in the way of his family or his business.

Although Mauricio was the tougher of the two, they both took the oath of Omerta so neither ever spoke with the authorities.

After Sergio and Francesca left, Roberto sat with his son.

"Father, I am interested to understand why you have allowed a woman to get involved in matters that have never concerned women. How will it look with the other families?"

Roberto knew this would concern Mauricio, not because of Francesca's lack of knowledge but her lack of understanding of their world. "My son, the old days have gone. Honour still exists, maybe in the form of fear and greed, but times have changed. Never in our history, or the history of our families in Sicily, have women ever been invited to our business. They gave us love, good food and, if lucky, a son." He gestured to Mauricio with a smile of pride. "But, my son, never underestimate the power of a woman."

"Father, the other families had advisors, men who understood the business, but never a woman — never. And look at you, father, you trusted no one, you were your own consigliore."

Roberto smiled as he cupped his son's face with his hands. "My child, did you never realise who my advisor was?"

Mauricio hung his head in shame. He had seen the sadness in his father's eyes, so how could he have not known? His mother had advised him all his life.

"I am sorry, Pa. I know Francesca will advise you well, but I worry for her too. She doesn't even know how our family works." He almost cried.

"Then, as her new brother, you will teach her."

Chapter Eleven

Francesca got to know Tyler very well over her short time of employment. She soon established that he was a sucker for sexy women and realised that his eyes followed her every movement. Notwithstanding the fact that he had a good legal and business head on his shoulders, he had no idea she worked for Roberto. Francesca's main concern right now was that he still didn't trust her with the files or his computer, which was disappointing but not unexpected. With the plan in place for Friday afternoon, she prayed that, all would go well; having come this far she wanted more than anything to get it right.

Francesca sat opposite Tyler, typing up dictated letters. She was surprised that, given the amount of flirting he did, it hadn't led to an offer of a date or at least a lunchtime drink. What she had not realised was the scheme that Tyler had planned, to put the Lucianis behind bars, was dangerous and risky. Therefore, although she was a small and delightful distraction, right now his mind was on the possible consequences of his actions. If he made one tiny mistake, then his life would be over, but not without hideous torture first. He had seen first-hand what Roberto's men were capable of – *with a nod from Roberto, Tyler's fate would be gruesome.*

Life as a lawyer for one of the most well-known business people in New York was easy. He was paid more than his worth and had the protection of the Lucianis. He only had to keep all the businesses above board and Roberto happy. However, his long-term goal was to give the Lucianis a false sense of security, to lure them into what they believed to be a safe lawyer-client relationship.

Francesca was dressed to impress, with a short skirt and soft, black, shiny stockings that made her legs appear even longer than they were, and she wore a white fitted blouse with buttons undone to reveal an ample bosom. Tyler noticed this, of course, as soon as she walked through the door. A connoisseur of anything under the age of twenty-five, with looks resembling Cindi Crawford, he was struggling to concentrate on his job. He was in the office before her today which, after two weeks, took her by surprise.

"Well, good morning, Francesca." He dragged out the sound of her name. "You look rather glamorous, I must say."

Francesca grinned – it was working.

Most of the morning she spent flirting, gently swinging on the swivel chair, with her legs crossed, and chewing on her pencil.

Tyler tried to concentrate. He needed to put the finer details in place, but she looked lovelier than ever. The sun streamed in through the huge windows and lit Francesca like an angel. He was tempted to shut the office, whisk her away to a plush hotel room, and spend the afternoon enjoying her body.

Dead on twelve o'clock, he got up and walked over to Francesca's desk, where he perched himself on the edge. Excited that her distraction worked, she was nervous at the same time, unsure how far he would go. He leaned towards her and she pushed herself further back into her chair. Suddenly, the door flew open and Tyler jumped to his feet to face a very excitable Sergio.

"Tyler, quick, quick," Sergio rushed over, grabbing him by the arm, much to Tyler's shock – horror in fact.

"All right, Sergio, slow down," said Tyler, trying to remove Sergio's arm.

"You have to come now, this cannot wait." Sergio's voice went so deep and firm that she barely recognised him. Unease crossed Tyler's face, and at that point Francesca realised just how much respect Tyler had for the Lucianis. There was no more to be said by Tyler; he left with Sergio, and Francesca sighed with relief.

*

She looked out of the window to see the two men get into the car and drive away.

Perfect, the plan went well. She knew she would have three hours exactly to search all the files.

The computer was still on and accessible because he'd had no time to close it down or even to lock his side draw which contained the key to the cabinets. Just as she accessed his personal files, the door opened. She froze, but then a huge wave of relief went through her body as she saw Mauricio, with all his charm, standing just outside the room.

"Need a hand, Fran?" he smiled, quickly entering the room and locking the door behind him.

She grabbed the keys from the drawer and threw them to him. "Yeah, I do. Go through the files and anything that looks odd, or out of place, or you don't understand, show me."

"Sure." Mauricio was like a child on Christmas Eve. As he went through each file, he would make some comments like, 'Fuck, I didn't know I owned a jewellery shop on Madison Square or 'Oh, Pops, you spoil me' and 'The fucking Chief of Police is living in a house owned by Sergio'.

Francesca laughed. "Maury, just concentrate and keep your voice low. I don't want him to find out."

He slammed the first filing cabinet shut. "When we get to the bottom of this, that mother's rat will pay, and I'm gonna fuck him up like never before has a man been fucked up," he growled.

"Maury, shut up. You'll blow it."

Mauricio went silent and returned to the second cabinet.

Francesca was winning; all of Tyler's files were contained in four main folders. Without even opening them, she emailed them to herself, like taking candy from a baby – but in this case, it was like snatching the life from under him. She checked his emails and copied them too and, after deleting the sent messages and double-checking there were no other files hidden, she had completed job number one. Now the computer had to be left alone to go over to hibernate. If Tyler were to see it active, he would know she had been looking.

"Right, Maury, have you found anything?"

He shook his head.

She started on the last cabinet, but everything seemed to be normal. It was full of title deeds and tax documents. *In fact, it was exactly the sort of stuff you would find in any lawyer's filing cabinets.*

Two hours had passed, and they were both feeling frustrated.

"Look, Maury, let's think about this. If you wanted to hide something, where would you put it?"

"Me? I'd fucking bury it."

Francesca sighed. "No, no. Listen, there is something in these cabinets that he doesn't want even me to see, and I'm his fucking PA."

Mauricio laughed. "Fucking PA you say." He emphasised the word fucking.

"Mauricio, stop it. Concentrate, will you?"

His tone changed. "Well, you wouldn't put it in any of the files, would you? Any one of us can come in here and demand access. My father owns this building, for Christ's sake."

Francesca nodded.

Slowly, she opened the filing cabinet again and removed all the floating files. "Mauricio, look." She pointed to the space between the bottom draw and the base of the unit. "Quick, we haven't got much time. Take out all the files from the first cabinet, but make sure they go back in exactly the same way."

They hurriedly got to work.

"Bingo!" she shouted.

"Hey, you, keep your voice down." Mauricio loved to tease her.

She pulled a leather pouch, roughly A4 size. It looked a hundred years old. Carefully, she removed the contents and stared at the old parchments. The contracts were written in old English and French. Attached to the paper work was a large map, folded into four quarters. She frowned, confused by the age of the papers and the content.

"What is it, Fran?"

"I have absolutely no idea."

"So now what, smart ass?"

"Shut up a minute and let me think… I am going to take a photocopy and figure this out at home. Let's just put this office back exactly as we found it and pray I have all I need."

Within a few minutes, they were done. Mauricio was surprised at her quick thinking, as she pulled out some Plasticine and took imprints of the filing cabinet key.

"Take these with you." She gave him the photocopies and the imprint.

Just as he unlocked the door to leave, Tyler was there, looking flustered.

Francesca felt sick. *She had been caught*; everything moved in slow motion.

To her surprise, Mauricio handled it all well.

"Hi, Tyler." His voice was calm.

Tyler looked shocked to see him. "Well, hello, Mauricio. What, uh, brings you here?" he asked, his voice faltering.

Francesca was now beginning to see clearly the relationship between Tyler and the family. He was genuinely afraid.

"I was looking for Sergio and I was told he was here with you." Mauricio held up the photocopies with the blank side facing Tyler. "I need him to look over some stuff for me."

Tyler looked at Francesca and then back to Mauricio.

"Well, he has just this minute dropped me off. We had a business lunch."

Mauricio, knowing that Tyler was trying to double-cross his family, decided to wind him up.

"I see, so Tyler and Sergio are doing business behind my back, eh? Wanna tell me about it?" Mauricio looked menacing.

Tyler stepped back, his face looking a little white. "No, no, Mauricio. It wasn't nothing like that, eh. He just wanted to close a deal on another casino, and he said he would meet with you later to go over the plans. He only wanted me to check the licensing details. You know, all that kind of stuff." Tyler's words were falling on top of each other, he was so nervous.

"And that takes you fucking three hours?"

Tyler frowned. "What, have you been waiting here all that time?"

"Don't be a stupid punk. Rudi at the club told me he left at a quarter to twelve and it is now three o'clock. What, you think I'm thick, I can't count?"

Tyler's mouth went visibly dry. "No, Mauricio, I don't think that at all – hey, would you like a drink with me while you're here? Maybe I could look over the papers for you?"

Tyler gestured for Mauricio to sit down.

"No, I'm busy." Before Mauricio left, he whispered in Tyler's ear, "You sure have a fucking horny secretary. If you don't want to fuck her, let me know, eh? I'll give her a go."

Wanker, thought Tyler.

Relieved that Mauricio was more jovial and light-hearted, Tyler smiled. *The worst thing he could do at this stage was to upset Mauricio; he was a loose cannon and would fuck you up as soon as he looked at you.* Once Mauricio was out of the office, Tyler hurried to the drinks cabinet and poured a large brandy. Unable to turn and face Francesca right now, he knocked back a double measure. He was embarrassed by Mauricio, he hated how they humiliated him in public. It wasn't a new issue. Being the most powerful Sicilian family in New York gave them the respect, and no one would argue or ever think of going against them. Lucianis main men, including himself, had witnessed serious beatings, torture and death. It was their way of keeping control. The consequences were harsh, but the rewards for doing a good job were high. Despite it all, he still despised the fact that they could make him look so irrelevant, so small, especially in front of a woman. He had wanted Francesca to see him as the big shot, highly respected in the business world. Women loved men in power. In the old days, back in England, he had women falling all over him – for the expensive cars and classy restaurants. But it all changed when he was sent to the States to secure a job within the Luciani Empire. Of course, his family had promised him the biggest chunk of the pie when the setup was a success, and Roberto and Mauricio were behind bars.

Tyler remembered the computer being left open and quickly rushed to his desk. Everything was how it should be, so he sent Francesca home early. He wanted to look in the cabinet to make dead sure that nothing had been disturbed. He'd had a close shave two weeks previously when a fax was sent to the wrong office but, luckily, he managed to get it back before Roberto had found it, or so he thought.

His family had insisted on keeping the original deeds, but he openly explained that it was for his own security and, since he was responsible for the riskiest part of the job, he needed to have them in his possession for insurance purposes. In reality, he did not trust his brothers, William or Charles, and he certainly had reservations about his nephew, Charles Junior. He was a strange child, a disturbed teenager, and a very dangerous adult. He never forgot the evilness in the child when he tried to set light to his puppy for messing on his blanket. Luckily, Tyler intervened in time and removed the pup to a safe home. As a teenager, Charles was intelligent but ruled by his inappropriate emotions towards his girlfriends, hence they didn't hang around for long and were lucky if they could escape his control without a bruise or two. Tyler had blamed his brother and his father for their infallible attitude and sheer hatred towards women. It wasn't that they believed in Victorian values, where women should be silent and their place was in the kitchen; it was much more extreme than that. They treated the opposite sex as lower class, an insignificant throw-away object, to be used and abused. Their own mother, once a beautiful serene woman, had become a bumbling wreck. The sons were urged by their father to treat her as an idiot. They grew up having no respect for their mother and she eventually went into an asylum, where she died alone.

The Enrights had already messed up once. They had Mauricio banged to rights, the setup had been perfect, and no lawyer in the land should have been able to secure a non-guilty verdict. However, William had placed too much trust in Launa to execute his exact instructions. He had assumed that, as her father-in-law, she would do as he demanded, but that was not the case. Behind his back, she busied herself, fought tooth and nail for his release, and won. But, luckily for Tyler, the outcome gave him more credibility. He had been ready to flee the country as soon as Mauricio was sentenced, but Roberto came bounding into the office and, throwing his arms around Tyler, he thanked him for recommending the best English lawyer to free his son. So Tyler realised he was in the right place at exactly the right time. Even so, now they only had four months to ensure Mauricio's incarceration. The contract would be read on first of January and it was late September. It was now up to him to pull off the next plan, *God help him if he got caught.*

Francesca was so relieved that today was over. She had no idea what the files contained, but the early finish would give her plenty of time to get some answers by tomorrow.

Mauricio had dropped the copies through her letterbox. He'd had a quick peek himself but made no sense of it.

She gathered all the office information up, walked into the living room, and put everything down by the computer. She was eager to see Bear. Once again, he jumped up to greet her – with each passing day, he got stronger. Every evening, before they both ate, she would run with him around the garden and, when they reached the far end, he would stop and look through the woods. So this afternoon, she decided to take him for a longer walk and go into the forest. He enjoyed the new sights and smells and showed it through the constant wagging motion of his long tail, now fluffier than before.

Her world had become unreal. The talk of power, greed and aggression had been all-consuming in her life recently, so she found solace in the company of her dog.

They ate early so that she could get stuck into her work.

She decided to go through the files that she had emailed to herself.

The first contained Roberto's contracts from as far back as 1945, which had been copied and scanned into the computer.

The second file was much the same, but the third file shocked Francesca. It was full of newspaper cuttings of arrests, murders, and anything that contained the name Luciani, and there were hundreds, again dating back to 1945. Tyler had somehow dug up bits of Roberto's past and scanned them into his computer.

There were pictures of Roberto as a young man, and his wife with their son. The picture of Antonio Luciani, Roberto's brother, lying in a pool of blood outside the FBI offices, made Francesca feel sick. The headlines ran a similar theme: '*Mafia man shot dead*'. Another headline: '*The Godfather, Don Luciani, is free of all charges*'.

She rushed to the toilet and emptied the contents of her stomach. Her head was spinning, trying to make sense of it all. *How could she really have been so fucking naive?* She had dismissed the fact that this very powerful Sicilian family, that everyone seemed to be shit-scared of, could be the Mafioso, but the idea still stared her in the face. She lived in a real world, for fuck's sake, she faced reality every day as a barrister. *Gangs like these didn't really exist anymore, did they? The seventies, early-eighties maybe, but not now, surely*. Her mind was racing; she went over everything from the last few months. *Was she now in so deep that she could not break away? Fuck it, they would have her shot*. Her hands trembled and her eyes watered. She tried desperately hard to focus.

The conclusion was to continue to do what she was doing and get this job finished as soon as possible, and then go back to England and try to live a normal life. Instantly she laughed. *What the fuck was normal?* How could her life ever be that? She was sent away as a child to escape murder, was left for dead by her husband, and was now working for the fucking Mafioso. Looking over the files, she focused on Angelina, her heart-shaped face with perfect eyebrows and thick lips. She had been every bit a beautiful woman, but then there was the horrific photo of her crumpled body, lying on the floor, with the rain washing away the blood from the gunshot wounds.

She decided to skip the rest of the paper clippings and go to the fourth file; it was full of emails from his family. She gasped when she saw a reference to her name: *Launa Enright*.

It had all had been set up. They had planned to use her to put Mauricio down for a long time. There was one email there from her husband even, saying that he would do away with her.

Dear Tyler,

I am really disappointed with the attitude of my wife who, it seems, is happy to undermine me, but I promise I will make her pay. I know it is no consolation for our family, but at least she will not be around for us to despise her.

I obviously made the wrong choice when I married her, but I can assure you it won't happen again.

Kind Regards,

Charles Enright Jr

Francesca read the email over and over again. She could not believe that this was such a callous and carefully organised plan. This obsession the Enrights had with Roberto and Mauricio was so powerful that they were prepared to go to these great lengths, even murder, to secure this plan.

She was more puzzled. Nothing made sense. *What did the Enrights have against the Lucianis that would drive them to this, or did they have something that the Enrights wanted?* Her head was full – she needed a break. She poured herself a coffee and decided to call home.

*

Mary was preparing breakfast for Joseph; his girlfriend had kicked him out of the house again for coming home legless. Dan and Fred hadn't come home that evening, which didn't worry her as this was a common occurrence. Running a club brought with it many pretty girls and so, more often than not, they would stagger home later in the day.

Just as she was buttering the toast, the phone rang. Joseph jumped to his feet, hoping that his girlfriend had changed her mind and would ask him to come back. It was Dan on the phone; his voice was low and gruff. "Joe, quickly, get Fred's passport, some clean clothes and our Dolly's address. Meet me by the garage on Turner Street and not a fucking dickie bird to the old lady."

Joseph didn't ask questions. He ran to Fred's room, grabbed everything, including Fred's address book, and he was out through the door before his mother could ask what was going on.

The phone rang again. Mary answered it, expecting it to be the original caller, Dan or Fred, and asked in a very annoyed tone, "What the hell's going on?"

Francesca was taken aback. "Mum, it's me."

Mary dropped the aggressive tone instantly. "Hello, Dolly, love, how 'ave ya been?"

Francesca wanted to say, *'Well, I've been set up, beaten up, and now hooked up with the fucking mafia,'* but she didn't. She just said, "I'm fine, Mum. Working hard, but I'm well. And you, Mum, how are you doing?"

Mary loved hearing her daughter's voice. It was so pretty.

"I'm good, darling. Your dad's well, and your brothers? Well, they're your brothers, need I say more?"

*

When Francesca got off the phone, she felt fresh and energised enough to take on the Enrights' emails.

There were so many that it took until two o'clock in the morning to get through them all but, by the time she was done, she had a very clear understanding of what was to happen – all the details of the plan between Tyler and Charles Enright Senior were in black and white.

Francesca nervously dialled the secret number and Roberto answered instantly.

"Roberto, I've uncovered their scheme but, I must warn you, the set-up is planned for tomorrow."

Roberto slipped into his shoes and quietly left the house. His Jag was waiting and, before anyone noticed, he drove away in the dead of the night. He knew he was taking a chance meeting with Francesca at her house, but the contriving lawyer had to be stopped; for all he knew, the plot could jeopardise all their lives.

The drive down to her home was quick. There was no traffic and, as he pulled into the small turning off the main road, he could see in the distance the house he took from the designer. He had known Francesca would enjoy staying there. It didn't have overlooking neighbours and so was private and discreetly situated. The huge, tall Canadian trees hid most of the property, like an enormous log cabin in the Rockies. It was hard to believe that five minutes' drive away was the hustle of city life.

Quickly, she ushered Roberto in. He looked around the large entrance hall, with its highly polished wooden floor and winding staircase. He never stayed here and so could not really remember the inside.

Francesca opened the living room door and led Roberto over to the small study area where she kept the computer. Bear came over to see who was there and gently lifted his lip to show his teeth.

Pointing to Bear, Roberto's eyes widened. "What the hell is that?"

Francesca nonchalantly smiled. "Oh, I've adopted a pet; his name is Bear."

Roberto nodded; he had no time for animals.

He sat in the armchair. "So, I have heard today you were magnificent. Mauricio said you are like a detective."

He looked tired so Francesca offered him a drink. She was thinking maybe a coffee, but Roberto wanted a brandy. He took a large gulp. Francesca sat back and admired him. It was two o'clock in the morning and he was dressed impeccably; his hair was neatly combed back and his shoes shined. She was looking at him as if he was a stranger. After all, he was not the man she thought he was. He was a mafia man.

Francesca printed off the emails of the plan and handed them to Roberto. She spoke nervously and, when he had read all of them and had all his questions answered, she decided she really had to tell him that she'd had enough.

"Roberto, I am so very grateful to you for all you have done for me, but when this is over, please may I return to England?" Her voice was soft and pleading.

He looked up in dismay. "My child, why do you speak to me this way? I am indebted to you. If you want to return to England, then I will see to it that you go back to a safe place."

Francesca sank in the chair. *Why had she felt afraid of Roberto?* Regardless of the headlines, he had never treated her badly. He had respect and gratitude. She was tired and thought that maybe she needed a good rest to see things clearly.

She stood up and poured herself a brandy.

"I'm sorry, Roberto, I don't mean to sound like this is a job, it's not. It's more than that, but I have had a shock today. In fact, I have had two. You saw the emails from my husband, well, that was bad, but there are other files too." She paused.

Roberto, being a heavy man, pushed himself forward on the chair to get up and follow her to the computer. She opened the file with the newspaper clippings and let Roberto see them. She scrolled down, revealing one after the other; it appeared to be an endless stream of them. Francesca herself had not looked at them all and then she stopped. There, in the final clipping, was Angelina. She was slumped at the gates of a large house with a bullet through her head.

"Oh my God," gasped Francesca, "I'm sorry, Roberto, for your loss."

Patting her shoulder, he whispered. "It's okay, I have seen these all before."

He walked back to his seat and drank another glass of brandy.

"I understand that seeing all those pictures is disturbing, but why do you seem afraid now? I am still the same Roberto as yesterday, or last week or last month, so I don't understand this fear in your eyes."

Francesca poured herself another drink. She needed to relax: today had been a turmoil of emotions and her mind was still in a state of confusion.

"Roberto, I never knew you were part of the mafia."

Roberto looked up in surprise. "What does it mean to you, Francesca, the mafia?"

Suddenly, she felt a little dumb, because she wasn't really sure what it meant.

"I guess the image that goes with the mafia is violence and crime."

"Yes, you are right," he replied.

Francesca was shocked. She almost expected Roberto to deny it but he didn't. Strangely calm, she didn't feel afraid, and she respected him for his honesty.

"Are you not in the least bit bothered that your life has been full of crime?" She didn't say it to belittle him, but to try to reconcile her perceived objections to the mafia with her own feelings of humanity for a man who had given her both love and affection.

"There is more to my life than that. For those few I have harmed, there have been ten times as many that I have helped. If those people who tried to stop my business succeeded, then there are hundreds of men who without my help would have lived a sorrowful existence."

He stopped and looked around the room. "You see this house? I gave this to you because you came to me in your time of need, and I did my best to help you become whole once more. If people stood in my way, I would not have had the means to help people like you." Francesca sat absorbing his words: they sounded so soft, so wise, and so normal. And now, her perceptions of violent men with Italian accents seemed to fade into obscurity, because she realised that it was her own ignorance at fault for having these false perceptions of Robert and all he stood for.

"My businesses are no longer criminal. I try to keep all my companies clean. I have thousands of men on my payroll and, imagine this for instance – Rudi, he works with Sergio, and he makes sure Sergio is protected because there are jealous people out there. Now take Rudi; his sister fled Italy, and she got very sick. He couldn't pay for her medicine, so I did. His sister left her two babies in Italy because her husband beat her so bad, she fled without them. I sent the boys over and they brought the babies to the States. Now I know that my Sergio is safe. Rudi watches his back all the time, but if Rudi let my Sergio come to harm, then what would I do, eh?"

Francesca nodded. She understood all that, but what worried her was owing favours.

"If you did me a favour, then I would owe you, and if I didn't pay up then would you hurt me?"

Roberto laughed. "You have watched the films, eh?" He leaned forward, put his arms out to her and hugged her. "My child, do you think my Mauricio would ever owe me? Or Sergio, do you think he would ever owe me? No, of course not. My family never owe me; you will never owe me. Before I help anyone, I tell them how they can repay me first, and not by doing anything illegal. I have men that work for me that enjoy the less tasteful jobs."

Francesca felt at home. What he was saying resonated exactly with her own life experiences. He was right, his words were real, she trusted him completely and, *so what if he was the Mafioso?* She thought about her husband, a law-abiding citizen, a pillar of the community, a prosecution barrister, and yet he took her womb, her face and, had it not been for the grace of God, her life.

The last few hours had been too much for Francesca and she began to sob uncontrollably. Roberto hugged her until she stopped and drifted to sleep like a baby in his arms. He laid her on the sofa and covered her over with a blanket, all the while closely watched by Bear. "You guard over her, dog, wolf, whatever you are." Then he quietly left. He had the letters between Tyler and Charles in front of him and he needed to make some plans of his own.

As he drove home, he thought about his wife, and remembered the day the police had shot her. They had been after him but it seemed that, back then, it was a set up too. He had no idea why Tyler and his family wanted him and Mauricio incarcerated.

Mauricio and Sergio arrived at Roberto's soon after four in the morning; both looked the worse for wear but soon livened up when Roberto explained Tyler's scheming plan. Mauricio once more hopped around the room, making all kinds of threats.

"Listen, Mauricio," shouted Roberto. "You need to go to France as soon as possible."

"Fuck, I hate that place."

"You must go to Bergerac. Although the cargo will leave Portsmouth headed for the States, I have contacted the Fredos and they have already organised for the ship to make a detour to France. You will meet my old friend Hugo Philip, who will take the cargo off and empty the contents, reload the ship with legal cargo, and away you go. I want you to be on the boat when the ship arrives in the Port of New York and New Jersy."

"Why don't I fly to England and meet the double-crossing bastard, Carlos Enrico, and take him out?" argued Mauricio.

"Because his name is not Carlos Enrico, it's Charles Enright, and he will recognise you immediately. They want us in prison, so do as I say."

Mauricio slumped in his chair, fuming at the cheek of the bastards.

"Uncle, what can I do?"

"Sergio, I need you to work with Francesca and make sure Tyler is away from the office tomorrow night, just in case anything goes wrong. I need him to believe the delivery has been made and is on its way here."

Sergio nodded.

*

Francesca awoke at around six o'clock. She was still fully clothed and on the sofa, with Bear by her side. She looked over to see the two brandy glasses, and it all came flooding back – *the files, the mafia, the set-up*. Quickly, she jumped to her feet to head for the shower. As she leapt up, her head started to bang. "If only you were human, Bear. I'd get you to make me some coffee." The shower was an instant relief from her sleepy haze. She slipped herself into a black trouser suit and headed towards the kitchen in the direction of the coffee. She had not reckoned on a visitor showing up.

"Shit, you scared me, Sergio. What are you doing here?" She noticed how tired he looked.

"We need to make a plan on how to keep Tyler away from the office this evening, just in case anything goes wrong. I know that the ship is almost there and Mauricio is on his way to France but one mistake and who fucking knows."

Francesca nodded.

She had the ideal plan to distract Tyler and keep him out of the office.

She changed into a more seductive suit, pure wool, black Chanel, short skirt, and low-cut jacket revealing just a small lace frill of her bra.

"Wow, you look good. That's definitely going to seduce him."

Francesca laughed and kissed Sergio on the cheek.

"Oh yeah, and what is that animal you have in the house? Is it a wild dog or a wolf, eh?"

"Oh, you mean Bear? He's my dog."

"Well, your dog loves to smile, eh?"

Sergio laughed, amazed by this woman. *Was she fucking mad?*

*

Back at the office, Francesca was first in. She felt rough and yet she knew she had to be chirpy to attract Tyler. It was amazing that he had written letters to her husband regarding her duty as a wife and acknowledging the actions of his nephew in killing her. She took a deep breath and tried to put it out of her head, but it was so hard. She had thought that maybe the Lucianis were mistaken, but now she realised that Tyler was just as much a sick bastard as her husband was.

She popped a couple of painkillers and set about making the coffee. Tyler marched in an hour late; he looked nervous and uptight.

"Good morning, Mr Enright, can I pour you a coffee?" she asked, practically oozing the words out in her sexiest voice.

Tyler was more distracted today than he had ever been. He was even wearing the same suit as the day before and had designer stubble that really didn't suit him.

He nodded to Francesca and sat back at his computer. He was busy typing away when she walked around to his side of the desk and slowly, deliberately placed the coffee next to him. In a flash, he turned off the screen.

"Thank you, Francesca." His voice was cold; she didn't feel him engage with her.

"Mr Enright, I don't normally pry into my employer's personal affairs, but I must say you look like you could do with a break, and I am trying desperately to find someone who will take me to see the New York sights, maybe have a bite to eat, and who knows what..."

Tyler looked over his coffee mug and stared at Francesca. She looked sexier than ever; he loved her short skirts and, *what the hell, he did need a break.* There was nothing else he could do today – the deal was made, everything was in place. It was all down to his brother now.

"Hey, why don't you take the rest of the day off? I'll go home, have a rest myself, and I'll pick you up around eight."

Francesca knew she needed to be with him from seven onwards.

"Why don't we make it earlier and eat first? I rarely go past seven o'clock for a bite to eat."

He was totally bewitched by her and so he agreed.

Chapter Twelve

Before Tyler was due to arrive, Francesca moved the computer into one of the bedrooms. It was very rare for homes to have a computer and she didn't want to answer any unnecessary questions. She made a special effort by wearing a black dress, plain but cut to define her figure, hoping to keep him interested enough that he wouldn't go home or back to the office too early.

Dead on seven o'clock, she saw his car coming down the hill and into her drive. *Cheeky sod,* she said to herself. She let Bear into the garden but, as soon as Tyler knocked, Bear was back in and on guard duty. She opened the door and was surprised by the transformation, from the scruffy drunkard this morning to a very elegant, smart appearance this evening. He kissed her on the cheek and handed her a small posy of red roses, along with his usual wink. The wink rubbed Bear up the wrong way and he curled his lip to show his pearly whites, adding a growl.

Tyler jumped back. "Shit, that thing looks nasty."

Francesca was annoyed. *How dare he walk into her house and insult her dog?*

"Go in the kitchen, Bear." She patted his head, and he instantly obeyed her command, much to the relief of Tyler, who wasn't too fond of dogs, especially one that resembled a wolf.

"Let me get you a drink," offered Francesca, in her sweetest voice.

Tyler nodded and continued gazing around the room, surprised that a secretary could afford such a beautiful home. Even his house wasn't this grand.

"How the hell did you manage to find this beauty?" asked Tyler, admiring the decor.

She looked up and realised he was referring to the house.

"Oh yeah, my friend in England; it's her holiday home and, since she is not using it this year, she let me have it."

That was easy, thought Francesca.

"Nice to have good buddies." As she handed him a glass of wine, they made a toast to friends.

"Maybe we could be good friends," whispered Tyler, as he winked yet again.

Francesca raised her very defined eyebrows and teased him. "Maybe, who knows?"

She giggled at Bear growling in the kitchen.

"Miss Francesca, I know a wonderful French restaurant to dine, and I thought we could follow with a bit of fun at the casino. I'm feeling really lucky tonight."

Francesca agreed. As they headed off, she smirked. *What a fucking bastard. Lucky, he thinks. Well, lucky if he lives until next week.* She could feel the rush of adrenaline that made her stomach churn. *When Roberto finishes with him, he will be one less Enright to worry about.*

*

The French restaurant was set back, away from the main drag, nestled in a side street; couples who entered were dressed in classy eveningwear. Box hedges, covered in tiny white lights, lined the entrance. Strong aromas from fried onions and garlic wafted outside. Her mouth watered. The table had been booked and a handsomely dressed waiter led them to a small private area. *Very cosy*, thought Francesca.

"Mr Enright, please let me take your coat and you, madam, let me help with yours too," said the waiter. Two other waiters approached the table, one to take the drinks order, and the other to read the chef's special menu.

Francesca was surprised by the attention Tyler received. He was clearly well-known by many of the other customers.

One man came over, obviously Italian, a big guy with a huge diamond ring on his little finger. "Tyler." He kissed Tyler on both cheeks. "Please send my regards to Mr Luciani and tell him my son is doing very well at the university, eh. Perhaps soon he will have your job," he laughed, joined by Tyler.

"I will, Mr Carponi," Tyler replied, politely smiling as he sat back down.

He was delighted, confident that she was impressed, which gave him a sense of increased anticipation that he would definitely bed her by the end of the evening. "Cheers." He raised his glass and, without the wine touching the side, he gulped it back.

"Let's order another bottle, hey. You choose this time."

Francesca went along with the spirit of things and scanned the wine list. "Oh yes, let's try this one, the Robert Mondavi 1974, a very good year for that region."

Tyler nearly choked. A secretary and wine connoisseur? "Shit, Francesca, you never cease to amaze me."

Then she realised that she should have kept her mouth shut.

"How did you know that, may I ask?" he asked, as he inclined his head and smirked.

"My father worked for a wine merchants, so I grew up with wine tasting."

Tyler was convinced and thought no more of it.

*

10 hours earlier – Back in London

Fred would never see it coming. Mad Mick's eldest son, nicknamed Piano, was waiting for him at the back of the club with his right hand man, Digger, and they had a car parked up and ready to go. It would be only a matter of time before Fred would be locking up and on his way home. Piano watched the back door to the nightclub with immense tension. He knew the one thing that would make his father favour him over his other brothers would be the murder of a Vincent.

Fred was a good hour away from locking up; keen to get the club in order before Dan, his eldest brother, showed his face. Dan had the club buzzing every weekend and was so organised that, come the next open night, the place was stocked up and spotless. So Fred liked to do the same.

He surveyed the punters knocking back the booze and smiled to himself – *it was such a great little earner that it wasn't hard to work at all, not when you've got good staff.* He cheekily patted one of the new barmaids on the bum and, instead of a tut, she gave him a smile. He raised his eyebrow suggestively, and she smiled again, mimicking him.

The McManners' boys had been plotting to kill Fred and had his moves closely surveyed for weeks, aware that he was alone at the club when they decided to make their grab.

Fred was looking forward to a good time with the new barmaid, Chanel, and decided to get the club cleared up, ready to lock up early. He rounded up the black bin bags, ready to take them out to the back. Usually the bar staff did this, but he was in a rush. As he dragged out four of them, with his back to the outside world, he didn't notice Piano, Mick's elder son, hop from his car. His mind was on Chanel. Piano pointed the gun at Fred's head and demanded he got in the car.

Totally off guard, it took Fred a few seconds to register what was happening. He turned to see who held the gun, praying it was a joke. *Piano, with ginger hair and acne scars, was one ugly bastard. A face that only a mother could love.* Yet that was funny because his mother didn't like him at all. He had been the worst son a parent could wish for. All through his teenage years, he had been encouraged by his father to treat women with total disrespect. When he was in the house, he made demands on his mother, grabbing her by the arms, pushing her into the kitchen, and ordering her to cook his food or wash his clothes. She did it, of course, because, like the other sons, he was a bully and, if she refused, he would slap her or kick her. So his ugly, spiteful face suited his personality, and his mother despised him.

Fred walked with Piano to the car, his legs feeling like jelly, the fear consuming him. Mad Mick's sons, otherwise known as the McManner brothers, were nasty – they had a reputation for the vilest acts. When they got together in any pub, the rest of the customers would leave. There would nearly always be a fight, a stabbing or, in some cases, torture inflicted on some poor unlucky soul. Fred looked at Digger, who smiled a twisted, slow, sarcastic grin. He felt his bowels moving, dreading the thought of what they had in store for him.

Piano got in the back of the car with Fred whilst Digger drove. The two bouncers hadn't seen Fred being forced into the car, but they did see the car being driven away, with Fred looking as white as a ghost sitting in the back.

It was sheer luck that Dan had decided to check on the club that night. He had just had the shag of his life with one of the girls who worked in the deli bar up the road from the club. Just before heading home, he pulled into the club to have a quick Jack Daniels and check everything was ready for opening on Wednesday.

He already had in the back of his mind that Mad Mick may go for Freddie. A week before, he had been making all kinds of threats saying that, since he didn't get Dolly, there was a debt still owing, so he would have the next best thing. Dan put two and two together and guessed it would be his youngest brother, Fred. Not a word had been mentioned to his mum and dad; *he would deal with it himself.*

*

As he pulled into the driveway of the club, he could see in the distance a red Mercedes, and the doormen all trying to get into cars. He knew that Piano had one just like it and, just as he went to get out of the car, Cody, one of the bouncers, came running up to him. "Dan, they've got your brother in that Merc. Sorry, mate, I thought it was your car parked up, they look identical." Cody pointed down the street.

"Get the boys to stay here, I'm going." And with that, he tore after the red Mercedes. Cody was right; it was the same colour, make and model as his own.

His heart pounding, he prayed that he would be able to rescue his little brother. He was angry and had been since he heard the threat. All his life he'd had to live with the worry of the McManners' family finding their sister but, not content with that, they now wanted another family member. He'd had enough now and, one way or another, he was going get his own back. Mad Mick was going to be a dead man and he would see to it – that was an absolute given. If they hurt one hair on Fred's head he would take them all out. After promising their mother all those years ago to stay away from the McManners, Dan had kept to his word. But it was different now: the threats would never end. It had been all right to stay clear of them because Dolly was out of harm's way but not now, none of them were safe.

Dan worked out that they were too stupid to realise he was following them. They drove Fred, with a gun to his head, all the way out into the sticks. Dan could just make out the outline of his brother in the back of the car. His heart was in his mouth, yet he needed to keep calm and think about what to do. Driving the long distance, Dan soon realised that Piano had no intention of shooting Fred in the car. He was taking him to a pre-planned execution site.

Mad Mick had made all the arrangements. He had been very clever in his plan. He knew his son would go along with it since he had brought his boys up to do as he told them. They never argued with him, mainly because they lived in fear but also because they had no scruples themselves.

The idea was to remove Fred's body the next day and put it in the concreted basement of the multi-storey going up in Hackney. All was arranged. His son and Digger, his son's accomplice, would leave the body in the barn, drive the Mercedes to the crusher, and then head off to Amsterdam for a few weeks until the heat died down.

They had not accounted for Dan following them, or the fact that Fred, taking the Mad Mick threat seriously, carried a gun tucked down the back of his trousers.

Dan drove along the country lane with his lights off.

As Digger pulled up at the barn, Piano ordered Fred to get out, with the gun still pointed at Fred's head.

To the utter amazement of Piano and Digger, Dan drove at them as fast as he could, switching on his full beam lights. Piano wasn't quick off the mark — blinded by the bright lights, he was left wide open. Fred pulled out his gun and shot Piano clean through the eye. He dropped to the floor like a sack of shit. Digger tried to run and Fred shot him too but only managed to wing him in the arm.

Digger fell to the floor, screaming like a baby and clutching himself.

Dan jumped out of the car, his adrenaline still pumping, letting out a high pitched laugh.

"Fucking 'ell, Freddie, I know you're good at darts but where did you learn to get a bullseye with a gun."

Freddie laughed nervously. He had surprised himself.

"Shit, Dan, they were gonna kill me, really kill me, 'cause they didn't find our Dolly, the sick bastards."

"It's all right, mate." Dan hugged Fred, who was shaking.

"They even told me how they were gonna kill me, where that fucking nutter Mad Mick was gonna bury me, and how they would make a toast to me over in Amsterdam."

Fred was trying to catch his breath from the excitement and fear of having the air knocked out of his lungs, and he was suffering from an adrenaline rush to the brain.

"Right, Fred, listen to me. You stay here, I'm gonna get Joe to get your gear, and then you're to fly out of 'ere, all right?"

Fred nodded, still out of breath and shaking. Dan hugged his brother again before he headed off to fetch Joe. "Oh yeah, don't let that fucker get away." Dan pointed to Digger, still reeling around on the floor.

"Shall I just finish him, Dan?"

"No, let me get me thoughts together first. I'm gonna get Joe. Don't worry, Fred, we will figure it out."

Dan had so many friends, many of whom were women, who were eager to please him.

"'Ello, babe, sorry for calling so late. It's Dan Vincent." The voice on the other end of the phone was a travel agent called Juliet who, when in England, often called Dan for a quick shag. He was handsome and not looking for commitment, but she loved him in her own way. "Hello, Danny Boy, don't tell me, you're gagging for it," she laughed.

"No, babe, this is serious business. Can you get my brother, Fred, on the next plane to New York?" His voice, although calm, still had a desperate undertone. Instantly, Juliet stopped joking and, hunting around for her pad and a pen, took down all the details.

"Right, tell your brother to go to my collection desk at Gatwick and his ticket will be there."

"Thank you, my darling, I owe you one."

"Actually, I'll have two," she joked again.

Joseph met Dan as planned at the Lakeside Shopping Centre, just outside Thurrock. "Blimey, Joe, you took your time. We need to get back to Fred now."

He jumped into Dan's car and off they went.

"Did you bring the money and his passport?"

Joseph nodded.

"And Dolly's address?"

"Well, I brought the address book."

Dan tried to explain to Joseph the series of events and the seriousness of it all.

"You know, Joe, sometimes I wonder about Fred — one minute he's the fucking brains of the family, next thing he's totally lost the fucking plot."

"It was so lucky, you know. If I hadn't stopped in the club earlier, our Fred may well have been brown bread." Dan shuddered as the realisation hit him.

Joseph was calm and tried not to get too involved in the nightclub business. He wanted to settle down and have a family but, every time he got with the boys, he was then in trouble — never would he get home sober, so he attempted to break away and lead his own life, but he was easily sucked into the party mood and excitement.

"So, Dan, when we drop Fred off at the airport, do you mind if I head off home? Only I need to sort things with Belinda." His voice was low and hopeful.

Dan nearly swerved across the road as, he flung himself around to see if his brother was really all there.

"What is it with you lately? Did you not get what I just told you? Are you fucking stoned or what?" Dan screamed.

"All right, bruv, stop shouting."

"Well, thick shit, let me go over it again. Our Fred was carted away by Mad Mick's son, you know, the one gormless-looking cunt. Jimmy is his real name but they call him Piano on account of his teeth. Anyway, him and his heavy, known as Digger, you know him, the ugly bastard with fucking great lug 'oles..."

"Yeah, I got that bit," Joe interjected. "But why do I need to come with you?" asked Joseph defiantly.

"Well, when you or I take Fred to the fucking airport, who's gonna guard Digger?"

Joseph sat silent for a minute. He was still trying to work it all out. Dan was exhausted and Joe was trying his patience.

"So if you drive Fred, then I'll stay and make sure Trigger and Piano don't move until you get back, is that right?" Joseph obviously thought he was being clever but got a sharp shock when Dan clipped him hard around his ear.

"What was that for?" he screeched.

"You are so dozy sometimes. First of all, his name is fucking Digger not bastard Trigger, and secondly, why would you want to guard Piano? He ain't likely to walk anyway now, is he?"

"Oh, I got it, you shot him in the legs," laughed Joe.

"Fuck me, you're thick, Joe. He can't walk anywhere on account of the fact that he has a bloody great big hole in his head – he's dead."

Dan held the steering wheel with one hand and hugged his brother with the other.

"It's okay, mate. I will sort it out. You just do as I say."

Joseph felt sick; he hated getting into heavy shit, and he classed murder as pretty heavy.

Dan took an unmade road off the dual carriageway and drove for about two miles. Luckily, trees surrounded the barn, so the cars were not visible for miles around.

Dan and Joseph arrived at the scene to find their little brother curled up in a ball, asleep.

"Fred!" screamed Joseph, who thought he was looking at a dead brother.

Fred abruptly awoke. "Hi, Joe." His voice was croaky.

Dan searched the barn. "Where the fuck is Digger?"

Fred pointed to where Dan was standing. Frantically, Dan looked around. "Fred, he's not here. Where is he?"

"Don't worry, he won't be far," replied Fred, shaking his head

Dan grabbed Fred by the shoulders and shook him. "He only has to get to the nearest fucking phone box, and we are fucked."

"Get off, Dan. He won't go far 'cause, unless his good arm is strong enough to drag himself to a phone box, he won't reach one."

Dan frowned. "What have you done?"

"I was dozing off when the bastard tried to go for me, so I shot him in both legs. Oh yeah, and 'cause he wouldn't listen, I shot his fucking ear off."

Dan rolled his eyes and wandered around. Sure enough, there was Digger, face down, behind the barn, both legs blasted, and half his face taken off along with the ear.

"Right, Joe and Fred, this is what we do."

Both brothers nodded.

"We put Digger in the boot of my car and drive you to the airport. Oh yeah, you fly to New York in about two hours." Fred nodded and Joe looked at the floor. He hated getting caught up in all this shit.

"Joseph, you set light to their Merc, remove the number plates and – see this petrol can? Pour it all over the body, make sure he is completely covered. I want Mad Mick to think that it's Fred's corpse, got it? Make a long trail with it, covering the blood behind the barn. I want all traces burned completely."

Joe nodded. He checked his pockets for matches. "Dan, why don't we burn both the bodies?"

Dan rolled his eyes again. "Look, with one body burned to a cinder, Mad Mick will think it's Fred, but if there are two bodies, Mick will have a pretty good idea it's not... got it now?"

Joe nodded, not wanting to even question the reason behind removing the plates.

Dan and Fred pulled and dragged Digger's body to the boot of the car. Holding both ends of the heavy weight, they hoisted him up and threw him inside, slamming the boot shut.

Joseph shuddered. He looked down at Piano, and imagined him sitting bolt upright like a one-eyed zombie. His face was even more grotesque – the bullet had literally gone through his eye and taken out the back of his head. He didn't waste any time. First, he poured the drum of petrol over the car and then, with his brute strength, he dragged Piano and threw him on the back seat, shoving some old blankets and straw over him and dousing the lot. In the corner of the barn were two other cans. He removed the lids and pushed them underneath the car. With his adrenaline pumping he ripped the number plates off the front and back and then ran a trail of fuel almost to Dan's car.

Dan tutted. "Careful, Joe, don't wanna blow us all up."

The barn was alight, and they were on the main road, before you could say 'London's burning'. The explosion could be heard a few miles away.

"Fucking hell, Joe, you should have joined the fucking army as a one-man band."

Joe, with that naughty school boy expression, grinned. He felt really chuffed that he'd been able to conquer his natural fear of violence and helped his brothers in their hour of need.

Dan gave Fred clothes to change into, his passport, and a load of cash, along with Dolly's address. He was last in the queue and just made the boarding. Dan hugged his brother tightly. "Look after yourself, and tell Dolly I love her."

Fred was relieved when the plane took off. He reclined in his seat in comfort, pleased that his brother had arranged a first class seat. Yet he was also concerned for his brothers and the mess he had left behind. He wouldn't properly rest until he knew they were safe.

*

The next morning, Mad Mick arrived at the area near the barn, and was angry. The place swarmed with police and the barn was burned to the ground. He didn't drive down the unmade road but instead made sure to stay well clear. Incident tape cornered off the area and police were on guard. Mad Mick stopped in the nearest pub. They always had the local gossip and besides, it served food, and police on duty were always hungry.

The landlord, an old fella, was quite excited when Mick asked what was going on.

"Well, from what the police told me, they were called to a fire there this morning. When the fire fighters eventually put the blaze out, they found a dead body, probably a man. There's practically nothing left of the poor lad. They are looking for a red Mercedes. Apparently, the old girl up the road saw one pull out of the road at the same time she noticed the fire, like."

Mick knocked back his pint of Guinness and grinned. *The little fuckers set that Fred alight.*

Well, I suppose it will save me burying the bastard myself, he thought. He had no idea that it was his own son lying there like a block of charcoal. And it would be some time before he found out.

*

New York

Francesca kept the conversation to flirty small talk. She really didn't want to give anything away.

They finished their meal with a surprise dessert on the house. Tyler loved the attention from the staff. It set him above the other customers and made him look important in front of Francesca who, he thought, was lapping it up. She has never had it so good, he stupidly surmised.

He guessed that as soon as he entered the casino, everyone would be making a fuss. He was, after all, Roberto's right hand man – again this was another of Tyler's false assumptions. He was simply the man that had the legal expertise to keep the business above board and dandy.

Roberto owned casinos in New York, and Francesca guessed they were heading to one right now.

The casino was enormous, and far more sophisticated than she had imagined. The women were dressed to impress, with diamonds dripping from everywhere, plastic faces, plastic tits, and they were generally taller than their short, fat sugar daddies.

"Well, good evening, Mr Enright. Good to see you, sir," said a very well dressed doorman.

Tyler nodded in acknowledgement but remained quiet, trying to act cool.

Prick, thought Francesca.

Just then, she spotted Sergio. He was in his suit, being hassled by a very pretty woman. He quickly turned to face her and his eyes widened. She had forgotten herself for a moment. She rooted herself to the spot, thinking that if she had been too friendly, Tyler would have guessed she was a plant.

"Hey, Sergio, did you make a decision on the other casino?" Tyler was loud and acting big.

Sergio shook his hand and pulled it so Tyler's face came to meet his.

"Don't ever discuss my business in public. If I need your advice, I ask you, eh." Then, he gently slapped his cheek.

Tyler felt uncomfortable and tried to laugh it off, but Sergio was angry. With the knowledge that Tyler was a sly bastard, and in the process of doing them over, he had to keep his cool. He thought about his cousin, Mauricio. If he had been here right now, he would have taken him outside and fucked him up.

Just as Sergio went to walk away, a commotion took their attention. Two women were being marched out of the door by another woman. They were all stunning, with long legs, short dresses, and plenty of hair, or hair extensions.

"Come back and I'll break your fucking legs, then you'll have no work."

The woman escorting the two other girls out of the club looked fierce. The back of her neck was tattooed. Francesca could just about make it out to be a dragon. As she came closer, she heard Francesca say, "Wouldn't want to get on the wrong side of her."

"Want me to fucking kick you out of here too?" The tattooed woman was now face to face with Francesca, with her hands on her hips, ready to start.

The words had an immediate impact on Francesca who, in her new life, would never take shit from anyone.

She looked the woman up and down and slowly, with an icy stare, she spat, "Try it, darlin', and I'll take your 'ed clean off your fucking shoulders." Her East End accent came back vigorously, much to the surprise of Tyler and Sergio.

Sergio grabbed the woman by the arm and marched her out the back door.

Once outside, he pinned her up against the wall with one hand and pounded her face with the other.

"I have given you the right to have your girls in my joint to make money out of my customers, and you go too far. You upset our lawyer's girlfriend, eh. Who the fuck do you think you are, eh?"

The tattooed woman had blown it. She had landed herself a comfortable role managing the prostitutes in the casino. She got a cut from each girl, and they were guaranteed work and security — now she had got too cocky and fucked it up. Her face throbbed.

"Hey, Sergio, please forgive me. I was stupid, it won't happen again." She was petrified. Most men thrown out the back door never came back; they were beaten, or worse. Two of the mob stood next to Sergio, just in case she pulled a knife.

"I never hit women, do you understand? Never. But you are no woman, you are a fucking scum whore. You insult my customers, you insult me, you insult our lawyer, and you insult Roberto."

Sergio took off his jacket and the woman lost all sense of herself, as the urine ran down her leg. He was disgusted by the way she begged for her life, sobbing, as snot bubbled out of her nose.

Sergio, a different person altogether from his cousin, decided to let her go.

"Get up from off the floor and get out of here. If you come back, I will forget that underneath the scummy whore is a female."

The woman nodded, staggered to her feet and fled for her life.

Francesca, meanwhile, tried to redeem herself. Tyler laughed, "Come on, tell me, where did you get that dodgy cockney accent from?"

"When I was at school I made friends with a girl from the East End of London who was sent to live with her aunt in Surrey. Her dad became very rich and so she had a privileged upbringing but never really lost her accent. So being her best friend the odd word would rub off on me. I think it sounds quite scary, don't you?"

Tyler laughed. "You're a cheeky minx, Francesca."

The bar stretched the length of the casino with twelve waiters ready to serve. To the left of the bar was a private area never open to the public.

Tyler ordered champagne from a waiter who knew who he was, and a bottle and two glasses were brought over to a table in the private area. Again, Tyler was showing off his sense of importance because this area of the casino was reserved only for the privileged elite of New York.

Sergio came over to the table and offered his apologies.

Francesca nodded in acceptance as if he was a stranger. "So, Tyler, are you going to introduce me?"

Sergio looked at Francesca and smiled. "This is Francesca, my personal assistant, but you have met before."

Both Sergio and Francesca froze, and then the penny dropped. "Oh yeah, when I came to the office yesterday. Forgive me." He took her hand and kissed it.

Tyler looked around. "Where's Mauricio tonight? I thought he would be here." Tyler knew Mauricio was at the casino every Friday without fail. He started to get hot under the collar.

"Mauricio had a date tonight." Sergio took a sip of water. "He is settling down these days and so Fridays are now reserved for his girlfriend."

Tyler felt a slight relief; but thinking about the shipment still put him on edge – *it would be taking place about now.*

Francesca remained quiet, afraid to say the wrong thing.

"So, he's still with that nurse, Kathy, then?" Before Sergio could answer, he went on. "What happened to that girl who was staying with the nurse, the one who was having the surgery?" Tyler had drunk two glasses of champagne and was feeling confident.

"Oh yeah, she moved on somewhere." Sergio shrugged his shoulders.

Throughout the evening, Francesca noticed more and more just how much respect Sergio had. It was apparent that Tyler was small fry compared to the Lucianis.

Sergio had the casino running like a dream and, with any sniff of trouble, he was there pointing to his men, making hand signs to eject certain customers. There was much whispering going on and it was clear, certainly to Francesca, that Sergio had the full respect of his casino staff. And all the while he would look over to see if Francesca was still there, alert to any sign that Tyler might suspect something amiss.

They played blackjack and roulette and drank more champagne. Francesca was starting to get really irritated with Tyler, as every so often he would overstep the mark and, when he won a card hand or doubled his money on the roulette wheel, he showed his excitement by smacking her behind or kissing her cheek.

Slowly but surely, Tyler was getting drunk. Francesca felt tired and was looking for an excuse to exit; *she only wished she had the knowledge that the shipment had gone to plan.* Just like magic, and much to her relief, Sergio looked over to her, smiling, and gave her the thumbs up.

"Tyler, I would like to go home now," said Francesca.

Tyler threw his last dice, put a heavy arm around her shoulder, kissed her on the lips, and said, "And that's for you." Pleased with himself, he had won a grand, and was now itching to have the shag of his life.

He waved goodbye to Sergio who nodded and, with a heavy arm, grabbed Francesca and swayed back to the car.

"Should you be driving, Tyler? Only, I'm quite happy to hail a taxi." She wanted to go home alone and felt nervous getting in a car with a drunk driver.

"Now you listen to me, my little sex kitten. I have been driving for years, I am a very good driver, and you are completely safe in my hands." He wasn't going home without his payback. She had been wined and dined, and now he wanted what he was owed.

Francesca felt sick. She had deliberately only sipped a small amount of champagne, whilst Tyler was knocking them back. She hated being in the company of drunk men, and he was becoming more and more like her husband. He was crude, continually and annoyingly asking personal questions, like 'how many boyfriends had she had' and 'her favourite sexual position'.

On edge by his conversation, she tried to laugh him off but his rudeness intensified.

"Tyler, you shouldn't ask me these personal questions. I am, after all, your PA, and so we shouldn't discuss our sex lives with each other." She tried to be nice about it, simply because her nerves were getting the better of her.

*

As they reached the drive, Francesca pushed the car door open as quickly as she could but, to her dismay, was held back by the seatbelt. Tyler hadn't put his on, and so he was out the door and by her side to help her. Of course, he was aware she had attempted to escape. She was not flirting anymore, she had not responded to his pecks or the arm around her shoulders, but she was not getting away so easily. He had spent a fortune this evening and, like all his many other secretaries who'd had the dubious pleasure of working for him, he was determined to sleep with her.

"I need to use your bathroom," whispered Tyler.

Francesca froze. *How would she get him out of the house once he was in?*

No sooner had she put the key in the door and he was behind, placing his hands on her hips, and guiding her into the lounge, as if it were his home.

"Tyler, come on now, get your hands off." Francesca tried to continue with the jovial tone. "The bathroom's over there." She pointed to the small toilet in the hallway.

He laughed, still swaying, as he staggered in that direction. While he was gone, she went to the kitchen to see Bear – he stood almost in a trance, ready to pounce.

"What's up, boy?" She ruffled his fur and realised he was tense. He looked ahead at the door.

"Do you want to go out?" She opened the back door but he remained. "Okay, boy, I'll leave you to sulk in the garden." She put his actions down to the fact that she had left and forgotten to leave the door open for him. As he walked into the back garden, she shut the door behind him.

She hoped that, once Tyler was finished in the bathroom, he would head home. She turned on the lights in the dining room and drew the curtains, getting everything ready before she went to bed. He was still in the toilet. She thought he might have passed out and went to check if he was okay, but the toilet door was open and Tyler was nowhere in sight. Her heart started pounding. She opened the front door to see if the car was still in the drive and it was. "Tyler?" she shouted up the stairs.

Silence. Suddenly she remembered where she had put the computer and that, if he found it, she would have blown everything.

Without thinking, she ran upstairs, leaving the entrance door open. As she headed for the room where she had hidden it, she passed her own bedroom, and then he jumped out and grabbed her, pinning her to the wall. Partially winded, she couldn't get her breath to scream. He had taken his jacket off and undone his shirt and now he pressed his mouth against hers. She felt a sharp pain as his front teeth bruised her lip. She anxiously caught her breath, but again he pressed his lips hard against hers, forcing his tongue into her mouth. She nearly choked. His breath was foul – a mix of cigarettes and champagne. She tried to push him away but he ignored her pleas. In her desperation to slide away from him, he gripped her even tighter.

"Come on, you want it. Don't play games," he spat.

The horror hit her; *he wasn't going to stop*. Just like her husband, she could not overpower him. Her legs buckled and once again her insides felt nauseous. Her head became hot, and she fought back from the dark depths of unconsciousness. *No way was this bastard going to take anything from her; how dare he help himself*. He was pawing her like a frantic animal, the sweat from his brow dripping on her face. He grabbed at her breast, squeezing hard.

"Stop, please stop," she begged.

Because she didn't respond to his advances, he put his hands around her throat and tightened. His face was contorted, his nostrils flared, and his incensed expression sent her into a panic. Her worst fear was about to happen; *he wasn't going to rape her, but kill her*. The adrenaline pumped furiously around her body as she tried frantically to hold on to life. She managed to summon up her last bit of strength and brought her knee up as hard as she could, catching him in the groin. He yelped like a dog and let go of his grip just long enough for her to get away. She ran heedlessly down the stairs, knocking all the pictures off the wall. As she jumped the last three steps, her ankle twisted but, like a fox, she continued to scramble – only he was there again, behind her.

"Where do you think you're going, you fucking little prick teaser?"

He grabbed her once more, throwing her over the couch. She tried to struggle free, but he threw himself on top of her and pushed her face into the cushion. She couldn't breathe. She needed to force her head up from the pillow to get air, but he held her down hard with one hand and, with the other, he slid his hand up inside her dress and viciously tore off her pants. He let go of her head to use both hands to pull her into position. But, as she pushed herself up, he hit her hard at the back of the head. For a split second, the room dimmed, but she recovered sufficiently to get her head free just long enough for her to scream. She hoped that someone would hear her.

He slapped her face. "Shut the fuck up, silly slut."

Shoving her face down again, he gave her another blow to the head. Her body went limp but she wasn't unconscious. She didn't want to have her face buried in the cushion because she knew she would die.

He found it easier to rip her legs apart. Before he could enter her, he heard a sound right by his ears – a low growl. He turned and saw a huge set of snarling teeth. Before he could blink, the jaws snapped shut, and the teeth buried deep in Tyler's cheek. Bear let go and lunged forward again, this time sinking his teeth into Tyler's arm.

Tyler instantly jumped away from the sofa, holding his face. Bear came at him again, giving Francesca time to get to her feet – but, before she could do anything, Tyler had grabbed the large glass ashtray from the coffee table and hit the dog across the head, sending him spinning into the fireplace where he remained still. Her heart sank in total despair. She had become attached to Bear and enjoyed having him around but now, just when she needed help, he he had paid with his life. He must have jumped the fence and come in through the front door. Consumed with hate and rage, it seemed that all her life her loved ones were taken away from her.

Francesca was afraid no more. Standing before her was the reason she had changed so much. Tyler represented all that was bad in her life, and now he had killed her dog. Her anger was so great that fear didn't exist anymore. She saw out of the corner of her eye her silver envelope opener — it twinkled like a bright star, the light from the chandelier reflecting off the blade, and in a split second it was in her hand.

Tyler, clutching his face, was livid. He lunged forward and in a very controlled manner she pushed the blade into his other arm, slicing through with ease as if she was spearing an apple.

Instantly he grabbed his arm in utter disbelief. She had just stabbed him. Francesca looked at the flesh hanging from his cheek — with no emotion she stood still and stared. Tyler afraid now, stepped back. "Give me the knife, Francesca. Come on, sweetheart, I won't hurt you." Just like Charles talking, his slow, soft voice echoing around her head, as if her husband was in the room with her, *was this deja vu coming to haunt her again?*

She looked over at her lifeless dog, then glared at Tyler.

"Come on, you stupid fucking whore, who the hell do you think you are? I'll have you cremated alive if you don't give me that fucking knife." He was desperate, never having faced a woman with so much hate in her eyes, and so he attempted another tactic. Even though he was in so much pain, he wanted to talk her around, get the knife and finish her off.

"Come on, darling, let's have a brandy."

Francesca was getting hot again but she didn't want to faint, for those were the same words her husband used the night he tried to kill her.

"You want me to have a brandy so you too can pin me down, slash my face to ribbons and cut out my womanhood, and throw me into the sea and leave me to die?" Her voice was chilling, her eyes as white as marbles, and her face as tight as an elastic band ready to snap.

He staggered back. His face, apart from the bite mark, was white. He looked sick.

Tyler was in immense pain but those words paralysed him — he may have had one too many drinks, but that was most certainly how his nephew had killed his wife. *She couldn't possibly be Launa, no way.* He was shocked. With his mouth open, he stared – this was no fucking secretary, for sure, so who was she?

"What's wrong, Tyler? You look like you've seen a ghost."

"Launa?"

"No, I'm Francesca."

Tyler thought he was going mad. The pain worsened. *After all, Launa was dead – no one could survive all that.* He had seen a wedding picture of Charles Junior and Launa, and Francesca looked nothing like her.

She continued to stare, enjoying the position she held, having Tyler at her mercy.

"I couldn't possibly be Launa. After all she would be fish food now, eh?"

Tyler felt his heart pounding. *How could Francesca know about Launa?* Light-headed from the amount of blood he had lost, he tried to focus.

"Launa died back in England. I am now Francesca." She smiled a very sick smile.

The phone was next to her. She made the mistake of turning away from Tyler to dial Sergio.

He lunged forward, this time to finish off what his nephew had started, but he was weakened by his injury and she managed to grab his hair, pull his head down and, with one forceful move, she plunged the knife into his eye, hard enough to penetrate the brain. The warm blood gushed from the socket and over her hand – that same warm feeling she felt when Charles had plunged the knife into her. She watched as he dropped to the floor and, slowly but surely, the twitching stopped. He was dead.

She poured herself a brandy and sat for a while. Her dog lay lifeless, and a tear rolled down her face. Her friend was dead; he had saved her from a night of hell, and now he lay there alone. She went over and gently stroked his head.

She dialled the number.

"Sergio, you had better come over here now." Her voice was calm and resigned. She sat back down and finished the large glass of brandy.

*

When Sergio arrived he let himself in. He was concerned because Francesca had sounded odd on the phone, and she'd hung up before she would give any explanation.

She heard him come through the door but remained sitting in the armchair. Unbeknownst to her, she was covered in blood.

Sergio stopped in his tracks when he saw a blood-drenched Francesca; instinct took over and he pulled out his gun and looked around the room.

"What the fuck is going on?" Then he saw Tyler lying flat on his back with half his face hanging off and the handle of a knife protruding from his eye.

She stood up and pointed to Bear. "The bastard killed my dog."

Sergio was astounded: there he was, looking at his lawyer with a knife in his eye, no sign of an intruder, and his Francesca soaked in blood, white as a sheet, but with a calm and demonic countenance. Something happened to him at that moment: he couldn't explain it – little did he know that from this point onward his life would change for evermore.

"Cesca, look at me, eh?" Sergio walked over to her; she faced him. "What has happened here?"

"I told you – that bastard, Tyler, killed my dog and I've stabbed him."

Dumbfounded, he put his arms slowly around her and hugged her. "It's gonna be all right."

Francesca nodded. She didn't really care anymore.

"Take off your clothes," whispered Sergio.

Francesca pushed him away. "What the fuck?"

Before she could finish, Sergio stopped her. "No, not here. I mean put them in a bag and get into the shower, clean yourself up, and I will take care of the rest."

Too tired to think for herself, she headed for the bathroom.

Sergio made some coffee and thought about calling Roberto, but the best move right now was to take care of Francesca, get the body out of the house, and go from there.

He looked at Tyler and tried to work out what had gone on. He looked grotesque: half-dressed, his cheek hanging on by a slither of flesh, and a knife sticking through his eye, he shuddered at the sight. *Fuck – getting on the wrong side of her;* she was just like Mauricio.

*

As he sat back, sipping the coffee and waiting for Francesca to reappear, he heard footsteps outside. He looked out of the window, whilst hiding behind the curtain. There, at the door, he saw a man trying to look through the entrance by the hall window. He had to be one of Tyler's men. Usually he had the mob, but now he was alone in the house with a dog-loving nutter upstairs and a peeping Tom in the front garden.

Without hesitation, he threw open the door, grabbed the stranger by the hair, and shoved a gun in his mouth.

"Get inside and don't fucking move or I'm gonna blast you to fucking Sicily."

Fred was stunned. *One minute he was in England being carted off with a gun to his head, next minute he was in the States staring down the barrel of another shooter; the only difference was that this gangster was better dressed.*

Sergio pushed Fred to the wall and pointed the gun at his head. "Who the fuck are you and what do you want. Before you answer – if you lie to me, I will kill you."

Fred was shaking like a leaf. He was staring into the eyes of a serious Italian gangster. There was a difference between the heavies in London and the heavies in the States, and Fred was shitting hot bricks.

"Hey, man, I don't want no trouble. I must 'ave the wrong house."

Sergio looked him up and down; the accent was British, there must be a connection. Francesca was British and the corpse was British.

"So who the fuck are you?" As the words left Sergio's mouth, he recognised Fred, not from a photo – in fact, he had no idea who he was – but it was the eyes which were so familiar.

"Sorry, mate, I don't want to disturb you. Just, I was given this address by my sister."

Fred was still holding the address book in his hand and, nervously, he handed it to Sergio.

Sergio didn't take it; instead, he stared at Fred.

"So who is your sister, then?" he asked, but then, before Fred could answer, a voice from the top of the stairs shouted down.

"Fred, what the hell are you doing here?"

Sergio looked at Francesca and then back at Fred. He put the gun back into its holster.

Fred was relieved when the gun was out of his face.

"Sis, is that you?" Fred was trying hard to see the woman who was walking down the stairs. She didn't look like his Dolly but the second she was in his view he could see her eyes and sense her. They hugged and kissed and Francesca introduced him.

"Sergio, this is my brother, Fred."

Patting Fred's back, he said, "Hey, I am so sorry. Francesca's brother is my brother." He hugged him, much to Fred's surprise.

"So you must be Dolly's boyfriend then?"

Sergio frowned. He hadn't heard her called Dolly before. "No, I'm her other brother from her Sicilian family."

Fred was seriously confused but took it with a pinch of salt. He'd had a hell of a last twenty four hours, and he was just glad to be with his sister and her Sicilian family, whatever that meant. He kept staring at Francesca.

"Cor, fucking 'ell, Dolly, you don't half look different."

She nodded.

"Listen, Fred, you can't stay here." She wanted him out of the house. This was, after all, her dirty mess and no one else's.

His heart sank. He looked at her grand entrance and thought that his sister had really made a good life for herself, and of course she couldn't have a dodgy East End boy in the way. Besides, he hadn't given her any notice and it was probably a bit too much to ask. After all, as much as she was his sister, there was a lot he didn't know about her. *Had she ever really forgiven them for sending her away as a kid?* Maybe it was a liberty to unexpectedly barge into her life.

The fright, when he had been dragged through the door, had made his mouth dry.

"It's all right, sis, I understand. Can I just have a glass of water first, and then I'll be off?"

Before Francesca or Sergio could stop him, he walked into the living room.

"Cor, Dolly, this is grand. You fell on your feet 'ere all right." As he was admiring the large luxurious room, he stopped dead. "What the fuck!"

Francesca grabbed his arm. "Fred, come on, you must get out of here."

Slowly, he turned to face his sister and Sergio. Sergio shrugged his shoulders and Francesca looked embarrassed. "Sis, what's going on?" Fred was now firm. "There's a fucking dead man in your house."

Francesca nodded. "Look, Fred, this is my problem, not yours. Please leave, I don't want you involved."

"Are you nuts? You're my sister. I'm already involved." He put his hand to his head. "So who killed him?"

Sergio jumped in. "I did."

"No you never. I killed him because he fucking killed my dog."

Fred was astounded; *his very own sister kills a guy because he killed her dog.* He shook his head. As he looked around the room again, he saw the dog lying by the fireplace. "Is that your dog?" He was almost laughing.

Francesca nodded.

"Fuck, sis, and I thought you were the clever one. That ain't no dog, that is a North American timber wolf!" He walked over to Bear and bent down to inspect the dog more closely and noticed it was slowly breathing. "Oh yeah, and he ain't dead."

"What!" screeched Francesca, dashing to Bear's side.

"Look, he's not dead. He has been knocked out, that's all. Go and get some blankets and keep him warm."

Sergio looked on in amazement. There, in the room, was a dead man in a gruesome state, and Francesca and her brother were fussing over a wolf, as if having a corpse in the house was normal.

"Hey, guys, guys, shall we deal with the important issue here?"

Fred got up and walked over to Sergio. "So, mate, what do we do, dump the body?"

Sergio nodded in bewilderment. *Most normal men wouldn't have even seen a dead body, let alone be happy to dump one. Well, apart from the mob.* But then, he had learnt tonight a great deal about Francesca's family and it intrigued him.

"So, sis, now you've gone and killed a man because he knocked out your dog, fuck knows what you would do if he hurt your family?"

Francesca was covering Bear with a blanket when she spun around and said, "The dog was protecting me. The cunt was trying to rape and murder me!"

"What?" shouted Sergio and Fred in unison.

"Oh, didn't I mention that bit?"

Fred walked over to the corpse and spat on it.

"Fred, help me wrap him up in this rug here and get him into the boot of my car," said Sergio.

"What are we gonna do with him, Serg?" asked Fred, as if this was an everyday occurrence.

Sergio smiled. He had taken a liking to Francesca's brother; he was straight talking, not afraid. He had a very deep honour for his family, and he liked the way he said 'we' as if it was his job to help.

"Well tonight I will drive him to the Owens funeral parlour; they will cremate him for me."

Fred laughed. "No, Sergio – really, what shall we do with him?"

"Like I say, I will take him to Owens and they will get rid of the body. They can put this body under another one in the casket and incinerate them together."

He was serious and so Fred stepped back thinking, *this is like the fucking Godfather films.*

As both men rolled the body up in the rug, Fred confessed that he killed a man the day before. "Yeah, funny, you know I shot the bloke in the eye, and the next day my sister stabs this geezer in the same place — must be a twin thing."

Sergio frowned again. *These two are fucking crazy. Her brother had just confessed he had killed a man and she had not even questioned it.* He guessed it really must be a twin thing. *This evening was too surreal.*

Bear opened his eyes and tried to get up. "Stay, boy," whispered Francesca, relieved that he was okay.

When Fred and Sergio drove off, with Tyler nicely rolled up in the rug in the boot of the car, she curled up next to Bear and went over in her mind the horrific events. She knew now that she was a different woman, having no remorse for Tyler's murder. In fact, she felt at peace that one Enright was taken out of her life, with just three more to go. She pondered over her brother's comments and shame clouded her. She never wanted her family to be involved in her mess. They had serious problems of their own. She wasn't perturbed that Fred had killed someone as long as he was safe, and she would make sure he stayed that way. *No one would harm her family again, not if she could help it.*

Chapter Thirteen

The next morning Fred was up before Francesca, busy making breakfast. She smelled the bacon and coffee wafting up the stairs and, reacting to this aroma, her stomach rumbled, so she hurried to the kitchen.

"How's the spare room — are you comfortable enough?" She kissed her brother on the cheek.

"Morning, sis. Yeah, I love the room, it's like a palace. I feel like I'm on holiday."

Francesca laughed. "What, a murder fucking mystery weekend?"

"Ha-ha, fucking funny." He handed her a cup of coffee. "Get your laughing gear around that."

Bear looked better than ever and excited to see Francesca — his tail wagged generously, and he seemed to be more alert.

"Bear looks well, Fred. What do you think?"

"Yep, he definitely is. You wanna see him run around the garden; he was leaping all over the place. But you look happier too, sis."

She nodded.

"Yeah, you've got a bit of a sparkle in those steely blues of yours." He handed her the bacon sandwich and then went on to ask if Sergio was coming over today.

Francesca then realised what he was getting at. She shrugged her shoulders and grinned.

"Sis…" He paused.

Francesca looked up over her coffee to see her brother's sad expression.

"Sis, it was hard growing up without you. I mean, I felt lost. It was like half of me was gone. There was an emptiness that nothing could fill." His eyes watered.

"I know, Fred," she whispered.

"Dole, there were so many times that I wanted to run away and live with you, not for any other reason than just to be with you… mad, eh? What I am trying to say, sis, is that although you were sent away, we thought about you every day and none of us forgot you."

Francesca nodded; a lump in her throat stopped the words from flowing.

"I was all right, Fred. I missed you all so much but Anne was kind to me, she really helped." Her voice cracked, holding back the tears.

"We have so much to talk about. I wanna know all about your life: the good, the bad and the ugly." His words slipped out before he realised that was not a good thing to say. "Sorry, sis, I mean…"

She jumped in. "Fred, stop, it's all right. I can tell you the good, but the bad and ugly – well, one day, Fred, I may be able to face it, but now it's hard."

He put his arms around her shoulders and hugged her. She felt complete, an odd feeling that had she missed for so many years, but it was back, and comfort engulfed her.

"You know what, sis, I don't want to delve into what happened. You will tell me when you're ready, but there's one thing I must tell you. The night you were attacked, I had to pull over in the car. I had a strange sensation and I blacked out. Kathy told me that, when you were rushed into hospital, the crash team had to bring you back to life. Dole, it was the same time that I fainted."

She nodded as if she knew. "Fred, I knew I was dying, and I wondered if you sensed the life leave me. I remember saying goodbye to you all before I was unconscious."

Fred was overwhelmed with emotion. The thought of her dying there, all alone, sent a cold wave through his body and, tormented with guilt, he sobbed.

"Hey, you, come on, don't cry. I am fine. Look at me, we are together, and soon I will be home." Francesca knew then that she had never been a distant memory. They had loved her as much as the day she left for her aunt's home.

"Let's get our teeth into some real business." She went on to tell Fred what had been going on with Tyler and the double cross to ensure Roberto and Mauricio's incarceration. Fred was back to his lively, eager self, and keen to get stuck in.

*

They sat at the dining table and looked over the contract again. It took a while before they could piece it together, since both their French was a bit rusty, and Francesca's corporate law studies were such a long time ago, but eventually they managed to translate the contracts.

Francesca sat back on her chair with her hands over her mouth and Fred just repeated the F word over and over.

"Fancy that, eh, a three-hundred-year-old contract," said Francesca calmly.

"The sly fucking bastards, no wonder they want Roberto behind bars," gasped Fred.

"I'm going to get Roberto over here now. This is a whole new ball game. Fred, are you absolutely sure this is the proper translation?"

"Oh yeah, sis, I wouldn't play guessing games with this heavy shit."

Roberto arrived with Sergio within the hour. Francesca was excited to reveal the findings – like finding the evidence in a court case that would set her clients free. She loved the feeling; it was the most satisfying part of her job. This was little different: she was so involved with both families and she had unravelled a three-hundred-year-old bond and a fifty-year mystery.

Roberto was just as excited to hear the news and, for the first time, she saw a completely different expression on Roberto's face – like a child opening a present.

"Right then, this may come as a shock..." She paused and took a deep breath. "But if you are the direct descendant of Gerard Fabien III on your father's side, then on January 1st, 1999," – she needed to pause as the excitement was taking her breath away – "you will be the owner of a substantial amount of land in France. The revenue from it, as it stands now, would give you millions of francs. In fact, you will be one of the wealthiest men in Europe."

"However, the conditions are that you must be a practising Catholic and a law abiding citizen, a common practice in those days, but a strict condition by which you must abide."

She sat back down and, along with Sergio and Fred, awaited a response from Roberto, who was now wide-eyed and silent.

Francesca couldn't read his facial expression and was impatient to ascertain his reaction. "Roberto, are you the direct descendant?"

Without hesitation, he nodded.

"You know this for a fact?"

He smiled a very angelic smile. "My family is so important to me and this goes back for hundreds of years. I was brought up the same way my father and his father and so on. I know who I am and where I came from and yes, I am the direct descendant." A tear rolled down his cheek.

"So tell me, Francesca, is this why the Enright family have tried all those years to put me and my son in prison? Why? Why would they do this to me? What interest do they have in all of this?"

Francesca looked to the floor. "They too are descendants — but not directly. They can only lay claim to this title if you are shown not to be a fit and proper Catholic or end up in prison. Then they would own the land and all the rights. The contract is undisputable; it is so rare yet they do exist. This one is probably the most powerful one in existence and no governing body, no council or court, can overturn it. The land and all its current properties are held by the church but, on the 1st of January, the titles will be placed in your name. You see, your great forefather had become a man of the cloth, yet he was so wealthy, and so his wealth was handed to the churches for three hundred years to do good, but in accordance with the agreement, it must be returned to his family... that being you or your son. Of course, since he was a religious man, you must not have lived an unlawful life. That bit is disputable but you would have to be found guilty in a court of law to have absolute proof of unlawfulness."

Roberto got up from the chair and walked over to the window. It was a habit, whenever he needed to see clearly; he would stare out into the open air.

"If I could have lived my life without the stress and worry of my brother, my wife and the boys, I would have gladly handed over the land. Look what those scum have done to us. You know something, my brain may not be so sharp these days but my memory is perfect. All the things that happened to me and my family in the past, all those times, I wondered why I was being set up, and I now know why."

Roberto drooped his head and cupped his face with his big hands. Francesca could feel his sadness and went to his side whilst Sergio and Fred left the room.

She had misjudged Roberto, thinking that he would be pleased that he would soon be the owner of so much land and money now that the Enrights' secret was out in the open. He was bitterly sad that his family's life journey had been partially governed by a three-hundred-year-old promise. The money hadn't meant so much in later years, only in the beginning, when he started out in life with his young bride, struggling and striving to make a good living. He would have gladly given it all up to have his wife and brother back.

Roberto took a deep breath and sighed.

He turned to face Francesca.

"My Angelina died carrying our second child, convinced the baby was a girl. Our daughter would have been your age, Francesca, and you are so much like my wife. She was clever like you. She was the one who always said knowledge is power and she was right every time." He cupped her face.

"I have a gift for you, my daughter. Both Sergio and Mauricio have one, but this one is made from some of my wife's jewellery."

Roberto pulled from his pocket a box that he placed on the dining table and slowly removed the lid to reveal what looked like a small gun. It was made of gold, with gems encrusted in the handle. He removed it gently and, with a firm grip, he pulled the trigger.

Francesca gasped and then smiled when the end of the gun produced a flame.

"Oh, how lovely, it's a cigarette lighter."

Francesca thought it was a bit of an odd gift, considering she only smoked very occasionally, but it was a beautiful-looking item.

Roberto smiled as he took Francesca to the French windows. He pointed the gun down the garden, cocked it and fired. Francesca jumped.

"This is very rare. There are four only and you have this one. Everything is handmade, and so the police will not view it as a gun but a lighter. It may save your life if you want it to."

Francesca took the gun gracefully. *One day it would come in handy: both Roberto and she had something in common and that was their hatred for the Enrights.* She hugged Roberto: he, in turn, felt something which had been missing in his life for a very long time – he could not rationalise it, but his thoughts turned to his wife and a tear left his eye.

He kissed her head and left.

Sergio decided to stay for a while and go over the contract again so he could understand it properly. When he was clear about what it all meant, he decided to change the subject. After all, it would be down to Roberto what the next move would be, and he guessed they would hold a family meeting when Mauricio returned.

*

Fred and Sergio spent the rest of the afternoon discussing business. Fred had not been slow in asking for a job. He had concluded that he would not be safe returning to England, and he didn't have a money tree in the back garden.

Sergio enjoyed the company of Fred and would easily find him a job. He needed people around him that he could trust, so he discussed the possibility of Fred managing one of the casinos. It would take the pressure off him and help Fred at the same time.

"I think you need to work with me for a while to get to know how it all runs, because it's going to be very different from running your nightclub back home."

"Serg, I can't thank you enough. I won't let you down, I promise, mate," beamed Fred.

They shook hands and clinked together large brandy glasses.

Francesca soaked in the bath whilst the men continued with business downstairs.

She tried to get the vision out of her mind. It was only exhaustion that had allowed her to sleep, but she knew that, once her life returned to normal, she would find it hard to stop the nightmares. She closed her eyes and could see clearly both her husband's face and Tyler's. They merged from one to another, until she saw herself plunging the letter opener into Tyler's eye. It was at that point she relaxed – most people would not react this way and, being a barrister, she knew it probably wasn't normal, especially if she was questioned by a psychiatrist. *She would be free when their faces no longer haunted her.*

*

Fred was dressed in a suit and looked very handsome. He had made the effort because he needed the job with Sergio, and so he went all out to impress him. Francesca decided to join them. She needed to take her mind off things and sitting alone would not be good right now. As they entered the casino, Fred's mouth was agape from the sheer size and glamour of the place – very different from the nightclub back in England.

"Shit, sis, this place is fucking enormous."

Francesca laughed. "Yeah, I have to agree, it's pretty huge."

He walked ahead, gazing like a child at the immensity of it all. Sergio walked over with his two guards either side; they tended to follow him around in the casino. In fact, it was only at Francesca's house that both Sergio and Roberto were alone.

He talked Fred through how it all worked, who was in charge of what, and who managed whom.

It was obvious that this business was far more complicated than running a nightclub.

Fred was baffled as to what part of this massive moneymaking machine he wanted him to manage.

Sergio patted Fred on the back. "Hey, you look worried. Don't be – this casino practically runs itself. I have the place divided into five sections and each section is in competition. Each manager is very competitive and good at their jobs; I only employ people I can trust and, well," he shrugged, "if they fuck up, they won't have the opportunity to fuck up again." He paused and looked Fred in the eyes. "Don't misunderstand me, to be under that sort of pressure they are paid well."

"So, Serg, what exactly do you want me to do?" He rubbed his hands together, a gesture that he was ready to get going.

Sergio laughed. "I want you to just stay with me and watch how everything works. It will take some getting used to, but you will be paid a good wage. You can start by joining me for a drink in the private bar."

Fred was enjoying himself; the women were beautiful and very attentive, especially the one who took his drinks order and ran her fingers along his jaw.

"Lacy, please do not flirt with him. He may well be your boss next week," dismissed Sergio.

The young cheeky waitress flushed red and tilted her head. "Sorry, Mr Luciani."

She turned to face Fred. "Sorry, sir."

Fred laughed; he realised that she was paid to make up to the punters.

Francesca fancied her hand at a game of blackjack and was quite happy to play alone. Just as she placed her last chip, she noticed two men beside her. They appeared smart, with white shirts and black ties, and to their left were three other men who stood guarding them. Listening to their accents, it was clear they were Italian. As she threw her chip onto the table, she couldn't help but overhear their conversation. The hairs on the back of her neck stood up. She concluded that the smaller guy near her was Mr Aldini. She remembered Sergio talking about the long feud they'd had with the Aldinis. In fact, she remembered that Tyler was cremated with the old man Aldini.

She could make out his intentions quite clearly.

"You see, this was all supposed to be mine. My father, God rest him, had left this to me in his will before it was taken from him. I am not my father. Honour? Honour? I will show honour when I take back this casino."

Francesca looked around to see if anyone else could hear but the blackjack table was bare. She headed towards the bar to warn Sergio, but Joe Aldini and his mob had beaten her to it.

She watched Sergio usher them into the private room. Fred had been left outside and smiled when he saw his sister heading his way.

"Hi, sis, enjoying yourself?"

"Fred, those men that have gone in with Sergio, they are up to something," said Francesca.

"It's okay, sis. Sergio's men are in there."

"How many?" snapped Francesca.

"Three. Why?"

"Because there are four men with Joe Aldini."

Fred slid open a drawer under the till and pulled out a gun. He quickly put it down the back of his pants.

"How did you know that gun was there?"

"Good guess, I suppose. I've got one hidden in the same place at home."

She rolled her eyes, opened her bag, and retrieved her new gold handgun. Fred laughed.

"What the fuck do you call that?"

Francesca frowned in annoyance; it was obvious Fred was not taking the situation seriously.

"This," she said, cupping the gun, "is the difference between life and death." Her serious tone made him realise she wasn't fucking about.

He looked around to see if anyone was looking. Francesca, like her brother, put her gun at the back of her trousers, and allowed her loose jumper to hide it well.

"Why are you so sure they want to cause trouble?"

"Because, my darling twin, I, like you, pick up languages fairly quickly and I overheard them discussing their plan in Italian. I just hope they didn't notice me."

Francesca planned to walk into the private room with Fred, armed with a tray of drinks. Francesca waited outside. She heard raised voices and, with her ear pressed to the door, tried hard to catch what was going on. She grabbed a tray full of refreshments. Her heart pounded. She looked over at Fred and ushered him to get ready. She heard shuffling and then a crashing sound.

Instantly, the pair opened the door to see Sergio on the floor and his men being held up. They all turned to face the twins. Joe, with the gun at Sergio's head, shouted for them to put the drinks down and leave the room.

Sergio was wide-eyed and petrified. Francesca held one hand up and said, "Please, sir, take it easy. I'll just put the drinks here." She pretended to put the drinks on the table but, as Joe turned back to face Sergio, she dropped the tray. The noise was so loud that all the men were unnerved. Fred, meanwhile, was working out how to overturn this situation. He spotted a small guy with a briefcase and a pile of papers under his arm. The small guy was a lawyer forcing Sergio to sign something. Each of Sergio's men was pushed against the wall with a gun stuck in their face. The only man not holding a gun was Joe Aldini's right-hand man, who had his foot on Sergio's neck, holding him on the floor while Joe pointed a gun at Sergio's face. In addition, there was, of course, the weasel-faced lawyer.

Francesca instantly pulled the gun from her back and fired it at Joe. The room was in a panic. She had surprised herself; it was a natural reaction to protect what she deemed as her family. She had caught his arm. Before the pain could truly hit him, he turned and aimed his weapon at Francesca. Another shot, this time leaving Fred's gun, hit Joe, and he dropped the gun. Francesca was now pointing the gun at the heavy holding Sergio to the floor.

As Joe screamed, Francesca swung around and aimed the gun at his head. "Call your men off or I'm gonna fuck you up."

Joe was stunned and furious but had been left with no choice.

Fred aimed his gun now at the lawyer, who was slyly reaching for something in bag.

"Drop it, you little fuck!" shouted Fred.

The lawyer had already grabbed the gun inside the briefcase and instantly fired it. The bullet went into Sergio's chest. The shock that he had just shot someone caused him to drop the gun and place his hands above his head. The lawyer was now in a state of panic. He had just shot Roberto's nephew and, even with the Aldini's protection, he was a dead man walking.

Francesca screamed at Joe's right hand man, who still held Sergio to the floor with his foot. "Get away from him!" She held the gun with both hands, aiming it now at the six foot six giant who still wouldn't release his foot.

She fired: in true giant style, he hit the floor like a sack of potatoes. The bullet had hit him clean through the heart. Sergio's men were astonished. It was their job to protect Sergio and the casino, but they had been taken by surprise. There had not been even a whisper that something was going down. They worried that Roberto would have them fired, or worse. To be shown up by a woman too – that would not sit well with their boss.

Fred grabbed Joe by the hair and dragged him across the floor, with little resistance, since Joe was such a wimp. The bullet wound, and the sight of his own blood made him feel faint.

"Now call your men off or I'm gonna blow you away!" he screamed in his ear.

The other men looked at Joe and he nodded. They put their guns away and instantly left – even Aldini's men were shit-scared of the Lucianis and were not going to stay around. They were under the impression that the casino takeover was a sure thing. Now Sergio had been shot, they were on borrowed time.

Francesca cradled Sergio in her arms. He was ashen and his body lifeless.

"Please don't die." The tears streamed down her face.

The men had made all the calls. The paramedics were on their way as well as Roberto. They quickly removed the dead body before the police arrived. Fred took Joe Aldini into another room, tied him up and gagged him.

"You can wait there and I'll see if I can get something for the pain."

His eyes widened. *He was bleeding to death and this English nutter was offering a painkiller.*

Joe Aldini, now reduced to complete humiliation, was going to be kept in a store cupboard by some fucking English waiter. He would rather have been brutally killed and have his body parts posted around New York than die an undignified death. *It just wasn't the Italian way.*

Fred returned with a bandage and a small cosh. "You're an ugly little shit. You think you're some kinda Godfather? Well you've gone and shot me buddy and pissed me sister off, so later, when I let you out, I'm gonna fucking piss you off, and ya muvver."

Joe couldn't believe the English waiter had such balls.

Fred threw the bandage at Joe and said, "Oh yeah, the painkiller," and with the cosh hit him hard enough on the chin to knock him out.

*

Francesca kept Sergio warm until the paramedics arrived. Roberto ran into the room, frantic. "My boy, my boy," he cried, as he knelt down beside Sergio, and prayed. The paramedic pushed them aside and, within minutes, Sergio was in the ambulance and speeding off to the hospital. Francesca wasn't going to leave Sergio's side.

Francesca was terrified he would die alone and never know how she really felt about him. She watched every move the paramedics made, willing them to save his life. Everything seemed to follow in slow motion like an old movie, which could be run at a slower speed, where even the voices appeared as though the characters were drugged and the speech slurred.

She remembered the first time she had met him. She had been so struck by his gentle manner when Roberto had been so hard, and how caring he was when Tyler tried to rape her. In fact, when she looked back, it seemed as though he was always there when she needed him, and he'd asked nothing from her. His soft, dark curls lay on his face, revealing the clear outline of his features. She noticed just how handsome he was. She wanted to see him open his beautiful eyes and wink at her, the way he often did, that let her know she was safe.

Roberto had arranged for his own doctor to be there when he arrived who, apparently, was a very good gunshot wound surgeon.

Sergio was rushed into the theatre, followed by a team of theatre staff, whilst Francesca and Roberto were ushered into the waiting room.

"I need to make some calls, my daughter. Please wait here and I will be back soon." His red-rimmed eyes looked full of the deepest sadness.

Francesca nodded. She wasn't going anywhere.

The minutes ticked away, as she rocked back and forth in her chair, hugging herself. Surprised by her sudden feelings towards Sergio, the tears kept rolling down her cheeks. Perhaps she had fallen in love with him the day they'd met, but she had put up a protective veil to prevent herself from being hurt. Right now, though, she was hurting more than she ever imagined.

The doctor appeared from the theatre an hour later. Peeling back his gloves, he looked drained. He rubbed his eyes and looked in Francesca's direction. He smiled, much to her relief.

Jumping from her seat, she rushed over. "How did it go, is he okay?"

Nodding profusely, he replied. "Yes, yes, he will be fine. The bullet has caused a considerable amount of damage to his lower left lung but we managed to remove all the offending parts and, with rest and medicine, he will live."

"Thank you so much," whispered Francesca.

Roberto had arrived to hear the last part of the conversation, and he immediately grabbed Francesca and hugged her. She could feel his shoulders moving up and down as he sobbed with relief.

Fred arrived a little later, after leaving Joe guarded by Sergio's men.

"Heh," smiled Roberto. "Look, it's my new son." He held Fred by the shoulders, looked him up and down, and then gave him an old-fashioned Italian hug.

Fred smiled. "How's Sergio?"

"He's going to be just fine," beamed Francesca.

"Thank fuck for that. For a minute there I thought…" He paused, ran his hands through his hair, and then went on. "Well, you know what I thought."

Francesca nodded.

"So what happened to Joe Aldini? Where is he now?" questioned Roberto.

Fred looked up. "Oh yeah, well I left him in the broom cupboard, tied up and gagged. He's either got a bad headache or he is brown bread."

Roberto shrugged. "Uh, brown bread?"

"Dead, Roberto. Brown bread means dead."

Roberto laughed. "You bloody cockney."

The police arrived and left again. When they found it was Roberto's nephew, they concluded it was pointless questioning him. His answer would simply be a stray bullet and they knew the Lucianis sorted out their own dirty laundry.

As Sergio came to, Francesca was there by his bed.

"Hello, stranger," she said.

His eyes focused on her face. He could see she had been crying. Then he said in a very faint voice, "Don't worry, Francesca, I wasn't going to die and leave you."

"So you heard me then? Only, I thought you were unconscious." She felt her face redden as she remembered the other words she had spoken to him.

"And I love you too, my angel," he whispered.

Her bottom lip quivered like a child, and a tear rolled from her eyes and onto his face as she leant forward to kiss him.

Roberto looked on and a warm feeling came over him. He saw the same expression in Francesca's eyes which, thirty years ago, he had seen in his wife's, the day she thought he may not pull through from a bullet wound.

Francesca left Sergio's bedside as he drifted off to sleep.

Chapter Fourteen

Roberto walked along the corridor with Francesca, discussing the way forward regarding the legacy.

As predicted, the FBI arrested Mauricio. He had docked their ship and its drug free cargo as planned. They were there ready for inspection on a tip off from Charles Enright. He had seen the cargo of drugs being loaded on the ship, and there should have been no problems. This would be the day that the Enrights would finally have the Lucianis behind bars. The land would be theirs, or so they thought. The Customs and Excise, along with Charles Senior, were rubbing their hands together. The FBI had wanted to take down the Luciani's cartel for years, and this was the best lead they had. But the tip off and the whole operation, seemed a little too obvious. Surely this was too straightforward? Mauricio wouldn't chance being on his own ship with illegal cargo, it wasn't his style. *Would they risk everything for a drugs run?*

Roberto knew that his son would be held by Customs and Excise, but his release would be imminent. With no illegal cargo on board, they had to let him go.

Mr Carponi's son had graduated with honours and had settled in with a law firm downtown. He decided to let the young lad go along and represent Mauricio. It was uncomplicated, and he just wanted assurance that Customs didn't try to set up Mauricio. Danny Carponi was delighted that he was representing one of the Lucianis, yet fully aware of the consequences. If he succeeded in doing a good job, Roberto may even let him work on his team. He left no stone unturned and, within two hours, Mauricio was out and in the clear. Charles Enright had not left any contact numbers with Customs, so they couldn't inform him of his mistake.

Francesca wanted the Enrights to believe that Mauricio had been arrested and banged to rights.

She sat with Roberto and Fred in Tyler's office.

It made sense that Roberto would be looking for Tyler if Mauricio was in trouble. After all, he was his lawyer. So if the Enrights contacted the office, the receptionist would say that Roberto was looking for him.

Of course, in the meantime, the idea was to email Charles in the guise of Tyler.

Roberto smirked as he asked, "So, what are you going to write in this email?"

"I will say that Mauricio has been arrested for carrying a large consignment of drugs and, since he is a member of a high profile family, this arrest will not be made public until the court case," she paused. "This will give us plenty of time to make plans."

She looked up to see both Fred and Roberto staring.

Roberto went through his usual routine, getting up and walking to the window.

"You are very clever, Francesca. This is a good idea and I see where you are going with this, by pretending you are Tyler and going through his emails to reel in the others."

Francesca nodded.

"I think it's a good plan, but that's where it ends. This gives me time to find this Charles, and his bloody brother, and deal with them as they should be dealt with."

Francesca jumped up from her seat. "No!" she shouted. She composed herself. "No, Roberto, I want to reel them in for myself."

He firmly shook his head. "This is my war, my history."

"You should have understood me by now, Roberto. Until I have rid myself of all my demons, I cannot start to live my life how I want to. And some of those demons go by the name of Enright."

Roberto put his hand around her shoulder and kissed her forehead.

The very quiet Fred piped up. "Sis, he is right; it's not your war. There has been a lot of blood spilt lately, and I don't think it's gonna do you a lot of good. I mean, I watched you in the casino – you just fucking shot two men like you were firing a fucking peashooter. Makes me think you are enjoying the bloodshed."

He looked to the floor, realising he probably shouldn't have said that. "I'm sorry, sis."

She shook her head. "It's all right, I know how it looks. But, Fred, you haven't walked in my shoes for the last few years of my life, or even been beside me where you should have been. So, I don't expect you to understand how I can be so cold. I love my family so much that it hurts every time I think of you. I became used to being so alone and loving people that couldn't show they loved me back because they weren't in my life. Knowing from such a young age that one evil man was responsible, and then to have the Enrights try to destroy me for their greed, and have my husband slice me like a butcher preparing meat, and throw me away into the sea to die, well..." She stopped to force back the tears. "Well, it has changed me. Life is not by any means a bed of roses and I can't ever stop and think of the consequences because those who hurt me, never did either. So I will get revenge on the Enrights and I will enjoy every fucking minute of it."

She looked at Roberto, who smiled with sympathy, and then back at Fred, who was crying like a baby.

"I'm so sorry, Dolly." He got up from his seat and hugged her, for what seemed like for eternity.

Roberto poured each of them a brandy and made a decision. "I have you to thank for so much. My Mauricio, Sergio – and you came into my life like an angel. You uncovered this age-old mystery and you want nothing from me, so this is what I propose. You may take revenge on anyone you feel has wronged you, and I will arrange for this to happen but, because you are family and are too important to me to lose you, I propose that we as a family do this together."

Francesca nodded and Fred smiled.

*

She wrote the email to Charles, who must have been sitting on top of his computer. Instantly, he wrote back.

> *Fantastic news, Tyler!*
> *I'll let the others know and get the ball rolling. Oh, before I forget, the ship is still in Roberto's name, I hope – only we really need him serving time as well as Mauricio.*
> *Just to let you know, your man didn't turn up last week with my package. Desperately needing some, as the last lot went in the cargo.*
> *KR Charles*

> *Charles*
> *Not to worry, the ship is in Roberto's name.*
> *My man is off the scene, but I have another good source.*
> *Keep you posted.*
> *Tyler*

She kept the reply short and sweet, just how Tyler would have done.

This was her opening. She thought of delivering a package of cocaine herself. She would meet face-to-face with Charles Senior, to take him out of the equation.

*

Fred and Francesca, with Bear for company, spent the evening in front of the fire with a takeaway. They were watching an American chat show when Mauricio came bounding through the front door. In an instant, Fred was up from the chair and grabbed his gun from behind the cushions of the sofa. Mauricio stopped in his tracks and laughed at the look on Fred's face.
Francesca ran to Mauricio, flinging her arms around him.

Fred put the gun down and nodded. "You must be Mauricio. Pleased to meet you, mate." Fred walked over, holding out his hand to shake the other man's.

Mauricio laughed. "Yeah, and you must be the brother I've heard so much about." He was fascinated by the resemblance. "You have the same eyes and, before her surgery, the same round face, so I guessed straight away!"

He shook Fred's hand then pulled him close for a hug.

"You two are more like twins, hyperactive, impulsive firecrackers!" laughed Francesca.

"You can talk, sis, or shall I call you Jesse James?"

"Well, guys, I go away for a couple of weeks and the terrible twins think they are the fucking mafia." Mauricio laughed loudly; his hair had grown and his tan was intensified. "Guess who's here to see you?" Mauricio opened the front door and ushered in Kathy.

Francesca greeted her with open arms and Fred followed suit.

"Well, I'll be buggered. If it ain't Freddie. I'm so pleased to see you both. Dolly, I had to come over, I've been missing everyone."

She looked Kathy up and down. "What have you done? You look different!" She was amazed at how Kathy looked; she had turned into a real stunner.

Her giggle took Francesca by surprise; somehow, she had regained her youth.

"I had surgery too, to hide those burn scars. That Calton is a genius."
Francesca's eyes widened. "Oh yeah, you look absolutely fabulous."
Mauricio kissed Kathy on the cheek. "She's fucking gorgeous."
Fred laughed. "I'd give you one."
Mauricio jumped in. "Hey, she's my girlfriend."

Fred put his hand up. "Don't worry, mate, she's more like a sister, and, as I was saying, I'd give you one if I was Mauricio."

Sergio was out of hospital, and Francesca agreed to have him at her home to nurse him back to health, with Kathy on hand to give his injections. Fred kept him amused and updated on the goings-on in the casino.

The relationship between them was awkward at first. Sergio wasn't sure if she had reacted the way she did because she thought he would die or if she genuinely loved him, and she felt like a schoolgirl. Now that she had admitted to herself her true feelings, her body was able to react. Her stomach had butterflies, and her heart raced when she looked at him.

One afternoon, whilst Kathy was at the hospital collecting his medicine and Fred was at the casino, Sergio sat at the table and waited for Francesca to join him for lunch. He was still very weak but able to sit with everyone downstairs. The day was wonderful, the sun shone into the dining room, and the smell of summer jasmines wafted in through the French windows.

Francesca sat opposite, placing a selection of sandwiches on the table.

He looked at her and winked. Her heart raced, and she sensed herself blush. She was afraid of her own feelings. Her first love, her husband, had betrayed her, when all she did was show him love, and she desperately wanted to trust again. *She couldn't let her heart be ruled by her head, not again, not ever.*

"Come here, Cesca," commanded Sergio, as he flicked his hair out of his eye.

As weak as he was, he looked strong and handsome. His appeal was more than his looks. He had a soft nature, which was a contradiction, considering his family's reputation. He had been kind to her without making it obvious he was doing her a favour.

He watched as she slowly walked towards him. He absorbed every curve of her body, the long slender neck, and beautiful full lips. He reached for her hand and gently he pulled her onto his lap.

"Do you really love me, Fran?"

She bit her bottom lip, trying to control her breathing.

"Yes, Sergio, I believe I do."

He held the back of her head and kissed her gently. She could feel her body responding to his touch and quickly she pulled away.

"What is it, Fran?"

"I can't, not just yet."

Sergio turned his head to the side.

"I do love you and I want to be with you," she confessed.

"I can feel a 'but' coming on."

Kneeling beside him on the floor, she held his hand. "I have so much to do before I can start anything with anyone."

Sergio shook his head. "I am not understanding this. What do you mean 'anyone'?"

Francesca stood up and, like Roberto would do, she walked to the window and gazed out.

"I have so many relationships that I need to start again – my mother, my father, my brothers, and I want to begin my life with you. And, yes, Sergio, there is a 'but'. I have to take care of matters in England – I must bury the past."

Sergio guessed what she was talking about. "Yes, I understand and I also understand that we need to achieve this together. I am coming to England with you and my men. You cannot imagine the hell we would go through if you were to go it alone. I am by your side, my angel."

Francesca shook her head. "No, you don't understand. I will not be on my guard if I am distracted by you and, trust me, you will distract me. I want you to love me as a woman of grace, not what I will be back in England."

"I know your intentions, Francesca. I know you so well and, even in your temper, you are still a woman of grace and beauty." He was pleading with her.

"Do you really, Sergio, or do you see a face and a body that you find attractive?"

Sergio laughed. "To ask me that question shows that you do not know me very well."

Francesca bit the inside of her lip, knowing he loved her for other reasons. "Sergio, let me ask you this – how would you describe a person who would continue to rip the flesh from a man that screamed and pleaded for his life, and then, when there was no more flesh left, roll that man in salt and spit on him?" She remained calm, still looking out of the window. The hairs on the back of her neck stood on end with the fear that Sergio would view her as a ruthless animal.

"I think that person had been so badly treated that the only way they can go forward is by a ruthless revenge."

She turned to look at Sergio's expression and was relieved to see that he was looking at her with those same loving eyes, not the eyes of a stranger.

"Francesca, I love you too much to let you go alone. I am with you even if it means I carry the sack of salt."

She threw herself into his arms and kissed him.

Chapter Fifteen

With the plans in place, she would meet with Charles Enright Senior, but first she needed to re-acquaint herself with her family. She had spoken with them on the phone but they hadn't seen her in person. She knew that her appearance would be a shock, but hopefully a good one.

Autumn weather back in London could be unpredictable, hence the fact that her suitcase was heavy. This was not a problem though as Dominic, her driver and right hand man, was there to help.

Reluctantly, Sergio agreed to let her go, but only because she promised that she was on a reconnaissance mission and nothing else.

She was surprised at how easy it was to smuggle her handgun through customs – its intricate and obscure design was fool proof, even through the x-ray machines. It then dawned on her that she had total trust in Roberto. It was a feeling she never believed would exist for her again.

*

The flight left Francesca tired and so she booked into a hotel for the night before going to surprise her family.

The Dorchester was as good a place as any. Dominic Capello had been a bodyguard for Roberto, but his job was to take care of Francesca. He was not to let on that he was a bodyguard, just a chauffeur. He was a tough-looking man, bigger than your average Italian, more like a Swede with black hair and a big square jaw. Word had spread that Francesca was one tough cookie. His nephew's guards had watched her take on Sergio's rivals without fear of death or repercussion. Few men would do what she had done. When Roberto had suggested he accompanied her to keep her safe, he laughed. "Roberto, excuse my boldness but may I say, Francesca could look after me if I needed help."

Roberto nodded and laughed. "Yes, this, my friend, is true. But although she is smart, and will not shy away from the bullet, she is still precious to me and my Sergio, and so I think it best."

Dominic nodded. He had been with Roberto since he was fifteen years old and had never let him down. Angelina practically adopted him after she caught him stealing salami in their local butchers. The poor boy was half-starved. His parents had come over from Italy and, within a week, a drunk driver mowed them down. Dominic barely spoke a word of English and had to fend for himself. She kindly took him in, gave him a bed and food, and he became their errand boy. Roberto had taken a liking to him. He was eager to learn to be part of the firm and so, by the time he reached seventeen, he had a suit, a pistol, and had learned to fight like a man. After taking two bullets, two blades, and one sneaky snake venom injection, he remained as strong as an ox.

Francesca amused him and the rest of the firm. She had become their hot topic of conversation, for it was unknown for women to be involved in their business. She was, for her ability and courage, given the respect and honour she deserved. The Tyler incident was not discussed, but Roberto made it clear she handled his legal business the Luciani way. It was left to his men to guess that her own hands killed Tyler.

The Dorchester hadn't changed since her last visit. It was still as grand as ever, though it seemed a lifetime since her previous visits with her husband which, in a different life, had been full of excitement and anticipation. She reflected briefly on those times: they had been so romantic, and on her state of mind then, when she had been so happy and so much in love.

"Care to join me for dinner, Dom? I'm having an early night, but I fancy a good meal first," said Francesca, who looked a little pale.

"Yes, ma'am, I'd love to." Dominic smiled, showing his perfect white teeth.

They left the luggage unpacked and headed for the restaurant. Francesca was aware of the gazes, and quite surprised, since she didn't feel fantastic. She underestimated how glamorous she appeared because inside she was still Dolly.

"I'll have the salmon," said Francesca, "and yes, a glass of champagne, please."

She looked at Dominic, who seemed to be struggling.

"Dom, what are you having?"

He stared at the menu. "The same as you."

She guessed he couldn't read English.

"Including the champagne?"

He nodded, thinking there must be something to celebrate.

When the champagne arrived, they chinked their glasses together, "Cheers." Dominic thought he probably shouldn't be dining with Sergio's girlfriend, but, on the other hand, he must not let her out of his sight.

"So what are we celebrating?" he asked, in a very thick Italian accent. His years in America had not removed or changed his way of speaking.

"Well, we landed safely, we are in a wonderful hotel, and I will see my mother and father tomorrow. I can't tell you how happy that makes me."

Dominic saw her face had softened when mentioning her family.

"I can tell you have missed them very much, eh?"

"More than you can imagine." Francesca spoke with so much emotion and intent, *unaware that Dominic felt the same.*

The meal was pleasant, as was the company. Dominic had been grateful that he could spend a little time with her since the Lucianis had a great deal of affection for her, and trust too. In fact, they trusted her more than they trusted anyone, so he felt privileged that they relied on him to take care of her.

Roberto had various properties and cars in England. The next day, Dominic went to collect the car and organise the cleaner to attend the house in Kent, put the heating on, and make sure it was clean and dust free, ready for her to stay if need be.

Francesca was up and fussing over her clothes. Her stomach was tingling with anticipation and excitement. She was on the cusp of something very challenging and very dangerous. It was a momentous moment for her, and one where the stakes being played were very high indeed. She had to focus properly on the plan in her mind – which had taken her many hours to put together – and where the chances of success were probably only fifty-fifty. But first, she had something very close to her heart to do.

Having gone through every dress and trouser suit she had brought with her, she eventually sat heavily on the bed and decided that it didn't matter; her mother and father were not judgemental. She scooped up the pale pink cashmere dress, along with her beige knee-high boots, and applied a small amount of makeup. Back in the States, she had been wearing business suits appropriate for a lawyer's office, but now she was their little girl, not one of the mafia mob.

Dominic pulled up outside the hotel in a black Jaguar. On the back seat, as she had requested, was a perfumed bouquet.

She hopped in. "How do I look, Dom? Not too pink, is it?" She was smoothing the dress down.

He raised his eyebrow, surprised how soft and serene she was.

"Eh, Belle, you look lovely in pink," he smiled. "Especially for your mother."

That's what I wanted to hear.

It didn't take long before they arrived at the East End. Francesca found it hard to recognise the streets. New developments were popping up over

Hackney Wick, Roman Road and Bow. The pubs her dad took her to, where she'd been allowed in the garden with a Coke and a packet of crisps, had gone. It wasn't as she remembered. The scrapyard Bill owned in the early days was just a piece of waste ground and now standing on the site was a board advertising luxury two-bed apartments.

Dominic turned into her street and her heart pounded. The Victorian houses were still standing and there was her mother's house – the best one in the street.

It had been a year since she had returned, but her memory was so vague. She did not recollect arriving and she barely remembered leaving to go to the States with Kathy.

"Just here," she said, asking Dominic to stop the car.

Slowly she got out, carrying the bouquet for her mother as if it were a baby.

Hoping they were home, she gingerly opened the gate and walked to the newly painted door. Her hands shook as she pressed the doorbell.

The time it took Mary to answer the door seemed like an eternity.

The door opened and Francesca stared at the best sight in the world.

Mary was so taken aback by the huge bouquet, she didn't notice her daughter holding them.

"Oh my dear, I think you have the wrong address," she said, still admiring the mass of pink roses. "I'm not expecting flowers and it sure ain't me birthday." Mary then noticed the girls' eyes; she tilted her head slowly to the side, and her bottom lip quivered.

"'Ello, Mum." Francesca tried to keep her cool but all too soon tears escaped and ran down her cheek.

The beautiful bouquet crumpled in the hug.

"I knew it was you, my Dolly, you're home." Mary tried to contain herself, but the feelings were so overwhelming.

"Did you really not recognise me, Mum?"

"Only you and the boys have those eyes and all the time I can look into them, I know who you are." She kissed her daughter and ushered her in.

Dominic sat in the car, watching. He wiped away a tear and drove to the nearest pub for a beer.

"Look at you," she kept saying. She admired her daughter's perfect figure and gorgeous face. "I can't believe you're here at last. I can hug you without hurting you. Your beautiful face was so, well..." – she paused – "But, eh, look at you now – you look so well. I can't tell you how happy I am, and ya dad, bless him, is gonna be over the flippin' moon." She kissed her face again.

"Ah, Mum, I can't tell you how much I've been looking forward to comin' home meself."

Francesca and Mary laughed at the way she turned off her well-spoken accent to her own cockney lingo.

"Uh, my gal, you don't need to talk like that. You are sophisticated and smart, and I like the way you sound. Ya know, you've done us proud." She winked at her daughter.

Francesca admired her mother, who was so attractive for an older woman. Mary had gained a few pounds but her hourglass figure was still there and her skin was soft, albeit with just a few wrinkles, but she kept herself looking fresh with her hair in gentle soft blonde waves, cut just above her shoulders.

"'Ere, did ya not think I might like to talk with me East End accent, seeing as I did nearly grow up 'ere? I might be posh an' all, but I am comfortable speaking like this. Ya know, it was tough in Surrey at that school, trying to speak like them. Guess now I can do both." Francesca nodded her head in achievement. "Oh and Italian, I can speak Italian so Sergio can't talk about me behind my back." She giggled.

"So tell me all about this Sergio then." Mary shuffled to the edge of her seat, eager to take in everything her daughter had to say.

Mary adored watching Francesca. The last time she laid eyes on her there wasn't much conversation. Francesca was so ill and the painkillers made her docile and slur her words. She remembered the horrendous gashes on her face, swollen beyond recognition. Now she sat before her mother, looking radiant and chatting like there was no tomorrow.

"Sergio is a kind man, very caring," said Francesca seriously.

"Yes, but is he handsome? Ya see, it's all very well being sweet and all but there's got to be a bit of passion like," Mary teased. She could see her daughter going red.

"Aw, Mum, he is handsome. He has those beautiful Italian eyes, you know what I mean, with the eyelashes that go on forever, and he has soft olive skin. His teeth are perfect and when he smiles his whole face lights up. He has a mysterious side to him though. You can't tell what he is thinking."

"He sounds a right catch," Mary laughed. "Well, you had to go across the pond to find him, aye? Ya dad's gonna be home for his lunch in about ten minutes; you will stay, won't ya?" Mary was so excited that the never-ending arthritis pains vanished.

"Mum, I'm in England for two weeks."

Mary was walking towards the kitchen when she spun on her heels. Her heart sank. Only two weeks, it wasn't long enough.

"I was hoping you were gonna say you were home for good. Only, we miss ya, Doll."

Francesca walked over to her mother and put her arm round her shoulders.

"Mum, I'm here for two weeks this time, next time I will be here for another two weeks, and then there's Christmas and I'll be here for a month. In fact, Mum, you'll probably see more of me than if I lived here permanently."

The kitchen hadn't changed much. The big table, made from solid oak, was still there in the middle with nine chairs surrounding it. Francesca barely recollected the house from a year ago, but she remembered it from her childhood.

"You've added two more chairs," noted Francesca.

Mary, making the tea, turned to face her daughter. She sighed. "Well, I might as well tell ya, our Sammy's in prison."

"Well, I guessed that, Mum."

"He has two babies, our Jack and our Ruby, and honest to God, Francesca, if you saw the fucking state of them, you'd wanna cry." She took a deep breath.

"Your chair 'as always been there and, well, your dad had two more made to match for when the little 'uns visit, but sadly that ain't too often and I worry, Doll. I have to keep my mouth shut or I won't get to see them at all."

Francesca was seething; her stomach churned and a pain shot through her. She would have to learn to control her emotions.

"I didn't even know they existed, Mum. I've got a little niece and nephew then?" Her face changed, and she looked angry.

"So why don't our Sammy do something about it?"

Mary hadn't seen Francesca get annoyed; it reminded her of herself.

"Our Sammy has to keep his mouth shut because she will stop us seeing them or she won't take them to visit him."

Francesca's mind worked overtime; *she may need to spend more time to sort out this problem. Her mother had gone through enough.* She thought about the pain she must have felt letting go of her only daughter. *No way was she going to let it happen with the grandchildren too.*

Francesca smiled when she heard the key in the door. "Quick, Mum, go upstairs, let me give Dad his dinner."

Mary hurried upstairs, happy to play in the game.

Bill aged well; he still looked smart — his hair had the silver streaks, but his eyes remained bright and wide. He hung his jacket in the hall cupboard and walked in to the kitchen. There, before him, stood a stunning woman holding a dinner plate. At first he thought, he was seeing things, but there was so much more to this vision. There she was, holding his dinner. Bill cupped his chin and stared; his heart told him he hoped that this was his precious daughter but his head just wouldn't confirm it.

Francesca tried to keep a straight face, until she saw her father's face drop in sadness. Quickly, she spoke. "Well, Dad, I made it meself."

"My gal." He stretched his arms wide. She put the dinner on the table and ran to them.

"'Ello, Dad."

"'Ello, Doll," he whispered, as he fought back the tears.

Mary joined them.

"Cor, Mare, I thought I was seeing things." He pulled a handkerchief from his pocket and wiped his eyes. "She looks so different, like a movie star."

Mary cried, watching her husband's joy. His smiles were rare since Dolly had gone to her aunt's home, but now he beamed.

They sat for hours catching up. Mary got the brandy out and they all enjoyed each other's company once again, thinking their own thoughts but eager to hear what had happened to them over the years Francesca had been away from her family. Bill didn't go back to work that afternoon. He wanted to spend every special moment with his daughter, knowing he would never get back the time they lost together.

"'Ere, where's the boys?" Francesca was itching to see them.

"Well, Dan and Joe will be at the club, and they'll probably get back around two or three in the morning. They had an early start because they were meeting the taxman," replied Bill.

"I am going to surprise them at the club."

Bill looked at Mary, then back at Francesca. "No, not a good idea. The threat is still there, babe, and sometimes those nasty McManners pass by the club and make a damn nuisance of themselves." He took a deep breath. "It only takes a sniff that you're around and that bastard will be after you."

Francesca rubbed her father's arm. "McManners? I never knew Mad Mick's surname, funny that. Anyway, Dad, please don't you worry about me ever again. Mark my words. Besides, look at me, not even you recognised me."

Bill laughed. "I did, I just didn't believe it, that's all."

The evening arrived in a blink and Francesca was ready to pay her brothers a visit.

"Now, my gal, promise me you will look after yourself." Bill hugged his daughter, fearing for her safety.

Francesca pulled the curtains and pointed to Dominic, sitting in the Jag.

"Dad, see him. If I can't look after meself, he will."

Bill raised his eyebrows; his daughter had protection, which was obvious by the sheer size of the man. He said no more and trusted she knew what she was doing. His little girl was a grown woman, and from another world, maybe tougher than his own. He admired her confidence and deep down inside he knew she was far harder than his boys. A lump wedged in his throat; *she was tough because, for whatever reason, she had to be.* He had not been there to protect her. The idea of her going to the posh school and becoming a lawyer gave him solace. Yet, in his heart, he recognised the dark side to her life, a side which gave her the edge and made her strong. *It was all wrong on every level; his Dolly should have been carefree, light in her heart, without that arduous look in her eyes.*

Dominic enjoyed his day, having made a crafty bet in the bookies, relished a really good pint of London Pride in the pub, and eaten a bag of the famous fish and chips.

He parked the car across the road from the club and opened the door for Francesca. The two bouncers at the door eyed Dominic up and down and realised he looked like a bouncer himself. Jason and Johnnie Lee were brothers, hard men, both ex-boxers, and had left the ring for the club. Dan had seen them box and knew, when he bought the club, they were the guys to watch the door.

Johnnie was staring at Francesca.

"What's up?" she said, annoyed.

He nodded for them to go in. Francesca was impressed with what she saw. The club was a fair size; the décor was bright and trendy, and there was a relaxed atmosphere. Dominic went straight to the bar to get her a drink, while she sat at a table, gazing around and trying to find her brothers. With the lights flashing purple and blue, she struggled to see clearly. In the corner were purple leather stools circling a black low-level table, and a man was sitting there laughing loudly. It sounded like Fred. She craned her neck around to see who owned that laugh but instantly recognised it was her eldest brother, Dan. He was entertaining a couple of page three models who were obviously enjoying his company.

Casually, she got up from the table and walked towards him. He looked up to see her heading his way and, with a glass in his hand, he said, "'ello, darling, and where have you been all my life?" He was never shy to chat up a good-looking woman.

Francesca smiled. She bent down and whispered in his ear, "Aunty Anne's."

Dan jumped back in shock. He fell off the stool and onto the floor.

Quick as a flash, he was on his feet and hugging her. The two women, who had just been the focus of his undivided attention, suddenly felt second best, so took their drinks and headed elsewhere.

"Fuck me, Dolly Vincent. My life, what a fucking sight for sore eyes!" He held her away from him to take a better look.

"You look amazing, sis."

Francesca was laughing. "Good to see you, Dan."

Dan was choked; he couldn't believe he was standing in the same room once more with his sister. She looked healthy and glowing – a far cry from the person he'd said goodbye to at the airport.

"Hey, where's our Joe?" asked Francesca, looking around.

Dan was still staring; he couldn't take his eyes off his sister.

"Over there, pulling pints. See if he recognises you." They laughed and Dan kissed her again.

Joe was still giggling when Francesca approached him. He had no idea who she was, but found it amusing that his brother had fallen on his arse.

"What can I get you?" he said, with a beaming smile.

"Well, let's see now, a kiss maybe?" She was finding it hard to keep a straight face.

Just like their mother, Joe put his head on the side, the way dogs do when they don't understand something, and his bottom lip quivered. Leaning over the bar, he whispered, "Dolly, is that you?"

Choked up too, she nodded. He came from behind the bar and hugged her and, being the most sensitive brother, tears rolled down his face. Dan joined them and ushered them over to a more private part of the club to an area that was partially hidden by a glass wall. Dominic remained in the corner, enjoying a pint of extra cold Guinness. The two page three girls made a beeline for him, assuming he had plenty of money.

Joe was still watery-eyed when Dan punched him on the arm. "What's up with you?"

Sniffing back the tears, Joe sighed. "Look at our Dolly, all grown up an' all, she should have been part of all this." He gestured to the club. "She should have always been with us!" He stopped sniffing and allowed a tear to roll down his face.

Francesca put her arm around him and said in a soft voice, "I was always a part of you, in your hearts. I am lucky to have my family still there to love me like I had never left, and I am back now, Joe. I am your sister and always will be. So those tears had better be happy ones."

She kissed his face as if he was a baby and he nodded.

"So I guess Fred has kept you up to date with what's been going on?" Dan was a little merry on five vodkas and he slurred his words.

"Didn't mention Jack and Ruby," she said sadly.

Joe and Dan looked at each other.

"We don't see, 'em," said Joe.

"How's Fred doing over there? And did he mention anything about why he came to you?" Dan was not thinking and Joe gave him a kick.

"It's all right. Fred filled me in and he is more than okay, loving the casino business, and the girls that come with it."

Dan laughed. "Fucking cheeky git. That's my job, pulling the birds."

"Yeah, I can see that." She pointed over to the two models chatting up Dominic.

Joe and Dan were unaware of the big Italian until then.

"Who's that geezer anyway?" asked Joe.

Francesca laughed. "Hey, don't go throwing him out, he's my chauffeur."

"Ooh, get you, a fucking chauffeur no less," laughed Dan.

"Do ya know what? I couldn't feel any happier. It's good to have you home, sis." He gave her another hug.

"We have got to watch those fucking McManners," whispered Joe nervously, looking around the club to check.

Dan nodded. "After they tried to do over our Fred, let's be honest, the slightest inkling you're here and they will be on us."

Francesca agreed. "Don't worry about me. I'm a big girl now, and I've got more than him on my side." She pointed to Dominic and pulled out her gun, lighting up a cigarette.

Joe stared at the gun and nervously laughed.

"Cor, Dolly, for a minute I thought it was real." He pulled a fag from the packet on offer and took a light from her gun.

"Joe, what makes you think it ain't?" she winked.

The two brothers looked at Dominic, back to Francesca, and then at the lighter.

"I told ya, I can look after meself."

Dan was taken aback by his sweet little sister; she wasn't stupid. The way she walked, talked and held herself, *she wasn't a soppy tart, oh no.* She was clever and not to be underestimated. He surmised that the big Italian wasn't just her chauffeur, and the lighter wasn't just a lighter. He enjoyed his sister's company. She was a true Vincent and more like a brother, just a very pretty one at that.

Joe was in awe of her. Dan, Sam and even Fred had always treated him as the baby and, listening to his baby sister, it was apparent she treated him the same, especially when she pinched his chubby cheek.

"Be damn careful though, sis. Take that scumbag, Charlie — thinks he's so special. You remember poor Rosie from the East India Dock Road?"

Joe nodded. "Yeah, I remember that incident — when Charlie took chunks out of her face with his pliers just 'cause she wouldn't date him. Evil muvver fucker."

Dan nodded, but to his surprise, Francesca didn't flinch.

"Yeah, and the other one, Stuart McManners, the ginger wanker, he had his own muvver fucked up. Apparently she left the old man, and being a bird basher, he got a couple of old prozzies to hold her while he beat her with a bat. The whole family have a screw loose, so Dan's right, make sure you take care."

Francesca held both their hands. "Listen to me, they are not going to hurt any of us again. Just wait, be patient and then see what happens."

Both brothers listened intently.

"I'm not just here on a family reunion. There are things I need to sort out, put right, but you have to let me get on with it. I don't want to cause any worry; believe me when I say I am well protected."

They knew there was more to their little sister than beauty and brains.

*

After spending a precious few days with her family, it was back to business.

Charles Enright had received emails from his dead brother Tyler. Luckily, he still believed he was alive.

He looked forward to meeting his new supplier. In the meantime, Francesca gathered as much information on Charles as she could and, to her surprise, Charles had a bodyguard called Adam, who boxed in the same club as her brothers and their bouncers, a well-known doorman in his time. After serving ten years for manslaughter, he got together with a local prostitute – Lindsey was her real name. She had originally come from a well-to-do family. She left home at the age of fifteen for the fast life in London and got herself hooked on smack. She loved the club scene but soon found herself skint and owing the dealers a ton of money. They put her on the street to work, and that's how he met her because she picked up punters from the Purple Club, where Adam was the doorman. He took her in, paid her debts, and before he knew it, she was pregnant. The doctors were surprised that she could carry the baby. She was as thin as a rake and whiter than a sheet of paper. Her hair was falling out in handfuls and yet she still knocked back the whisky and smoked forty fags a day. Adam was furious. He tried to get her to stop and look after herself but she was on the road to self-destruction, and all he could do was watch and hope his baby would be born undamaged.

Lindsey went into labour in the early hours one morning and, by the time they reached the hospital, the little boy arrived, but weighing only four pounds. Adam, a strapping man with huge hands, held his tiny baby and named him Jamie. The nurses laughed; he looked so minute in his dad's hands. A week later, the doctor allowed the baby home. Lindsey, meanwhile, had packed her bags and scarpered, leaving Adam, the baby, and London.

Francesca discovered that his little boy, now eight years old, had a tumour. Adam had contacted various surgeons to see if it was operable but to no avail. She needed him to be on her side for her plan to work.

Roberto gave Francesca the names of his English contacts that still owed him a few favours, who were big into smuggling – whether it be people or goods. So Francesca arranged to have two of them to take Adam's son to the States that week. She made sure he was well looked after.

The plan worked a treat. Francesca knocked on the door of Adam's flat, whilst Dominic sat in the car, and the other two men waited patiently in another. A young woman in her early twenties answered.

"Hello, how can I help you?" she said, with the sweetest French accent.

"Hello, I am the health visitor. I am here to collect Jamie for his hospital appointment. Adam will meet me there." Francesca walked past the French girl into the flat without waiting for an invitation. Unsure what was going on, the nanny asked, "Who are you?"

"I am the health visitor," repeated Francesca. "Did Adam not tell you I was coming? Only I am in a hurry. He has a doctor's appointment in fifteen minutes and we cannot afford to miss it." Her words were stern enough not to argue.

"And I will need his current medication and passport to show the doctor." The nanny nodded and, without hesitation, grabbed the drugs and paperwork, then shoved them in a bag.

"Thank you very much," said Francesca.

The nanny was so used to Jamie's constant trips to the hospital, and Adam's plight to find a surgeon, that she let him go without any further questions.

The boy looked sick, his little round face grey, and there were dark circles surrounding his huge blue eyes. Francesca wrapped another blanket around his shoulders and kissed him on the forehead.

"It's all right, Jamie, I will take care of you. Your dad will meet us soon." The pasty little boy just nodded.

The two men gently helped him into the car, placed pillows under his head, and more blankets over his tiny body.

Francesca whispered to Jamie, "Do you like Disneyland?"

Jamie's face lit up and he smiled.

Dominic took Francesca to get a coffee before they returned to the flat.

"I will come with you, to meet Adam," he stated.

"If you must, but I can do this myself," she snapped back.

Dominic rolled his eyes. He knew that if Roberto got wind of this and she was alone, he would fire him.

"I would just feel happier."

Francesca looked at him and nodded, aware he had been paid to do more than drive her around.

Adam parked his black BMW dead in front of the Jag. Francesca watched for a minute. It was him; the description was spot on.

"Let's go," she said.

As they both stepped out of the car, Adam stopped him in his tracks.

"You must be Jamie's father."

Adam was taken aback. He couldn't see the connection: a woman that looked like a catwalk model, and a lump that looked like the Godfather.

Apprehensively, he nodded. "Who wants to know?"

Francesca held her hand out for him to shake, which, like a gentleman, he took.

"Shall we take a seat in my car?" she suggested, and gestured to the Jag.

Adam felt uneasy; but, without resisting, he sat heavily in the back seat of the car, waiting to discover what all this was about.

Francesca looked into his eyes. He appeared soft, with a very likeable face, but his reputation, as one hell of a hard man, was well known in criminal circles.

"What do you want?" he said calmly, although his hands were shaking.

"It's like this, Adam – I need you to work for me." She smiled. Her beauty drew in Adam, for a second.

"I already have a job and I am happy where I am, thank you very much."

The Enrights paid him well, and he needed the money and security, especially to help his son.

"No, no, no, you don't understand." She grinned sarcastically. "You don't have a choice."

"What makes you so fucking sure I don't have a choice?" His expression changed from soft to downright scary. Francesca hadn't even flinched when he spat the words in her face.

"Your son has secured that for me."

His could feel the blood pumping fast through the veins in his neck as he lunged forward, with his hands around her throat. Dominic had the gun in Adam's mouth before he could blink. Adam instantly released his grip.

"Don't you even think about fucking with me." She pulled out her lighter and lit up a cigarette, blowing the smoke in Adam's face.

"I have your son and so I think that means you will work for me."

Adam put his head in his hands and cried, "Don't hurt my son, he is sick, he needs his medicine, he needs..." He was blubbering uncontrollably. Francesca felt a lump in her throat; *the poor man was only doing his job*, and she hated herself for doing this to him, but she needed guaranteed assurance.

"You do as I say and your boy will be back with you as soon as the job's done," she said coldly.

"All right, what do you want me to do?" He was calmer; he could not afford to mess up with his son's life on the line.

*

Francesca went over the plan, which was straightforward, and Adam nodded to every request, until she mentioned the date.

"Oh my God, you can't do that to me! Three weeks? Jamie is so sick, he may not last that long." He cried again. "I swear to God, if you hurt one hair on his fucking head, I will kill you with my fucking bare hands."

Francesca expected no less.

Before he got out of the car, she grabbed his arm and said, "I'll make you a promise." He turned, hoping for good news. "You do as I say, from now until the job is done, and your son will be treated as if he were my son. If you fuck up, well, you won't see him again." She let go of his arm and, with his shoulders slouched, he bowed his head and walked back to his flat.

Francesca was silent all the way home.

Adam felt a light relief when he discovered that Francesca had taken Jamie's medication and the nanny had mentioned that she had wrapped another blanket around his shoulders. It gave him the hope that she was a woman of her word, so he would go ahead with the plan.

The first meeting with Charles was straightforward. They agreed to meet in a country pub called The Bull's Head in Sevenoaks. The car park was always dark since the village had neither streetlights nor CCTV.

Francesca was already seated inside, sipping a glass of red wine. In the corner was Dominic, enjoying a Guinness. Fred had given him a list of all the things he should try in England but as soon as he got to Guinness, that was it, and he stuck with it.

Charles walked in with Adam, and Francesca instantly recognised him. She hoped he did not recognise her. She stood up and Charles walked towards her in his usual self-assured manner.

"Oh, I say, you must be Francesca. I've heard so much about you," said Charles with a pompous attitude.

Francesca cringed as he shook her hand. He hadn't changed, and clearly he still fancied himself. *Was it her newfound strength or her hatred for them that made her wonder how in the world she'd ever respected them?* She smiled at him, but the grin was her self-satisfaction. She had overcome the fear and need to please the Enrights. The weak, defenceless Launa had gone, a shadow from her past. Francesca was the strong, unforgiving, ruthless woman created by the McManners and the Enrights. *They had made a monster and with every bone in their body, they would regret it.*

*

They sat at the table, eyeing each other up.

"I must say, you are not a typical..." He paused, thinking it was not a good idea to mention drug dealer. After all, she could be the police.

"Business woman?" Francesca inclined her head to the side.

"Um, yes, business woman," he replied, intrigued by her.

"My brother mentioned you would bring a sample of your work." He looked to see who was in the pub but, apart from an Italian in the corner, it was empty.

"Yes, as we agreed on the phone," she replied, in a calm and collected tone.

Charles was getting excited. He was about to have a snort and his new dealer was a fine-looking specimen. Maybe he could kill two birds with one stone. No, he thought, the urge for a toot was greater; he could wait to bed her.

"Well, where is it then?" He was impatient. Francesca smiled; she was in control. Charles had a serious cocaine addiction and he was itching to have a toot. She had often wondered why Charles was so twitchy and, looking back, it should have been obvious he was an addict. Not that it affected his work though; he maintained a good reputation in the courtroom.

"You can have your gear when I have my money."

Charles glanced at Adam and back at Francesca. Unlike his other dealer, she was organised and controlled. The last supplier was on crack himself.

"I need you to meet me in Knole Park; no one will see us there."

It was there that the first deal was made. Francesca had made sure that the kilo of cocaine was of the highest quality. Adam helped her source it. He'd also informed her of how Charles had shot the previous dealer. He wanted to do everything right by Francesca, as she was the only person that had control of his son, and he wasn't going to cross her. The problem was, Charles had been greedy and owed far more than he earned. He wanted to find a supplier that he could knock off, and she was to be his next victim. Adam knew Charles' plans; the Enrights had no reason not to trust him completely. Yet if Charles killed Francesca, he would never get his son back.

Splitting open the bag, she popped a tiny amount on her index finger and offered it up to his nose. His eyes never left the line of pure white powder. Quickly, he snorted it. Francesca wiped her hand with a baby wipe and almost laughed at how pathetic he looked gagging for a line of coke. Charles looked at the single bag in the boot of the car and decided it wasn't worth knocking her off for such a small amount, not when she could supply the finest cocaine he had ever tooted.

"He's got your cash." Charles pointed at Adam, who pulled out a wad of notes.

Adam handed over the money and smiled.

"Now then, Francesca, same time next week, shall we say?" His eyes were bulging.

"No, not next week – the week after," she replied. She hadn't planned on such a quick return.

"What? Look, lady, I need the gear next week or the deal's off." He was panicking, he had promised his Russian mob a few kilos by the end of the month.

"Well, the deal's off. Besides, I've got a few Russians interested, so take it or leave it." She was in control and she loved it.

Charles was angry; the Russians were his customers and he would not have a young tart push him around.

"All right, all right, I'll see you in two weeks, but I want twenty kilos of the same gear, no less, or the deal's off."

She handed Charles the bag and left.

On the way back she stopped off at Adam's flat and posted the money through the letterbox. He had been true to his word; he came up with the goods and was there with Charles to take care of business, just as she planned. Adam was relieved to see the money back in his hands to pay the dealers.

Chapter Sixteen

Two Weeks Later

Francesca, dressed in her neat, tight-fitting Armani suit, capturing the eyes of most men, strolled nonchalantly past the 'Nothing to Declare' sign. One of the customs officers, a flash young man known as Niki, eyed her up and down, wishing he could do the honours of a strip search, but he sighed. She was obviously a business person; she reeked of money, judging by the quality of the clothes she was wearing. It was his job to look at appearance and body language; he had no reason to pull her in to get a closer look. Shame, he thought. She was every inch a beautiful woman – long, slender legs, high cheekbones, and platinum blonde hair that shone and extenuated her steel-blue eyes. Dreaming of how he would undress this specimen of pure sophistication, she turned and glared a stony cold stare straight at him. He blushed as if she had heard his thoughts. Quickly, he diverted his eyes, pretending to be interested in the man directly behind her. She smirked to herself; *he was a fool*, but then she thought many people were fools, and those were the type she found irritating.

Dressed in a suit, Dominic carried two large suitcases, unaware of the customs officer staring his way. He was concentrating on carrying the two heavy cases for Francesca.

"Sir, could you come here please?" said the customs officer.

He cringed at the thought of being delayed by a pompous officer, but was relieved that he didn't have anything on him which would incriminate him.

Dominique walked over to the long table and, as if Francesca had eyes in the back of her head, she spun around and joined him.

Niki then felt hot under the collar, not having realised that the two were together.

"Who do the suitcases belong to?"

"They are mine," replied Francesca, in a cool tone.

The officer felt uneasy by the confident monotone of the woman's voice. "Do you have anything to declare?"

With a long icy stare into the officer's eyes, she said, "No," and remained transfixed.

Niki, usually full of charm, and an expert in the art of flirting, fidgeted on the spot. The tables had now been turned, and he felt awkward and wanted to walk away.

"Will that be all, Officer?" asked Francesca, still staring into the young officer's eyes.

"Um, oh, yes. Yes, that will be all."

Without another word, both Dominic and Francesca left.

*

Outside, the rain poured and the wind howled. Francesca took a deep breath and stepped back inside.

She had only been back in the states for two weeks but had fallen into the comfort zone of the warm weather, but now she had to get used to the unpredictable nature of the British rain.

Dominic smiled. He liked Francesca; she had the eyes of an angel but the soul of a devil. He admired her confidence, and how she managed to wrap people around her little finger with just a glance. They waited inside the arrival lounge for Adam.

Adam had driven Charles to meet Francesca at the airport as planned but, as they pulled up outside the arrival parking, he then needed to make an excuse to go inside.

"For fuck's sake, why do you need to go to the toilet now? I want you here with me when she walks out. I don't trust that fucking bitch!" shouted Charles. He was gagging for a snort and nervous at the thought of what he had planned.

"Look, Mr Enright, I had a dodgy curry last night and, unless you want me to shit meself, I need to pay the men's room a visit."

Charles rolled his eyes. "Okay, just fucking hurry back."

Quickly, he shot inside the airport and spotted Francesca with Dominic.

"Here you go. Charles is outside in the car, so give me five minutes and then walk out." He handed over a small parcel.

"Is everything in place and as we planned?" she asked.

"Yes, and is my boy all right?" His expression was full of sorrow and it played on her heartstrings.

"So far so good," she replied.

Adam returned to the car, and to an irate Charles.

"Did you see her?" His voice was anxious.

"No, I will drive around the block again before we get a ticket," replied Adam.

Francesca waited a few minutes before walking out through the exit as arranged.

"Dom, take my bags to the Dorchester. I have a room booked and please have a meal taken to my room for eight o'clock."

Dominic nodded and hailed a taxi.

She saw his black Mercedes pull up and casually she strolled over.

Charles Enright greeted her as she stepped into the car. *She pitied him in a sick sort of way; he had once been a very clever QC and now he was just a loser hooked on Charlie.*

"So, Francesca, we meet again, and I must say you look rather charming."

Francesca smiled sarcastically. She hated his haughty Oxford accent – his over-the-top plum in the mouth – still, she used the same accent and fancy words when needed. No one would know her real roots, the East End of London, unless she decided they should.

"Cut the crap, Charles, I'm not into flirtatious conversations."

Charles had forgotten for a second just how confident this woman was. Shit, she was not to be messed with; his stomach churned as he saw a gun being pulled from her bag. Pointing the gun at her own face, his eyes widened. She pulled the trigger and lit her cigarette.

"So, Charles, do you have the money or have I wasted my time?"

"Oh, I have the money. Do you have the goods?"

She nodded and pulled a small packet from inside her bra.

"I have a small sample of the cocaine. Try it first and if it's not up to standard, I will take it elsewhere." Again, she smirked, knowing very well that the cocaine was of the purest kind.

Charles, without a word, tipped a small amount onto the back of his hand and snorted. He wiped his nose and smiled. "This will do nicely."

Francesca looked away, sickened by the sight of it. She wanted him to overdose so much that his heart gave out, he keeled over, and was marked a junkie, *but perhaps that was too good for him.*

The exchange was to take place in a secluded wood in Kent. She had previously organised a car to be there with the drugs inside the boot. Charles, slightly high on the shit, tried to banter with Francesca, but this irritated her even more.

"Charles, who's your driver?"

"Oh no, my dear, he is not my driver, he is my PA – well, bodyguard if you like. You see, sweetie, even you're dangerous," he smirked. His stomach churned again. He was afraid of her. After all, in the cocaine business only the toughest survive – a woman with wealth and the purest coke was scary, and he knew she could have only got to that position if she was dangerous. Now, as they entered the woods, he consoled himself with the thought that she was in a position of pure helplessness, alone in Kent in England, and of course before any switch took place they would both search each other for a gun. He was as safe as houses.

Her car was there as planned.

Charles looked at the car, slightly puzzled. "Where's your driver?"

"I haven't got a driver; I had my car taken to the location. I am not driving around with a case in the boot of my car that could put me away for twelve years, am I?" She shot him a sarcastic glance.

Both stepped out of the Mercedes and did the acceptable body search. The driver, Adam, stood by Charles' car, watching as Francesca removed the suitcase from hers. Charles removed his briefcase and both were opened. Charles demonstrated that all the money, all two hundred grand, was in used notes and Francesca slit open the top bag for Charles to try.

"It's okay, Francesca, I trust you." And why wouldn't he? This was the second transaction. However, now he had found another dealer at a lower rate and this would be the last transaction. He didn't give a shit about Tyler's reputation. After all, his main aim was to find a source of the purest cocaine to fuel his own addiction. If it was not the best, she was a dead woman anyway and he would not be out of pocket. They swapped cases and returned to their own cars.

Francesca put the briefcase in the back of her car and removed her gun-shaped lighter from her bag to light another cigarette. Charles placed the suitcase in the boot of his car and grabbed his loaded gun, which was tucked under a concealed flap. Now he would kill her; the snort of cocaine made him more confident and aggressive to go ahead. Normally he would instruct his PA to take care of the dirty work, but he wanted to do the honours and finish this lady off himself. *The idea of a woman having so much power disturbed him. His idea of women was to play good lady wives and carry out small talk when entertaining and, of course, to entertain in the bedroom, but anything other than that was wrong. Whoever allowed her to become so influential, and have the power to scare the wits out of him, should be shot.* Putting a bullet through her beautiful face would do all of humanity a favour. Gripping the gun, he felt a sense of elation, real power. He wanted to watch her squirm.

Pointing the gun at her chest, he shouted, "Take your last drag, Francesca."

Without any expression on her face, she said, "Oh Charles, you are so bloody predictable."

His heart pounded and the burning contents of his stomach rose to his throat. This woman is fearless. He wanted to blow her away but the clicking sound of his gun did not fully register. *No, it cannot be.* He vividly remembered loading it himself.

"You pompous fool, Charles."

Thinking fast, he spun to face Adam. "For Christ's sake, man, throw me your gun."

"What? This one, sir?" replied Adam, pointing the gun at Charles' head.

Before he could answer, the bullet discharged and Charles' brains decorated the two-hundred-year-old oak tree.

Casually, as if she was taking an afternoon country stroll, Francesca walked over to the crumpled body and grinned, dropping a locket into his pocket. *Two down.*

"Adam, are those the shoes I told you to wear?"

He nodded.

"Good, walk around a bit, would you?"

The six-foot bodyguard did as she said. He didn't know this woman at all but he knew enough not to cross her. She was clever all right; all her plans were finely tuned. She had arranged for his son of eight years old to be sent to America while he carried out this job. Of course, she had to be sure that she could rely on this man, and her life depended on it. Well, so he thought.

Adam drove Francesca back to London, but remained silent. He had done as she asked and all he wanted now was his boy back. He was all he had in his life. Eight years of fatherhood had taken him from the world of contract killing to bodyguarding; it was less money, but it gave him peace of mind. He was, however, a well-respected man in the East End.

"I have something to show you, Adam. Pull over here."

He did as she said but his knees felt weak and his heart began to pound. There were no bullets left in his gun and her lighter looked too much like the real thing. He took a deep breath and prayed that his son would be all right without him.

"Here, Adam, I know you must be missing Jamie so take a look at these."

His heart sank. *What had she done to him?* Slowly, he turned his head to see what was on her lap and instantly he felt relief when he saw she was holding photos.

They were pictures of his little boy in Disney World, having the time of his life. His face looked white, and he still looked weak, but he was happy.

"I have flight tickets for you to go to New York tonight. Once you arrive, you will be driven to the hospital. I have arranged for Dr Lan Su to carry out the operation to remove the tumour on Thursday; he is the country's leading neurologist. Kathy has made all the arrangements for you to stay in the hotel close by, and I will join you in a few weeks. Once little Jamie is fit and well to leave the hospital, you may stay in a cabin by the lake. Kathy has set up a bank account for you so you can enjoy your stay."

Adam sat, staring at her in disbelief; he had mistakenly thought her to be the devil in disguise. Even her voice, that cool tone, sent shivers up his spine. Her steel-blue eyes were expressionless as if she could take your very soul. For a second he thought it was a trick and was freaked out, but then she said, "Adam, it's okay, there is no ulterior motive. You did as I asked and I look after those who look after me. Besides, Jamie's a lovely boy."

Her face softened and her words sounded genuine. He smiled and nodded. "He is all I have and when you had him sent to the States, I thought..." He paused. "Well, you know what I thought."

"Well, Adam, that was the idea. I knew you would do the job all the time I had your son."

"You must have been sure I'd do it," said Adam, feeling rather confident.

"You owed us big time. Mauricio hasn't forgotten how you helped the Enrights to set him up and, well, it's payback." She paused and took a drag on another cigarette. "Let's get something straight, shall we? I trust no one, do you understand?" The words came out like bullets. She pulled away her jacket, revealing a bulletproof vest. "Oh, and this," she laughed, holding up her gun-shaped lighter, "I'm not James fucking Bond, but never underestimate me." She fired the pistol through the small gap in the passenger door window.

Adam's eyes widened. He was a fool to think she was ever likely to be off her guard, and made a mental note never to be too confident in her company again.

Francesca smiled. "Look, Adam, I need good men around me who I can trust with my life, and those men will have rewards. You, for instance – I can do well for your boy and you know as well as me that, without the top surgeon, your son will die. So, now you have seen what I am capable of, you won't cross me, and I will stand by my words too." She paused, glancing up to meet his gaze, then added, "There is one thing I will say as I don't want to get a bad name for myself – I never have and never will harm a child. Oh, and make sure you put the shoes and the gun where I told you."

He nodded, elated that his son was alive and safe. He was going to do exactly as she asked before his flight to the States. She had kept her word and so would he.

She had, of course, done an extensive background search and knew all about his previous work and his child – his likes and dislikes – but still, there was more to this man. She was content in the fact that she had found her own muscle. It was great having Sergio and Mauricio's men around and feeling protected, but it was even better having an English one that at least understood the culture.

*

Adam slumped heavily into the seat, awaiting take-off, and went over and over the last few hours. She was a remarkable woman, so cool and collected. He expected a tough cookie but not as dangerous as this, or as glamorous. He tried to get her image out of his mind and concentrate on his son. He knew she was part of the Italian mob and she was loyal to them, and he liked the way she worked. The Enrights had been pigs to work for and when he was asked to switch sides he would have probably done so without having his son used as collateral. But the Enrights would never have helped in this way. They didn't give a flying shit that his son was on his death bed. At least Francesca had arranged for the help for his son that he so desperately needed. He would always remember that, and be loyal to her.

Chapter Seventeen

The rain still pouring, Francesca shivered, standing at the gates of Wormwood Scrubs. She remembered the last time she had been here, holding her mother's hand and waiting to visit her father. It had seemed so much bigger back then, with its castle-like appearance. She grinned as she remembered her mother saying her father worked there for the Queen. She had pretended to believe it but her mother was not aware just how much she could read, despite her young age. At the age of eleven, the teachers had begun certain tests on Francesca to find out her level of intelligence, and they took full credit for her academic ability. Mary, Francesca's mother, always assumed that her only daughter would be successful in whatever she took on.

Standing in the queue waiting for the officer to let them inside, she looked around at the other visitors, who were women as a general rule. There were two types. The young brigade consisted mainly of young women wearing skimpy nightclub clothes, with bare snow-white shoulders and tattoos, on which were scrawled the name of their partner plus the odd 'Mum' and 'Dad' in huge red hearts. In some cases, these particular tattoos were seen as a sign of commitment. Wearing skin-tight jeans and cleavage-exposing tops, they dressed to impress, to look good for their men. Most of the girls were pushing prams and dragging on cigarettes.

There was also another type of visitor who belonged to the more high-end 'club'. These ladies wore designer clothes, strings of gold chains and had sunbed tans; they were the wealthier kind, whose husbands were inside for money laundering or organised crime.

But still, they all had one thing in common: they were there to reassure their partner that they weren't messing around with other men and would loyally await his release from stir, however long the stretch may be.

Francesca gritted her teeth as she overheard the two girls in front of her making up a story to tell one of the girl's boyfriends. The girl, roughly twenty with long blonde hair, twitched and bit furiously at her lips. She could tell instantly that she was on speed and felt sorry for the skinny creature. The pity swiftly changed when she saw two little children, roughly four years old, possibly twins, run over to the woman, excited that they had found a caterpillar. The children were unbelievably dirty. The little girl had huge knots in her hair and the little boy had a black eye, and both their clothes were ready for the bin.

"For fuck's sake, you two, will ya stay 'ere wiv me? If I lose me place in the fucking queue, I'll fucking do ya."

They looked to the ground, held each other's hand and didn't move.

Spiteful bitch, thought Francesca.

As she watched the two children, she noticed a remarkable resemblance to her own family. The little girl had the very same steely-blue eyes and dimples and the boy had thick black wavy hair.

The queue became longer and the rain heavier. Francesca pulled up the collar on her cashmere coat. The two children looked frozen. The little girl wore a summer dress and a dirty cardigan, obviously too small, and her tiny fingers and knees were blue from the cold. The boy had a grey tracksuit halfway up his ankles and baggy around the knees.

Her heart went out to them. They looked roughly the same age as her niece and nephew although, sadly, she had never met them.

The guard at the gate began to check the visiting orders. He stood with his beer belly hanging over his black trousers, just nodding and pointing. When he got to Francesca, who clearly looked out of place, he questioned her. "Ma'am, are you here on a legal visit?" She still had the presence of a confident barrister.

She shook her head and handed him the visiting order.

He thanked her and told her where to go, taking one last look as she entered the prison. Once inside, she was led to the waiting room.

Francesca watched the two little scruffy urchins. Their mother stood by the side of the chair they were seated on and tried desperately to fix her makeup, but she made a mess of it as her hands shook so badly. Francesca spotted, through the bars in the waiting room, an officer with a sniffer dog.

The dog barked, which grabbed the attention of the girl, so, as a three or four-year-old would, she stood up to look through the door. As she did so, she accidentally knocked into her mother, who by now was uptight because her face looked worse than when she started. In a fit of anger, the mother lunged out at the child and, with the back of her hand, sent her rolling across the floor. The thud of the child's head as it hit the floor echoed frighteningly.

Francesca felt her chest cave in and her breathing tighten. She began to think that maybe the two children were her brother's. After all, she knew that his girlfriend had been sent a visiting order as well. Her anger increased, and she tried desperately to contain her temper, and turn her thoughts to a plan. She wanted more than ever to smash the woman to a pulp, but she would do worse than that. She was sure now, having looked closely at the children, that they were her own flesh and blood and prayed that she would have her suspicions confirmed.

She went to the dingy toilet, knowing they contained drugs' amnesty bins, a last chance to hand over any illegal possessions before the actual visit. It was a serious offence to take drugs in to the visitors. Posters everywhere outlined the consequences of imprisonment, which led to some of the visitors losing their nerve at the last minute and pouring their drugs into the bins.

Checking that no one could see her, she lifted the lid of the bin. There were empty sweet wrappers and Coke cans but, just under the Mars bar wrapper, she spotted a small parcel. Quickly, she grabbed it and rushed into the toilet cubicle. It contained a brown powder, heroin. Francesca grinned. Inside her own handbag, she had a packet of mints. She shoved the parcel into the packet and, with a handkerchief, she wiped the box and held the corner with her fingernails.

As Francesca walked past the skinny woman, she knocked her and dropped the packet of mints. The woman swung round, ready to have a slanging match with whoever had pushed her. As she looked Francesca in the eyes, she bowed her head. *There was something about Francesca that put her off; she looked familiar, but her eyes looked menacing.*

She looked at the floor and saw the mints. Instantly she picked them up.

"'Ere, love, I think these are yours." The skinny woman was holding the packet with her fingers wrapped around them.

Francesca nodded, and took the packet from her hand, using her long, well-manicured nails. As the woman turned to get back to applying her makeup, Francesca dropped the packet into the skinny woman's handbag.

The little boy was comforting the girl. Francesca had a sickening feeling, as if her stomach was being twisted. She looked at the girl's face then realised that the tiny child was too afraid to cry.

Francesca went over to the little girl to get a closer look.

"She's all right, love, leave her. Always getting in the fucking way, that one."

Francesca gently moved the hair away from the child's forehead to see the mark and then saw that there were two other, older-looking, bruises. The woman, still busy applying makeup, was totally oblivious to her surroundings.

"And what's your name?" asked Francesca, in her sweetest voice.

The child was afraid to speak. Her brother spoke up. "Her name's Ruby Vincent but our dad calls her Dolly."

Francesca almost gasped. These two little children really were her own flesh and blood. So many emotions ran through her mind: hate, anger, revenge, but also an overwhelming love for the little children. She wanted to cradle them in her arms and hug them tight but she couldn't let on just yet who she was.

It would be in the visiting room that she would meet her brother for the first time in sixteen years.

He had spoken with her when she arrived back in England after being in the States for so long.

The prison allowed phone calls, and that's when he told her the truth about his imprisonment. He was serving time because he had taken the rap for his girlfriend. He was sentenced to five years for possession of a large stash of cocaine. His girlfriend, Jesse, was pregnant with their daughter and their son was new-born, so he decided, for the sake of his babies, that he would take the rap.

Francesca's mother had feared that her only grandchildren were badly treated and, when she did get to see them, they always had bruises. Of course, if she'd said anything, Jesse would have stopped all visits with her and Sam.

It suddenly dawned on her that as soon as Jesse went through the search section she would be arrested, and the kids would be taken into care. It was standard practice and she as a lawyer had witnessed it first-hand.

Her mind began to race. She needed to get the kids into the visiting room before Jesse. Then, once they made the arrest, Sammy - as their father – had the right to hand the children over to her.

This meant that she would have to introduce herself now, so in a loud voice for Jesse to hear she asked, "Did you say Vincent?"

Jesse heard her and turned to face Francesca. "Yeah, that's right. Why, who are you then?"

"I'm Sam's sister," she replied.

Jesse stopped dead still. "But you are supposed to be in Spain." She wasn't sure of Francesca but tried to smile sweetly. She pointed to the children. "Well, there you go, that's Ruby, and he's Jack." She stood both the kids up. "Say hello to ya aunty, then."

Jesse looked very uncomfortable. Her partner's sister was so sophisticated, graceful and yet very self-assured. Jesse was unnerved and intimidated by her.

Both children smiled.

"Can I hold your hand, Aunty?" whispered Ruby, looking up at what she saw as a huge Barbie doll.

"Me too," said Jack.

Francesca grabbed both their tiny little fingers and prayed they wouldn't let go.

The officers opened the metal door and called five names.

"Jameson, Ebb, Vincent..." Francesca followed the others but remained in front, still holding the children tightly. She was searched first and ushered to the next door.

Jesse, having her handbag scrutinized because the sniffer dog had shown an interest, acted unperturbed because she had no idea that it contained the planted drugs.

"Wait for me," she called out in her croaky fag breath voice.

"I'll get the tea and snacks for the kids," shouted Francesca.

Jesse nodded. She didn't have any money on her and she hated watching all the others eating crisps and sweets, drinking tea and having her kids sulking because they couldn't have the same.

One of the officers held up the packet of mints. As he opened it, wearing his gloves, out fell the small parcel. Jesse was still putting her shoes back on, and sorting herself out, when she saw the officer nod to another officer who was leaning up against the wall. She looked at the packet and tried hard to recall where it came from, knowing it wasn't hers.

She was read her rights.

"That's not mine, I swear it. I never seen it before in my fucking life."

"Then, madam, it won't have your fingerprints on it then."

"No it won't..." She stopped dead. She suddenly remembered Sam's sister taking the packet from her with her long fingernails.

The final grey door opened and Francesca, with the children, walked through, but not before both women took a long, hard look at each other.

She expected Jesse to scream for her children, but she didn't.

The visiting room was just how she remembered it as a child. The walls were grey, three officers sat at a desk, and other officers walked about. The table and chairs were strategically placed to be viewed by the guards.

*

The room was practically empty, with only two other visitors in front of Francesca, and they sat down and waited for the side door to open.

Ruby and Jack acted much more lively out of their mother's sight.

Jack looked at the door that they had just come in from.

"Is Mummy coming, Aunty —" He stopped as he didn't know her name.

"I'm Aunty Francesca," she smiled at the little boy. "No, Mummy had to go home."

Jack didn't ask again – neither did Ruby.

The side door opened and in came the inmates. They stopped one at a time and scanned the room for their visitors.

Francesca didn't know what Sammy looked like and he certainly would not recognise her.

"Daddy, Daddy," shouted the children, when the final inmate emerged. Taller than Fred and thinner in the face, he had the same steel-blue eyes and the most adoring smile that instantly spread across his face when the kids ran into his arms.

He kissed them, hugged them, and then he looked over towards a tall, beautiful-looking woman. She certainly stood out amongst the other female visitors, but he couldn't for the life of him work out who she was.

Francesca stood up and Sam walked towards her, holding the hands of both the children. Then he saw the Vincent trademark – the steel-blue eyes, looking at him with so much love.

A tear sprang from her eye and she flung her arms around him.

"Dolly, is that you?" he whispered, as he held her at arm's length for a clearer look.

She nodded. "Yes, Sam, it's me all right. I just had to have a few alterations."

"God. Look at you all grown up and..." He started to get choked up. "Our Dolly, eh."

Ruby quickly jumped in. "I'm Dolly as well, ain't I, Daddy?"

Francesca's heart went out to the dear little girl with her infectious lisp.

"We've got an aunty now, Daddy, ain't we?"

Sam looked at his five-year-old son. "Yes, my boy, you have an aunty. You always did have."

They sat down and smiled, squeezing each other's hands.

Suddenly, Sam realised that his girlfriend wasn't there. He looked over at the tea bar to see if she was queuing for drinks.

"Where's Jesse?"

Both the children looked at Francesca. She didn't want to talk in front of them, so she pulled out a ten pound note and sent them to the tea bar for sweets. Both the children ran as fast as they could, in case their new aunty changed her mind.

"What's going on?" asked Sam, in a very soft voice.

"Are you in love with her, Sam?"

He looked down and shook his head. "Dolly, if only you knew." He sat, still shaking his head.

She hugged him. "Sam, I think I do know."

He looked up and watched how in control his sister was.

"Sam, I am a lawyer and I can get you out of here, and the kids taken away from Jesse."

Sam jumped in before she could finish. "My kids are my world, I have to keep her happy, 'cause if I don't I'm not gonna see 'em. She's a fucking evil bitch, and I fucking know she ain't good to those babies, but the only way I get to see 'em is if I don't make a fuss. She's got me and those little 'uns by the short and curlies."

Francesca could feel her head getting hot; it was anger that came over her.

"Not now, no fucking more, Sam. I'm getting you out of here and with your kids, where you belong."

"It's no good, Doll, I've got another few months, and who knows what she's gonna do when I get out."

There was silence for a while.

"Sam, I've got something to tell you. She's just been caught with drugs on her and she will probably do time."

"What?" screeched Sam. "Fuck, the social will take the kids. Oh my God, this gets fucking worse."

Francesca squeezed his hands. "No they won't. You are their father. When they come in here in a minute, which I'm sure they are going to do, you tell them I'm looking after them."

Sam's eyes widened and he nodded.

"Look at me, Sam. I'm getting you out of here and you will have custody of those kids, watch me."

Sam knew she could. He hadn't seen her for most of her life and yet the bond was there; he knew she was going to get him out and get him his kids back.

"Aunty Francisco, look what we got, sweets and Coke, and the lady gave me lots of money back."

The two children held out their hands, proud of their purchases and pleased as punch that they even got change. Francesca was totally charmed by the pair, with their cockney accents and sweet little ways. The fact that they couldn't say 'Francesca' was even more endearing.

As Francesca was paying for two coffees for her and Sam, she noticed two prison officers and a woman approaching their table, so she hurried back.

One of the officers, an older man with grey hair and a softer face, spoke first.

"Sorry, Sam, but we had to arrest your girlfriend. She was carrying Class A drugs, and a fair amount too. Now, we know you're not one of our heroin addicts, so we are assuming that she has tried to bring it in for someone else, or it's her own. The social services are here and are ready to collect the children when you have finished your visit."

"Your bird will be taken into custody," said the smaller officer.

Francesca put her hand out to the officer who was taken aback. He wasn't used to visitors shaking his hand – in fact, he wasn't used to visitors that looked like her.

"Hello, Officer, I'm Francesca. There is no need to concern the social services. I'm their aunt, and I will be taking them home with me."

The officer shook her hand. "Well, I'm sure that will be fine." He looked at Sam, who now had stood up.

"Thank you for letting me know, and don't worry about my children. My sister will take care of them."

The three of them left and Sam smiled.

"Well, Doll, you certainly know how to handle people. He was like putty in your hands."

"Well, I must say he treated you with respect. They are not normally so polite."

Sam laughed. "The thing is they know in here what's what, they have a bloody good idea about her, and they know I shouldn't really be in here."

The children were oblivious to it all.

"They are so sweet, Sam. I'm gonna enjoy looking after them and I know Mum's missing them."

"I know she does. She says Dolly is just like you." Sam was watching his daughter with eyes of devotion. "And little Jack, well, he is like Fred. Talking of Fred, how is he?" he whispered.

"Having the time of his life running a casino now, you know." They both laughed.

"Sam, when you get out, come with me back to the States with the kids. I need you all to spend time with me and my family."

Sam hugged her. She looked again like the child he'd said goodbye to in Surrey.

The bell rang and it was time to go.

The children hugged their dad, and tried hard to hold back their tears. He was so pleased to have his long-lost sister back in his life and to get him out of prison.

The black car pulled up outside the prison gates and Francesca ushered the children inside.

"Aunty Francisco, is this your car?" asked Jack.

She nodded.

"Wow."

"Why don't you drive it then?" asked Ruby.

Francesca laughed and tickled the pair of them. They giggled.

*

The journey took about an hour before it eventually pulled into a long, secluded drive.

The car stopped outside a large Tudor house. There were no neighbours for a mile each side, just the way she wanted it.

Sergio was waiting inside. As he opened the door, he took a step back. Before him stood Francesca with two small children, who were dishevelled to say the least.

The entrance was grand with shiny polished wood flooring and a huge chandelier hanging from the ornate plaster moulded ceiling.

"Come in, come in." He bowed, pretending to be a butler.

The children were a little unsure and they gripped Francesca's hand even tighter.

"Come on, let's go in and have some hot chocolate and fudge cake," giggled Francesca.

Jack and Ruby didn't know what fudge cake was, but it sounded really delicious.

Sergio raised his eyebrow and stared at Francesca, waiting for an explanation.

She was beaming.

"Ruby, Jack, meet your Uncle Sergio."

"'Ello," said Jack.

Ruby, still holding Francesca's hand, waved gently with her other.

"These two little monkeys are my niece and nephew, and I will tell you all about them over dinner when they are in bed."

Sergio slowly nodded and kissed Francesca on the cheek.

Chapter Eighteen

Christmas was just around the corner, and Jack and Ruby were very excited. From the day they met their aunt, their little lives hadn't been the same. Sam was due to be released early on good behaviour, and the custody order was in place for the children to be handed over to their dad on release. In the meantime, Francesca and her mum shared the responsibility.

At times, Francesca felt a twinge of guilt when the children asked about their mother, knowing she was responsible for her incarceration. However, as soon as the children behaved oddly or would say something strange that demonstrated they had been ill-treated, Francesca would smile and feel content, knowing her own flesh and blood would be safe from now on.

She learnt more about her brothers as the days and weeks passed by. She was told how her brother, Sam, became an angry youngster when Dolly was sent away. He'd served time before for violence, as did Fred and Joe. Sam, who was the sweet one, wasn't anymore. Joe's temper was dangerous and Fred became a fiery live wire. Mad Mick had a lot to answer for and the more Francesca heard about her family's tormented lives, the more determined she became.

Sam found the rest of his time in prison easier to contend with, knowing his sister was back and his kids were being looked after.

Mary was in her element. She was a good and loving mother, so having the chance to love and spoil her grandchildren was more than she could ask for. Little Dolly was the image of her Francesca when she was young, and Jack was a mixture of all her boys rolled into one.

They were loved by everyone and began to look it too. They were happy and more confident.

Bill was the same; he too adored the grandchildren and Jack was his right-hand man. If Bill stopped dead, little Jack's nose would be up his arse and that was the family joke. They referred to Jack as Bill's shadow.

He also loved his granddaughter and tried to spend time playing all the little girly games with her. Mary knew why; he'd never been able to get over the time he had lost with his own daughter. But, as soon as Francesca walked into the room, Bill's face would light up, listening to every word, embracing her when she arrived and hugging her when she left. He could never get back those precious lost years, so he tried to make up for it every time he saw her.

This was to be the best Christmas ever. Francesca was staying in England for a while, Sam would be home, and Fred would join them at some point still to be decided. He still had to keep out of the way for fear that Mad Mick would realise the dead body was his own son.

Luckily, so far, Mad Mick had no idea, and word went around that his son and his henchman had killed Fred and gone off to Amsterdam, where they were nicked. The rumours were started by Dan and spread fiercely around the clubs, eventually falling on Mad Mick's ears.

Mary and Bill looked forward to their family Christmas. Francesca was having the dinner at her secluded hideaway in Kent. Nothing could be more perfect.

The temperature fell and the weather report said snow. Bill decided to take Jack to the yard to keep him quiet, and Mary planned to make fairy cakes with Ruby.

Mary's house was warm and cosy and full of sweet smells from cake baking. Ruby liked to decorate them using silver balls, sugar flowers, and hundreds and thousands. Mary loved her little granddaughter so much that she could get away with anything.

"Nanny, Nanny," she squealed from the living room. "It's snowing."

Mary looked out of the window. "Well, would you look at that?"

"Quick, Nanny, I need my boots! I'm gonna make a snowman."

Mary laughed. "Listen to Nanny." She bent down to look at her very excited grandchild. "It's not thick enough to make a snowman and you will have to wait until Granddad comes home and he can take both you and Jack out to play in the snow."

Ruby flared her nostrils. It was the first time she had ever seen snow except for on the TV.

She was disappointed; she had just become used to grown-ups saying yes, and it had taken considerable effort to encourage Ruby and Jack to ask for anything. Their mother had said constantly, 'If you ask, you don't get', so for Christmas Jack and Ruby never said a word. They went to bed Christmas Eve thinking that by not asking for a single thing, Father Christmas would bring them lots of toys. They were so disappointed when the morning came and at the end of the bed were two Mars bars along with a very drunken mum, sprawled out half-naked on the bedroom floor. Their tiny socks were empty, with not a fairy light or a mince pie in sight.

Jesse had sold the toys sent by Mary and Bill to feed her drug habit. She gave the children cruel reasons why they shouldn't have them.

A week previously, Mary and Francesca took the children to Hamley's to decide which toys to buy them but, as they wandered from floor to floor, the kids looked sad and uninterested. Francesca sat them down in the coffee bar at the top of the shop and demanded to know why they wouldn't look at all the lovely toys.

Jack spoke up. "Toys are for children that don't have brothers and sisters, and I have my sister."

Ruby nodded and sucked her thumb.

"You can have toys that you can play with together," said Mary.

Ruby shook her head. "No, 'cause if I want toys, Mummy says it means I don't want my bruvver."

Both Mary and Francesca felt so sorry for the children. It was apparent that, along with the bruises, were mental scars. Jesse had been cruelly manipulating them.

"Well, how about I make a promise to you?" whispered Francesca.

Jack and Ruby nodded in unison.

"I promise that you will always be together as brother and sister, and you can have toys too." Both children looked apprehensive. "I will write to Father Christmas and make sure that he brings plenty of toys that you can both share."

Jack looked at Ruby, and they both smiled.

As they toured the shop again, now with much more enthusiasm, the idea of toy sharing went out of the window. Jack inspected all the monster trucks and diggers – anything that resembled the machines at his granddad's yard – and Ruby eyed every style of Barbie, all the dollhouses and anything to do with cooking.

"Well, Father Christmas has a very long list to choose from," said Mary, who was now exhausted.

Francesca sent Mary back upstairs with the kids to get a tea and rest while she placed an order. The shop assistant followed Francesca around, writing down the codes for each toy on the list. "And this is the address and, before I forget, can you have all the boy's toys wrapped in blue and the girl's wrapped in pink."

The assistant nodded.

Just as Francesca went to go back to the coffee room, she spotted, in a glass cabinet, a beautiful porcelain doll. It had dimples, thick, wavy brown hair, eyes of steel-blue and, to her amazement, the doll had a name tag — 'Dolly'.

"Before I go, can you wrap that doll — and the small blue bike over there with the stabilisers — can you wrap that too, and I'll take them now."

The car pulled up outside Hamley's and they all jumped in. This time they looked clean, tidy, and dressed ready for the cold — very different from the two little urchins she drove home from the prison that day.

"What's in those boxes, Aunty Francisco?" asked Ruby, who loved her pretty aunt.

Francesca put her finger on her nose and winked. Ruby smiled, curled up to Francesca, put her thumb in her mouth, and drifted off to sleep.

When they arrived back at Francesca's house, Mary settled herself deep into the soft leather sofa and watched as Sergio brought the bags in from the car. She had no idea what was in them.

Francesca carried Ruby in and Adam, her new driver, carried in Jack. Both children had slept all the way home but now, once inside the house, they began to wake up.

"What's in the boxes?" asked Jack, who tried to have a peek, knowing they had come from the toyshop.

"Well, whilst I was looking at all the toys and putting together a list for Father Christmas, there was a letter for me in the shop."

Both children were perched on the edge of their seats.

"And, well, it was from Father Christmas and it says," — she paused to unravel a crumpled piece of paper — "Dear Jack and Ruby, it has come to my attention that, for the last year, you have been exceptionally good children, and so you may have an early Christmas present!" She pointed to the two boxes.

Both children leapt from their seats and, with beaming faces, tore at the wrapping paper.

Sergio and Mary looked on at Francesca, who was unaware of their stares. Sergio fought to hold back the tears; *she would have made the perfect mother if that bastard hadn't taken away that chance.* Mary, watery-eyed, watched her daughter in admiration.

The children bonded with Francesca very quickly and really looked forward to spending time with her and Sergio in their mansion in the country. But it was soon time for them to return to their nanny's house in the East End. She needed to prepare for Christmas and Mary had to get back for Bill.

Jack had time to ride his bike up and down the hallway and Ruby dressed and undressed her new baby doll. They had been so excited at their new gifts that never before had they giggled so much.

"I cannot imagine what it's going to be like on Christmas morning, with these two little monkeys," laughed Sergio, as he chased them up the hallway, them squealing with delight.

Adam packed the car up, ready to take Mary and the children back to London.

"Bye, Mum, see you Christmas Eve." Francesca hugged her mother, and kissed the children, who were excited that they were allowed to take their toys with them.

"It looks like snow," said Sergio, looking up at the sky.

"They predicted snow at the end of the week," replied Mary, as she slowly eased herself into the car.

*

The cakes were nearly done.

"Dolly, do you want to wash your hands, ready to put the sweets on the cakes for Jack and Granddad when they get in?"

Ruby watched the snow falling heavily, longing to go and make a snowman.

"When will Granddad be home?" shouted Ruby, now becoming a little impatient.

Mary walked into the living room and pointed to the clock on the wall.

"Now, you see that big hand. When that reaches number twelve, that's when Granddad will be home."

Ruby lost interest in the cakes and continued to watch the snow and the clock. Five o'clock came and went, and there was still no Granddad. Mary hadn't taken into account that the snow on the roads would delay them.

Busy preparing the evening meal, Mary had not paid attention to Ruby.

Little Ruby decided she could wait no more and pulled her coat from the hallway closet and tugged at her tiny pair of pink wellies. Quickly she put them on, struggling because they were on the wrong feet. On tiptoes, she turned the door handle and hopped outside. She grabbed at the snow and shivered, never having experienced it before, and was surprised at how soft it was, but also how painful it was when she held it for too long. She stepped back into the house to grab her doll; she wanted it to see the snow too.

In the pocket of her coat she found her gloves, and quickly went to work trying to compact the snow and build a big snowman that her brother and grandfather would be proud of.

In her own little world, Ruby played with the snow, unaware of the silver car that pulled up alongside the front garden.

A man got out and looked around. The street was quiet; there was not a soul in sight. He watched the child for a few seconds before making his move.

"Hello, little snow queen." He tried to speak in a soft voice, but his voice was croaky from too many fags, excessive booze and shouting.

Ruby looked up. She remembered one of the Barbie dolls on the television being called snow queen and a smile lit up her innocent face.

"So you are the snow queen?" the man asked as he edged forward.

Ruby nodded.

"And what's your other name, snow queen?"

Ruby giggled. "Dolly."

The man gritted his teeth. "Is that your baby over there?" The man pointed to the porcelain doll.

Ruby smiled and nodded. "It's my early Christmas present from Farver Christmas."

The man leant over Ruby. "Are you looking after your new dolly?"

Ruby turned to pick up the doll but, just before her tiny fingers had a chance to grip her precious toy, the man grabbed her, muttering, "And your granddad should be looking after his."

Ruby screamed out, "Nanny!" before he had a chance to cover her mouth.

Mary was holding the tray of cakes when she heard the tiny child scream. The cakes fell to the ground as she charged towards the door, just to see the silver car wheels spinning as the driver tried to get away in the snow. Mary knew instinctively that her granddaughter was in the car. She ran screaming at the top of her voice, managed to grab the passenger door, and tried in vain to open it. She could see her terrified granddaughter staring back at her helplessly, with eyes wide open in disbelief. As the car eventually gripped the road, Mary was thrown helplessly to the side, hitting her head hard on the kerb, causing a deep gash.

The fear for her granddaughter kept her conscious and she screamed the most heart-wrenching sound. "Help, someone help!"

Vomit rose up and hit the back of her throat. Panic had blinded her and she fought to get her breath. Just as she got back to her feet, Bill pulled up in his car. He could see his wife was in trouble; she was white and obviously shaken. Her screams were high-pitched and hysterical.

He ran to her side. "Mare, Mare, what's up?" He helped her get steady.

"He took Dolly." She pointed up the street. "Silver BMW."

The words went over and over in his mind. *Not again*, the pain was too much. *His daughter and now his granddaughter.*

"Go, Bill, get her." She knew he had to hurry.

Mary sat back on the kerb and Bill flew off in the car. He shouted to Jack, who by now had hopped out of the car. "Jack, get Nanny indoors and call your Uncle Dan."

Bill tore off up the road, sliding from kerb to kerb, trying desperately to catch up with the silver BMW which was, by now, nowhere in sight. The tears streamed down his face, the air was still, and huge snowflakes fell from the evening sky. His heart pounded as he prayed, '*Please, God, don't let him hurt her.*'

Back at the house, Jack became the man. He helped his nan to a chair and then rushed to the phone. He quickly looked through the address book – in big letters, it said 'Dan'. He dialled the number next to it.

"Yeah, hello," shouted Dan down the phone, as the music in the background was too loud.

"Uncle Dan." He waited.

Dan realised it was his nephew, Jack. "Turn the fucking music off!" he shouted at the new DJ, who was testing the sound.

"What's up, boy?"

"Uncle Dan, Nanny's been run over and Dolly's gone. I'm 'ere with Nanny but she's got blood everywhere."

Dan could feel his body go cold. He knew it was Mad Mick; the feeling came from the pit of his stomach. Joe walked over, sensing right away something was wrong.

"Get your car, Joe. Go to the house and phone me when you get there. Muvver's hurt."

Joe looked blank. "What's happened, Dan?"

Dan grabbed his car keys. "I think that cunt Mad fucking Mick has got our baby Ruby."

Joe gasped. "Oh, fuck no!" he screamed. "Not our Ruby."

He headed for home, wailing like a baby. Joe had never been the thinker in the family; he just did as he was told. But his love for the children was so great that it ripped him apart to think of Mad Mick hurting his precious niece.

*

Joe hit three cars on the way home but managed to arrive in one piece.

The red-eyed, blubbering Joe tried to pull himself together before he reached the front door.

His mother was bleeding badly and her face was grey.

She was still conscious and sobbing, which set Joe off again. "Let me get you cleaned up."

Mary was still very unsteady but, as daft as Joe was at times, he was good with first aid. If he hadn't come from a tough East End family, he would probably have been a nurse.

He pressed a wet cloth on the back of her head to stop the bleeding. However, she was now being sick.

Joe helped his mother to the car.

He phoned Nellie before leaving and picked her up on the way.

"Nell, will you stay wiv me muvver and our Jack while I sort out some business?"

Nellie knew not to ask too many questions and did as she was asked. She loved the Vincents and had remained good friends with Mary all those years.

Mary was slumped in the back of the car, going in and out of consciousness, when Nellie jumped in. She would do anything she could to help.

"All right, Mare, love, I'm here. I'm gonna sit with you in the hospital."

Little Jack sat quietly; he had never seen so much blood.

"Don't worry, Jack, Nanny will be fine, just you see." Nellie was ready to take charge; it was the least she could do.

Out of the blue, Jack spoke. "Someone has taken my sister."

Nellie gasped. "Joe, is that true?"

Joe was concentrating on getting his mother to the hospital and getting back to his brother to work out a plan.

He nodded. Nellie could feel the pain her best friend was going through; it was Francesca all over again. Nellie put her arm around Mary and hugged her.

"It's gonna be all right, girl," she whispered.

Dan drove frantically to the car yard owned by Mad Mick. The lights were off and there was no sign of life.

He sat outside and waited, racking his brains and trying to think of a way to find his niece.

The car phone rang. It was Francesca.

"Dan, where are Mum and Dad? I keep phoning but there's no answer." Her voice was cool and calm. She had no idea what was going on.

"Fran." He paused, trying to think of the right words to say.

Francesca's heart started to pound; the tone in his voice said it all.

"Fran, Mad Mick's taken little Ruby."

She dropped the phone. Her head was pounding like it would explode; her face heated up, and she could feel the ground coming towards her. This time she couldn't control it and blacked out.

Sergio rushed to her side. "Fran, what's the matter?" He helped her to the sofa and waited for her to regain consciousness.

Fred had arrived safely in England and Francesca was phoning to let her parents know. But, when Fred walked into the living room to join his sister, he found her slumped in Sergio's arms.

"Fuck, sis, what's up?" He grabbed her head and looked into her eyes as she slowly came to.

The phone was still on the floor with a muffled voice calling her name.

Fred grabbed the receiver. "Who is this?" he snapped.

"It's me, Dan."

Dan should have been excited to hear his brother's voice, but the whole picture was so bleak.

"Dan, what's going on? Francesca's as white as a ghost here."

"Fred, Mad Mick has got our Ruby."

"No, no, the bastard! Oh my God, he can't have."

"Me and the ol' man are looking for him now."

Fred dropped the phone and hopped around the room.

"The fucking cunt." He ripped at his hair, not knowing what to do. "I'm gonna fucking kill him, the cunt!"

Francesca got up, but very unsteadily. She gradually focused her eyes to see Fred screaming and crying and Sergio in the background talking with two men. Roberto had sent his own men over to England to accompany Fred and Mauricio. Their safety was still top priority. He wasn't sure if the Enrights had any other plans.

Mauricio, who had flown over to join them for Christmas with Kathy, came running into the living room, still dripping wet from the shower. He and Kathy had taken the same flight as Fred and were slightly less jet lagged. Kathy was asleep and, even through all the commotion, she remained that way.

Francesca got back on the phone.

"Dan, are you sure it was Mad Mick?" she sobbed, trying to make some sense of all this.

Mauricio grabbed Fred. "Fred, what's all the noise, eh?" He tried to stop Fred from blowing a fuse by grabbing his face. "Fred, calm down. What's happened?"

Fred started to sob. "That bastard."

Mauricio looked over at Sergio, who nodded. He was still talking to his men.

Sergio stepped forward.

"We will get her back, but now we must make a plan." His accent was more Italian than ever.

Francesca snapped out of her daze. She already had a plan to take down the McManners, and now it was time to put it into action.

Dan was still parked up outside the yard when his father, Bill, arrived.

Bill was grief-stricken and he could not control his sobs. Dan held his father and they cried together.

*

Joe drove to Mad Mick's yard but, because he was a little slow, he hadn't realised that Mad Mick had sold the old yard and moved premises to Greenwich, Charlton and Hackney. Bill and Dan only knew of the one yard and Joe only knew about the old one.

The old yard was derelict before he had sold it. He turned it into a site for the collection and dumping of aggregate, a big money-maker. The books looked good, and so he sold the company to buy three scrapyards that were strategically placed to carry out his illegal rackets. Each son now had a yard of his own. Eric, the largest of the four, happily married with two children, tried to keep the illegal smuggling and storing of arms to a minimum. He enjoyed the family life, so ducking and diving was less appealing these days. He didn't really care that much for his father, who carried deep grudges and wouldn't rest until those who did him wrong were well and truly punished. He secretly believed his father really was mad, but he did as he was told for fear his father would turn on him.

Then there was Stuart, smaller than Eric, but a fiery-tempered man just like his father – only with fewer morals. Piano was the eldest child and the least intelligent. He was thought to be in Amsterdam but hadn't contacted anyone, which obviously worried Mad Mick. Of course he wasn't anywhere, except in a bag at the morgue marked John Doe.

The youngest son was Charlie, the apple of his father's eye. He was the good-looking son, who took on his mother's looks. His brothers, on the other hand, had the misfortune to take after their father's hideous features...

Chapter Nineteen

Mick, his sons thought, had gradually gone mad. His obsessive personality took over his life. His wife, Betty, had left him. He was convinced she was having sex with all the neighbours and anyone she spoke to in the street. The abuse was unbearable; she couldn't take anymore, not at her age.

He would not let her out of the house without calculating the time her trip should take – any minute longer and she was back in the dog house. She was not allowed to wear makeup, and she couldn't speak unless spoken to.

She was a small woman, attractive in her younger days, and married Mick because he was a charmer. It certainly wasn't to do with his good looks because, with his red hair and pointed features, he was certainly no oil painting. To add insult to injury, his very white, sickly skin, which only turned pink in the sun, didn't attract the women.

Eventually he lost it and, when his right-hand henchman helped her carry the shopping into the house, he decided there and then he was having an affair with her, so he took a kitchen knife and stabbed the man in the leg. As the poor guy reeled around in agony, Mad Mick wiped the blood with his finger and smeared it over his hysterical wife's face. That afternoon she turned into a different person. She picked up a cast-iron saucepan and hit him around the head. She left the same day. For some reason he let her go and she never looked back.

He was obsessed with revenge, particularly on the Vincents, and Bill was only one name on a long list. His reputation, as being a hard gangster, had preceded him in every club, pub and criminal hangout. No one wanted to mess with Mad Mick or his sons. He believed he was invincible, and his lucky break came when he took a shortcut past ole' Billy Vincent's house and happened to clock a small child playing in the front garden.

The snow had caused a delay on a shipment which Mick had organised and this had seriously pissed him off. A few too many glasses of whisky waiting in the cold yard fuelled his anger and, seeing a child in the garden of his worst enemy, he believed all his prayers had been answered at once.

The youngster, such a cutie, would obviously be the apple of her grandfather's eye. He drove away with one thought on his mind, which was how to dispose of the body. She cried quietly in the back of his BMW. He thought this was unusual for a small child – his own granddaughter of around the same age would have screamed the place down.

He drove into the dark, eerily quiet yard. There was nobody in sight and it was unlikely there would be anyone around. The old car pits had not been filled in just yet. No one entered the site. It was an ideal place to leave her there to freeze to death, as her tiny body would easily go unnoticed.

He drove around the back to where the old diggers and sand piles were. He opened the passenger's door and grabbed the frail little girl by the arm. She was terrified and, in a tiny whisper, asked, "Where's my nanny?"

Mick looked at the child and grinned. "She's probably dead now."

Ruby was so scared that she wet herself. Mad Mick dragged her to the pit and looked down. It was too deep to climb out of, and there was no chance that she could escape. Besides, a good hard clump and she would be dead.

She looked up into Mick's eyes. "Please can I see my nanny?"

He was angry with himself that a Vincent child had allowed him to feel a touch of guilt. So, without a flinch, he hit her hard across the head and she fell into the pit. She lay on the floor and the snow continued to fall.

Mick looked up at the skies. No one would find her just yet. He would leave her there until morning and fill in the hole himself.

'*Thank you, God.*' He punched the air, satisfied that he had finally avenged his enemy. The murder of Fred was just interest gathered over the years. This child was the real deal. *They would suffer this time.*

Ruby lay lifeless in the dark pit – her tiny body was slowly covered in a blanket of snow.

Mick drove home, more drunk than he realised, and he slumped in front of the TV, with a warm sensation of satisfaction.

*

Francesca had been planning her revenge against the McManners' family for a long time and had every detail finely tuned. But she hadn't anticipated that it needed to be actioned now. No one had seriously expected Mad Mick to kidnap the baby. They believed he'd had his pound of flesh with the disappearance of Fred's body, even though he was unaware of what had actually happened. However, they still watched their backs, in case he wanted more.

Adam, her driver and right-hand man, had gathered information on Mick's family over the past few weeks – a job for which he was being paid very well. He'd had every one of Mick's boys watched and all their routines noted. This was something he was good at. He enjoyed the detective side of his work.

Francesca gathered them together and, like a sergeant in the army, she gave them their instructions. "Mauricio, get your men and find Eric. I need him back at Mick's yard bound and gagged."

Mauricio nodded. "Alive, I take it?"

Francesca glared. "Too fucking right, alive. He is my number one bait."

She looked at Sergio, who stood with his arms folded. He still looked weak. "Sergio, will you take your men and find Charlie? He will be the most difficult."

He nodded as he stroked her cheek. "And you, Fran, what will you do?" Sergio was worried. Her expressionless face concerned him.

"Just do what you need to do, I will be fine." For a second, her face softened.

Fred, still reeling, worried Francesca. "Fred, listen to me, you have to stay calm. Don't fucking blow it, not now." Her harsh voice startled Fred into reality.

Adam spent a few minutes going over descriptions and timings with the men before they left.

Mauricio had associates in England who he called upon whenever he needed any back-up. They met him at the agreed spot.

The instructions were clear and precise. Francesca had prepared for the moment she would come up against her nemesis, and her weeks of planning had to pay off. She had promised herself, and her family, that she would make things right, and that she would see to it they lived a free life, not forever looking over their shoulders and always dreading that phone call. This had to be the final act: never having to hide again.

Mauricio found Eric easily, as a creature of habit. Every Friday evening he would go to the late-night florist in Church Street, buy a dozen roses, and pop to the off-licence where he would buy a bottle of champagne.

Sitting with his associates in the café across the street, Mauricio waited, hoping that the snow hadn't put him off.

Sure enough, around seven o'clock, a brand new Audi pulled up outside the florist and a large guy, roughly thirty years old, went into the shop and walked out with a dozen red roses. Two of Mauricio's associates, Pauli and Rizler, jumped out of their seats. Mauricio grabbed their arms. "No, wait and see if he buys the champagne – we must be damn sure that's him. We can't fuck this up." Slowly, they sat back down. Then he went into the off-licence and bought the champagne. Mauricio nodded.

As they walked towards him, he stopped in his tracks, ready for trouble.

"You must be Eric." Mauricio smiled, and put out his hand to greet him. The two men either side of Mauricio smiled. Eric was not unnerved; they seemed friendly enough.

He put the flowers and champagne in one hand and stupidly held out the other to shake Mauricio's hand.

He grabbed Eric's hand with the one hand and with the other pulled from his pocket a stun gun, pushing it into Eric's side. The charge to his side left him paralysed, and he fell to the floor like a wooden pole, still clutching the flowers and champagne.

Rizler and Paulie, two rather skinny men with rat-like features, were dangerous. They took on the dirty jobs which paid well. Although they were Londoners, they knew exactly who they were dealing with and didn't dream of crossing Mauricio. Rizler grabbed the stiff Eric and, with the help of Paulie, they managed to put him in the back of the car, where they tied and gagged him.

Relieved that it had gone to plan Mauricio said, "One down, two to go, eh."

Eric's faculties shortly returned, but he had absolutely no idea what was going on.

"Just sit still and quiet and you won't get hurt," muttered Rizler.

They sped off and headed for the yard.

Dan had pulled himself together when his sister called him back on the car phone.

"Now, Dan, listen very carefully to me – and trust me, okay?"

Dan nodded, despite being on the phone. He was happy to go along with any idea at this moment, since he couldn't even think straight.

"Dan, I need you and Joe to get Stuart. Bind the bastard up and gag him, then bring him to Mick's yard. Dan, I'm going to pass the phone over to Adam. He will give you more details."

"All right, Doll, I'll see you there. Take care, love." Dan went into automatic pilot, his sister took control, and he didn't question her.

Adam gave Dan all the info he had on Stuart.

Stuart loved a good drink and entertained the pubs around the Greenwich area. Dan had to get him somehow and take him, still alive, to the yard. In the meantime, Bill had no idea of the plan; Francesca needed him out of the picture. She couldn't bear her father to see her in action. Dan suggested he drove around looking for the silver BMW. Bill headed off; he couldn't sit at home twiddling his thumbs. More importantly, he could not go home without Ruby.

Dan met up with Joe at the Cutty Sark and looked in each pub for the piss-head Stuart. It took six minutes to find him. He had come into their club in the past; winding them up, asking if they had buried their sister. Dan had, in the past, kept his cool to protect his family, but he would not be doing this now.

Stuart stood outside the pub, chatting to a young French girl. She was obviously being sucked in by his drunken charms. Dan's heart thumped as he bit down on his bottom lip and headed towards the ginger-haired, weasel-looking lad. Joe marched alongside Dan and, up until now, hadn't said a word. He was not good with words and the anger inside made him worse. Stuart turned to see the two Vincent boys marching his way. He propped himself up on the cement moulding outside the gloomy pub.

"Well, if it ain't the Vincent sisters." He knocked back the last of his beer and grinned, showing his chipped teeth. The young French girl hurried off, sensing serious trouble. Dan and Joe said nothing. They walked up to Stuart, and Joe promptly pulled a gun from his pocket and held it up to Stuart's nose. Dan shoved his gun in Stuart's back.

"So, ginger cunt, whose bullets do you want?"

Stuart held his breath. The Vincents were hard, but they never fucked with him or his family. He felt weak at the knees and stuttered, "'Ere, all right, boys, just joking, like. Know what I mean? No harm meant." He shook all over.

"Get the car, Joe," said Dan, who was more concerned with the look on Joe's face than Stuart himself. He knew that if Joe lost the plot and shot Stuart, the plan would be fucked. Joe didn't move.

"Joe, get the fucking car now!" he screamed.

Joe snapped out of his trance and ran to fetch the car.

Stuart shuffled uncomfortably.

Dan pushed the gun harder into Stuart's back. "Move, you ugly fucking cunt, and I'll shoot ya. Got it?"

Stuart stood stiff; he had never witnessed so much anger in a man's eyes before and never expected it from a Vincent. He prided himself with a cavalier attitude that no one would dare threaten him. *He was the big shot with the reputation.*

"Look, Dan, I dunno what's going on, like, but I ain't done nuffin' wrong, I swear."

Dan didn't move. "Shut the fuck up." He didn't shout this time, but just whispered in a way that sent a shiver down Stuart's spine.

Joe sped around the corner and stopped in front of the pub. Dan pushed Stuart into the backseat, where they tied his hands behind his back and then headed for the yard.

In the meantime, Sergio went with his men to find Charlie, the youngest of Mad Mick's sons. Time was running out; the plan was to meet at the yard at the same time. Charlie was not where he was supposed to be. They headed to the last place on the list and Sergio prayed, for little Ruby's sake, that they would find him.

The whorehouse was the final chance, but it was still very early. Charlie popped in there after eleven o'clock on a Friday – it was only seven thirty. They had checked the pubs but, unlike Stuart – who drank from five o'clock – Charlie was a late starter. Sergio had been sitting in his car for a while when a young guy walked by.

"Hey, boss, that guy there looks like Charlie."

Sergio turned to face his man in the backseat. "What the fuck? How do you know what he looks like?"

"Sorry, boss, only the description said a tattoo on his neck and a tattoo of a sword on his hands, and that guy there has both."

"Well, let's see, eh?" Sergio stepped out of the car onto fresh untouched snow and let out a high-pitched whistle. "Hey, Charlie, it's me, Sergio."

The young man turned to face Sergio. He rolled his collar up on his thick sheepskin coat.

"Do I know you?" shouted Charlie, walking towards Sergio, trying to see if he recognised the caller.

"Yeah, of course you do. You remember Rose, don't you?" Sergio gestured to the car and pretended he had a woman in there. "Rose, don't be silly, Charlie remembers you."

Charlie was completely taken in and believed Sergio was some old acquaintance – he messed with so many women that Rose could have been any one of them. As he got to Sergio, the guy in the back of the car, Rudi – Sergio's trusted right-hand man – lunged forward and head-butted Charlie. His nose split open and he wobbled. Rudi grabbed him and threw him into the back seat.

Sergio called Francesca on her car phone and checked in.

"We have all the men now and we are at the yard."

Engulfed by anger, Fred struggled to get his breath.

"How the fuck can you stay so calm, sis?"

"Fred, my anger is deep and vast and I am focused on what I need to do to get our little Dolly back. That son of a bitch won't ruin both our lives."

Fred was annoyed that she was calm. "Ruin our lives? Sis, she might be fucking dead," he cried again.

"No she's not, Fred." Her voice was flat and direct.

"How the fucking 'ell do you know that?"

She knew he couldn't cope if he really believed little Dolly was dead. "Trust me, Fred, I know, okay," she shouted back.

He stared at the controlled woman next to him. She was nothing like the sister he left behind in Surrey. She didn't look the same, talk the same, or act the same, but he didn't care – he had total faith in her.

*

They arrived outside a big white house opposite Danson Park. It was Art Deco design, rather unusual, but it was the right address. Francesca pulled herself together and suggested Fred did the same. They hoped that one of Eric's children would open the door.

Adam had been following all the brothers and Mad Mick, and he'd noted all their moves. Every Friday night Eric would knock at the door instead of using his keys. Usually the kids would open the door and in he would go. Francesca nodded for Fred to ring the doorbell, keeping away from the window.

Sure enough, the little girl answered and, as quick as a flash, Fred grabbed her mouth first and scooped her up. She, too, was only about three years old and looked terrified. Fred and Francesca sat in the back of the car with the child as Adam headed to the yard.

Francesca tried to comfort Millie, Eric's first born; she cuddled her and eased her fear by telling her she was going to see Daddy.

As soon as Francesca called Sergio to let him know she had Eric's daughter, Eric's phone rang. His wife was calling frantically to tell him that their daughter had been kidnapped.

Sergio removed Eric's gag.

"You tell your wife she is with you and you had to return to the shop – you forgot something… If you don't say it we will kill your baby, eh." Mauricio poked Eric in the chest, who nodded wildly. Anything to protect his family.

"Hello, love, I'm on my way back to the shops with Millie. I forgot the champagne." He tried to stay calm.

"You fucking halfwit, I was worried to death. I thought someone had fucking snatched her."

*

Mick's sons, rounded up like sheep, stared at each other without a clue as to what was going on.

Charlie spoke first. The others still tried to work out who had captured them. "Who do you bunch of knob heads think you're dealing with?" Even with his busted nose, he still maintained his cocky attitude. Frankie stood behind Charlie, ready to place the gag around his mouth but, with the outburst, he gave Charlie a real forceful slap around the back of his head – hard enough to cause him to lose his balance. "Shutta ya mouth, show respect," barked Frankie, in a husky Italian accent.

Frankie placed the leather gag in Charlie's mouth and tied it so hard that the corners of his mouth split open. He squirmed as the excruciating gag ripped into him. His body lost the tautness, and he sat unsteadily on his chair. His two other brothers watched in fear. They had no idea as to who the hell the Italians were and what their fate was to be. It was no secret to them that they had gathered themselves a fair few enemies over the years, with no thanks to their father. Stuart really was a coward when it came to it. He more or less hid behind his father's name and any beatings which needed to be done were never administered by him. He would take along a crew, his father's henchmen, and wait until the victim was on the floor, practically dead, before he would put the boot in.

He kept his mouth closed. He wanted to say to Charlie, 'It's the Vincents, they are behind all this,' but his mouth froze shut. The gag was coming his way and he felt the pain before it arrived as, like Charlie, there was no gentle handling. Frankie had pulled from his pocket another leather wad and given Stuart the same treatment.

Eric was made to sit without the tight gag put to his face. Stuart and Charlie's eyes darted around the room. They tried to see who they knew, desperate to get some clue as to why they were here and what their fate could be. Stuart wondered if their father had been in on it. After all, this was his yard. Nothing made sense.

Mick's yard was big. Scrap metal, covering an acre of land on which his warehouse sat right in the centre, was used to house his best car engines along with his dodgy stock, which were his big money earners.

The men heard the car pull into the yard and they all waited in anticipation for the door to open. The Italians knew exactly who to expect and they stepped away from the prisoners. Francesca stepped out of the car. The air was cool and she pulled her coat tightly around her body. Fred jumped out, still impatient, whilst Millie, Eric's daughter, was kept inside in the warm with Adam. As she entered the building, Mick's sons stared at her in wonder. She was tall, and dressed in a suit and long black coat, wearing black leather gloves. Charlie was surprised to see a woman. She walked slowly and deliberately and he realised as soon as she glanced his way that she was Dolly; she had the same eyes as the Vincents.

Stuart gasped when he saw Fred standing there, as large as life.

"What's up, Stuart, me old mucker? Thought I was dead, did ya?" He was nose to nose with Stuart who, by now, was as white as a ginger boy could be.

Fred was losing it; his voice sounded erratic. "And you, Charlie boy, bet you're fucking pleased to see me." He walked over and spat in his face.

Charlie's temper was like Fred's — up and down — and he stared back, daring Fred. He was the ruthless one, believing he was invincible, just like his father.

Francesca slowly walked over to Eric, who sat wide-eyed and petrified. Being the bigger brother, broader and with more meat than the average man, he should have been the hard case, but his eyes gave him away. They were as soft as shit when it came down to it. He had only gained his reputation because his father made him fight. 'Don't fucking talk your way out of shit, shoot your way out, you fucking big girl's blouse,' his father would say. He could have a good fight too, but deep down he hated it; he didn't get the same gratifying pleasure his father got from seeing men plead for their lives. He drew the line at torture though, and his father overlooked it, as long as he was still prepared to give a bareknuckle ruck and use the odd chain. However, he couldn't be his father and hang people up on the butcher's hook. Eric was wary of Francesca; she had a definite presence about her. The men in the room, without words, were taking their direction from her. Never having met a woman running her own racket, with so many hard men watching her back, he was scared but, at the same time, morbidly curious. It was strange because it had always been others that feared them. Now the tables had been turned, and it was they who were being forced to sit facing their killers. He prayed they would not be tortured in the way that they had tortured their enemies. The thought of being cut into pieces and having his skin peeled, or worse, made him feel faint. He watched Francesca, with his phone, walk towards him, and the edges of the picture began to close in. The realisation that they had his daughter jolted him into reality, and he managed to stay seated without sliding onto the floor.

He expected her to have a typical East End accent like her brothers. He was wrong.

"Call your father and use whatever knowledge you have to get him here now." Her voice was cool as she enunciated every letter, a sign of a good upbringing. Her eyes stared deep at Eric. As his bowels moved, he thought he was going to shit himself.

"If you are not successful, then, well, I take it you adore little Millie?" Her words stopped and she stepped back.

Eric shook in his chair as the others watched on.

"My Millie, where is she?" He didn't come across as aggressive. In fact, he seemed quite passive.

"She's in my car. Do as I say and she will stay there, nice and warm. If you choose not to, then she will become cold very quickly."

Eric, absolutely certain that Dolly was serious, wasn't about to gamble with his precious daughter's life. But, on the other hand, he couldn't second guess his father's thoughts: he knew one thing for sure, and that was that he was cold and callous.

Francesca had dialled the number from Eric's phone. The wind began to blow up and whistle through the warehouse. Eric didn't trust this evil woman but did as she said without question. He watched the men around the room who appeared to be guarding her – who the fucking hell were they? Most of them looked Italian; even the Vincents blended in well, with their Mediterranean features.

"Dad, it's Eric."

Mick grunted down the phone.

"I'm at the yard." *The yard meant Mick's yard.*

"What the fuck are you doing there?" He was still half-asleep.

"Dad, you'd better get over here. Mum's here clearing out the stash. I can't stop her."

Mad Mick jumped up from the sofa and was in his car in seconds. The idea that his wife was back to clean him out enraged him. The snow was still falling and his thoughts returned to the little girl he had left in the pit and he smiled. *One revenge and another one on its way.* He was planning repeatedly how he would fuck his wife up. He hated her more than he hated anyone.

Francesca smiled. "There's a good boy. Now, you sit quietly."

Eric nodded like a child. The other brothers had been gagged in case they gave the game away.

She knew that the sons didn't have a clue where her niece was so she decided to wait for Mick.

As he pulled up at the gate he noticed one car and concluded that his son had scarpered. Good, he thought, at least he wouldn't get in the way. As he marched towards the warehouse, he could hear a rustling sound coming from the pile of tyres to the side of the building.

He turned to see a smartly dressed Italian man holding a gun to his face.

"Who the hell are you?"

Frankie didn't answer. He nodded for Mick to go inside.

Mick was fuming; he hated being taken by surprise, especially if a woman was orchestrating it. Mick still thought his wife was behind it. Grudgingly, he stepped inside. He gasped when he saw three of his sons lined up, tied to chairs and gagged. The lights were on and the whole warehouse looked huge this evening. His mind raced as he tried to take everything in. Frankie pointed to the chair in the middle of the room that faced his three sons. Mick tried to clock all the men before he sat down.

Charlie and Stuart glanced at each other. They had hoped their father had got wind that they had been kidnapped and was making a plan to rescue them. *Now they were fucked.* Stuart was choking. Fear got the better of him and his stomach's contents were now rising up with such force that they projected through his nose, but the gag blocked the vomit from leaving his mouth. As he tried to swallow it, more came up. Mick, seeing his son struggle, tried to get to him, but was stopped by Dan, who was ready to kill Mick with his bare hands. "Where's our baby, you fucking cunt?"

Mick realised who had him by the bollocks: the Vincents...

He looked around at each man, trying to work out who was who, and then he paused when he came to Francesca. He stared for a while, unnerved by her reaction. Walking up to Mick, she smiled. He glanced back at Stuart, who was no longer choking.

"Yes, Mick, I am Dolly... You know, the most precious thing to my father."

He looked at her in amazement. He had hunted her for years. He turned from her to look at Fred, whose veins now protruded from his neck. The rage caused him to foam at the mouth. Then realisation sunk in; it was Fred who was supposed to be burned to death by his son Piano.

"Where's my boy, Piano?" he spat back, fearing the worst.

"Where's the child you stole?" demanded Francesca, as she walked over to him, ready to bargain.

He grabbed her by the throat and threw her to the floor. Sergio jumped over the chair and grabbed Mick by the hair. Fred lunged forward and kicked Mick in the chest. The men all pointed their guns at Mick's head, as he curled into a ball to protect the newly broken rib. He looked pathetic; it was obvious that Mick had been the ultimate bully but never been hurt himself. Sergio hit Mick across the cheek with the butt of his gun.

"Don't you ever touch her again."

Mick cowered back, his eyes full of fear. The beads of sweat appeared on his brows and top lip, and the blood drained from his face. He wasn't sickly white any more - just grey, the colour that skin turns when you know your fate.

Fred dragged him back onto his chair. Francesca was on her feet, completely unperturbed. She slapped him hard across his face. It was the first time that he'd been hit by a woman, except the clump from his wife before she left. This slap, though, was more of a sign of humiliation, not meant to hurt physically but mentally. It was a slap that said, *'I have you by your balls and your fate is now in the hands of the woman you hunted since she was a child'*. He knew he was going to die – her cold eyes were emotionless, which told him all he needed to know.

"I said, where's the baby?"

Mick laughed aloud; why would he let them win now? He had served a lump inside over their father and a debt like that needed to be repaid. He was going to die, that was clear enough, but he would take a Vincent with him. Fred punched him off the chair again, splitting his lip. Mick wiped his face and laughed. The punch had stung, but it was the knowledge that he would leave the yard, his yard, in a body bag, that made him hysterical. After all, knowledge is power. And he knew something that the Vincent family desperately wanted at this moment.

Francesca was losing her cool and, as she stared at Mick, he smirked back.

"She's dead," he laughed.

Before Fred could hit him again, Francesca pulled her gun from the back of her trousers, pointed it at Charlie, and fired. The bullet hit Charlie in the middle of the chest. The chair, with him still tied to it, hit the floor. The blood squirted from the sides of the old school seat, to the disgust of Stuart. Mick's euphoria was suddenly gone. The realisation that his precious son, his favourite boy, had been shot dead, shook him to the core.

He shook his head in disbelief and screamed. Dan and Joe stood rooted to the spot. Fred stopped shouting and Sergio winked at her.

She pointed the gun at Stuart.

"No!" Mick put his hand up. "No, please don't shoot. I'll tell you where she is." His voice was full of desperation, a change to his spiteful character.

She cocked the gun and spoke slowly– she was utterly calm and emotionless.

"I don't believe you." Then she fired another shot. This time the bullet went straight between Stuart's eyes. The chair stayed where it was but the mess from the back of his head covered Eric and the cardboard boxes behind. Everyone was shocked; they hadn't expected the first shot and this second blow unnerved all of them.

Mick threw himself onto the floor, begging. "Please, no more. I'll take you to her, I promise."

Joe jumped in. "Where is she then?"

The room was silent.

"She is at my old yard, in the pit."

Joe ran towards his car parked around the back. Fred followed.

Dan took Fred's position, standing next to Francesca. He put his hand on her shoulder, shocked at how calm she was.

*

Joe knew a quick route to the old yard. Regardless of the snow, he tore through the streets towards the old aggregate site. Within five minutes, his car was screeching through the gates. Fred prayed that his little niece was still alive.

They ran to the first pit but it looked empty.

"Ruby!" called Fred.

His heart sank. There was no reply. The second pit was empty. Fred shook his head.

"That fucking lying cunt, she ain't 'ere."

Joe grabbed his arm. "Hold on a minute, there's another one here, I'm sure." The brothers headed in different directions and both ended up in the same place, behind the sand pile, looking into the third pit. Fred jumped down and saw a small, crumpled body, covered in a layer of snow. He held his breath as he bent down to retrieve the still and cold body of his tiny niece.

Slowly, he scooped her in his arms as if she was made of glass.

He was so afraid to look at her face and was convinced she was dead. He held her out for Joe to take her.

"Is she…" Joe couldn't say the words.

The child was so cold Fred assumed the worse.

He shook his head.

"Ruby!" screamed Joe, as he grabbed her from Fred. He held her tight, kissing her blue face.

Fred held his head down. He felt as though he would never return from that black hole.

Ruby's tiny hand touched Joe's cheek.

He held her out in front of him and her eyes opened.

"Joe-Joe, I'm cold." Her tiny voice was barely audible.

Fred almost flew out of the pit.

"She's alive! She's alive!" He snatched her back from Joe and they ran to the car.

"Quick, Joe! Open the door, get her in."

The tiny body was frozen; her lips and fingers were blue. And there was a nasty bruise around her head with a gash above her eye.

Joe wrapped her in his coat and put the car heater on full blast.

"Keep talking to me, baby," said Joe, trying to keep her conscious.

"Where's my new baby doll, Uncle Joe-Joe? I fink that man took it."

Joe and Fred cried as they looked at their tiny niece. So strong, a real tough cookie.

"You can have as many baby dolls as you want, you just promise me one thing," said Fred.

Ruby nodded at her new uncle. She guessed he was an uncle since he looked just like her others and he kept kissing her as they did.

Fred met Ruby a year ago, just before he went to the States, and fell in love with his dear little niece. Of course, she was too young to remember.

"You promise me you will get better and never go out of our sight again."

She nodded and the colour began to fill her cheeks.

Fred drove back to the yard. He wanted to take Ruby home, but he knew his sister needed to see her.

Dan and Francesca paced the floor in front of Mick, who was pleading for his life and the life of his last living son. Francesca smiled. He was suffering just as she and her family had.

They heard the car pull into the yard. Francesca felt sick, not from the blood or shootings but fear that they would find her dead or not at all.

Fred ran into the warehouse, out of breath.

"She's alive, sis! She's alive!"

Dan dropped to his knees and cried.

Sergio smiled at his cousin Mauricio, and Francesca's nausea left her body.

Joe carried the child into the warehouse, wrapped in his coat. Francesca looked over and instantly spotted the gash on her head.

She looked at Mick. "You fucking evil bastard." Her East End accent had returned, which surprised Sergio. Dan got up from the floor and took Ruby, checking her over.

"Joe, take her home," whispered Dan. Fred nodded and handed him the keys.

Mick was still snivelling, and snot ran from his bloody nose.

"You shouldn't have marked her face." Francesca's voice was almost demonic. She pulled a small flick knife from her pocket and, without warning, ran the knife down Mick's face, slicing his eye. No one expected it. Least of all Mick.

Screaming in pain, he spat at Francesca.

Sergio was enraged and grabbed Mick by the back of his hair. With the other hand, he grabbed salt from his pocket and rubbed it into Mick's face.

He screamed, pleading with them to stop.

Francesca smiled at Sergio. He was a man true to his word and she loved him.

Joe took Ruby and fled away from the carnage. Then there was silence — even Mick stopped screaming. A car had pulled into the yard. Mauricio shouted, "It's the cops."

Mick, for a split second, thanked God; he would be saved by his enemy, the Ole' Bill.

Dan put his hand up — no, if they suspected trouble there would be more than one car. They waited as the door slowly opened. Dan's pounding heart was relieved to see his father.

Bill didn't say a word. He walked over to Francesca.

She bowed her head in shame; she had never wanted her father to see her this way.

He took the gun from her hand and kissed her on the cheek.

"No more, Francesca." His voice was firm.

"I have wanted to kill you for so many years, Mick, and I thought the day would never come. I told you a hundred times that I was not the one who grassed you to the Ole' Bill, but you wouldn't listen. The threats you sent to my wife, the horrendous letters you wrote describing how you were going to torture and kill my daughter, the fear you put into our family, was something you can never put right."

Mick stared directly into Bill's eyes. For years now he never feared Bill because he always had the upper hand, but now he was surrounded by a mob he didn't recognise and a man with a reason to kill him.

Just like his daughter, Bill raised the gun and put a bullet clean through Mick's chest.

Bill instantly felt relieved; the one thing that had kept him awake at night and haunted him every day was gone.

He turned to Francesca and hugged her. "It's over, Dolly."

She looked at her dear father and was glad he had no idea it was only the beginning.

*

Mary had already returned from the hospital, and was sitting by the fire, nursing a cup of tea, when Joe arrived with Ruby. Nellie was trying her best to console her, and poor little Jack didn't know what to do. He recovered his sister's doll from the garden. Like Ruby it was covered in snow with just the dark curls visible.

Mary looked at her grandson and her heart went out to him. He appeared so lost being only five years old. His little world was more confusing to him than ever.

Joe had Ruby, still wrapped in his coat, and he struggled to put the key in the lock. The rustling sound made Jack leap from his chair and run to the door. Mary was still weak as she tried to call to Jack to stop him going. Her voice croaked and died off. Nellie jumped up and followed Jack.

He pulled the door open and saw his Uncle Joe holding a big overcoat and it took a second before he could see his tiny sister inside wriggle, in some discomfort.

"Ruby," he squealed.

Mary heard her grandson, and with her head pounding, she got to her feet.

Joe carried the bundle into the living room to see his mother, who was shaking with relief. She pulled the tiny tot from Joe and squeezed her.

"Nanny, you're squashing me."

Mary couldn't speak; she was so overwhelmed by the latest turn of events.

She placed the child on the sofa, looking at her bruise and the cut above the child's eyes.

"Look, Nanny, Ruby's cut her head."

Mary looked at Joe. "What did he do to her, Joe?"

Joe looked at Jack and back to his mother. He shook his head.

Mary knew it was bad; Joe obviously was not going to say anything in front of Jack.

Jack sat on the settee next to his sister and held her hand. It was a habit they had formed when they needed each other.

Ruby sat up and looked around the room. She began to cry but without the noise – her bottom lip quivered and large tears rolled down her face.

"Does your head hurt, darling?" asked Mary, who was suffering from a bad headache herself.

"No, my head don't hurt. That naughty man took my dolly and now it's gone."

She put her face into her hands and cried.

Jack remembered the doll and ran upstairs. He grabbed the toy from Ruby's bed, where he had placed it earlier, and ran back down the stairs.

Ruby looked up and, even with the tears rolling down her cheeks, she managed a smile.

"Fank you, Jack." She hugged the doll, put her thumb in her mouth, and curled up to go to sleep. Nellie was running around making hot water bottles and cups of tea.

"Thank God," she said.

Advised by the hospital to stay overnight due to the possibility of concussion, there was no way Mary could, not when her granddaughter's life was on the line. The doctor in casualty gave her ten stitches and allowed her to go home.

She didn't ask Joe any more questions – not whilst Jack and Nellie were present. Thoughts, however, raced through her mind.

Soon Nellie left and Jack went to bed, content in his mind that his sister was safe and well.

*

Mick was slumped in a pool of blood. The only one alive from his family was Eric.

Francesca removed his gag.

"Please, please, kill me, but don't touch my girl."

Pauli and Rizler, along with Sergio's men, were loading the dead bodies in the back of the cars. Sergio and Fred had organised the boys to take them to the pits at Mick's old yard and bury them.

Francesca bit the inside of her lip.

"Do you know what my parents went through all those years, believing that your father could at any time find me and murder me?"

Eric looked to the floor and nodded. He was helpless. His father was a nasty piece of work and his brothers were sick enough to go along with it, even the plan to kill Fred. However, he didn't believe for one minute that Francesca would know he wasn't the bad one — *how would she?* He was wrong. Francesca was a lawyer; she left no stone unturned, so she was well aware that Eric was not like his father and brothers.

She pulled out her knife again.

Eric closed his eyes.

She cut the rope that tied him to the chair.

He looked up. What was she going to do with him? He stared at her, trying to read the mind of this formidable woman.

"I will let you go, but remember this — if you grass, then I will make sure your Millie will live the life I had to live, because someone will come for her — and you wouldn't want that, eh?" The last part was said with an Italian accent.

Eric looked around the room; he hadn't noticed how many men there were before. It brought home to him the power of this woman. It made no difference though; he did not intend to grass on anyone. He was the only son that hated his father and he wasn't very keen on his brothers either.

He looked straight into her eyes and said, calmly, "I promise not to say a word."

She nodded.

Millie was playing cat's cradle with some string and chatting away to Adam about her nursery school. Eric pulled her from the car and Mauricio drove them back to his Audi.

Eric felt as though the whole event was surreal. It had happened in slow motion and now he was back in his Audi, his daughter still chatting away, and the roses were there, ready for his wife. He drove home and tried to imagine it was just another Friday night.

Sergio took Francesca's hand and walked her to the car, whilst Dan and Fred, followed by their father, drove back to their East End home.

Mauricio's men made all the necessary arrangements to clear the mess and leave no trace of bloodshed.

Before Bill and his sons left the yard to go home to Mary, they agreed to keep the night's events low-key and never to mention that Francesca was even there.

Joe was in the kitchen, pouring a stiff brandy. Mary walked in a few seconds after he set the bottle down. "So, Joe, what happened?" She sat at the kitchen table. Her legs were still heavy so she struggled to stay standing.

He had no idea where to start. He didn't know what he should say to his mum. After all, his brothers always kept the skulduggery stuff quiet.

He poured her a tea and sat down too.

"Joe, tell me what happened. Where did you find Ruby?"

Just as he took a gulp of his brandy, there was the sound of a key going into the door.

Joe jumped at first; he was still a little nervous, especially after all the unpredictable bloodshed.

It was Bill; he walked over to Mary, who was still rather pale.

"All right, my gal?" he whispered.

Mary smiled. She still looked at her husband the same sweet way she did all those years ago when they first dated.

He sat at the table and took a drink from Joe. Dan and Fred walked in and Mary stood up to greet her son, who she hadn't seen for a year.

"Mum, it's good to see you." He was calmer now and planted a big kiss on her cheek.

"You look good, my love. Your sister's obviously looked after you well," she said in a faint voice.

"Yep, she sure has."

The boys sat around the table.

"So will someone tell me what happened – how did you get our Ruby back?" She searched the eyes of each of her sons for answers.

Bill spoke up. "I managed to find Mick, and let's just say he will never bother us again."

Mary guessed what had happened but decided not to pursue the how or by whom questions. As long as her family were safe, she didn't care.

Fred went into the living room to check on Ruby. She was lying down, still staring into space.

"'Allo, little princess, and how are you feeling?"

"Don't wake her up," said Mary.

Fred laughed. "She's already awake."

Ruby sat up and put her little arms around Fred's neck to hug him.

"I'm all warm now, see, and I got my dolly back."

Bill came in and picked up Ruby. "You're safe now, and that nasty man's never gonna touch you again."

Mary, Bill and the boys sat in the living room, drinking brandy. Francesca and Sergio eventually showed up. Mary was over the moon to have all her family in one place.

"I won't stay long, Mum, but I just wanted to check you and Ruby were okay. Only, Dan told me what happened, and I came as quick as I could." She hated lying to her mother, but it was far kinder to leave all the mess outside the home.

"Aunty Francisco, where's your pretty gun?"

The room went a deadly quiet as everyone looked at Francesca, hoping she would come up with a bloody good explanation.

Francesca pulled the gun from her bag and the boys looked at the floor. Even Bill was dumbfounded.

"Here it is." Quickly, she clicked the lighter switch and a small flame popped out of the end.

"Dolly, how could you?" snapped Mary. "I didn't know you smoked."

"Mum, I only do it occasionally when I really have to."

Dan and Fred smiled at each other. Their sister was a real gem - just like the ones on her gun.

Chapter Twenty

Sergio was exhausted. He had not fully recovered from his bullet wound. The surgeon had recommended that Sergio should not leave the States and travel to England, but he'd been too anxious to let Francesca travel home alone.

Adam drove them home to Kent and then went off to be with his son.

Mauricio was already in bed with Kathy who had still managed to sleep through the whole commotion.

Francesca sat in the kitchen looking out across the immense open space to the back garden and the land beyond. Sergio took his painkillers. The leap over the chair to bash Mad Mick had left him in agony.

"Hey you, come here." She was perched on a stool up at the breakfast bar, gazing at the whiteness, with everything covered in a glittering, white, magical dust. The sky had cleared, and the moonlight shone an inviting glow across the hill in the distance.

"What a view."

Francesca made two Irish coffees and waited for her man to join her.

He stood watching her outline in the evening light, her satin nightdress smooth against her skin.

"Yep," he smiled.

She blushed, realising he was staring at her and not nature's postcard.

Sliding the coffee towards him, she smiled a slow, seductive smile.

Sergio was more in love with this beautiful woman than he had ever been. He'd watched her in the yard, and had been impressed by the way she had handled the men. Her cold exterior hid the real, warm, passionate person she was. Everything she did was controlled. There was no bargaining with this woman. She knew what she wanted and God help anyone who stood in her way.

He slid his arm round her waist and yanked her from the stool. The time was ready: she had held him off long enough. She wanted him to take her, but she had to be sure.

He smothered her neck in kisses as he ran his hands up and down her sculpted back. He could feel her tight body responding to his touch. She pressed her lips firmly against his, experiencing a tingling sensation running through her veins. As he gently pulled the thin lace straps from her shoulders and over her arms, the full-length nightdress floated to the floor. He looked at her body for the first time. She watched his expression, hoping he liked what he saw.

He ripped his shirt trying to get it off. He wanted to feel her skin against his. She helped him take off his clothes, his body more defined than she had imagined. With his strong, muscular arms, he lifted her up, carried her to the bed, and laid her down, kissing every inch of her body as she writhed in ecstasy. He was slow and gentle but she wanted passion – she had waited a long time for him. Their bodies entwined, as tight as olive trees wrapped up in a scene of permanence, as they made love. Francesca had been conscious of the way she looked, her sex appeal, the consequences of a brutal husband having knocked her confidence. But now she felt totally at ease with her body and her inner self.

After a long soak in the bath, both Francesca and Sergio drifted off to sleep.

The evening's events would have traumatized most people. However, Francesca found great comfort in her achievement. For the first time in her life, she was free – *well, almost free.* Just before she fell asleep, she saw her husband's face contorted with rage. It was still a vision that haunted her, and yet she curled up in Sergio's arms feeling safe and protected.

*

Christmas Eve arrived and the Vincents descended upon Francesca one by one. Mary was in the kitchen baking Christmas cookies with two very excited children.

Mauricio was up in the loft, looking for the decorations, but the old toys and memorabilia distracted him. His father bought the house back in 1964 and used it for the odd English holiday with the boys. Sergio's father often brought them here when they were young, especially if things were getting dangerous back in New York. The mansion was redecorated before the family returned, to the delight of Francesca, who looked forward to being near her family and living in comfort.

Guarded with iron gates, the house contained ten bedrooms, each with en suite bathrooms, and there was a huge lounge, with a large inglenook fireplace. It was perfect for Christmas, with the hearth decorated in a thick foliage garland and glowing red fairy lights.

Mauricio eventually came down from the loft, carrying bags of decorations. Ruby stood at the bottom of the ladder and clapped her hands in excitement.

"Uncle 'Ricio, can I decorate the tree?"

He scooped her up and carried her into the living room. "You will have to put the decorations on the bottom, and I will put them on the top."

She flared her nostrils.

"Now, Belle, what's the problem?" He bent down to tickle her chin.

With her sweet lisp, she put her hands on her hips and said, "If you decorate the top, then I won't be able to put the angel on."

Mauricio laughed. "Belle, Belle you are too cheeky. I will lift you up and you can put the angel on the top."

Ruby clapped her hands together again.

Of course, all the coloured baubles ended up on the same branch, but everyone clapped and said she had done a good job.

Jack, proud of his cookies, offered his granddad first pick.

Dan arrived with Fred. Usually they would not be home until Christmas dinner – the nightclub was always open until late, a dead cert that the boys would be cashing up well into the early hours. This year was different though. It would be the Christmas they all shared, one they had all longed for.

Roberto, however, remained in the States, as he had a lot of business to attend to. On January 1st, he would be the rightful owner of a substantial amount of land in France. His team of lawyers, not associated with the late Tyler Enright, worked on the details in preparation for the handover.

Bear moved into Roberto's home and was spoilt by his Italian maid, Rose.

The only other person missing was Mary's sister, Anne.

She had moved to Australia with her Jewish friend, once she believed Francesca to be happily married, unaware of her niece's predicament.

Francesca was smitten with Sergio and everyone could tell. He was very attentive, pinching her behind, kissing her neck, and popping the odd sweet into her mouth. They had cemented their relationship. Mary nudged Bill; he looked up over his paper to see his daughter tickle the back of Sergio's neck. He smiled at his wife.

"Let's hope he loves her as much as I love you, Mare." He squeezed his wife's hand.

"If he does, she will be one hell of a lucky woman."

Joe arrived with his big surprise.

Francesca had arranged with Joe to pick up Sam from the Scrubs. He was allowed home for four days, starting Christmas Eve. It would only be another two weeks and he would be home for good. She had kept it a secret from the family. It was to be the Christmas present for them all.

Joe came through with his arms full of presents and, in response, the children jumped up and rushed to help their uncle, their eyes wide with anticipation.

"I've got one more present for all of us," Joe beamed.

Little Ruby clapped her hands together again.

As Joe went back out to the car, everyone sat on the edge of their seats, wondering what he could have for them all.

Francesca's eyes welled up watching her mother's face as Sam walked in. The children screeched and jumped all over him. Sam was surprised to see his children so plump and looking a picture of health. Mary got to her feet and hugged her son. "Oh, my boy, it's so good to have you here. This has made my Christmas perfect, thank you," said Mary, who was fighting back the tears of joy.

"You have our Doll to thank for that."

Ruby and Jack tugged their father in two different directions, excited to show off their new toys, the Christmas decorations, and of course the freshly baked cookies.

They spent the evening around the fireplace, playing games and drinking warm mulled wine. When the children finally went to bed, Francesca got to work, bringing the presents down from the loft and placing them under the tree.

Mary shook her head. "Francesca," she said, enunciating every letter of her name, "You've gone right overboard; look at all those presents."

"Oh, Mum, those kids haven't got any toys. This will make up for all those Christmas days I missed."

Mary smiled. "Well, they are going to be two very happy bunnies tomorrow morning."

"And that's how they should be," replied Francesca.

The evening ended at one o'clock, when everyone decided to call it a night. Sam snuggled deep into the king-size luxury bed and looked to the side, out of the leaded window, across the field to the snow-covered hill, and he felt as though all his prayers were answered. His two children were asleep in the room next door, and the rest of his family would tomorrow sit around the huge dining table and enjoy their first Christmas dinner together in sixteen years. He drifted off to have the best night's sleep ever.

Ruby woke up around two o'clock. "Jack, Jack," she whispered.

Jack stirred. "What's matter, Ruby?"

"Jack, did you ask for anything for Christmas?"

He lay silent, thinking for a moment. "No, I only said I liked those things in the toy shop. What about you, did you ask?"

Ruby couldn't remember. "I fink I might have asked for a Barbie. I know I said I liked the Barbies."

Jack thought about the situation. "It don't matter, Ruby, we got our daddy, eh?"

Ruby turned over, with her thumb in her mouth, and thought that this Christmas would be good fun, not like Christmas with Mum, who went down the pub and left them with chips and a bottle of lemonade. She shivered at the thought of living with her mother, and the cold nights that she spent curled up in bed with her brother in sheets that stank, and in her nightdress that was so tight around the arms the elastic dug in and caused sores.

"Jack, we won't have to go back to Mummy's, will we?"

He went cold, dreading it, and thought about his big strong dad and his pretty aunty. "No, Ruby. Aunty Francisco won't let us."

"I'm sorry, Jack. If I asked for a Barbie, I'll say I didn't mean it."

Jack, as young as he was, knew his little sister worried about what she might have said.

"Move over, Ruby." Jack climbed into her bed and cuddled her.

Ruby sucked her thumb again and dozed off to sleep, dreaming of being just like her aunt when she grew up.

*

Mary was the first to get up. She crept down the grand staircase and enjoyed being alone in this impressive house, with its huge kitchen and double range cooker. The turkey and beef were prepared by the butcher and easy to just pop into the oven. Mary was surprised to see the vegetables already peeled and in large catering pots. Satisfied that everything had been prepared, she sat with her tea and looked out of the French doors, soaking up the peace and tranquillity. Her head was still a bit sore, and Kathy had suggested the stitches should come out tomorrow. As she daydreamed, a big, strong hand pinched her shoulder.

"Good morning, my queen." It was Bill.

They sat staring out of the window, comfortable in their own silence. The others began to rise. Francesca was first and, to everyone's surprise, the last to get up were the children.

Sam finished his cup of coffee and couldn't wait any more. "I'm gonna wake 'em." Mary went to stop him but decided not to.

As he entered their bedroom, they were already awake and looking utterly miserable.

"What's up, you two? It's Christmas!"

Ruby got up and hugged her dad. "Father Christmas didn't come to us again." Her little fingers pointed to the end of her bed where she had hung her sock, and at the end of Jack's bed there was one of his.

Sam laughed so loud he collapsed on their bed. Scooping them up into his arms, he said, "Father Christmas has been and decided to put the presents under the tree because they are too big to fit in those little socks."

The children rushed down the stairs to see the tree adorned with presents of all shapes and sizes in pink and blue.

"Is there one for us?" squealed Jack.

Francesca kissed both the children and whispered to Jack, "All the blue presents are for you." Ruby's eyes were wide like a bush baby as she waited to hear a whisper from her aunt. "And, Ruby, all the pink ones are for you."

The children opened their presents, giggling and adoring every gift.

The adults exchanged gifts. Kathy had the best present to give. She waited until dinner was served and she proudly stood up and faced Mauricio, who was slowly getting merry on champagne. "I would like to give Mauricio his gift."

Fred, also merry, jumped in. "Kathy, I think you gave him his present last night, from all that noise coming from your room."

Kathy rolled her eyes and the rest laughed. She handed Mauricio a card. He looked around the table at the others to see if they had any idea. He ripped opened the envelope and read, *'See you in six months' time, Dad'*.

Mauricio read it over again.

"Kath, are you?" He paused as she nodded. He jumped up and kissed her. "We are having a baby." Everyone clapped and offered their congratulations. Francesca was over the moon; her dearest friends were having a family.

Mauricio excused himself to phone his father.

The call was in Italian.

Sergio excused his cousin. "I am sorry, but when Mauricio gets excited, he goes off in his own language and forgets where he is."

Mary was so pleased for them. "Oh, don't worry; it's lovely to see him happy."

The day was a perfect success. The food was cooked to perfection, the drink went down at a pace, and the children played contentedly with their toys.

*

Boxing Day arrived, along with the newspaper.

Francesca was the first up and, as she sipped her freshly brewed coffee, she scanned the latest news. She smiled when she read a large section on the arrest of William Enright for the murder of his brother, Charles. It had described William as a long-standing judge in the high court. They believed the motive to be greed as they were to be the beneficiaries of land in France. A note in a gold locket found in Charles' pocket, had stated he was afraid that his brother would make an attempt on his life. Walking shoes, along with rare pollen, were discovered in Williams's garage – the rare pollen was only found in the wooded area where they found Charles' body. Police also recovered the gun in a trough in his neighbour's stables. The paper also reported that the judge had no alibi.

Francesca was so relieved; her plan had worked. *No lawyer in the land could get him off that charge – he was bang to rights, and it would make a mockery of the judiciary system if he was freed.*

She had another sip of her coffee and admired the view.

As she turned the page, there, staring her in the face, was a picture of her husband. He held his head low, walking away from the court.

'Charles Enright QC, son of William Enright and nephew of Charles Enright Senior, declined to make a comment'.

Francesca's heart felt as though it was leaving her chest. She took some deep breaths and calmed herself.

Her thoughts returned to her father-in-law – another evil bastard. He had tormented her and been the instigator in all her husband's cruel goading. He would have a tough time in the nick, especially when faced with inmates that he had sentenced himself.

Chapter Twenty-One

With Christmas out of the way, Francesca started to plan her future. She enjoyed being back in England, but she also enjoyed her home in the States with her dog and Roberto. Fred itched to get back. The girls were all over him there, especially with his cockney accent and the respect the Italians showed him. He walked around as if he owned the place and Sergio didn't bat an eyelid. He would eye him up and down and grin, knowing that Fred was in his element, and not causing any harm at all.

Sergio busied himself sending his men to get as much information regarding Charles Enright as possible. The newspaper cuttings were sent to Roberto, who was elated by the fact that his archenemies got their dues.

He ruffled Bear's fur. "Your momma's a Mafioso through and through." Then he realised he was talking to a wolf, but it didn't matter. He had grown quite fond of him and wondered why he'd never let the boys grow up with pets.

Sergio stared at the picture of Charles. For ages, he had wanted to kill the man with his bare hands. However, another clip of Charles and his four-year-old son on the next page captured his attention. Sergio frowned. *How could Charles have a four-year-old son?* He was married to Francesca at that time. He felt an urgency to speak with her. If she had a son, why would she keep it a secret? He began to shake at the thought of a deception of that magnitude.

"Francesca." His voice was firm; she was in the living room sweeping up the pine needles from the floor. The heat from the log fire caused the tree to dry out.

Standing in the kitchen doorway, she studied his expression. He looked serious. "What is it, Sergio?"

He pointed to the newspaper and walked to the French doors to get some air.

Francesca scanned the paper again. She had already seen the headlines and picture of her husband.

She stared at the page that Sergio left open.

There, in the corner, was another photo, this time with Charles holding the hand of a little boy, his son.

"There must be some mistake. How could he have a child? We were married – I can't believe it."

The child in the picture did look like her husband. Her mind raced. How could he... then the realisation set in; he treated her like shit, yet all the time he was living a double life. Her heart began to race and she needed to sit down.

Sergio watched her reaction.

"So that child is not yours, then?"

Francesca was sitting on the bar stool, trying to take it all in. As her anger welled up, she spat back at Sergio, "What do you fucking take me for? If you think that I would leave a child of mine with a fucking monster like that then, Sergio, you don't fucking well know me at all." She began to cry, with her head in her hands.

Sergio realised he had fucked up. Of course, she would never have left her child.

He tried to comfort her, whispering his apologies. She was not concerned with Sergio. Her tears were for herself. Her husband had taken away every hope and dream of her having a baby the night he ripped out her womb. Her heart ached for the child she would never have.

"My Francesca, you must try to put this behind you. The Enrights have been taken care of, so now you have to move on with your life. I think we should take some time to go for a holiday, somewhere warm and beautiful."

Francesca heard Sergio, but the words just whirled around inside her head. She was not going to be happy until her husband could not haunt her again, whether in a newspaper clipping or in her nightmares. So something needed to be done about it.

Sergio cooked her some eggs and bacon and fussed over her for the rest of the morning.

At midday, Francesca put on her coat and decided to go for a drive. She looked around her and inside herself. The snow had now melted, leaving a grey slushy mess and, unhappily, she saw this reflected in her own fragile state of mind. The magic of Christmas, with the glistening white powder, all the lights and decorations, and the joy surrounding her family following all the recent events in her life, had now dissipated like the snow disappearing from the garden. She saw in front of her a picture that was both dull and gloomy, but also one which needed to be put right if she was ever to have real happiness for herself and her husband.

Sergio was anxious that she had wanted to be alone.

"She will be okay, probably wants to clear her mind," said Mauricio.

Mary and Bill returned to their house with Jack, Ruby and Sam. Dan, Fred and Joe lay in bed, taking advantage of the rest, whilst Sergio paced the floor. This wasn't like Francesca – she seemed lost.

"She will be all right, eh. Look, Francesca can take care of herself; she's only gone for a drive."

Sergio grabbed the paper and flung it under Mauricio's nose.

He scanned the words 'four-year-old son'. "What does this mean? Francesca has a son, eh?"

"No, Mauricio, he is not her son. Now can you see why I am so worried she will act without thinking this time? She looked strange today, as if she would take her own life."

Mauricio stared with his mouth open. "We must find her then," he replied.

*

Francesca drove to the Sussex cottage where it all began. She wanted to face her demons one last time.

The weather was miserable, even for this time of the year. The sun hid behind the clouds and the seaside town in East Sussex looked bleak. As she drove along the coastline, her mind flashed back to the last time she followed the same route. He had been with her in the Jaguar, and she remembered how it glided along. She recalled feeling intimidated and afraid of his unpredictable temper. He had been quiet all the way to the cottage, which had unnerved her.

Now, as she pulled up to the remote drive, her chest tightened as though it would cave in. There were no other houses for miles. The cottage was partially hidden by fir trees which waved furiously in the wind. She heard the sound of the waves smashing against the cliff face. The vast garden behind the house came to an abrupt end, where a sheer drop marked the boundary. It must have been there that he threw her body into the sea. She remembered, the first day she viewed the cottage, that one of the most appealing characteristics of the garden was the way it rambled wildly to finish with a cliff edge. Many a summer evening she sat there with her husband, as they dangled their legs over, enjoying the ferocity of the waves smashing against the rock face. They would watch the sunset and later they would look at the stars. How different that feeling was now and those recent memories of the garden sent shivers up her spine.

She turned the ignition off and stepped out. The wind got stronger and the bitter cold tore at her face. Her long coat flapped around and she pulled it tighter whilst she walked to the entrance of hell.

There were no other cars and the lights were off.

Francesca always hid a key under a large pebble at the back of the house. She kicked it over, and there, covered in sand, was the front door key.

Looking around quickly, she slipped the key into the big oak door and turned it until it clicked open.

Once inside, the smell of damp, masked by potpourri, lingered. The hallway looked just the same: the deep red carpet and curtains, the dark oak table with the welcome light, and his family's portraits displayed in the entrance. *Funny,* she thought, *that lamp was left on permanently.* Without it, the room seemed uninviting and cold.

She sheepishly crept into the living room. The furniture was as she had last seen it but the carpet was new. The cream rug and all the photos of her had gone. She felt as though she was intruding, yet this was her house, not her husband's. She had every right to be there.

She stared at the floor, where he had pinned her down and tried to end her life. Of course the carpet would have gone. It must have been covered in blood. *They say you don't remember pain itself,* but she did. Whether it was twinned with mental pain or not, it still hurt.

The boiler in the kitchen came to life and made Francesca jump. She was surprised that the central heating was on. She shivered and suddenly needed a drink to calm her nerves. She found the brandy in the drinks cabinet along with the glasses. Another flashback came to her – *his face grinning, that memorable evil smirk, as he made her drink from the glass.*

She poured a small amount into the cut crystal tumbler, sat in the armchair, and waited.

Such a long time ago, a lifetime ago, yet it seemed like yesterday. The smell, the sounds of the sea, her hands clutching the glass, and all that was missing was her husband. Now she was Francesca. Her time in America gave her the strength, mentally and physically, to face her demons. She had planned his demise repeatedly in her mind. Every plan was different. She thought about poisoning him, and watching as he squirmed around on the floor, clutching his throat, but then that was too much like the movies. She contemplated stabbing him repeatedly, him looking at her, whilst he held the bread knife protruding from his stomach.

She laughed to herself – *leaving the glasses on the side may put the wind up him.* She thought about the central heating again; *why would that be on?* Her husband always made sure everything was turned off before they headed back to London – except, of course, the hall light. Maybe he rented the cottage out, and, in a way, she would be trespassing. Her mind ran away with her.

All the time she lived in America, she felt so safe and protected. Her home was warm and so inviting and she realised that, although there was business in England to attend to, back there was her home. Sergio was so kind and loving, Mauricio so generous, and Roberto made sure she had everything she needed. Every material thing was luxurious; the love from the Lucianis was endless. They all gave her respect just for being alive. She compared this to her married life with Charles and the Enrights: She was always expected to show her worth, to be at their beck and call, to deny her own needs for theirs, to achieve high standards for their own purposes, and never acknowledge that she was a person in her own right with her own aspirations. She could not slip up in any way: they never praised the good, only ridiculed the bad.

She took a deep breath and gulped back a large mouthful of brandy.

There were no guarantees that Charles wouldn't walk into the cottage. She closed her eyes and tried to visualize his face when they first met but she couldn't, it was just so contorted like a monster.

The winter months were generally spent in London or abroad, somewhere hot, so she guessed he wouldn't arrive. She drank another brandy and began to warm up.

The cottage, which she loved so much the first time she had laid eyes on it, was now a shell that had been witness to a terrible scene. She hated the cottage for it held such an awful, dark secret. The day she left it was the day Launa died.

The room was filled with ghosts haunting her, the loving face of her husband turning into the devil – taunting her, spitefully torturing her mind and her body.

She willed him to walk in, to see her, to recognise her. She wanted to watch him squirm.

Francesca was not afraid anymore. Launa was gone, and she was now the child born to an East End family again.

There was a storm ready to set in. She could see the dark clouds in the distance, and also a bright light which was now shining through the dining room window and, with her nerves firmly on a knife-edge, she realised that a car was pulling into the drive.

She remained seated and took another sip of brandy. She could hear the crunch of footsteps on the sand and pebbles. They stopped as they reached the door. She listened for the sound of a key in the lock. The hairs on the back of her neck stood on end. Feeling for her lighter, she was excited yet terrified. The door opened and in walked Charles, looking rather dishevelled, his long hair wildly blown all over the place, and looking in need of a shave.

As soon as he entered the living room, he threw his briefcase down and almost jumped back when he clocked her.

At first Francesca froze, not knowing if he recognised her. Even with the large brandy, she felt her body shaking.

"You fucking people don't give up, do you? Now Mrs Whoever You Are, this is trespassing. Get out of my house before I call the police." His face wasn't angry-looking, just tired.

Francesca was rooted to the spot and her brain was working overtime. *Who did he think she was?* She wanted to laugh. He didn't look terrifying or like a monster.

"What do you mean 'your house'? I understood this house belonged to Launa?"

Charles was livid. "Who the hell are you and what are you doing here?" He shifted from foot to foot nervously.

Francesca was not used to seeing him like this, not with her anyway. Self-assured, she stood up and placed the brandy glass on the coffee table.

He leaned forward, took the glass, and demanded she left.

"I don't know who the fuck you are but this is my house and you are leaving."

He went to grab her arm, but she stepped back.

"I wouldn't do that if I were you."

Her voice was familiar. Something about this very sharp woman made him turn cold. She smiled. "Sit down, Charles. Let's talk."

He was mesmerized by her calm manner, her seductive voice and, of course, her obvious beauty.

She sat in front of him, handing him a glass of brandy. He took it and drank. "So, are you one of those persistent reporters or what? Tell me."

"Reporter," laughed Francesca. She realised then why he was at the cottage in the winter. The reporters would have made his life hell. His father's case, so high profile, they would have hunted him down for any juicy titbits.

He stared at her for a second. She looked at the silver threads at the side of his hair. His face had sagged and his eyes were not so bright. Her head got hot again. The anger gripped her and, desperately, she tried to control herself.

"So, come on then, if you're not a reporter, who are you, and how did you know Launa?" He gulped back the brandy.

"Why, Charles! You speak as though Launa was dead."

He stopped for a second. He had let his guard down. "Look, what do you want? Only, I am a very busy man."

She sat with her coat open, baring her long slender legs. Charles looked her up and down, lusting over her curves. Yet, as he gazed into her eyes, something told him he knew her.

"I just wanted some legal advice and Launa was always good at that. She did say you might help me. After all, this matter is probably more up your street." She sipped her brandy and licked her lips, taunting him. Crossing her legs over and running her hands through her hair, she gave him mixed messages. Francesca toyed with him, giving herself the sense of being in control. Sex would have been the last thing she would ever have with him. The notion repulsed her, yet she knew he was a lady's man, a womaniser. Whether a highly educated man or a punch-drunk East End boxer, a womaniser meant only one thing – they could be easily distracted, and right now Charles was definitely fazed.

"So, you were friends with my wife." He slipped up again.

"Charles, why do you keep talking about her in the past tense?" She smiled slowly.

His heart began to race. How could he be so stupid?

"So, how about it, eh?" she laughed.

He completely fell for her act.

"Yes, I think I could help you with legal matters." He looked her up and down. "In fact, I could help you with anything you wanted. Your name is?"

She leaned forward and offered her hand. "My name is Francesca Vincent."

He quickly took it and smiled. "So, Francesca, how can I help you?"

He wanted to get the formalities out of the way and get on with the familiarities. She looked hot; her lips were plump and inviting, and her body was posed in a very seductive position, with her back arched.

"Well, it's like this. My husband, a very wealthy man, met another woman." She paused.

"Go on," demanded Charles, who guessed it would be another divorce case.

"My husband, a clever man, decided to try to kill me."

Charles nearly choked on his drink. "What?"

"He tried to kill me and now I am in a position where he thinks I'm dead and, well, Charles, as you can see, I'm very much alive." Her voice teased as she ran her hands down her body, showing Charles that yes, she was very much alive.

"I see that." He paused. "Well, really, Francesca, all I can suggest is you go to the police and they will arrest him for attempted murder."

She sniffed the air.

"I was thinking of killing him myself. You see, he has so much money, and knows people in such high places, that he would certainly get off and I would be left worrying about my life."

Charles began to feel sick. The woman was hypnotic but with a sickly undertone that made him uneasy. His thoughts returned to Launa and how he killed her, *yet if this woman had spoken with Launa, perhaps she wasn't dead.* He shuddered and his mind galloped — *if this woman knew his wife, then surely she would know about what he had done to her and the way he tried to kill her.* Poor Launa, he had loved her once. She wasn't like the others. They had been nobodies, scum of the earth — their deaths meant as a gift to society — but Launa had not done as she was told, and he had a compulsion to end her life too. When he saw her cheeks burst open and the life leave her eyes, he didn't enjoy the elation, or the euphoria, as he had with the others. Yet when he carried her lifeless body and threw it into the sea, he knew then that there was no going back. He had rubbed his hands together, just as if he had thrown the last piece of rubbish on the fire, and walked away.

"Francesca, when did you last see my wife?"

She smiled, because she had got to him. "Today."

Charles looked shocked. His mouth went dry and his head started spinning. *Nothing was making sense these days.* First, his uncle was murdered, then his father was arrested and charged, and now this woman claimed she saw Launa today.

He gulped the brandy and Francesca smirked. She enjoyed seeing him panic.

"Where was she?" he asked gingerly.

"Charles, I see her every day."

He shook his head, running his fingers through his hair, and gulped back the remainder of the brandy. It all seemed surreal; *no one would have survived those injuries, the fall, or the deep sea.* It had been icy that night. She would have bled or frozen to death if she hadn't drowned. *This woman was a con; she was trying to wind him up.*

"Look, who are you?"

"Like I said, I am a good friend of Launa's."

Charles was frustrated. It was the first time in his life that he felt helpless. He had no idea what was going on: this beautiful woman sat before him, yet she was unnerving him. "Francesca, please tell me how you know my wife."

"Well, she represented my adopted brother in court. She might have mentioned him."

He perched on the edge of his seat, still wearing his jacket, and hanging on to her words.

"His name is Mauricio Luciani."

Forgetting himself, he screeched, "What? You are Mauricio's sister?"

Francesca was smiling and her eyes were wide, full of life.

He began to panic, knowing that the Lucianis were part of the mafia. His family had retained every bit of information on them. They had committed themselves to ensure that they left no stone unturned. But this was shocking – *how could they have missed an adopted daughter?* This was so complicated – *how could Launa be connected to the family of Mauricio?* As far as he knew, she had represented him in court and, on the same day he was released, he flew back to the States, and that should have been the last time she ever saw him. He was desperate to understand this huge web of connection, but he was tired and, hard as he tried, he could not work it out.

He decided to act ignorant of the matters surrounding their family tree and the land in France.

"Yes, Launa did a very good job in that particular case." He was not giving away any more information. After all, what was this woman really up to? If he kept quiet, she may give more clues.

"Look, Francesca, it was really lovely to meet you, but I don't think I can help you with your case. I'm sorry. I am fully booked for a while." With that, he stood, a gesture for her to leave, but she remained seated.

"Charles, how's your Uncle Tyler? I must say, you do look so much alike."

He was beginning to shake now. The chicken pie he'd had for lunch was churning in his stomach and he felt sick. She knew far too much.

"How do you know my uncle?"

"He is our lawyer back in the States." She smiled again.

"Look, Francesca, it's very nice to meet you but I must insist you go now. I really do have a lot to do." He swallowed hard, trying to hold down the vomit that kept rising to the back of his throat. He felt as though he would faint.

"Oh, Charles, please sit down and have another brandy. We have a lot to talk about. Now, where shall I start?" She paused. "Oh yes, how about we start at the beginning?"

He turned his head to the side. "I'm not sure where you are going with this. What do you mean, let's go back to the beginning?"

"The prostitutes in London."

This was like a dream — well, a nightmare. How could Mauricio's adopted sister have any idea about his little prostitute clean-up scheme? He thought about the book *'The Christmas Carol' and how the ghosts of Christmas came back to haunt Scrooge. Was this happening to him? No one could know all that she knew, unless she wasn't real.* The adrenaline started to pump and he now thought he was really losing his mind. She winked at him and for a second then he saw Launa sitting there. It was too much. The name Francesca started to ring a bell, and he knew the name. *Where did he know it from?* It was the house, the title deeds. He never understood after Launa had gone, why she had bought the house in the name of Francesca Vincent.

His nostrils flared and then, without warning, vomit shot from his mouth and out of his nose. He lunged forward but started to choke.

Francesca jumped to her feet and felt for her lighter.

Charles wiped his nose with his wrist.

"Oh dear, you have vomit on your Rolex." She stared into the deflated eyes of her husband. A shiver ran up his spine. He tried to clear his throat and pull himself together.

"So then, Charles, tell me: how many prostitutes was it?"

Charles didn't answer. He let her speak. He wanted to get the strength to take her down.

"So you don't want to talk about those women you murdered? Then let's discuss fish food."

The words *'fish food'* circled his mind. He had told Tyler that Launa was fish food.

Charles instantly concluded that Tyler had defected to the other side, and the only reason this woman knew everything was because of him. He felt betrayed now, and the anger gripped him. She too would be fish food, like Launa.

There was an eerie silence between them. Francesca watched her husband's face change. It was grotesque, just as it had been that night he tried to kill her. She put her hands behind her back and grabbed the lighter. Charles now had himself together and was ready to make his attack. As he lunged forward, she brandished her gun. He stopped in his tracks, staring at the gold weapon, not sure enough to be convinced it was a gun or a toy, but not willing to take a chance.

"Where's your knife, lovely lashes?" taunted Francesca. She had always called him that since they were first together, and when she had thought they had been totally in love, but she could not have been more wrong.

Charles felt as though he had been hit around the head with a bat. Weak at the knees, this was a feeling he had never experienced before. Her voice changed again. She was like a chameleon.

"Launa?" He put his hands to his mouth. This was worse than seeing a ghost. She looked so unlike her. Yet those eyes, the deep steel-blue, and her voice — he knew it was her. The Launa he remembered was a bumbling wreck, eager to please, running around trying to say and do the right thing, always there and in the way. He had been proud of his wife — the way she had so casually wiped the floor with her legal opponents, and her beauty, which was so natural and simple, but not to be underestimated, because her intelligence was far beyond her innocent looks. The woman in front of him now was complicated. He looked at her, really looked at her, and didn't like what he saw. He felt frightened for the first time in his life. It was as if his brain just couldn't comprehend that his wife had survived and was standing there looking like a Hollywood star.

"What's up, Charles? You look like you've seen a ghost!" she laughed.

She was still holding the gun, and he was not going to take a chance at lunging forward.

Charles wiped away the vomit from his face with the back of his shirt sleeve. He saw the yellow sick on his watch.

"What's up, Charles? Can't handle a tiny bit of puke on your Rolex? Then again, this time it's different — it's your own vomit and not mine." She laughed again.

Now his stomach had settled, he decided the best plan would be to act sorry and get her to drop her guard.

"My Launa, my lovely Launa, it really is you? You don't know how much I regret what I did. I can't sleep at night, I can't eat, I can't believe what I did. I must have been out of my head. My God, will you ever forgive me?" He forced a tear.

Francesca looked him up and down and laughed. "Fuck off, Charlie boy." She was now talking like a true East Ender. "Don't even go there, you mother's cunt. If you think for one second that your silly performance will make me forgive your stupid ass, then dream on. I know and you know that you wanted me fucking brown bread. What you didn't bank on was me surviving your butchering, not forgetting the rough sea out there. So give yourself a break with the dramatics and be bloody honest."

Charles couldn't believe this was happening and his exhaustion was not helping him to think straight. He needed to get that gun off her and finish what he had started.

Francesca was calm. She pulled a packet of cigarettes from her pocket and casually placed one in her mouth. Charles watched every move, ready to pounce. His was so on edge that, when she used the gun to light it, he jumped. She laughed and drew in the smoke, then blew it in his face. He laughed at the relief. He could snap her neck and throw her in the sea. An evil grin spread across his face, and Francesca guessed he was going to go for her. His hand knocked the cigarette clean from her mouth as he slapped her face. The other hand held a tight grip around her throat, but to his horror, she smiled. He looked deep into her eyes; *he could smell fear, but it was his own.* She was smiling, and the lighter was pushed into his stomach. He knew then that he had fucked up as the bullet discharged, shot through his liver and made a mess of the crisp, cream coloured walls. Letting go of his grip, he held his stomach and fell to his knees.

Francesca held the gun to his head. "Get up."

Charles was in shock. There was no more vomit left, but blood rose up to the back of his throat and he pleaded for her to get him to the hospital. "Get up, you stinking rat, or I'll blow your fucking brains out." Her tone was cold and calm. He could hear the words going around in his mind and tried to fathom their meaning. All he wanted to do was get help, knowing he would be dead within an hour. "Please help me, Launa. You don't want to kill me really." He wasn't acting this time, he pleaded. The tears flowed and his voice wavered.

She grabbed his arm and helped him to his feet. He got up unsteadily and walked with her, believing she was going to take him to the hospital. The back door was pushed open and slowly and, in agony, he walked through it. They were halfway up the garden, when he realised she was not leading him to the car. The blood was now soaking his trousers, the pain was immense, and he was weak. He dropped to his knees and begged. "Please, Launa, don't do this. Get me to a hospital. I won't press charges. I won't say it was you." The snot bubbled from his nose.

Launa didn't hear him, as she was headed for the cliff.

"Get up. I want to show you something." She was still pointing the gun to his head.

In resignation, he used his last ounce of strength to do as she said. They reached the cliff edge and there he slumped to the floor.

She casually sat down with him. Pulling her coat tighter around herself, they both sat looking out at the sea as if it was a romantic date. She wanted to show him what the sea would look like when he was floating in it half-dead.

He was sitting down because he was bleeding to death and she sat beside him. She wanted to watch him die.

"So, Charles, tell me about your son?"

*

Meanwhile, Sergio had woken her brothers up and explained the situation. They agreed it wasn't a good idea to ignore it. They would need to find her. He knew about the cottage and knew it was along a particular stretch of coastline, but he didn't know the exact address.

"Fuck it, let's all drive in different directions and we will look out for her car," said Joe, who surprised himself. Normally he would be the one taking the orders.

"What makes you so sure she went there?" asked Dan, who was still half-asleep, with a mouth like a camel's armpit and hair sticking up in all directions.

"She's there all right," Fred piped up.

The boys nodded in acknowledgement. If Fred thought it, then it had to be right.

"She said he had thrown her off a cliff, so I guess we look where the cliffs are. Does that make sense?" Sergio was unsure if the coastline was huge or if there were only a few with cliffs.

"Yeah, I know where the cliffs are in East Sussex. It's not difficult to find. There are a few cottages dotted around there, so my guess is she is in one of them. Follow me," said Fred excitedly. At stressful times like these, Fred could be something of an enigma. His countenance suggested he was really enjoying the moment, such was the look of excitement on his face, but in reality he was experiencing just the opposite. He dashed around, trying to find the keys, and then Mauricio held them up. "Here, slow down."

Fred snatched them and rushed to the car, quickly followed by Sergio. They both jumped in the black BMW and the others followed. The nights were drawing in and it was dark at a quarter to four. Fred was racing through the country lanes. He could drive like a lunatic when he needed to. Sergio was silent but then he was a man of few words. One of the things Francesca loved about him was that when he did have something to say it was clear and not full of shit. He was intelligent and composed, and she admired him far more than he really knew.

*

"Who is the child's mother?"

Charles knew now that he was done for. He had lost far too much blood and, although he wanted to live, he knew he was in his final moments.

"Who is she, Charles?" Francesca sounded so sweet, as though her human side had returned from the demon holding the gun.

He tried to focus on her face but she was a blur.

"Mackenzie, all right?" he managed to mutter.

Francesca snapped out of her gaze and stared in disbelief. "Your stepmother?" She could hardly believe what she was hearing.

"Yes," he nodded. He was weak and his voice was barely audible.

He was a sick bastard. She looked at Charles lying on the floor, dying, and felt nothing except relief.

Francesca was surprised by his answer. She knew Mackenzie was married to William but they were living separate lives. William had other women and she knew Mackenzie had other men. She wasn't as old as her father-in-law, yet she wasn't as young as Charles — it was just absurd. Even so, it didn't shock her, nothing could any more. The prostitutes that were murdered were always a mystery until the murderer — her own husband — horrifically sliced her face. Events became a little clearer in her mind when she began her journey of recovery. The missing pieces of the puzzle all began to move themselves into place — all the late nights, the times when he left the house in one shirt and returned in another, the way he scrubbed himself with disinfectant, the knife she found in the car, it all began to make sense. She shuddered when she thought she had been married to a serial killer for years, and never realised this until he attempted to murder her.

"Goodbye, Charles," she whispered, as she kicked his heavy body over the edge and into the sea below. He didn't struggle or attempt to put up a fight. *Maybe the monster within him had left, and he was ready to leave this world.*

The headlights shone past her as she stared out to sea. Somewhere in the background, she could hear car doors being opened and then shut. The men ran towards her, hoping desperately that they would catch her before she jumped.

It was Fred and Sergio that got to her first. Sergio placed his arm round her waist and Fred took the gun from her hands. She was freezing. Sergio hugged her tightly and kissed her cheek. Looking over her shoulder, he saw what he thought was the face of her husband just before it disappeared for good below the ice-cold waves of the sea.

"It's over, my angel. It's over," he whispered.

She smiled.

"I can live in peace now." She looked at the loving eyes of her brothers, including Mauricio. She classed him as her blood and Sergio as her future husband. Never before had she felt so safe, so content.

Fred cried, "Fuck me, sis, I thought you was gonna jump."

She shook her head. "I won't give up on life that easily, not when I've got all of you to love me. No, Fred, I was saying goodbye to my last demon."

Dan looked at Joe and nodded. They knew what she meant.

Her eldest brother hugged her as the others watched on. "Dolly, we would have taken care of him. You didn't have to do this."

"You all are my big brothers and when I was little I always depended on you because I was the baby sister, but then I was an only child when I lived with Anne, and I had to learn to depend on myself. One day I will fit in again, just be patient."

Fred knew exactly what she meant, as he was the other baby, and always had his brothers to lean on. Looking over the cliff into the cold, uninviting sea, he trembled at the notion that she had been thrown down there and survived. The realisation hit him; his sister had been to hell and back. She had endured so much in her short life, all at the hands of evil men — *no wonder she could be so ruthless.* The blade in Tyler's eye, the McManners' shootings, and now her husband thrown in the sea: all this without a morsel of remorse or regret. The waves smashed at the cliffs, the wind howled, and the bitter cold chilled him to the bone. He experienced an odd feeling of wanting to jump, to endure her pain.

"Fred, come on, let's go," whispered Francesca in his ear, as she studied his face. It was as if she knew.

The house was cleaned up and sold. Charles' car was crushed and the body was never found — *he really had been fish food.*

Francesca curled up in Sergio's arms and slept like a baby. Her dreams were of sunshine and flowers, holidays and wedding bells.

Epilogue

The wedding took place in glorious sunshine. The gardens were adorned with huge arrangements of pink roses. Ruby, dressed in layers of pinks frills and with flowers in her hair, paraded around like a fairy princess, enjoying all the fuss.

Nellie and her daughters flew in by private jet, along with Old Sid and his wife, Shirley. None of them had been to the States, nor had they travelled anywhere in such luxury. With no expense spared, the friends and family of Francesca were treated like royalty.

Bill and Mary moved in with Roberto two weeks before the wedding to help with all the arrangements and Francesca's brothers stayed at her home.

It was to be the wedding of the year: the East End family united with the Italian family at Roberto's huge mansion. The garden was set up with an enormous marquee in which were placed row upon row of white chairs, and outside, the lawn was decorated with flowers. The rose arch at which they would stand, and take their vows, had two elaborate crystal fountains on either side. Roberto, being one of the richest men in France, and one of the most highly respected Italian families in America, spared no expense. However, what he wanted more than the extravagance was the gathering of his closest friends and family. The guests from England were there at his expense. They enjoyed every moment of it and dined on the occasion for months afterwards, describing to their friends the wedding of a lifetime.

As the limos drew up at the gates, Sarah, Nellie's daughter, gasped. "Fuck me, look at that. You would think Francesca's a movie star." The guards in black suits and earphones watched everyone. Theirs was not the only limo pulling up. Behind them was a long entourage of expensive cars.

"To think, our Kathy lives like this. Do you reckon old Mauricio is a bit of a mafia bloke or what?"

Nellie laughed. "Don't be so daft, you. Your problem is you've watched too many films. Her Mauricio is a rich fella, owns many businesses, and you know our Kathy was never one for a criminal. She likes the simple life." She smiled to herself as her heart skipped a beat. She was excited to imagine her Kathy living with all this grandeur – and to think, all those years ago she nearly burned to death in that fire.

"I can't wait to get me hands on our new baby – and what a pretty name, eh?" squealed Nellie, as she rubbed her palms together.

Jane, Nellie's other daughter, reapplied her lipstick. She never dreamed that the wedding would have been so elaborate and she hoped Mauricio had a cousin or someone she could saddle up with also.

Old Sid sat back, clutching his wife's hand, as the limo glided up the drive to Roberto's grand home. He had a lump in his throat, which was hard to believe since half of his throat was missing. Not having any family of his own, he classed the Vincents as his and he was overjoyed that Dolly had sent a special invite – private jet, five-star hotel, two-week stay and front row seats on the day. Proud as punch, it was as if Francesca had been his very own daughter. Shirley sat upright, revelling in the experience. She had always loved the finer things in life and, the trip to the States had been 'pure posh', as she would say.

"Cor blimey, Sid. There's money here, all right. Look at the security. Are they all for Dolly or is the President visiting?"

Sid laughed. "Shirley love, our Dolly is marrying a very wealthy man, and 'cause of the type of business they run, well, he needs a bit of protection."

"'Ere, he ain't part of that mafia, is he?"

"Just 'cause he's Italian and minted, don't mean he's the Godfather," he replied, but the thought had crossed Sid's mind.

The guests arrived in their droves, with everyone looking immaculately turned out. Bill and Mary were at the house with Francesca, adding the final touches. The days leading up to the wedding had seen Francesca shop for the perfect dress, but this time it was with her mum. As proud as any mother could be, Mary had watched her only daughter trying on wedding dresses and soaked up the delight. Mary enjoyed helping with the arrangements, the choice of flowers, the cake, and her speciality - the catering. She had needed some advice from Roberto, since most of the menu would be Italian. Mary knew good food when she tasted it, so she enjoyed tasting samples from each catering firm, joined by Roberto, who had the same palate. Francesca loved to see her mother so happy, fussing over the finer details.

Mary stepped back to admire her daughter in her beautiful white dress, a simple silk dress, with rows of diamonds covering the bodice. Her hair, now longer and restored to its original colour of a raven's wings, fell in loose curls, framing her face. A dainty crystal tiara perched subtly on her head, and her soft makeup accentuated her blue eyes.

She was ready to walk up the aisle and meet her husband-to-be.

Bill stood at the door, looking younger than ever. He had sold the yard and enjoyed his new hobby, fishing. The relaxation had removed the harshness from his face. He was handsome and fit; the sun had brightened his complexion, and he looked like an older brother instead of her dad. He tried to stop the tears welling up by taking deep breaths. His daughter looked as though she had stepped off the cover of *Vogue*. She held herself so high, full of confidence, and huge smiles for everyone. Mary kissed her daughter and quickly wiped the lipstick left on her cheeks. She used the same handkerchief to wipe a tear that dropped from her eyes.

"Aw Mum, Dad, you're gonna set me off, and I can't look like a panda marching up the aisle."

Mauricio checked the surveillance. He wanted everything to be perfect. With so many Italian families arriving, he needed to be sure he was on top of the security, every second of the day. Kathy rested in the kitchen, glad of the break from the baby, whilst Roberto, dressed in his finest navy blue suit, diamond cufflinks and crisp white shirt, swanned around the guests with his bundle of pink frills. He was the proudest grandfather ever. Unlike the other family heads, who would never be found holding a baby, he wouldn't put her down. She made life mean so much more now.

Mauricio had been overjoyed when Kathy went into labour, and Roberto had rushed to the hospital to be by his side. "My son, from this day on you will be a different man. You will be a father and you will experience a love like never before, and that love, my son, never goes." He had looked his son up and down. "Look at you, Mauricio, my son. I love you more than my life and soon you will know what that feels like. You will be a great father." He kissed his son and sent him into the room to hold Kathy's hand.

When the baby arrived, Mauricio cried. He had never felt an emotion like it and ran into the corridor to tell his father.

Roberto couldn't wait. He wanted to see the new grandchild; Mauricio was so emotional Roberto hadn't waited to ask if it was a boy or a girl. He pushed open the door, to find Kathy sitting upright, with the baby in her arms.

"Come in and say hello to your granddaughter, Angelina."

His heart pounded with pride as he crept over to the bed.

Roberto looked down at the baby and back at Kathy.

"Oh thank you, thank you so much." The tears rolled from his eyes. He gazed at the tiny, perfect, pink bundle and whispered, "Angelina, you are just like your grandmother."

At only six weeks old, she was spoilt rotten. Roberto wanted to see his granddaughter every day so Mauricio and Kathy moved into his mansion. When the guests arrived he paraded her around, as if she was the only baby in the world.

Ruby and Jack played in the garden, pretending they were getting married under the arch. Dan, Fred and Sam were on the pull, eyeing up the young Italian women and joking about their mothers.

"Dan, look at it this way. You clock the mother and you will see your bird in twenty years from now," Fred laughed.

"Oh yeah, see that tasty bit over there that you had your eye on? Well, her mother's that big bird over there." He pointed in the opposite direction. "She's got a fucking beard."

Sam and Dan roared with laughter.

Joe arrived by limo, happy to be back with his girlfriend, who was just showing a neat bump. Dan nudged Fred. "'Ere, would you fucking look at that?" Fred glanced over at Joe, who was having his face wiped by his girlfriend's handkerchief. Sam rolled his eyes. "They are happy though. He needs a bossy bird, 'cause he hates to think for himself."

The waiters served champagne and canapés as the guests started to get to their seats.

Anne arrived with David Moss, all the way from Australia. Her business was doing well, and she enjoyed her new life, yet she did miss Francesca and couldn't wait to see her. She would just have to wait like the others.

The Italians were loud when they embraced one another, not to mention very expressive. The Londoners were more reserved, perhaps because this wedding was so far removed from their typical do's; a church hall, a DJ and a prawn vol-au-vent.

Mary arrived ahead of her daughter, eagerly greeted by her sons. They all fussed over her. "You look beautiful, Mum."

She smiled shyly. It wasn't often these days that she got dressed up, but today she wanted Francesca to be proud.

Anne saw Mary out of the corner of her eye and ran over, arms outstretched. Mary was taken aback for a moment, as she didn't recognise the tanned, tall bombshell. "'Ello, sis." She beamed with excitement.

Anne hugged Mary so tightly she could hardly breathe.

"Hello, Anne. I'm so glad you came. There's so much to talk about, lots to catch up on and you look really lovely." Mary was holding her arm.

"Well, Mare, I'm over here for a few weeks, and I can't think of anything better than a good cuppa tea and a long chat with me skin and blister."

Mary laughed loudly. She was so surprised at how her sister had changed.

Then she went quiet for a second, before a tear sprang from her eyes.

"You know, Anne, I only asked one thing from you, and that was to love my daughter as if she were your own."

Anne took a deep breath, dreading what Mary was about to say.

"And you did that, and so much more. Our Francesca is the most wonderful woman, and I know you had a lot to do with that. I don't know how I can ever thank you. I just hope she gave you as much joy as she gives me."

Anne hugged her sister.

"Mary, I could never have taken your place but believe me when I tell you, Dolly coming into my life made me the happiest woman. I loved every minute, and I can't ever thank you enough. She was the child I never had, and what a gift she was."

They sat together to watch Francesca walk up the aisle. Sitting nervously, they squeezed each other's hands. It was the closest they had ever been.

As everyone took their seats, the music began to play. Sergio stood by the arch, with Mauricio by his side. They looked like two handsome princes, both wearing navy blue suits and white shirts that accentuated their summer glowing tans and black wavy hair. Sergio looked particularly distinguished, and all eyes were on him. In the crowd were young Italian women, members of significant families, who had been particularly disappointed that he was to be wed. Both the Luciani boys would have been the perfect catch: with status, wealth and respect came honour, not to mention their good looks.

Kathy beamed with pride as she admired Mauricio, soon to be her husband — *well, as soon as he got around to popping the question.*

Her very proud father helped Francesca from the car. Ruby stared in wonder as she handed her the dainty bouquet.

Bending down, Francesca whispered in her ear, "You look like a princess, Ruby."

Her tiny face lit up as she followed her aunt and grandfather up the aisle. She smiled, as proud as punch to be the one and only special bridesmaid, walking behind her beautiful aunty. Jack walked beside his sister, holding her hand, and he smiled sweetly at all the guests. The family looked at Jack with pride; he was a real little gentleman.

Bear had managed to get out and join the celebrations. As always, he made a beeline for Francesca and, to everyone's amazement, he followed her slowly up the aisle and sat next to Mauricio. The crowd laughed.

Sergio turned to face his bride to be. She was the most perfect woman he had ever laid eyes on and, with her hair falling around her face and now back to her natural colour, she looked even more beautiful. Her father walked slowly, holding her arm as if he was holding a china doll. He kissed his daughter again on the cheek and whispered to her, "I have never felt more proud as a father than I do today."

Francesca tried to hold back the tears. She wanted a smile on her face when she married her husband.

Sergio felt a tear ready to fall and quickly wiped his eyes. Of course, it didn't go unnoticed and, by the time they had started saying their vows, all the front row was snivelling, including Roberto, who was still holding the baby.

He stared into her steely-blue eyes as she said, loud and clear, "I do."

The Sequel...

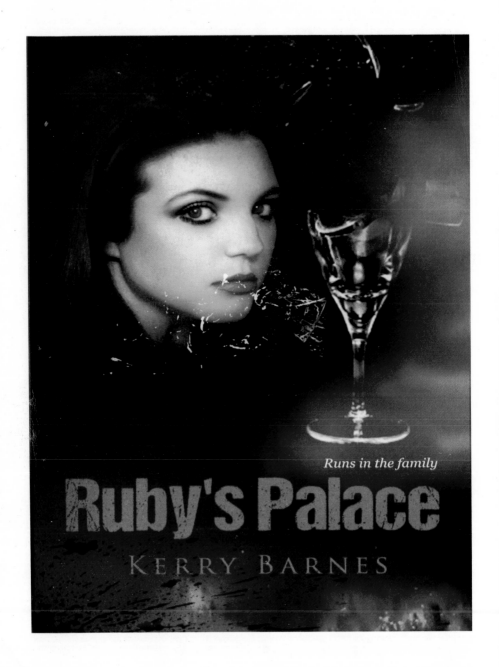

Runs in the family

Ruby's Palace

KERRY BARNES